Stirring Up a Storm

Stirring Up a Storm

a Storm

TALES OF THE SENSUAL, THE SEXUAL, AND THE EROTIC

Edited by Marilyn Jaye Lewis

Thunder's Mouth Press
New York

STIRRING UP A STORM
Tales of the Sensual, the Sexual, and the Erotic

Published by
Thunder's Mouth Press
An Imprint of Avalon Publishing Group Inc.
245 West 17th St., 11th Floor
New York, NY 10011

FOR BOB CATO

1923–1999

In gratitude and fond memory

Acknowledgments

$\mathcal{I}$ AM MOST indebted to my agent, Helen Breitwieser, for her continuing input, suggestions, and generous spirit. Her enthusiasm for this project has kept me excited from the word go. And to my publisher, John Oakes, who gave me a lot of leeway and whose ideas sent this anthology in a more rewarding direction than I had envisioned on my own.

I also wish to thank Michael Hemmingson for his customary selfless suggestions and support that helped get this ball rolling; Jill Terry, for tireless emails of enthusiasm over the course of the project; Gary Adler, for his generous scanning hours without ever charging me a dime. My continuing gratitude to Janice Eidus, for all her encouragement, ideas, suggestions, and for letting me ride a little on the coattails of her impeccable reputation—as well as for sharing a little tea. This anthology wouldn't be quite what it turned into without her!

Above all, I want to thank the writers in this collection who shared their incredible stories with me. There would simply be no book without them. For that, I am nothing less than a little awed and very grateful.

Contents

Introduction

$\mathcal{I}$S IT TOO early in our relationship as sophisticated editor and erudite reader to admit that while editing this lofty anthology you now hold, I was frequently listening to Helen Reddy's 1972 classic "I Am Woman" at top volume in my headphones? And without irony, mind you, but rather with an unbridled sense of awe and joy, as if everything that was important in life was at last coming back to me. Reminding me of how I'd first felt at age twelve when "I Am Woman" was #1 on the Billboard charts and I listened to its tinny jubilation on a transistor radio, the tiny plastic plug wedged in my ear when I'd sneak out of my bedroom at 2 a.m. to restlessly roam the dark streets of our safe little suburban Ohio neighborhood. I was unable to sleep. I was too excited by life, by whatever it was that was coming at me at top speed and I didn't want to miss a minute of it. "If I have to/ I can do anything/ I am strong/ I am invincible/ I am woman." Yes, indeedy. In those days, my future was heady stuff.

Naturally, this was long before I knew about things like artistic sexism, extreme cynicism, utter disillusionment, or worse yet, feeling all-consumingly enraged at the world at large for its lack of acceptance of "my art" in it. Or perhaps enraged at myself for the type of "art" I insisted on producing—I have always referred to my writing as literature, but a whole lot *more* people have generally dismissed it as porn and, to my general shock and disbelief, assigned it a very narrow avenue for publication.

It made me feel like howling, "But Genet was *celebrated* . . . in a way."

"Yes, but he was gay and that was France. And Cocteau had a lot to do with it."

Ah. Well. Okay then. Here's my book and just, well, send me a check. Thank you.

Coming of age in the '70s unwittingly set me up for a lot of erroneous assumptions about American society. As a teenager, I could walk into any Little Professor bookstore in any local mall and find a plethora of sexually explicit books; photo books, nonfiction books, and novels. There was so much going on in those days. Too much, perhaps, so that it clouded my vision. It took years before I realized that the '70s were in fact a cultural fluke for mostly-Puritan America and that few of those sex books I perused at leisure were penned by women. By now this is, of course, old news but it doesn't mean the initial realization of it was any less staggering or woeful. What was I supposed to do with my ambitions, then—I mean *besides* move to France, exhume Cocteau, and somehow exhort what was left of his corpse to get back into publishing?

Well, this isn't meant as a feminist manifesto or anything. It's just a collection of terrific, engaging stories written by women from wide-flung backgrounds, each story dealing specifically with the sensual or the erotic. And every story in this collection fills me with a sense of glee. It doesn't mean that some of these stories aren't decidedly dark or cautionary, because a number of them, my own contribution included, certainly are. And it isn't that I think I can only make "a statement" by subtracting the male contributor. It's just that throughout time, as we all know by now, the male voice has been traditionally more acceptable whenever it came to writing about sexual or erotic topics. The same acceptability hasn't been the case for women until only recently.

A number of the women contributing stories here are

considerably younger than I am. I'm sure they approach their craft without feeling as if women aren't thoroughly entitled to express whatever they want to express, fully expecting to have it published somewhere—perhaps not fully grasping what a recent cultural paradigm shift that is. And there are also several contributors here who have been around long enough to have been profound influences on me in my still-formative years; Rosemary Daniell is a prime example. To be able to include a sample of her groundbreaking poetry from her early '70s collection, *A Sexual Tour of the Deep South*, is nothing short of thrilling for me—if only as personal proof that my future did at last meet up with me, it just took its own sweet time getting here.

There's so much going on in erotica publishing today that's exhilarating. Strong confident voices; all imaginable sexual persuasions, male and female. And still the erotica genre has yet to fully make itself known in the mainstream. I believe the consistent quality of all the writing in this anthology helps blur those lines between erotic fiction and any other type of fiction. Not to presume that any one reader will accept all the stories with the same level of appreciation. Fans of explicit erotica might be quizzical of a story with a more "sensually suggestive" tone, and god knows vice versa. But the chance to bring such a wide group of women writers together under one cover without the fear of censorship even among ourselves is, for me, a personal triumph. It's less a way of addressing the naysayers in my own past, those folks who urged me not to waste my talent on smut, that there was no market for it. And more a way of celebrating all the women storytellers who had visions similar to mine and who ploughed ahead and stuck it out; writers who seemingly couldn't do otherwise. We are at last in "numbers too big to ignore." We are strong. We can write anything. And to illustrate my point, I've put together this book. I now unleash it on you, gentle reader. Enjoy!

—*Marilyn Jaye Lewis*

5 January, 2004

Lauren Henderson

I'M NAKED.

I have never felt so naked in my life.

It's been a steep learning curve for massages, this holiday. In the West, the masseur always covers your private parts with a tactful small white towel before setting to work, holding one discreetly to mask you if you need to turn over, and usually you get to wear your thong as well. Shiatsu positively requires you to wear long-sleeved cotton clothing, for God's sake. Clearly, the Japanese are considerably more decorous than the inhabitants of the Indian subcontinent. Last week, the five of us piled into an Ayurvedic massage center in Habanaruwa, where tiny smiling sari-clad women said firmly: "All off! All off!" while gesturing at our bras and knickers, and then worked dark green, pungent oil into our skin and scalps with light sweeping movements that were, apparently, intended to help our circulation, but instead left us feeling unsatisfied and greasy. Betta, pulling ruefully at her soaked hair, said that now she knew what seabirds caught in oil slicks felt like.

So no one but Lucia and I were up for another massage the next opportunity we had; the others preferred just to lie on the beach for our last full day of sun and sea and sarong-sellers, while I walked over with Lucia to the little stone pavilion lapped by a tiny stream, set in the stone-walled garden we had found the day before, quite by chance, with a small poster beside it offering Keralan massages. We had booked by phone for this afternoon, and because it was a male masseur, Luci wanted me to chaperone her to her appointment—she was taking the first slot—just in case he tried to behave inappropriately.

Ten minutes later, I was back, giggling so hard that they could hear me coming. They all sat up on their loungers, squinting into the sun, curious to hear what had set me off.

"I just left Luci in the arms of this *heartthrob*—" I started.

"Oh my god, and she was so nervous about being massaged by a guy—"

"Well, she looked nervous when I left, but jolly excited, too, I can tell you—"

"What did he *look* like?"

"Lean, young, dark, dark eyes, skin like hazelnuts, rising up with the grace of a panther from the mat where he'd been meditating, pushing back his long hair from his frankly madly handsome face—"

(I had practiced this description on the walk back to the beach.)

"Oooh, long hair—"

"You should have seen Luci's *face*!"

But an hour later, her face was blurred, as if his massage had smoothed her features into primitive clay. All I saw were her eyes, bright and dazed, as if she were in the aftermath of the best trip she had ever had.

"I'm not going to tell you anything," she said, gliding past me. "Just that it was the single most erotic experience *of my entire life.*"

"Did you have to take all your clothes off?"

"Oh *yes*," she breathed.

I was determined to be cool, matter-of-fact. No visible nervousness for me; I was damned if I would be the shy Westerner blushing at less physically-repressed foreign ways. He had tied his hair back; he was wearing a white vest and pajama-style bottoms, fitted enough so that I could see that, though thin, he was all lean muscle. As he padded toward me, barefoot, it took all the cool I had not to take a step back, because his closeness made me dizzy.

He slipped past me to close the pavilion door, and I started untying my bikini. Never before in my life had I taken my clothes off in front of a gorgeous man within two minutes of meeting him, after only a brief exchange of names, nationalities, and "how long have you been in Sri Lanka?" It felt shockingly transgressive, deliciously naughty, as if I were paying him for sex. Immediately, two narratives started to play out; one, where, on my last full day of holiday, I went for a therapeutic massage, icing on the cake to my relaxation; and the other, where I stripped and lay down on a mat on a stone floor in a yoga pavilion surrounded by a narrow moat, in a green shady garden just behind the beach, and closed my eyes, waiting for a pantherine streak of young Indian manhood to do with me what he would.

It was five in the afternoon, and sunlight poured gently through the cobalt panes of glass onto the stone floor. As I settled my body onto the mat, I felt two thick streaks of sun falling and settling across my shoulders and buttocks, heavy as sleeping cats. I was dazed already with the shock of being naked, dazed with the sun and the fact that he was about to touch my body, the sound of him kneeling down beside me. Oh, delicious. No wonder Luci had said this was the single most erotic experience of her life.

Oil streamed across my back. For a long moment he didn't touch me, just let the oil run down my skin, into the crease between my buttocks, where it collected, sinking down into the crack, tickling at my pubic hair, scented with jasmine. He waited long enough for me to shiver briefly with the anticipated pleasure, exactly as if I were obeying a lover's instructions to lie down naked, close my eyes, and take everything that he would do to me without a murmur of protest. Jesus. I reminded myself, delighted, that this entire massage was going to cost me only twenty dollars—twenty five, if I tipped in lavish American style. He hadn't even started, and I already knew that I would pay ten times that, just for this moment, these sensations. I suddenly realized why men paid for sex.

And then he touched me, and my ability to think vaporized, as if that touch on the base of my spine had pressed a button, sending every lucid thought boiling up in steam which promptly shot out through my ears and evaporated, leaving only sensation. I was melting, drowning. He knelt over me and stroked hard from one shoulder to the opposite buttock in a rhythm that pressed me down into the mat, my breath synchronizing with his movements. He worked his fingers round my tight shoulder blades as if he were unstitching, unpicking, every snugly wound spot of tension, feeling for the knots, pulling on them to see how tight they were, sliding his fingers gently, painfully, into their center and tugging them loose.

It hurt; I bit my lip; I wouldn't have asked him to stop for the world. He commented on how tight I was, and I was pleased to hear my voice sounding so casual and unaffected as I said yes, my shoulders were terrible, even after ten years of yoga. He said if I came to him for two weeks he would cure my shoulder tension for good. I believed him. Then he started massaging my buttocks and my eyes rolled up in my skull and we stopped talking. He ran his long, heavy strokes from the top crease of my thighs, down the tender muscle of my calves, to the soles of my feet. Sand on my skin from the beach caught in the oil; his hands were rough and dry, an old-fashioned masculine calloused sensation that contrasted sensually with the smooth strokes, the delicacy of his touch. The sand was like a body scrub, polishing me down till I was perfectly smooth and oiled and scented with sea salt and jasmine.

I felt as beautiful as a harem girl. I could have woven a hundred fantasies, imagined myself on a marble floor in the *zenana*, being prepared for the sheikh who owned me by my secret lover, the harem masseur who pretended to be a eunuch so he could at least be near me, touch me, an exquisite, tortured pleasure as he worked my skin into perfection for another man to enjoy . . . but I didn't have any thoughts left, any brain power. I was gone, tripping, and the only consciousness I had was this sensation of being absolutely . . . perfect. I felt worshipped, beautiful; I had felt both those before, but never like this. Never like this. By the time he whispered softly that I was to turn over, I was absolutely convinced that I was the most gorgeous, sensual creature who had ever existed. I was all the Venuses rolled into one, and I was myself, and as I turned over, eyes closed, and felt the oil slicking down my breasts, as he touched me to rub it in, I knew that he thought so, too.

His breathing didn't change, his touch didn't alter; I knew that whatever he was doing to me was the standard massage he gave to every female client. His fingers on each breast as he brushed down from one shoulder to the opposite hipbone didn't linger, weren't salacious, didn't flick my oiled nipple with their rough pads as they passed. But I knew I wasn't fantasizing his response to me. I knew by the energy in the room, rising, gathering, flowing up from my nakedness and wrapping around us, as if I were some magical creature, enveloping him in a cloud of mystical smoke, forcing him with every stroke he made on my body to see me as not just flesh and bone and muscle and ligaments, but sensuality, pure and simple. I felt like a goddess. It poured out through my pores, my breath, and I made him see me as a goddess too. My back arched infinitesimally as he stroked over my breasts, reaching up to his hands, offering myself; I felt my thighs part just as slightly. He knelt over me, pushing my shoulders down; I raised my eyelids just slightly, for a glimpse of his face, and its expression of extreme concentration, the full lips drawn together as he worked on me, was somehow as intimate as if I had spied on him making love. I shut my eyes swiftly, guiltily, and as his body reached over mine, his weight on the caps of my shoulders, his vest gaped open, hanging down to brush my chest, and I smelled his body odor, musky and rich as fertile cinnamon earth, nutmeg and cumin and salt sweat. I smelled his excitement, the scent of his sweat, and I knew he wanted me.

I don't have a perfect body. That's the point. If I had, I would take this for granted. Or would I? Do those women who have perfect bodies know what they have? Or are they made insecure precisely by their own perfection, counting millimeters in their waist measurements, panicking when they see tiny bulges over the top of their bikini bottoms as they sit up? I work out and I diet and I can do cartwheels and handstand forward rolls and Pilates sit-ups and a backbend that is actually getting pretty damn good after years of practice. But I have a metabolism as slow as Lent passing; I'm not lean; and despite those Pilates sit-ups, my stomach makes considerably more than a tiny bulge over the top of my bikini bottoms. And at that moment, in the scent of jasmine oil and the heat of the late-afternoon sun on my eyelids and his hands on my back, encouraging me to sit up, did I care?

I didn't even notice. I sat up, legs straight ahead of me, and felt myself leaning into him, my spine arched right from the base to my skull, bending like a bow with him the archer. My head tipped a little back, and I felt my lips curve into a smile as I remembered that just a few minutes ago I was lying on my back as he encouraged my hips to open, my knees bending, the soles of my feet coming together so he could push my thighs to the ground, opening my sex as he worked his knees onto my thighs to press them even further down against the tightness of my hips, and I had let him do it. No resistance from me, no shock, no hardening, just laughter bubbling up inside me as I lay back and my cunt opened to him, my breathing never changing, his hands never slowing.

You might think I was insanely arrogant to think that he wanted me, with all the women he must massage each day, each week: me, with my imperfect body, my unmade-up face. But as he squatted behind me and pulled me back toward him, my head against his chest, his thumbs moving slowly across my forehead, into my hairline, pulling the skin across my cheekbones away from my nose, caressing me like a lover even while he made the standard, sweeping gestures of a face massage I had had many times before (though never while sitting naked practically in the lap of a young man), I knew, and I waited, and I sensed that he didn't want to stop touching me and was spinning out this face massage twice as long, three times as long as he would normally have done, because this was the end, and he couldn't take his hands off me, and even if he had finally managed to do it, pulled back, and said, "That'll be 20 dollars, please. I hope you feel relaxed," I would have known, I would, and when instead he placed his palms against my forehead, guiding my skull back onto his chest, and took a long, deep breath, and then bent to whisper into my hair: "Lauren? Can I kiss you? Please?" I wasn't remotely surprised.

⌒

IT WAS THE most erotic experience of my life.

⌒

I COULD END it there.

Or I could tell you what happened afterward, but only if you understand why I put that sentence above, directly after describing the massage.

OK.

Well, I didn't let him kiss me, not then and there, because I knew that if we started kissing we would probably be making love a minute later, and I knew I had no defenses left, absolutely nothing. I was naked, covered in oil, lying in a stranger's arms, in a stone pavilion with cobalt windows, drunk on sex and sunshine and the smell of him. I was sure he didn't have a condom, not here anyway; and I had just enough sense left to take a deep breath and tell him that now I was going to put my clothes on. A bikini, a tiny sarong. I would have said I felt half-naked in those on the beach, before he had his hands in the juncture of my naked thighs, his thumbs digging into the muscle. Context is all. Now I had my breasts and my bottom covered, I felt, by contrast, the picture of respectability.

And then, then we kissed. His mouth looked like strange fruit with a mauvish blush, a full round plum set in his nutmeg skin, but it wasn't as soft as I had imagined it. I had thought the plum would melt under my mouth, ripe to bursting, but he kept his lips oddly firm, a hard pressure that boded well, perhaps. Then he came for a drink with me and the girls, and then I invited him to dinner with us, and after dinner he and I walked on the beach and he kissed me and stroked my breasts and pulled down my top, and I laughed and laughed to think that he was the first man ever to have touched my naked breasts before he kissed me, and then we went back to the room he was renting for the season, blue walls, blue tiled floor, a little blue bathroom off it with no toilet paper, just a spray on the wall to wash yourself down with, and we had sex.

Which was, by no means, the best I had ever had. It wasn't even the best one-night stand I had ever had. Nothing, I suppose, could have lived up to the massage; and if I was expecting hours of sensual caresses and soft strokings, I should have known better, because, after all, those were his profession, and now he was off-duty, and nobody wants to bring their work home with them. It was gymnastic instead, not particularly sensual nor relaxing.

At six in the morning he had to go out for an hour—to see off a friend of his who was leaving for Colombo, he said. After he left, unable to get back to sleep, I pulled on a T-shirt and sarong and wandered outside, into the blue-green light before the dawn. The house he lived in was surrounded by trees, whose thick heavy branches filtered the faint light and gave an odd, Indian-fairy-tale aspect to this moment. I sat on the front stoop, a concrete block, and petted a poor skinny dog tied up by the door, who jumped all over me at first, ecstatic at the attention, but soon settled down with his head on my feet, twitching his ears happily as I scratched between them. An old man in the madras sarong all the men here seemed to wear, bright squares of blues and greens and yolk-yellows knotted at their skinny, skinny waists, passed by on the cinder path and, noticing me, stopped by the gate and leaned on it, staring unashamedly at me for a few minutes, his narrow chest and spindly arms and knock-knees shaming me by contrast with my well-covered bones, my muscle earned at the gym, not from necessity. Dawn began to break, the blue-green sky suffusing with gold streaks, warmth slowly rising off the ground. I watched the sun come up and then, suddenly exhausted, I went back into the silent house and curled up on his thin mattress and fell asleep at once.

That day I had to leave with the girls for Colombo and the airport, and though he asked me to stay, it would have been near-impossible to change my ticket . . . and the sex hadn't been wonderful . . . and I felt it would be all downhill from here. And his kisses had been strange, too: he just pressed his lips hard against mine without ever using his tongue, and when I slid my tongue into his mouth he told me I "kissed weirdly." So we said good-bye that afternoon on the little terrace of my bed-and-breakfast, with the Sri Lankan waiters staring at me, the foreign tart with her local pick-up, and I massaged his dry, dry hands, wanting to give him a gift of sorts. In return, he told me that never before had anything like that happened to him with a client. And though it didn't really matter, I almost believed him.

In Italian, the word "storia" means "love affair." When you talk about anything from a fling to a serious relationship with someone, you say that you had a "story" with them. So this is my Sri Lankan story. We saw an elephant on the beach on New Year's Day, just standing there, seeming quite indifferent to our presence, before it lumbered back into the jungle again, and five days later I was naked, covered in oil, in the arms of a young man. If nothing else, it was a grand start to the New Year.

Sky People

Tulsa Brown

"*But* WHAT IF it happened to *you*, Sybil?" I said. "What if the spacemen took you into their saucer and flew you to their home planet, or the moon? Imagine if you looked out the window and saw the earth!"

"I'd wave," Sybil said. She was driving, wearing cat's-eye sunglasses that were just like Ava Gardener's.

"No, you'd want to tell everybody about it," I insisted. "And if the spacemen gave you a message to deliver—"

"I'd tell them they had the wrong Patterson. My brother is the famous fiction writer."

I grinned and let it go. For a nonbeliever, Sybil was a pretty good sport. If she hadn't been my sister, she would have been my friend.

We were on our way from Gaberville, California, to the Mojave Desert, for the Annual Great Rock Interplanetary Spacecraft Convention. It had been organized by George Van Tassel, who really *had* been on the flying saucers, and had met the spacemen, face-to-face. I'd read all his books and subscribed to his newsletter, where he posted the telepathic communications he was still receiving from the Space Brothers.

That's how I knew we were standing on the threshold of a new era. In just a few years—by 1960, surely—the world would be a very different place. No matter how the aliens phrased it, their message was always the same: Love. Intergalactic, interplanetary, inter-everything. They said it so often and so emphatically, I knew there was a deeper meaning, one that filled me with glimmering, tingling hope. When the space beings finally revealed themselves, the world would change. And I really needed it to.

I was going to be a writer. I had a typewriter, a black, square-shouldered Royal 330, and I wrote in my bedroom. I loved the solid strike of the keys on the paper, a clackity-clack that vibrated the desk, a happy horse at a trot. Sometimes I could make it gallop, and on some blazing, red-eyed nights, I was the whole horse race, thundering around the track.

"For God's sake, what is that fool *doing* up there?" My father would stomp to the bottom of the stairs. "David, do you want to come right through the floor?!"

I wanted to be famous. I had just turned twenty and two of my stories had already been published in *Saucer!* magazine. I had written three-quarters of a novel, *Six to Save Orion*, in which rocket commander Jack Drake and his five crewmen are stranded on a planet where the heavy mist itself is sentient. . . .

"Good story," the editor of *Saucer!* said. "Where's the girl?" He was short, rumpled, bristly, and bald, a man who kept a bottle of Listerine on his desk, and a different bottle in the drawer.

"The girl," I repeated.

The editor rolled his eyes. "Listen, if you get a girl into the story by the end of chapter three—give her some bazooms, mind you—I know someone who'll publish this. You just have to finish it. And don't forget the tits."

My best friend, Chris, read *Six to Save Orion* right before he left for university. He read to the end of what I had on a Sunday afternoon in August, the two of us alone in his garage. The air was cooler than outside, hushed and heavy with the smell of motor oil, grass clippings, and forgotten wood.

There was a row of narrow windows above his father's workbench. Chris leaned against the table and read in the slanting beams of light, dust motes swirling leisurely around him. We were both wearing T-shirts, but his looked better than mine, stretched by a body that had laid sod all summer, for a landscaper. His brown hair had been streaked gold by the sun and it tumbled over his forehead, needing a cut. His father said he looked like a beatnik. I thought he looked like a god.

I waited, listening to him breathe, to the rustle of the pages, and my own heart. At last Chris looked up.

"This is great!"

I could hardly speak in the gust of joy. "You . . . you think so? It's only a first draft."

"You put me right there. I was on that planet with Jack and the guys. It was *real*," Chris said excitedly. He talked and I drifted closer, devouring every word. Finally, he laid the stack of paper on the workbench. "I even know how it should end."

"How?"

"Like this." Chris put his arms around me in a tentative, trembling embrace. I was surprised but reached up to hug him back. He clasped me hard against his body then, and the revelation shook me: I'd wanted this all summer, I'd wanted it forever.

I was terrified, and thrilled. I could hardly believe I was pressed against the body I'd stared at for so long. My sweaty hands curved around the strong muscles of his back, my fingertips meeting at the V of his spine. I inhaled him, the warm, summery scent of his skin mingled with the dank metal smell of his father's tools, and my mouth watered.

My hard-on was rising at rocket speed.

"Think about baseball," was my father's standard advice regarding hard-ons. But when I felt Chris's rigid length pressed against my hipbone, the Boston Red Sox could have hit a grand slam to win the World Series and I wouldn't have cared. His lips brushed my cheek in a kiss, and I turned my head to return the same, and caught his mouth instead.

Heat hurtled down to my balls. Chris kissed me back hard, a

hungry, searching probe that opened my mouth and pulled the deep sound of my secrets up into the air. I felt him fumble between our bodies, struggling to pull up both our T-shirts, and my knees almost buckled. The thought of pressing naked against my best friend had only been a wild dream, and now it was an urgent reality. Nothing could stop us.

Except the door. The tiny, metallic click drove us apart like a wedge, threw us against the workbench, hearts pounding.

Chris's father stood in the garage doorway, a dark, ponderous shadow surrounded by the white blaze of the real day. He looked at Chris, then at me. I tugged my shirt down.

"I need a wrench," he said. Chris scrambled to hand him one.

"Five-eighths, not seven-sixteenths!"

I cringed at the thunderbolt; it was aimed at us both. When his father had the length of steel in his hand, he pointed it at me. "You'd better go home, David."

Chris glanced at me, the bold lust faded to a frightened plea. I grabbed my manuscript and squeezed out past his father, so fast I hated myself for it, sick alarm and lingering arousal slapping me like alternating wet rags.

My letters to Chris came back, unopened. My story *Six to Save Orion* languished, untouched. I knew how it was supposed to end now, but I didn't know how I could do it. I needed the world to change, and soon.

⁓

Welcome Space Brothers!

The sign was ten feet by twelve, secured to the front of a platform, which rose twenty feet up the side of a boulder that was seven stories tall. Against the massive chunk of granite the structure looked rickety, boards leaning like straws in a winding, spindly staircase. I studied it through binoculars, nailed in place by awe. This was where George Van Tassel would stand tonight as he channeled communications from the aliens.

"Their message to the world," I told Sybil.

"But not 'til ten o'clock." She checked her watch. "Let's go get corn dogs."

We worked our way through the crowd that was part carnival and part convention. Some people had set up tables to sell the books they'd written, and held out hand-drawn illustrations of what they'd seen. Everyone had a story to tell.

"And the female crew members are very much like earth women, except for their third breast. Their uniforms consist of short pleated skirts and sweaters, the texture of which resembles angora . . ."

". . . then Ashtok said to me, 'Go forth, and share our teachings with your brethren. Be ready for the time when we call for you.'"

I had to stop at every booth. Sybil threw up her hands and deserted me, heading for the food vendors. I wasn't hungry—I was being eaten alive by envy. Had everyone been on a flying saucer except me?

I stopped at the booth of a man selling Radiatrons. He was wearing one himself—a metal band that wrapped snugly around his skull at the forehead, with spokes radiating outward, each capped by a small silver knob. He said that it could turn anyone into a radio receiver for the aliens' transmissions.

"If they choose your channel," he added hastily. "But of course they're more likely to choose someone who's already equipped for reception."

I picked up a Radiatron, my heart running lightly. Sybil would shoot me—it cost ten dollars, half our gas money home. But if it worked . . .

A man gripped my arm. "You don't need that."

He was so dark and striking I thought he was Navajo, until I remembered Native Americans didn't grow beards. His had started out as a moustache and goatee, but now stretched up in a rough ridge of stubble along his jaw. The deep tan of his skin had been varnished by both sun and wind, and his hair was layered with dust, and long enough to touch his shirt collar. He was broader and shorter than me, not muscle-bound but solid. Below his walking shorts, his strong, hairy legs bristled with animal health.

On Main Street, Gaberville, he would have been stopped by the police for sheer scruffiness. But here, against the rocky, wind-carved desert, he looked more right and real than anyone I'd ever seen. I felt like a tall glass of milk standing next to him.

The Radiatron man glowered. "Are you questioning the integrity of my invention?"

"Not at all," the stranger said, and released my arm. "My method is just simpler."

"Then you're receiving messages from the spacemen, too?" I blurted.

His eyes were extraordinary, gold-flecked brown, coyote colors.

"The natives used to call them the Sky People," he said. He cocked his head and smiled, then backed away and slipped into the crowd.

His pace was brisk. I had to lope to catch up.

"You're pulling my leg," I said.

He grinned. "I pull a lot of things, man, but never legs."

"Tell me about your method, how you receive communications from . . . the Sky People."

"Hell, you can *try* it."

We were at the edge of the crowd, where the desert had become a congested, impromptu parking lot. The stranger pointed at a rocky hill that rose up near the giant rock.

"Follow the path around that hill, and you'll find my camp. It's only a half-hour walk. Come out tonight at dusk. We'll watch the sunset, and see what happens." He raised his eyebrows. "What they say."

"But George Van Tassel will be channeling tonight."

"And tomorrow night, too. Trust me—it's pretty much the same show."

I was knotted in coils. I'd driven hundreds of miles to hear Van Tassel, and maybe see a flying saucer. Yet this dusty, shaggy stranger seemed to hum a mysterious song that only I could hear.

I laughed nervously. "I don't even know your name."

"Richard. Call me Rich." He thrust out his hand and I clasped it. "Dave."

He lifted his hand as he walked away. "See you later, Dave."

I waved back, faintly stunned. I'd never called myself by that name before. No one had.

I changed my clothes twice in our cramped little camper, combed and combed my light brown hair, trying to flatten the stubborn wave. I set out into the desert an hour before dusk, buzzing with anticipation.

In minutes the sound of people had fallen away behind me and I was alone under a vast, quiet sky, the rocky hill rising up in black and gray on my left side. I wondered why Rich had chosen to set up camp so far from everyone else.

When I rounded the hill, I saw his car first, then the green tent with the open flap, and then his naked body. Just twenty yards away, he was standing in a low silver washtub, bathing. I dropped against the rough incline and pressed myself into the rocks, hoping to vanish like a chameleon. It took me three seconds to remember I had binoculars.

Pulses of slick, squeezing guilt didn't even slow me down. Heart thudding, I peeked out over a boulder and adjusted the focus, drawing him tight to my face.

He soaped himself with a sponge and it was glorious: luxuriant black hair laying in flat whorls over his wet skin, white foam frothing up suddenly, then meandering in slow trails down the bronze landscape. He'd already washed his hair and it clung to his head in a dark, gleaming helmet, the ends twisted into dripping tails. My gaze lingered on his strong thighs, tight abdomen, and the soft, meaty penis that bobbed and quivered every time he moved.

My erection came up quickly. I shifted the bulge and fought the urge to stroke myself.

Rich rinsed and toweled off, then crouched down to shave, the mirror propped on a chair. I stared at his back, the muscles that undulated when he moved, the long, tantalizing trail of his spine, and I had an unexpected thought: the spacemen wouldn't care if he was clean. He was doing this for me.

The surge of hope almost undid my zipper. I had to call up the Red Sox, the White Sox, the Cardinals, and the Cubs.

The earth had tilted by the time I ambled into his camp, the white glare of the day burnished gold, shadows spilling in long trails. Rich was dry and dressed, and had set up two wooden folding chairs. A six-string guitar leaned against his.

"Have a seat," he said cheerfully, and gestured at the sky. "The show's already started."

A glorious vista was unfolding, endless blue sighing to pink, blazing to orange along the edges of the clouds. Yet even as I gazed at the panorama, I saw his naked, wet, soapy body standing in the tub, as if the image had been burned into my retinas.

Rich said he was on his way to San Francisco; I said I was writing a novel.

"That's so cool. Tell me about it."

I did, in shy, halting half-steps. When he picked up his guitar and began to strum, I stopped.

"No, no, keep going!" Rich said. "You make it sound like poetry. My friends and I do this all the time, in coffee houses."

Twilight fell and the stars came out. With his music and my story, we transformed *Six to Save Orion* into a poem and a song. I was exhilarated, dizzy on my own words and Rich's handsome, eager face.

Finally, we just talked. Rich lit a kerosene lamp and plucked soft, aimless notes that wound through our conversation. I asked about the natives' Sky People, and he told me about the petraglyphs, ancient carvings on the rocks, just twenty miles from here. When he said some etchings looked like spacemen, wearing helmets and throwing bolts of fire, I leaned forward, tingling.

"And yet you think Van Tassel is a liar?"

"I think people stood in this desert and saw things they couldn't explain, long before you, me, or Georgie ever got here."

"But somebody communicates with *you*. You said you had your own method."

Rich put the guitar aside, grinning, and pulled a twisted cigarette from his pocket.

I felt as if I'd been drenched in cold water—a whole washtub full. That was reefer, I was sure of it, and marijuana led to madness. I'd seen the films in school. I pushed up to my feet, seasick in the wave of disappointment.

"I thought you were talking about something real," I blurted. "You're a beatnik, a dope fiend."

"And how much 'real' did you expect to get with a ten-dollar piece of tin on your head?" Rich put the white reed between his lips and lit it with a wooden match.

"I came a long way to hear what those people had to say. I'm missing it because of you!"

"Listen, there'll be at least five speakers before Van Tassel." He took a drag. "And you know what he'll do, Dave? He'll talk to himself for fifteen minutes, pretending that all the different aliens are trying to channel in at once. Then he'll tell us the Space Brothers are going to land and show us a new way, fill the world with *love*. But in the meantime, please send money."

I was silent for a moment, stung. Van Tassel did ask for donations, in every issue of the newsletter.

"But don't you want the world to change? Don't you think people should just . . . love each other?"

"That's *exactly* what I think." The lamp cast swaying golden light over his face, but his gaze was steady, coyote eyes lit by a different glow. We both knew that if I was leaving, I'd already be gone.

I sat down again.

"If you never do anything, what will you have to write about, Dave?" he said softly.

My first puff of the reefer was an acrid, burning gust that made me cough and sputter. It was worse than unfiltered Lucky Strike.

"Here, stand up," Rich said. Face to face, he took a drag and blew smoke into my open mouth. This time the taste was grassy, earthy, easy. Again and again I inhaled his smoke into my own lungs, our mouths separated by inches. When the reefer was finished, it took me seconds to realize I was still staring at him.

His face was enthralling. The freshly-shaved skin looked soft and luminous; his goatee and moustache were a sharp, alluring bull's-eye around his ruddy lips. He had hold of my arm now, the warm, familiar clasp of someone who knew me. I felt a rush, the sudden whoosh of driving over a hill too fast.

Kiss him.

I blinked, astonished. Who'd said that?

Rich smiled. "What are they saying?"

Whoosh.

I leaned forward and opened my mouth over his, easily, fearlessly. I could hardly believe this daring man was me, yet in the same instant I knew it was more true than anything else. I was a bold explorer, Jack Drake's older, braver brother.

His mouth was velvet joy. I pressed into it hard and deep, reveling in the wet fusion, the brusque prickle of his moustache. I entered him with my tongue and heard the thick, happy surprise in the back of his throat. His hands slipped under my jacket and shirt and stroked me in strong, thrilling encouragement. I ran my fingers through his long hair, closed my fists in it, amazed at the silky, resilient texture. I'd never known a man who had hair this long. I wanted to put my face against it, but on the way there I got distracted by his ear. I tugged the fleshy lobe into my mouth and began to suck.

The sensation was slow, liquid lightening from my mouth to my groin. As a kid I'd never sucked anything, not even my thumb, but the pleasure of that simple motion struck deep, ancient chords. I thrust against his thigh, moaning.

"Let's . . . go inside," Rich panted.

The glow of the lantern turned his small, dark tent into Aladdin's golden cave, or the secret core of some fiery planet. We pulled off our clothes as if they burned us. The sight of him seized me fresh, his swarthy nakedness, his erection that rose up like a taut, belligerent animal. When I reached for him, he stopped me, eyes gleaming.

"Wait."

The tent itself seemed to be breathing. He made me stand, hands at my sides, while he traced my body with his fingers. I'd always thought I was too scarce, a loose, lanky sketch waiting to fill in. He made me feel like sculpture, a work of art.

"Shoulders," he said, and caressed them. "Pecs." He drew his hands down my chest, thumbs along my breastbone, fingers fluttering over my nipples. Until that moment I'd hardly noticed them, but they hardened abruptly, awake.

"Abdomen." He stroked through the light forest of brown hair. "Cock." He gripped me.

I groaned out loud, swaying in the rush of sensation and sound. That word was the smack of sex itself, and it reverberated through my flesh. *Cock.* It was the throbbing center of my body, the center of the universe.

And now Rich had it in his mouth. He was on his knees, eyes half-closed in bliss, sucking me in the yellow lamplight. I was engulfed by wet, rippling heat, delicious pressure that stroked up and down my shaft. I cradled his face between my hands and watched the ruddy flesh slide in and out of the dark bull's-eye. *Cock.* A churning meteor gathered between my legs and I prayed to God and baseball to hold it back.

Red Sox, White Sox, Cardinals, oh, Jesus . . .

But Rich knew me better than I knew myself. He pulled away in time and led me to the roll-out mattress, then skillfully entwined himself with me. I was amazed at the simplicity of it: his mouth between my legs, my mouth between his. Even on his clean body, the scent was sharp, as distinct and powerful as the word.

Cock.

I took it eagerly into my mouth, and the thrill was magnified a hundredfold as he enveloped mine, too. We were a perfect, blazing circle of suck. There was no prayer for this, no team in the world could hold it back. I bucked mindlessly and the comet came hurtling out of the darkness, a streaming, unstoppable joy. I shuddered and writhed as I rode it, still sucking hard, and in seconds the pleasure came full orbit and exploded, hot and tart, in my own mouth.

By and by, the tent stopped breathing. Rich and I lay with our shoulders touching, fingers peacefully intertwined. The night seemed unearthly calm. I could feel the vast silence of the desert sky right through the canvas above me.

"It's not too late," Rich said.

I rose up on one elbow to look at him.

"If you still want to see Van Tassel, I know a shortcut."

His kindness caught me in the chest. I kissed him hard, courageous and certain now. I was Jack Drake's older, braver brother—Dave.

The moon was bright and high, illuminating the rocky hill in stark silver. That was fortunate because we couldn't have carried a lantern or even a flashlight up the slope. Rich led the way and I followed, hand over hand, nimble with hope. This was a magic place, even the ancient people had known it. I thought of them climbing this hill or another just like it, under the same moon.

My muscles burned by the time we reached the summit. I was panting, heart pounding, lightheaded in the rush of triumph and vertigo. I seemed to soar between the endless twinkling sky and the desert far below. The people and cars were as tiny as toys. I had a sudden, dizzying thought—at this moment, *we* were the Sky People. I tried to tell Rich but he hushed me, and tugged me down on my knees beside him.

"Listen," he said, and pointed to the Giant Rock, which looked a lot smaller than I remembered it. I finally noticed the animated little man on the platform, and heard his tinny voice echoing through the loudspeaker. George Van Tassel was communing with the Space Brothers.

"*Now* who am I talking to? Well, somebody else keeps butting in! Confound it, you keep switching on me. Let's settle on who is to do the . . ." His voice lowered abruptly. *"I am Knut from the planet Zorkon. I bring you love."*

This time the words struck me fresh. I felt a sensation in my chest that tickled like a string of bubbles, then bloomed into a fountain, a geyser. I leaned toward Rich to smother the sound, and he reached his arm around me, pressed my face against his warm neck. I laughed and laughed, convulsions that shook us both.

Everything had changed.

The Gift

Kim Addonizio

I FIND A dildo on the street: thick and slightly curved, flesh-colored, dark fluff around the balls. It looks so convincing that for a second I think it is a real penis, and I feel a sense of vertigo. It's brand-new, wrapped in white tissue which has ripped open. There's a thin blue-and-white-striped ribbon tied around it, and red scotch tape with little Christmas tree designs holding the corners.

I look around to see if there is someone nearby who might have dropped it. The street is full of people entering and leaving stores, carrying oddly-shaped packages, or dragging enormous bags full of gifts, no doubt intended for loved ones, yes, it is clear that everyone but me has loved ones to buy for. The dildo could belong to anyone. It looks elegant and expensive and forlorn, lying there so vulnerably, perhaps about to be stepped on, trampled underfoot, a smudged heel mark left on the still-pristine tissue; perhaps it will be kicked aside, to lie all night beside a garbage can, or even placed inside it with the reek of old hamburger wrappers to which well-chewed gray gum clings.

I can't bear these thoughts, I bend down to cradle the object in my hand. I think for a minute of its rightful owner—perhaps some woman like me, a woman who is lonely, isolated in fact, a woman who has no one to be with at Christmas. Maybe she bought herself a present, a present she would wait until Christmas morning to open; maybe she would take it to bed and close her eyes and moan and rock back and forth on it saying "John, John" (for that is his name, the man who walked out on me at the start of the holiday shopping season, leaving me devastated, perhaps even suicidal, who knows what I may do next), and then she would come, her legs stiffening, her juices flowing, and she would begin to cry afterward and perhaps fling it across the room with a curse; but now I have deprived her of all that, I have picked it up and put it into the pocket of my long black coat and hurried home with it.

Now it sits—or stands, rather—on the dresser, freed of its wrappings. It glows in the light of the lamp, its veins seem to pulse, a rosy aura suffuses it. I take off my clothes and approach it, something seems to radiate from it—a sense of ease and power, a kind of self-satisfaction, a kind of . . . lust—yes, it is clearly lust I feel. I seize it in my hand, I fall to the floor with it and writhe around, it throbs under my palm, swells and hardens as I pump it faster and faster. My orgasm builds until I explode all over the rug; come spurts from me, one spurt, another, I lie exhausted holding it in my hand, I pass out from the sheer pleasure of it.

I wake up, not knowing how long I have been unconscious. Maybe minutes, but maybe years; I could be an old woman, finished with sex forever, content to sit on a sagging plaid couch and stare at the television in an ugly room with no visitors day after day; I eat candy bars from the vending machine, at night I take pills and lie awake listening to the radiator and the nurses' shoes going by my door and the person in the next room trying to breathe with his weak collapsed lungs. I stagger to my feet, feeling strange and dizzy, I look in the full-length mirror and see that I am not an old woman at all; I am a young man.

I have a large penis, thick and slightly curved, dark hair around my balls. I yank at it and feel it at the base of my belly, I look at myself in horror. I would gladly turn into something else—a werewolf, a vampire, I would happily be like Gregor Samsa and live out the rest of my life as a dung beetle. But I am a man. And already, as I look at myself, the horror begins to fade; I can no longer think or feel anything but—yes, again it is lust I feel, I touch the head of my penis and it quivers, it longs to dive into the bed sheets and thrust, over and over, it takes me with it, I come all over the sheets yelling and thrashing about.

Afterward I sleep deeply. I wake the next morning and think it has been a dream, perhaps I am delusional, perhaps the doctor was right after all and I should begin taking Prozac; but truthfully I feel better than I have in weeks, and besides I have a hard-on; I lie there dreamily pulling on my penis, and come again in the sheets which are already a little stiff and sticky. I think of doing the laundry, it has been so long since I have washed the sheets, or my clothes, or cleaned the apartment; I have been so depressed over John's leaving. But I do not want to clean today. No, I want to take a shower and eat a large breakfast and take my penis out into the world.

Now the streets look different, the shoppers so hurried, so pathetic in their desperate efforts to find just the right gift. I walk confidently, feeling my penis bulge against the zipper of my jeans; it is my companion, I will never feel lonely again, it will accompany me everywhere. I thank God for this gift of a penis, my beautiful wonderful penis, tucked so cozily inside my silk underwear, nestled like a little wren; I see an attractive man and the wren begins to grow talons, it lifts its great wings and follows the man with its fierce eagle eyes, it wants to swoop down and carry him off to my apartment and feast on him for hours.

I follow the man down the street, into a store where he fingers scarves, looks at expensive earrings, takes down pretty kimonos from a rack. I remember that I am a man, too, and suddenly a wave of revulsion rises in me, the thought of dragging him home with me is crushed and drowned by the wave crashing over it. I am normal, I say to myself, normal; there is nothing wrong with me, I have never been a woman or wanted to make love to a man, I must wipe all that from my mind—especially the image of sucking on a penis, the joy of taking it into my mouth, licking the clear liquid that forms a bright drop at the tip, swallowing the slightly bitter fluid as I kneel before John, as he strokes my hair and says Baby, oh baby—I must erase all that.

I hurry from the store, and now I see the women, their breasts bulging inside sweaters, or hidden under coats, their asses moving just ahead of me like beacons to guide me, I think of their cunts and their smells, their soft inviting mouths. The eagle circles and circles, hunger gnaws at its belly, and now a kind of terror: I must find a woman, a woman who will have me, suddenly my penis is profoundly lonely and cold and sad.

I go into a bar and the terror is greater; there are women here, all around me in twos and threes, my penis is about to leap from my pants. I want to go up to one of them, to lean her back over a table and plunge into her, but I must stop myself; I drink beer after beer to quell my anxiety, to try and think of a way to do this politely. I stumble to the back of the bar, into the men's room, stand at the urinal and watch the arc of piss, golden and fragrant, and I am so fascinated by it I forget about the women. I go into a stall and jerk off, sitting on the toilet, and then emerge calm and in control once more. I return to the bar and continue to drink. I talk to no one, I think bitterly about my life, my past lovers, I resolve not to ever love anyone again; somewhere in the deepest recesses of my brain I remember who I am, I know that something is wrong, but it no longer matters. I get gloriously drunk, so drunk that everything goes black and disappears . . .

I wake up in a strange, but prettily decorated, room. I am lying in a canopy bed, tiny lights are strung around it, blinking on and off; Bing Crosby is singing "White Christmas," and I can smell sugar cookies baking somewhere. I want to reach between my legs to see if I still have my penis, but I can't move my arm very far. Perhaps I have had a stroke, and there is no hope I will regain my bodily functions; I am in a hospice, no one will visit me but volunteers doing their Zen practice, who will sit beside me to experience dying close up and tell me I must learn to let go. Forget John, they will say; life is but a dream, they are saying, or someone is singing; yes, a little girl is singing "Row, Row, Row Your Boat," in a high, pleasant voice.

Now she is standing over my bed, but her face is huge, impossibly huge; surely I am dying, and this is the angel of death, wearing enormous wings and a white gown and holding a plain wooden wand in one hand, a glittery silver star stuck to one end of it. She reaches down for me, and lifts me, naked, into the air. She sets me on the dresser, and I see in the mirror that I am supposed to be female, I have long slim legs, a tiny waist, but I have no nipples on my otherwise perfect breasts and nothing between my legs but a sort of hinge, no sex at all anymore. I try to open my rosebud mouth to scream, but it is painted shut, it smiles happily back at me. "Merrily, merrily, merrily," the little girl sings, and begins to brush my hair.

Non-Stop New York Ecstasy (1981)

Beverley Glick

*M*ARC ALMOND HAD been teasing me for months about what we could do when I joined his merry band of hedonists in New York. As a long-time friend and supporter of his band Soft Cell and a trainee fetish queen to (six-inch-heeled) boot, he couldn't wait to show me off.

I had always thought of the adorable yet highly-strung singer as 100 percent guycentric but recent events had given me cause to wonder if he really was pink to the core. A new recreational drug called MDMA—street name, Ecstasy—had had a profound effect on him: so much so that he had bonded with his supplier, who called herself Cindy Ecstasy. He even announced their "engagement" live on American TV.

Hell, surely Marc wasn't bisexual? I'd always believed it was strictly a case of BDSM voyeurism and an appreciation of the feminine aesthetic with him.

I put it out of my mind as I exited the terminal building at Kennedy and rendezvoused with Stevo, Soft Cell's deeply mischievous manager, who treated narcotics like sweeties.

He was waiting for me in an enormous black limousine with a colossal chauffeur who was so tall the sunroof had to be kept permanently rolled back.

We had barely cleared the airport perimeter when Stevo pulled out his bag of pharmaceutical delights. Anything seemed possible: I was in a surreal road movie, and Lurch was behind the wheel.

Stevo stuffed some black and blue tablets down my throat (I asked no questions) and we began to drain the bar of alcohol. The rush was intense. "I throw myself upon the mercy of Manhattan," I said, dramatically.

Soft Cell were the toast of the city. "Tainted Love" had joined "Rock Around The Clock" as one of the ten longest-running hits on the American charts. This gave Marc and his sidekick, Dave, the golden key that unlocked almost any door they wanted to open, and behind most of them was an unlimited supply of alcohol and class-A drugs. And they wanted to share it all with their friends.

I was in the mood to experiment, with no consideration of negative consequences. Marc gave me a white capsule of Ecstasy just before we arrived at Danceteria, the nightclub hosted by Rudolph and his impossibly voluptuous wife, Diane Brill. When was this stuff going to hit? What would it do to me?

My brain failed to alert me but its chemistry was already changing. I didn't register the weirdness of the bearded man with the camera. He asked if he could take pictures of my shoes— electric red patent stilettos with four-inch heels. It seemed the most natural thing in the world to agree to stand on a glass-topped table in the middle of a throbbing, super-hip club to show off my ballet-honed arches.

"Take as many photos as you like," I said, dreamily, imagining myself to be starring in an eighties version of Warhol's Factory.

In an instant any notion of inhibition had slipped from my conscious mind. And the beardo was zooming in on his lust objects.

"Would you mind posing for me in the kitchens?"

"No problem," I said, clambering on to a stainless steel draining board as chefs rushed past beneath me.

They smiled and congratulated me on my excellent choice of footwear and unusual hosiery (one leg black, one red) before putting the finishing touches to another main course.

I was several feet off the ground. The drug was stripping away the veils between myself and others, and the parts of me that I usually held back from the world.

Marc observed me like a sculptor admiring his handiwork. He had many New York buddies operating on the fringes and was keen for me to meet and greet. Among them was a professional Dominatrix by the name of Terence Sellers, who had recently written a book called *The Correct Sadist*.

The impossibly aloof and imperious Terence—whose working name was Mistress Angel Stern—frequented the clubs of Manhattan with her fellow female correctionists. She terrified me, but my successful stint as a foot fetishist's model had attracted the attention of one of her cohorts—a ghostly, etiolated girl dressed all in black with penetrating eyes. She approached me as the pink light of the club became painfully neon.

"Hi. I saw you posing for the foot guy," she said, oozing cool. "You enjoyed it. Looked comfortable up there."

"Yeah, I loved it," I burbled, floating. "I could have gone so much further. . . ."

"How do you mean?" she probed.

"Like maybe digging my heels right into his back. . . ." I replied, playing up to my designated role.

"Really? He'd have dug that! You might enjoy doing my job . . ." (Was she serious?)

"So you really are a Dominatrix?" (I needed to know.)

"Yeah," she said, perfectly languid.

"Wow. Do you really get off on inflicting pain?" (As if I didn't know.)

"Sometimes. Depends on the client. But you have to remember who's paying; they call the shots, you just make 'em," she explained.

"I've always fancied totally getting into the dominant role, really playing it out. . . ." (I was sounding far too much like a novice now.)

"Yeah, it's like acting, but you have to love it, without getting emotionally involved. Could you take it?"

"I think I could. . . . Why?"

"I sometimes take on trainees. Would you be into that?"

(My awareness had expanded so much that I could hear, feel, see, taste, and smell more than I ever had before. I felt so in tune with this woman; I was convinced I could do what she did and be who she was. I was inside her, without having touched her. It was extraordinarily intimate—delicate, beyond sexual. Now I understood why Marc might have wanted to marry Ms. Ecstasy.)

"Yeah, I'd seriously be into that . . . can I call you?"

"Sure."

An alternative existence flashed before me.

⌒

LEAVE LONDON, GO to New York, become a professional hit girl's apprentice. Yes, it could work for me.

I already had the wardrobe, after all: one back-zipped, studded black rubber skirt; one backless PVC skirt (with complicated strap arrangement); one leather miniskirt; one black leather handcuff belt; one black rubber molded corset with suspenders; one studded black leather conical bra (to reveal nipples); one homemade black leather corset; one pair black, one pair red rubber stockings; two pairs long black rubber gloves; one pair black patent thigh boots (uncomfortable); one pair red, one pair black patent stilettos (four-inch heel); one pair fifties-style red Sex shoes (designed by Vivienne Westwood); one pair black Cover Girl stilettos (six-inch heel—latest purchase); one black, one blonde Cleopatra wig; one black "Betty Page" wig (with cute fringe); two pairs handcuffs; one pair thumb cuffs; one black leather whip; one riding crop; one antique cigarette holder (for attitude rather than smoking).

And the *piece de resistance* was ready to be unveiled. A friend had been working on designs for a couture rubber collection and I was his muse. The frock—or should I say construction—wore me.

Crafted in black latex with red trim, it was strapped tightly in four places across the front and laced right up the back to reveal the entire cleavage of my rounded buttocks. Beneath, I wore red rubber stockings. On top, red stilettos, a black rubber peplum jacket and a black and red plastic peaked cap with chain, over a severe black wig.

The ensemble begged a response and never failed to elicit one. "Oh my God!" shrieked Marc. "You look absolutely fantastic! We'll have to take you somewhere to do that dress justice."

"Where?" I asked, sheepishly.

"Just you wait . . . I want it to be a surprise! But first, you must take this . . ."

In the cold Manhattan night, my head was in a tingling haze, my body pleasantly confused by my second skin, not knowing whether to heat up or cool down. Acutely aware of my epidermis, I felt the rivulets of sweat running down to the most delicate section of my inner thigh. "That's what wearing rubber is all about," I thought, ". . . complete erotic commitment."

(I remembered the time I was getting ready to go out to Skin Two, the first fashionable fetish club in London. To a soundtrack of hi-NRG dance music, I fastened my latex stockings to my rubber corset and had a spontaneous, rippling orgasm: look, no hands . . .)

"Here we are," shrieked Marc, waking me from my reverie, "L'Esqualita!"

Latino heavies toting machine guns guarded the entrance. "Jesus, Marc, what's this? Are we starring in a remake of *West Side Story*?"

"No, don't worry. It's a Puerto Rican drag club and I know the owner. We're welcome."

The honchos waved us through but we were the only ones speaking English. I drifted in, a vision in black and red, to find I had serious competition: a gash of crimson here, fabulous fuchsia and frills there. Transvestites in full flamenco gear swirled around the stage as delirious Spanish families stuffed dollar bills down their fake cleavages.

We screamed, we danced; we were embraced into this color-coordinated cacophony. "Suck me and see—I'm juicy," a voice said; thank God it was only in my head.

Our strange little gang moved on. A squat, mustachioed Spanish guy on the street outside stroked my arse, but in a good-humored way. I needed to be tenderized: we were off to the meat market.

The Hellfire was Soft Cell's hellhole of choice. Essentially a gay club, it also specialized in S/M scenarios, all sexes welcome. No boundaries except mutual consent.

Marc, Dave, Stevo, their DJ friend Anita, and I ventured into the red-tinged gloom. Bodies were barely discernible in the half-light; wooden swing doors provided the only privacy in the cubicles throughout the club. This was a Wild West saloon in Dante's *Inferno*.

In the corner, a naked man was strapped to a St. Andrew's cross, awaiting attention from a woman dressed in a leather harness, flicking a cat-o'-nine-tails in the direction of his exposed genitals.

Behind a swing door, a clone in leather chaps pumped furiously up and down. I didn't stop to see what was underneath.

In the middle of the room, a Rubenesque woman in her middle years perched on a stool, naked folds of skin and blubber spilling over its brim. A queue of men waited patiently and politely for her to suck their cocks; her dribbling grin said they were in for a gummy treat.

The atmosphere was heavy with the acrid aroma of rubber, leather, perspiration and pheromones. But I knew the manner of my dress guaranteed that no one would approach me with disrespect.

As I glided into the caverns of the club, a group of voyeurs began to gather around Anita and me. She immediately entered into the spirit of role-play.

"Lick your mistress's heels clean, vile worm, or She will grind these metal tips into your pathetic, unworthy flesh."

Soon, several tongues were vying for space on my patent leather spikes, administering a surprising all-over custom shoeshine.

Meanwhile, each tongue's owner hastened himself jerkily toward *le petit mort*, as if his life depended on it.

When this willing group of onanists had finished their oral cleaning work, they had to start all over again, having deposited strings of sperm pearls on the highly polished surface of my stilettos.

"Lick that disgusting mess off immediately and make sure you swallow every last revolting drop. . . ." (Did I say that?)

Marc, bless him, was watching over my shoulder. He had become a voyeur of the voyeurs. Before we became inundated with the ejaculate of every man in the house, we beat a hasty retreat. I was still dripping.

"How perfect," I mused. "Marc and I bonding over other men's spunk. . . . Now he'll have to marry me."

~

I FELL OUT OF the Hellfire as dawn was breaking. I jumped into a yellow taxi waiting outside, not even wondering why it might be there.

"Have a good night there, ma'am?" asked the driver.

"Yeah, it was amazing. So friendly and, erm . . . open." (I still was. . . .)

"Do you like to use a whip?" (Here we go . . .)

"Well, sometimes . . . it depends who I'm with." (Hedging . . .)

"I bet you hit real hard . . ." (Gulp . . .)

"That depends what situation I'm in. . . ." (Deflecting . . .)

"Do you wanna get into a scenario? I could take you someplace now. . . ." (Think. Quick.)

"That's sweet of you to ask, but I'm afraid I can't. I'm about to start very strict training and I have to be disciplined. . . ."

That shut him up and made me moist.

But I needed to peel off my persona: she was a demanding bitch. Shorn of my demonic black and red, standing in front of a mirror in a Howard Johnson's motel, I looked like a ghostly, etiolated girl. I dreamt about her, of being inside her. But I couldn't find my way in.

Coming down, I thought of adventure, of making that life-changing call, of opening doors in my head. I thought of the man who had made it all possible: a mad, camp superstar who was my friend and co-explorer.

Marc wasn't bisexual: hell, no. But the girl I had become was.

(Adapted from *Hit Girl: My Bizarre Double Life in the Pop World of the Eighties*, by Beverley Glick, copyright 2004)

Cruise Control

Janice Eidus

$\mathcal{V}$INCENT DESTEPHANO, WEARING his lightweight khaki suit, sitting alone at a table in a hotel bar on West Fifty Seventh Street and staring at a redheaded woman wearing a sleeveless black dress, had a revelation: *his was a life on cruise control.* He'd never thought about it quite that way before, but it was true. In Charlottesville, where he now lived, it was easy to take the smooth and steady course, with no bumps on the road, no sharp and unexpected curves. He loved Charlottesville, its comfort, architecture, history, and privilege. Privilege, especially, struck Vincent as a beautiful thing.

Pouring himself a second glass of white wine and staring at the woman, who was sitting a couple of tables over, and whose bright red hair shone even in the dimly-lit hotel bar, he wondered for the first time whether it would be good for his children to grow up taking such privilege for granted, or whether they would become weak and spoiled. He'd wanted them to go to good schools, to live without fear and violence. Most of all, though, he wanted them to belong somewhere. As a boy, growing up on the streets of the Bronx, he had never felt that he belonged.

But he'd found a way out: working two part-time jobs, he'd put himself through law school in Baltimore. Now he worked for a small firm in Charlottesville, which, as far as he was concerned, was another planet from the Bronx, located in another galaxy. He had a sweet, blonde, blue-eyed wife named Katie. They had two children: James, who looked like Katie, and Lisa, who looked like Vincent, with dark eyes and hair, olive skin, and strong features. Sometimes Vincent watched Lisa as she played with her blonde girlfriends, and she stood out, like a gypsy child.

Vincent was trim and muscular. As a boy, he'd played stickball on the streets. Now he played tennis three mornings a week. He liked the discipline of tennis; he liked anything that made him feel in control. His parents had prided themselves on being out of control, on being volatile and hot tempered. Every night during dinner in their cramped, dark apartment on Gun Hill Road, there were curses and arguments, and sometimes the shattering of plates and glasses. His two sisters, Anna-Maria and just plain Maria, frequently fled the table in tears, their meals half-eaten, their black mascara running down their faces. Sometimes, after dinner, his father would take the strap to him.

His friends in Charlottesville frequently asked him questions about his Bronx childhood; it was such a curiosity to them. He romanticized it, making it sound palatable and familiar, a situation comedy on t.v.: the larger-than-life Italian Mama and Papa with their hearts of gold, always eating spaghetti and chicken *cacciatore*.

Pouring himself a third glass of wine, he watched the red-headed woman, who was now reapplying her red lipstick, which was even brighter than her hair. He promised himself that this would be his final glass. But, being back in New York, even for two days, depressed him, and the wine made him feel better. His widowed mother, old and sick and superstitious, wanted, at last, to return to her people in Sicily. He had been called in to help. He'd spent the last two days going through stacks of papers, trying to remain calm, even when his mother went on and on about how the ghost of his father came to her every night, mad as hell at all of them, but especially at Vincent, who had moved far away from the family, who had deserted and betrayed them all.

The redheaded woman was raising her arms over her head, stretching. Her movements were feline, full of confidence. She was the only woman at a table full of men. He recognized her, in a way, although he'd never seen her before. She was one of them, one of *the girls*, as he called them. As a teenager, he'd been drawn to them, to that type: the lone female in the group of guys, the one girl the boys felt so at ease with, they drank and bowled and played cards with her. The girl was always pretty, slightly rowdy, very smart, and sensual beyond her years. Not indiscriminately sensual, of course. The girl was never the tramp.

Anna-Maria, his younger sister, was not one of the girls. She had married Louis Colucci from the Gun Hill Projects. They had three kids, and they still lived in the Bronx, on Arthur Avenue. They'd wanted Vincent to stay overnight with them. But it had been on Arthur Avenue that he'd been beaten up one hot summer night by a gang of boys from a rival high school, and it was there, the next night, that he'd returned with his own friends from Gun Hill Road for vengeance, armed with baseball bats and switch-blades. No, he didn't want to spend an evening on Arthur Avenue.

His older sister, just plain Maria, had also never been one of the girls. Maria had been less fortunate than Anna-Maria. Mickey Piscatello had gotten her pregnant while she was still in high school. Mickey had gone on to become a big-time drug dealer in Las Vegas, abandoning her in the process. She'd raised her child alone, in a one-bedroom apartment in Yonkers, on a secretary's salary. She had no extra room for Vincent. So he was staying, instead, in this snazzy hotel near Carnegie Hall, with its dimly-lit hotel bar, where the waiters all affected British accents and glided swiftly along, almost as though dancing, and where, no matter how hard he tried, he just couldn't stop staring at the redheaded woman.

After he'd started college, and had begun separating from his family and the streets, he'd given up the girls. The girls were too restless, too flirtatious and quick-witted, too passionate and demanding. In order to become the kind of man he so much wanted to be, he'd had no choice but to give them up.

And he hadn't really minded. He never thought about them one way or another, after he'd met Katie. Katie, born and bred in Charlottesville, had never gone barhopping with the guys, had never sat out on a stoop drinking beer, smoking and cursing and flirting. She'd gone to Sweet Briar, had majored in Home Economics, ridden horses, been in a sorority, and dated fraternity boys. Her single act of rebellion had been marrying an Italian guy from the Bronx. But Vincent made it clear to Katie's parents right from the start how much he hungered to enter their world, how much more he valued their world than his own, and they soon accepted him. Really, Katie barely understood how different his background was from her own. Not that she was stupid. She was, however, sheltered, and her imagination couldn't include that which she didn't know existed. Besides, he didn't talk much about his past, about Gun Hill Road, about violent fights with baseball bats, about sniffing glue from paper bags in parking lots late at night, about having a father who cursed at you and then took a strap to you when you weren't even sure what terrible crime—or, perhaps, what mortal sin—you had committed. The few times Katie had met his parents and his sisters, she'd just been bewildered.

But this redheaded woman in the hotel bar, sitting with all the men, laughing so loudly, so flirtatiously, well, it annoyed him that he couldn't stop watching her. She was probably in her early thirties, not really a girl at all. She wore her sleek, shiny hair in a geometric bob, like a twenties' film star. Her jewelry was all silver: a large necklace in the shape of an elephant; long, dangling earrings; and serpentlike bracelets coiled along each of her bare upper arms.

He had never been unfaithful to Katie. Lots of his friends in Charlottesville fooled around while their wives looked the other way. But he didn't want to. First, there was the issue of morality. All those confessions at the Immaculate Conception Church, across the street from the Projects, had left their mark. Second, none of the women he met down in Charlottesville had ever tempted him much. There was nothing they could offer him that Katie didn't already provide.

The redheaded woman took a long sip of her drink. Briefly, she rested her head on the shoulder of one of the men, a man with a blonde beard and a turtleneck sweater. She definitely wasn't on cruise control. She and the men ordered another round of drinks and laughed some more. He felt stodgy and stale in his Southern-gentleman khaki suit, with his dark, wavy hair so neatly combed.

The waiter appeared. "Sir?" he asked Vincent politely, in his quasi-British accent, lifting the empty wine bottle from the table. Despite himself, Vincent ordered a second bottle. He glanced at his watch; it was late, midnight, and the girl's party appeared to be breaking up. One by one, the men rose and kissed her good-bye. She remained at the table, alone. A moment later, she stood up and walked over to him. "You've been watching me all night," she said. Her voice was soft, but she spoke boldly and directly, which was the way the girls always spoke, he remembered.

"Yes," he said. He'd been wrong in thinking that she hadn't noticed him. He felt all the excitement, all the unruly and pent-up energy, of a teenage boy.

She sat down next to him. He offered her a glass of wine, but she shook her head. She called the waiter over. "A campari and soda," she said. She turned back to Vincent. "Why?" she asked him.

"Why?" he repeated her question, not understanding. Her eyes were an intense, bright blue.

"Why have you been watching me all night?"

"You're so pretty." He surprised himself by his boyish candor. "Also, you remind me of girls in my past."

"But not in your present?"

"No. Not in my present." He let the statement hang there. She could interpret it however she wanted—that he yearned to have someone like her in his life, or the opposite. He wasn't sure which he preferred. "Why did you come over to me?" he asked.

"Because you were watching me." She made it sound as though

it were the most obvious thing in the world. She sipped her Campari and soda.

"The way you look," he pointed to her exotic bracelets, suppressing an urge to reach out and stroke the bare, pale, slightly freckled skin of her arms, "you must be used to being watched." He did one of those clichéd male numbers—gazing at her body suggestively—and immediately felt embarrassed. But she didn't seem to notice, or care.

She nodded. "Well, I didn't come over just because you were watching me. It's also because I don't want to be alone. All of my friends were going home, and I didn't want to go back to my apartment. Also, *you* sort of remind me of someone in my past, too."

He felt even more embarrassed, so he changed the subject. "What was the occasion for your get-together with your friends?"

"It was a celebration for Joey Gardner, the playwright, maybe you know, he had a play off-Broadway a few years ago, 'Moving Forward'?"

Vincent shrugged, and smoothed the sleeve of his neatly-pressed jacket. Of course, he didn't know.

"Anyway," she went on, not seeming to mind at all that he'd never heard of her friend, "Joey just got a big grant. First time ever. I can't tell you how many times he's applied for Guggenheims and NEAs, for instance. And the group of us who were out tonight, we all met a few years ago at an artists' colony upstate, and we keep up with each other, celebrate each other's successes, you know."

"Why didn't you want to go home?" he asked. He felt strangely comfortable asking her such a personal question.

She frowned. "I just broke up with the man I've been living with for eight years. It was my choice, but even so. . . ." She looked into her glass.

"Are you a playwright, too?"

"No. I'm a poet."

Some of Katie's girlfriends had recently formed a poetry-writing group. Katie had been thinking of joining, too. By next year they'd be bored of poetry, and they would discover pottery or quilting. He didn't fault them for it. But he did sense that this woman was the real thing. Even though, with her black dress and exotic jewelry, she could just as well have been some bohemian dilettante, but he knew she wasn't. He continued to feel like a teenager around her: intimidated, nervous, and yet, very bold and very aroused, all at the same time.

"Where did you grow up?" he asked, trying to place her. Maybe if she told him about her background, she'd seem less magical, less arousing, less threatening.

"Brooklyn," she answered, as though eager to help him out in his quest to demystify her. "Sheepshead Bay. There's nothing at all poetic about my past." She smiled, and her teeth were slightly crooked. "I started publishing my poems in very little magazines right after I graduated from college. I *still* publish my poems in very little magazines." She laughed. "But I've also got three books out, with good presses."

He could place her now. In high school, she'd been the editor of the literary magazine. She'd dressed all in black back then, too. She'd definitely been *the girl* in her crowd, the one who'd hung around with the hip boys, the boys who also wrote poetry. He'd been aware of those girls, of course, but he had his own crowd, his own girls. In his crowd, nobody wrote poetry.

"Where did you grow up?" she asked.

Maybe she was as drawn to him as he was to her. Maybe she was also hoping to demystify him. He didn't hesitate. "The northeast Bronx. Gun Hill Road."

"Gun Hill Road," she repeated, making the three words sound almost musical. "I have a friend who grew up on Gun Hill Road. Lucy Zucchino," she said.

He stared at her. He had been friendly with Lucy's older brother, Petey Zucchino. Petey had been one of the few other guys from the neighborhood, who, like Vincent, had managed to earn high grades, and yet somehow also to pass muster with the tough boys. Vincent remembered little Lucy, too, a cute kid with braces and early-budding breasts.

"Lucy and I met at my health club," the woman went on. "We swim together three mornings a week. She's a photographer for a New Jersey newspaper, and she lives uptown, near Columbia." She tapped her glass with a long red fingernail and looked thoughtful. "You know, she *has* mentioned her older brother to me. He lives out in L.A. I think he's a film editor."

Suddenly, Vincent very much wanted to see them—Lucy and Petey Zucchino, who'd both survived those mean streets, unlike so many of the others. Billy Reticliano had become a junkie. Joey DeCroco had died in Vietnam. Rosemary Rizotta, who'd once been so lively and pretty, still lived with her parents on White Plains Road, afraid to go out by herself ever since she'd been brutally raped by a gang of boys in Bronx Park on the evening of her twentieth birthday. It made his heart soar just to think about Lucy and Petey. He wanted to throw his arms around them and say, "We are the survivors! The pioneers!" He knew it was a crazy, drunken thought, but, nevertheless, he felt love at that moment for Lucy and Petey Zucchino.

He also felt something akin to love for this redheaded woman, this bearer of such good news about Lucy and Petey. He wanted to throw his arms around her, too, to hug her tightly to his chest. Instead, he held tightly onto his wine glass, and began telling her all about how he used to hang around with Petey Zucchino in the old days. He told her about how, when he and Petey had been about twelve, they'd been caught trying to steal cigarettes from old Mr. Riccio who ran the corner candy store, and how Mr. Riccio had gotten them to sweep the floor for free in the store for a month after that by threatening to tell the cops on them. Then he found himself telling her about his superstitious, old-world mother in her black dresses and stockings, and her insistence that the ghost of his father came and cursed him out every night. He told her about his father and the strap. And about Anna-Maria and just plain Maria. About Katie and his two kids, and how he lived on cruise control in beautiful, historic Charlottesville, Virginia, home of Thomas Jefferson and Monticello. And about *the girls*, and how he'd always been drawn to them.

She sat quietly, her elbows on the table, sipping her second Campari and soda. Her expression was serious. When she finally leaned back and spoke, her voice was soft. But again, she was direct. "Do you like living on cruise control?"

"What about you," he asked, instead of answering, "do you like *your* life?"

She didn't hesitate. "Well, I like writing poetry. Even though there's no money and no glory in it. I mean, nobody reads poetry anymore, right?"

He certainly couldn't remember the last time he'd read a poem. But he didn't say anything, and she didn't seem to expect him to.

"Of course, some poetry," she went on, "can lead you to a certain respectability, to a tenured academic post somewhere. But my poems are more raw and sexual—more wicked."

"*The girls*," he said, "are always wicked. It comes with the territory."

She went on. "But the man I just broke up with, well, in the end I didn't like him very much. Or who I was when I was around him. He's a lot older than I am. He's a poet, too. But the last few years, he wanted me to stop writing. He'd become too respectable, a man of letters, a big shot academic. My work began to embarrass him."

He wanted to lean over and kiss her, to tell her that *he* would never, never ask her to stop writing, that he would die for her right to create sexy, raw poems. It was time to go, he thought. Time to say that it had been a pleasure to meet her, time to wish her good luck with her poetry and her love life, and then to depart. He paused, and said, "Would you like to come upstairs to my room with me?"

"No."

The wind went out of him, as though she'd punched him, hard, in the stomach. On the other hand, he felt relieved, too. She was making it easy for him. There was no temptation. She didn't even *want* to go to bed with him. She'd just been chatting with him, making idle talk, killing time. His revelations about his life had meant nothing to her. She traveled in circles where people revealed themselves all the time. In New York City, total strangers shared their life stories on the subway each morning. Her lack of interest in him was liberating; he could keep on living on cruise control.

"I'd rather you came back with me, to my apartment," she said.

He laughed aloud with the pleasure of it all, with the roller-coaster-like emotions she was bringing out in him. He felt exhilarated. He felt boyish. He felt terrified. What if Katie called him at the hotel in the middle of the night? What if there were an emergency at home? He had no answer. All he knew was that he was going home with her, with *the girl*, a redheaded, blue-eyed poet from Sheepshead Bay who swam three mornings a week with Lucy Zucchino from Gun Hill Road.

"My name is Barbara," she said, as they stood outside the hotel and hailed a taxi together. "Barbara Stock."

"Vinny," he said, helping her into the taxi. "Vinny DeStephano." It had been a long time since he'd referred to himself as Vinny, instead of Vincent.

Her apartment was in Chelsea, on the top floor of a small building wedged between a twenty-four hour greengrocer and a Mexican restaurant. He followed closely behind her, up the five long flights of stairs, wondering if she could feel his breath upon her neck.

She led him into her living room. He looked around, surprised that the room appeared so cold and inhospitable. Nobody in Charlottesville decorated their homes like this, with geometric, sharply-angled steel and black furniture. It was "postmodern," he decided—a word he'd read in magazines—but then he decided that, after all, he liked those sharp angles, those edges and hard lines, precisely *because* nobody else he knew would like it.

"Something to drink?" she asked. "All I have is a can of Pepsi and a can of ginger ale."

"Ginger ale," he said, sitting down uncomfortably in one of the chairs.

She went off to the kitchen, and he tried to adjust his body to the angular chair. One of her books was lying out on the square steel coffee table: *Spectrum: Poems By Barbara Stock*. It was a slim volume. The cover illustration was of a bright red cloud floating in a turquoise sky. He turned the book over. In the author's photograph on the back, she looked even more like a twenties' film star than she did in person; her lips were poutier, her eyes more luminous. Above the photo, there was a quote. "Barbara Stock's poems," he read, "do what all good poems must do—they force you to question your vision of the world." He opened the book. "For Al," he read, "who has taught me so much about the ambiguity of poetry. And also in memory of Rick, who taught me so much about the ambiguity of life."

Al, Vincent guessed, was the older poet. He felt irrationally jealous and resentful of Al. He felt a tough boy's urge to fight Al, to take him out on Arthur Avenue in order to establish his claim on Barbara Stock. As for Rick, whomever he was, he was dead, so there was no reason to take him out. He closed the book. He didn't feel ready to read any of her poems.

She returned with the two sodas. She'd stuck a curved plastic straw—a child's straw—into each can. He felt more boyish than ever as he sipped his soda through the straw. When she inserted the straw between her own red lips, however, it struck him as anything but childish. It was so erotic, so arousing, that he had to look away. "Listen," he said, not looking at her, "you said, back at the hotel, that I reminded you of someone in your past."

She was sitting across from him in a chrome chair identical to his, although she seemed comfortable in hers. She spoke so softly he had to lean forward to hear. "That's right."

"Who?" he pressed. "Who do I remind you of?"

She looked up. "You remind me of my first love," she said. "Of my one great love."

He was struck by her language. *Her one great love . . .* he'd never known anyone who spoke like that, or at least, who spoke like that and sounded genuine.

"In high school," she went on, slowly, "I was the editor of the literary magazine. It was called *The Ladder*. I hung around with the other kids on the magazine staff, the kids who wrote poetry and short stories, you know the type."

He refrained from smiling with the knowledge of how right he'd been in his assessment of her. He simply nodded.

"I had boyfriends. Boys who quoted Camus and Kerouac. To use your expression, I was one of *the girls*. I smoked pot with the guys, went to museums and foreign films and hung out in the Village with them, all that. But there was always something missing for me. There . . . was this boy. I would see him in the hallway. I would see him in the cafeteria, sometimes hanging around with his friends outside the school. He was tough, Italian, he hung out with the bad crowd, the boys who were always in and out of trouble, who ended up expelled from school. Boys who did hard drugs, robbed liquor stores . . . well, *you* know."

Again, he nodded. He knew.

"He and I were absolutely worlds apart." She sighed. "Listen, this part of my life, when I try to tell it to anyone now, it just sounds like a Grade B movie. Are you sure you want to hear?"

He nodded, watching her as she sipped her Pepsi and crossed her legs and slipped off her black shoes, which, to Vincent, looked like the delicate slippers a ballerina would wear.

"Well, I kept noticing this boy. He and I would exchange glances. I would flush when I saw him. . . . I never told anyone about him. This went on for *two years*, you have to understand, all through tenth and eleventh grade. Two years is a really long time when you're a kid. Finally, early in the fall of my senior year I couldn't stand it anymore. I walked right up to him. It was three o'clock, and he was standing in front of the school, lighting up a cigarette. 'Why are you watching me?' I asked him."

"That's the same thing you asked me," Vincent said, surprised.

She nodded. "Yes. The same thing. And he answered just the

way you did, too. He said, 'Because you're so pretty.' And then he said, 'Let's talk.' I just couldn't believe it. This bad boy wanted to *talk* to me. I brought him home with me. Both of my parents worked. His name was Rick Giampino. He was one of seven kids. His father was an unemployed gambler. His mother drank. I read him my poems, and he listened so seriously, more seriously than any other boy had listened to me before, and we made love. I mean, we were seventeen, and we made love that very day, all afternoon. And after that we saw each other as often as we could. But we hid our involvement. We knew that everyone—his family and friends, my family and friends, our teachers, everyone— would try to break us up. And of course the tension of having to hide our relationship added a fierce eroticism to things. . . . And then I got pregnant." She paused, sipped her Pepsi through the straw. Her voice grew even softer. "I was on the pill, but I'd grown careless. When I found out I was pregnant, I fell apart. I didn't tell my parents, or my friends. I didn't tell Rick, either. I just refused to see him, and I wouldn't tell him why. It drove him crazy. I totally rejected him."

"Why?" Vincent asked. She seemed to be leaving something out.

"I don't know," she said, without expression. "I've asked myself that question every single day for years. Why? I've asked therapists. I've asked my friends. I used to ask Al, the man I lived with. He said it was because I had gotten myself into a situation I couldn't control and unconsciously I wanted out of it. But I don't know. I just don't know."

Vincent was silent. He was surprised that poets—people who spent their entire lives exploring feelings—didn't always know why they did the things they did.

"I carried very small," she went on, "and my mother didn't figure it out until I was in my sixth month. I was sent away. I had a girl. I gave her up for adoption. Sometimes I dream about her, that she's all grown up and that she looks exactly like Rick. When I returned home, Rick had another girlfriend, a girl from his crowd, a girl with a drug problem. I heard that he'd also gotten into drugs.

A year later, he overdosed and died. For years, I felt responsible for his death. Sometimes I still feel that way. Al hated it when I used to say that. Sometimes I fantasize that Rick is alive, that he didn't die, that he kicked drugs and that he lives a quiet and simple life on cruise control some place far away, like Charlottesville, Virginia. And that I'll run into him one day in a hotel bar on West Fifty Seventh Street, or someplace equally farfetched."

He rose from the chair. He kneeled down in front of her and he ran his fingers through her sleek red hair.

She sat very still. "To tell you the truth, I'm terrified right now."

"Of me?" He continued to stroke her hair.

"Yes. I mean, you're not Rick. What you are is a complete stranger. And I've let you into my home. You could be a murderer, a. . . ."

"I'm not," he said. He kissed her.

She kissed him back without any hesitation at all. She placed her thin, pale arms on his shoulders.

They kissed for a long time, and then he followed her into her bedroom. He watched her undress. Her pale, narrow-waisted body was unbearably beautiful. Standing there, watching her, he understood why they had come to be together, why they were going to make love. In each other's arms, they were both seeking forgiveness and absolution for their past sins—the real sins, and the imagined ones. He hoped that after they made love they didn't feel even more like sinners than before. He began unbuttoning his shirt. No matter where it led him, though, he was going to do it, he was going to follow this dangerous and unexpected curve in the road.

Awake

Selma James Blair

I HAVE ALWAYS been afraid of the dark. I have been afraid of so many things in this lifetime it is a wonder I have made it to the age of forty-three with a hair on my head. My Aunt Anna used to joke that she was "going to brush her hairs now." I don't remember if her hair was actually so thin as to warrant that expression, but it conjured an image of her as Popeye, with three thin hairs on a bald pate. She had fingers like a gnarled bonsai. She is dead now. At the end, Anna was a penniless amputee writing to my mother for money. She lived in Atlantic City. She died alone there. Perhaps in the dark. I am afraid of this. I try to make out the face of a younger her captured in a glamorous portrait my mother keeps. It only makes me sad.

I am trying to settle my thoughts as I blink confusion away. My eyes adjust to the room. It is always the same bare wall and scratched alder writing desk. The desk with its bills and books and papers remind me of the thank-you notes I have yet to write to all the ladies who made the Garden Club Autumn Luncheon such a success. (Although I do not think Elaine Heslop deserves one after those comments she made.) I must get to those first thing in the morning. The thought nags that Elaine might bad-mouth me at the club for neglecting to use proper etiquette with the late notes and all.

Tangled in the sheets next to me is my husband. I can see the slope of his shoulder more clearly with each even breath he takes. I turn my face to his form. The mass of him feels like a bag of moist clay. The weight is that dense. I do not know the time because I am afraid to rise up on my elbows in order to check. That might wake him and I mustn't do that. I am afraid of disturbing him. I have nothing important to say.

Like so many nights for the past thirteen years, I feel trapped. If only I were alone, I could turn on the light and read, or pace the floor with a mug of coffee in hand. But this man, my husband, is sleeping and there is not that freedom. So I lie still, begging my brain to slow my heart. It is beating too fast. Something feels wrong . . . an unexplainable guilt. What have I done? I am so thirsty. I drank too much wine again. I curse myself for having the third glass. Always too much wine and then there is the waking, and the headache, and the regret. My lips are so dry. It is sometime in the middle of the night and I can hear the familiar click and whir of the heater. Water would be nice. If only I could just sit up with the light on, then I might feel better. My God, am I sweltering. The nausea is hopping about my gut. Ugly, stupid me. My cheek finds a cool spot on the pillow and I fall asleep.

When I find myself awake again, there is a faint blue cut of light around the square of the thick vinyl shade. It will be morning soon, I reassure myself. He will be off to work, or at least in the shower and I can creep out of bed and begin my routine.

This is when the dull thud settles on my chest. I do not find any relief in my routine. This is a different kind of waking than the panicked Ferris wheel of random thoughts I usually have. The dry lips and thirst are the same, but something is completely different. I fumble through the covers to find my heart. I rest my right hand there like I am saying the Pledge of Allegiance. "Oh my God," I whisper. I am going to be in the ground. This realization stuns me. I breathe in and out almost imperceptibly. I will be dead. My hand goes to my mouth and covers it. I take a deep breath this time. I don't recall ever noticing the smell of my skin before. It is faintly metallic, but sweet and powdery. A memory comes to me of my husband. When we first met, I kissed the fleshy palm of his hand and was delighted it smelled like peanut butter. That was just the way he smelled and I was touched.

I clap my hand tighter to my face so I cannot breathe in. I try to clear my head. Moments pass without a thought and then I struggle for air. When I let my hand slip to my neck, I miss the sensation, the pressure on my face the way someone might miss a kiss from a clumsy child. Every breath, every blink, every physical sensation only reminds me that I will be dead. People always said that "we all die alone." That expression infuriated me. I am married for Christ's sake. "Not necessarily," I would mumble while searching through the tight folder of my handbag for a hankie or a pen.

What a fool I have been. I do not want to wake the man next to me. Of course I am dying alone. I will be dead. I will be in the ground. I am using these words as a mantra, repeating them so they might lose their effect.

Then comes the sting of tears. Quickly, I begin to recount my day.

Coffee with non-dairy creamer. A phone call to my husband, asking him what he thinks his father wants for his sixty-eighth birthday. He tells me anything I pick will be fine. I pick at a muffin on the counter and throw the rest away. Random errands. Buy a new headband at the boutique Margot fancies. I pick out carpet samples for the laundry room. There was the girl at the bistro. Brown hair and long legs in old blue jeans and moccasins. She was tan with a full mouth and green eyes. Long fingers, too. I am not attracted to women, I know, but she is gorgeous. I stayed to watch her talk to her friend, or maybe it was her boyfriend. Although they seemed too intimate to be a couple. I ordered a glass of pinot noir and waited. After a few sips, I felt less afraid to sneak looks while I nibbled at my goat cheese salad. When I gulped down the second glass, I began to understand how odd a place is a restaurant. A group of strangers sit in each other's company and eat. Like a trough with napkins. I fidget with my silverware. I can see myself, fish-eyed and inverted, in the bowl of the spoon. I look cute that way, like a goofy toy. I wipe at the corners of my eye and keep peeking at my girl. She looks in her twenties and seems so comfortable. She eats and talks with equal relish, her long limbs sprawled every which way while she pays complete attention to her friend.

The waiter asks if I would care for anything else. I ask for the check as well as another glass of wine. A longing tugs in my throat and I finish what is placed before me. I slowly gather my things. I should do more errands, but I am drowsy from wine and afraid I will do something foolish. I make my way across the room, praying that nobody notices me. When I reach the door, swaddled in my pilled cashmere, I turn and gaze clumsily at her. She is dipping bread into a plate of olive oil. She takes a bite and smiles. On her chin is a golden smudge where some dripped down. She looks beautiful. There is that tug again. I brace myself and leave.

Get gas while swaying at the pump. Turn into driveway and thank the baby lord Jesus for getting me home safely. I park and sit. I do not remember much of the rest of the day. It turned dark. My husband came in after I was in bed. We did not speak. I feigned sleep.

This day is what got me here. I will be dead and I will never have that girl look at me. That girl does not look afraid. Her friends hug her tightly, I am sure. Everybody wants to hold the pretty girls. It is the luck of the draw, I suppose.

The light is creeping into the room now and I am drifting into the gray. My heart is even and I let the tears come. Shutting my eyes I hold my belly. It feels so foreign. I slide my hands under the elastic waistband of my putty colored panties, allowing myself to wriggle free. I pretend she is next to me; that we are friends and in the near dark, we look alike. She is not asleep, but playing a game where we wait to see which one of us is able to hold out the longest before reaching for the other's hand. I break the silence first. "I love you" I say. She shifts and searches for my hand. I win.

"On Bourbon Street"

Rosemary Daniell

"She's got tits as hard
as your fist! Yes sir!
She's tough enough to fuck!"
Mother he's speaking of
me your Sonshine Precious
Boy now a party of parts—
fake hair & silicone an
Ideal Doll. Here it's always
Christmas glitter& tinsel—
I'm gift-wrapped forever.

Wearing a bed jacket with
feathers I've been probed in
Baton Rouge purged in New York,
shared a room with a matron
from Westchester watched her
stitched lids twitch as I
begged the nurse for a pad—
instead of the sweet nail
you played with I now have

a gash: Mother I'm mailing
you my old sex in a box

& I know you'll be thrilled
to hear what I've learned: to
pose in sequins & boa to
smear on a new kind of mouth—
Ma! I've got Revlon
Reds the Maybelline Blues—
I'm painted-on perfection
a mannequin from Frederick's
the Queen of Bourbon Street.
As bright as a Hiroshima
postcard Saint Teresa in
a G-string I dance on high
in this bar & except for
the bruises of needles when
my little fanny swishes I'm
as cute as can be Mi O Mi!

I'm DYNNAMITE! I'm Spanish Fly!
I magnetize! *Mother Mother*,
I've got it down by heart now:
the shove to my knees the dirt
in my face the nail through
my sex I'm your daughter
At last I'm a woman!

"Cystitis"

Rosemary Daniell

Blood, you've nailed my clit—
now sting down the small channel
where, in healthier days,
piss flows, clear & pale.
Passing water, I flash easy
streams instead of your crimson
rush, these tears down my cheeks!

Blood, when I swallowed him,
I swallowed diamonds that sank
& sank, cutting my bladder
to this pocketbook full of
you & pus, a small hot purse
embroidered with stones, passed
on by old wives. Mother, the Word.

Blood, you blazon my death:
". . . cancer . . . her belly packed in ice . . ."
White-hot catheters arrive
on trays, carried by an army
of nurses commanded by doctors

wearing badges inscribed,
"Qualified Judge: GOD'S AGENT."

Blood, I'm caught on your cross
as any farm girl who wakes
in sulfur & haste, begging
mercy for the hand up her skirt
during church, for *later*
in an old Buick: the smell
of rubber, THE SIN, THE SIN.

Blood, I confess, but too late:
in spite of my hot bath, my meal
of tablets, white & chalky,
my fault comes out in *the* spot—
in "a touch of the gravel"—
in "the honeymoon disease"—
in my lover's face, forgotten—

yes, Blood, I'm lightning struck!
in this motel room with Bible—
by the voice of Barbara Walters—
in this stall of blue & tile—
as I squat in your urgent flame,
hellfire of one-night stands,
of women who want too much.

The Psychiatrist's Vacation

Lynda Schor

I'M WAITING OUTSIDE the psychiatric clinic where I've just had my weekly group session. I've never waited outside before, but this evening my husband and children are to meet me here so that we can walk together to the church where my daughter is going to have her flying-up ceremony from a Brownie to a Junior Girl Scout. I'm leaning against a parked car, fantasizing that at the moment my husband walks up to me with the three children beside him my doctor will emerge from the building and see them.

"Are these your children?" she will say. "How great they are," surprised that anyone as sick as I am could have such a fantastic family, even though the little girl is hiding behind me and the baby is crawling all over the ground, pretending to be a dog. I've often imagined Dr. Marcus seeing me with them, so that I can say, in effect, "See what I've done?" Tonight there's a possibility that it will happen.

My doctor comes out. She's very tall, slender, and wearing a white pantsuit, which has the look of a doctor's uniform while remaining extremely elegant. She's walking beside a man who is even taller, definitely wearing the white jacket of a doctor, and extraordinarily handsome. It's a shock to see her come out of that door with a man. He doesn't even glance at me—perhaps because he'd have to lower his eyes too much as I'm fairly short, but the fact that he doesn't make the effort even out of curiosity makes me feel unimportant. Dr. Marcus nods at me, but she seems annoyed that I've seen her with someone, that some element of her private life has been revealed, and perhaps she thinks I've waited on purpose. At my age people don't do that. Her annoyance makes me feel like a child, and I become very small as I say, "Have a nice vacation," which I've already said inside. I feel like a worshipful third-grader saying goodbye to her beautiful teacher at vacation time, as the two of them, looking like Barbie and Ken, walk briskly off somewhere.

About two minutes too late for the great confrontation, my family comes toward me across Seventh Avenue. They're also very short. Harold is holding the two boys by the hand, and Alex is walking alongside in her Brownie uniform, which was too long and now too short, her Brownie beanie perched, not elegantly on the crown of her head, but directly on top, covering half of her bangs and pushing the rest down over her eyes. How she can see that way amazes me, but perhaps she shares that ability with certain breeds of dogs. Besides, we've discussed the beanie before and she's adamant about how she wants to wear it. She hands me the bag with the can of juice that we've promised to donate to this ceremony. Harold hasn't even washed the boys, no less given them a bath, and they have city summer dirt all over them, topped by limp, sweaty hair and heat rash blooming along their necks and hairlines.

"She should carry that herself," says my husband, referring to the juice. Can he be actually starting an argument on the responsibilities of children when they make a commitment to something? As it is, he has to carry the juice while the three children scrap about who gets to hold which of my hands, pulling me this way and that. I feel very passive in this situation, which occurs quite often. Maybe Alex feels some pity for me, as I'm more than usually disheveled. I don't know what goes on under that Brownie cap, but she consents to hold Harold's hand, and then there are just enough hands left for the boys, once they choose sides.

"She should carry the juice herself," I say, as the two of them walk a bit ahead of us. I notice that my daughter toes in when she walks and is growing some faint fuzz on her legs.

I'm still disturbed about seeing my doctor going off to Bermuda and Florida with that handsome man, and in such a hurry to get going. Though I might have supposed she would be going with a man, it's a very different thing to actually see her with him. It disturbs me that she picks someone so fantastic looking, who is also a psychiatrist. Her annoyance at seeing me forces me to realize what a miniscule part I play in her life. Maybe she scorns the mess I've made. I'm just part of her job. Perhaps those doctors sit and laugh about us all day. I can assure you she wouldn't be in my position. To imagine her being pulled apart on the street with various hand wipings on her clothing, and the grubby grime of asphalt parks ingrained permanently on her sandaled feet, the clearer it is to me what a mess I've made. There comes someone Alex knows. It's another Brownie, with her mother and another woman. They are also tall, though obese, but dressed up in stockings, high heels, blouses, vests, skirts that look too hot, hair bows, and brooches. I notice that Nadine is carrying her own juice.

We're sitting on wooden bridge chairs in quite a large auditorium in the basement of the church. There's a stage and a water cooler. As usual, things are not going to begin on time, so my daughter is running wildly across the stage with other Brownies bursting from their uniforms. The boys are running wildly by themselves, alternately making one another cry and taking drinks from the water cooler. I'm torn between trying to deal with them and ignoring them, but for the most part I'm sitting on the bridge chair, crossing, uncrossing, and recrossing my legs as I peruse other families who come to Girl Scout ceremonies. Someone collects seventy-five cents from me to pay for some kind of sash that is placed over my daughter's shoulder when the time comes.

I'm thinking about Dr. Marcus's purse, which is very revealing.

It's large, as she is, and, being a summer purse, is white—a note of conventionality—and has, due to its size and type of leather, a casual softness, which causes it to sag provocatively without losing its respectability. The way she leaves it open on the desk, fairly far from her, indicates a certain healthiness, and a certain proprietariness, as if the desk and room belong to her, which they do only in a way; they really belong to the hospital. It also indicates trust, symbolically and actually, when she casually goes out of the room and leaves it sitting there, open as before, without even glancing at it. This is in great contrast to me, sitting in my low seat clutching my purse, also soft, but smaller and brown, in my lap, directly on top of my thighs. Then again, there's nowhere for me to casually throw it, except on the floor or hook it over the back of my seat, but when I decide to do something different with it it will have to come naturally.

When Mr. Fowler, the Brownie leader, calls a name, all the children on the stage sing a Brownie song which ends with something like ". . . and now so-and-so flies up." When it's my daughter's turn, she apparently takes it quite literally, and hooks her hands under her arms, with her elbows out, and flaps her way across the stage toward the lady who is holding her sash and Junior Girl Scout trefoil pin, saying "Tweet-tweet."

While I hear twenty Brownies each repeat the Girl Scout Pledge separately, I picture my doctor at dusk on Condado Beach in Puerto Rico. Even though she went to Bermuda and Florida, Puerto Rico is my only reference. No, she's not on the beach looking at the lights of all the big hotels, she's in the middle of the lights; they flicker around her in the dusk like fireworks, celebrating her vitality. It's very quiet except for the sound of the waves crashing softly, barely visible anymore. Dr. Marcus, in a white bikini, and her lover are walking back to their hotel. As they near the large buildings, awnings out invitingly, lights from the lobbies illuminating tropical plants growing profusely but carefully, the sounds of the waves recede and once in a while there is the sound of a car. There are faintly visible dots of salt residue on her black hair, which is parted in the middle, and her skin retains the faint glimmer of suntan oil.

I'll tell you one thing about my doctor: even though she's beautiful and in a position of control (she would never take a lot of shit from a man, live in dire poverty, and have three children), she has no sense of social conscience, no desire to change things. Though she's a psychiatrist, I know she isn't motivated by a need to help humanity, but by vanity and a desire for status and wealth. I'm sure she doesn't go on peace marches to Washington or join food cooperatives. I'm also positive that she eats only protein, like steak and shrimp, broiled lobster with a bit of butter sauce, salads, and fruit. She probably drinks cocktails and wine, but would never consume three Entenmann's crumb cakes at one time, in frustration. Her life is not confused by various and sundry conflicting ideologies; she knows what she wants and how to get it. And what she wants is very simple.

This is a long and tedious ceremony for two little boys who are both sleepy. They want to run around, while a large woman in a green Girl Scout uniform makes a long speech about all the things Girl Scouts do together. I'd like to let them run around and just listen to the speeches myself, but I can tell from the demeanor of the people around me that I'm going to be held responsible for their actions. Rummaging through my soft, brown purse, I find two bent oatmeal cookies, which should keep the boys quiet for the moment that it takes for them to devour them. Timothy begins to cry because there's a nick in the cookie and he doesn't like imperfections. Since I won't allow him to pull Zachary's out of his mouth in order to exchange with him (besides, since Zach has already taken a bite, his is imperfect, too), he rips his leather sandal, the one we went all the way to Avenue B to get at half price.

I picture my doctor in the dining room restaurant of the Caribe Hilton, at a small, black table with her handsome psychiatrist lover, drinking sangria, an elegant rotund glass pitcher, half filled with the richly colored drink, which has an abundance of thinly sliced fruit floating on top, moving gently, a thin line of green from a lime or apple slice becoming visible now and then through the condensation on the pitcher, which, when it becomes too moist, forms drops which descend heavily and sensually. She's wearing a cocktail dress. (No, it isn't white, it's black.) She's also wearing a pin. The pin is a giveaway as to how conventional she really is. The dress, like most of her clothes, looks fine on her and is fairly simple, but at the same time very conventional.

Once in a while, during our group sessions, I could see that she has oily skin. That's reassuring. One time I noticed that she was getting cheek wrinkles from her nose to her mouth. Perhaps she isn't as young as I think.

When my husband and I went to Puerto Rico with knapsacks and stayed only in small hotels and guest houses without showers that are meant for Puerto Ricans, and wore one pair of jeans and one shirt for a whole week, Dr. Marcus thought that was wonderful, but I'm sure that she has one whole area in her large suitcase set aside just for her makeup. I can tell that she feels perfectly at home in that flamboyant dining room with its neoclassic crystal chandeliers. But they aren't still or even subdued, the two of them are laughing and having a ball.

Thank God it's refreshment time. While we were listening to the speeches someone was surreptitiously arranging all the donated cookies, pretzels, and cans of juice, each with two triangular punctures, on two wood-and-Formica tables. There are suggestive stacks of various design paper cups. The children have rapidly moved in and are unabashedly stripping the dishes of cookies. I'd like to stay with the pretzels so I won't spoil my diet too much, but once I've eaten a pretzel I decide that the diet's spoiled anyway, so I go on to bigger and better things. I am very cordial as I devour mountains of chocolate chips and Oreos in my nervousness. Between swallows I am asking Mr. Fowler, whose bald head is perspiring, whether he will be in charge of the Junior Girl Scouts or stay with the Brownies. He's leaning forward, moisture dripping from his large bald head like the condensation on the pitcher of sangria. He's making an enormous effort to be likable.

Flattered that he wants to be liked by me, I'm making an effort to be likable too. The only reason we're talking is to show each other that we are likable. I'm wondering how we're going to make it home with three exhausted children—one in an obsolete Brownie uniform and two crabby boys, one with only one sandal.

Their room is very dimly lit, but it has a luminous quality, and faraway sparkles of light from other hotels are very sharp because it's a clear and beautiful night. It's also very quiet and once in a while one becomes aware of the sound of the surf. Dr. Marcus is looking out the window. She's wearing bikini underpants in a paisley pattern; in the dimness only the electric-green, irregularly etched outlines are visible. She's long and slender, and the endless tract of her back is broken by the back of a flesh-colored brassiere, the soft, natural kind which causes her fairly large breasts to hang a bit low, which doesn't mar her beauty, but rather enhances it because it's so natural. A hand reaches out and gently grasps the rounded edge of her shoulder. It's a sensual hand because it is slender, but defined and muscular, slightly tanned already; however, what makes it such an exciting hand is its decisiveness and firm gentleness (or gentle firmness). Dr. Marcus responds, but with just a touch of wryness, as she gives one of her smiles, with an almost imperceptible little chew first. Like a voyeur, I can almost feel the magnetism between them as she is gently turned toward him and they face each other with a bit of space between. For a moment they don't move, just use their eyes to increase desire until they're in each other's arms, but still gently. There's no need to rush anything because the feelings are so intense. There is a slightly sardonic smile on his incredibly handsome tanned face, as his black hair is softly pulled by Dr. Marcus, to keep her balance as she lowers herself next to him. I guess that, though she's his equal in looks and status, because he's a man he expects her, a woman, to worship him. I guess she has her problems, too.

Dr. Marcus is lying on the bed, staring at the large overhead fan, which imparts a tropical atmosphere to the room even though it's air conditioned. Her body retains the sensation of being in the waves and, totally relaxed, she can feel as if she's floating, but with the support of the large, cool bed, which is always already made whenever she needs it. Suddenly, encroaching on her image of the fan is a burst of hot breath, a face with an upside-down mouth. A large piece of someone's hair falls into her eyes. As an immediate reaction, she almost pushes the face away and gets up, angry at a self-centered intrusion on her own demulcent world, but the impulse passes instantaneously, and already she's responding to the gentle sexuality of her lover, who's running his tongue around her salty hairline and allowing her to remain absolutely still and passive. Probably he enjoys her passivity. He continues for so long that she wants very badly to kiss, to feel his lips with hers, but finds it pleasurable to lie there perfectly still, almost aware of the relaxed state of every part of her, and wait. She's learned that waiting is sometimes more exciting than actively getting what's desired. Perhaps because he's a doctor, he knows exactly how gentle to be and where to put his tongue as he holds her open with the palm of a hand that he's partially lying on, imparting to it a protective weight, as his tongue slowly, with no heaviness, traces lightly around Dr. Marcus's already erect clitoris. She has a desire to move her hips, but doesn't. Then he touches her with just the tip of his tongue for a moment, and moves it around slightly, sliding it so softly that it barely touches, then he suddenly relaxes his tongue so that it becomes a large, flat, wet thing, pressing and pressing. Dr. Marcus can feel waves of voluptuous sensation emanating from her thighs, pulsing outward until they're no longer distinguishable as waves. Her body feels swollen, is flushed and palpitating, radiating heat. Then her lover, as if in answer to her desire to move her hips, lifts up her behind from underneath with both hands and thrusts his tongue deeply into her.

I doubt that I'll go to my group therapy anymore. How can I be expected to relate to someone who's just interested in money, fun, and status? But maybe I'll force myself; since I'm over-scrupulous (one of my problems), I don't want to be the victim of some kind of psychiatric resistance.

Perhaps because this is their last night here, Dr. Marcus's lover seems less controlled than usual. In fact, it's with total abandon tonight that he makes love with her, so much so that his breathing, which makes a ticking noise at every large inhalation, probably from some mucoid obstruction, goes unnoticed by him. Now he's pressing down on her with all his weight, his mouth over hers, one hand squeezing her breast, the other under her buttocks, ramming into her rhythmically with such frenzy that, though their lips are pressed together, the room still resounds with echoes of his grunts and whistles of air being pushed out of her body as if in some last frantic effort at artificial respiration. For Dr. Marcus, though she's passionately aroused, her sensations of pleasure are mixed with pain at his uncaring force. His teeth press into her lip, and his hand is squeezing her nipple harder and harder. Even more than physically, this excites her as a new manifestation, a new unfolding and revealing of this person to herself. She finds herself responding with similar abandon. She holds his buttocks hard and gyrates her hips. Her moans are added to the other sounds in the tremulous tropical night.

Is it a mark of unreality that I simply can't seem to fantasize any conversation between the two of them, but only the most satisfying sexual confrontations?

She enters the small room where we hold our group sessions, appearing taller than ever because I'm already scrunched into my leatherette seat. She looks the same, only suntanned; Malibu Barbie. She really looks better without a tan. As a doctor, she must be cognizant of the fact that exposure to the sun ages the skin. I try not to reveal anything this week, as punishment, but during one painful moment I blurt, "I'd like to see what you would do if you were married and had three kids."

Which is stupid anyway, because when she gets married she'll be able to afford a babysitter and a full-time maid, plus a cook.

She laughs, "So I'm not married, and I don't have any kids, huh." She laughs again. I'm so weak that for an instant she almost has me fooled. I picture her rushing off with that psychiatrist, who now becomes her husband, to pick up their kids from their sitter so that they can get them ready in time to get to the airport. But no, I couldn't be wrong, this new fantasy just doesn't fit. She was just making an effort to throw me off the track because she wishes to remain enigmatic.

Champagne and Darling

Bianca James

(For Bella M.)

"*E*VERY TRULY BEAUTIFUL woman has a perfect flaw."

These were the first words Marcelle ever spoke to me, a serpent's hiss between shiny red lips.

I glanced up from my drink and saw lidless green eyes staring right at me.

"A flaw makes a beautiful woman seem approachable," she continued.

Marcelle was equal parts snake and feline: heart-shaped face, lanky body sheathed in strapless black silk, wild auburn hair unbound in rope-like twists. She was the most beautiful woman in the bar, and I couldn't help but think, "What would she know about being flawed?"

It was then she turned to face me.

I gasped, and she smiled. It wasn't so much the missing left arm, as the shamelessness with which it was displayed: milk white shoulder fading into a smooth mound of scar tissue. While it seemed rude to stare, it appeared that Marcelle was intentionally flaunting her missing limb. It was as arousingly inappropriate as a miniskirt worn without panties.

"You could do it, too, you know," she told me.

I thought she meant losing an arm, and I blanched.

She laughed a little. "No, I mean stop hiding underneath all that dark clothing. You've got a beautiful body."

I froze until the words registered. I had been told my entire life that I had a beautiful face. I cringed when people said this, as if the phrase was silently punctuated by "It's a shame you're fat." But in Marcelle's eyes, thirty extra pounds was a perfect flaw, icing on the cake.

Marcelle had a tailor create a corset that squeezed my waist to a sadistic twenty two inches, and silk dresses in shades of cream, pale pink, and beige. Matching stiletto heels and cosmetics. Lastly, she gave me a name: "Champagne." I laughed, until I realized she was dead serious.

Marcelle took me shopping, then she took me home. Velvet skin on skin, sharp hipbones cutting into my tender flesh, her silicone cock parting my wet lips. Marcelle promised me love that was pure and untainted.

"Men are only good for two things," Marcelle told me, as her hips moved against mine, "Money and cock." She thrust a little deeper with the word *cock*, and I gasped. "Expect no more, no less.

"It's a myth that a woman loses her power when she opens her legs. The important thing is to keep your priorities straight. Never fall for a man's lies. Play them for all they're worth, then leave before morning. Save your love for me, who will not betray you."

We spent all day in bed together. It would have been enough for me, but nothing was enough for Marcelle. She was predatory as a shark, and seduction was her way of life. She had to keep moving, cutting a swath through the crowd with the black silk fishtail of her evening gown.

Marcelle showed me how to work a room. The importance of making an entrance. The air stood still when I helped Marcelle take off her coat, the satin lining slithering over the scar tissue, leaving it bare and exposed.

Marcelle taught me how to spot the wealthiest man in the room. She determined which men would be given a phone number, a gentle rejection, or a night of no-strings attached sex. We did body shots and cocaine with hard-bodied college boys while milking wealthy businessmen for diamonds and fur coats. We partied with rock stars and porn stars; we inducted beautiful, stupid socialites to a world of sapphic delights.

But when the night was over and the makeup washed off, there was always Marcelle's naked body against mine. "I love you," she'd whisper as we drifted off to sleep and I'd hold her a little tighter. No one slept in that bed but she and me. We never brought anyone back to our apartment; we never slept anywhere that wasn't the apartment. Even if we were out partying until noon the next day, we always took a cab home and slept it off together.

Marcelle made all things possible. Marcelle knew the rules of the game, Marcelle knew when to stay and when to bail, but most importantly she was always there for me at the end of the night, to give me the love and comfort that was missing from the hungry maw of the clubs and bars.

Our days were spent sleeping, fucking, shopping, and preening, our nights spent "working." We were not whores in the truest sense of the word, but sometimes it felt that way. Marcelle was content to live a life of idleness hiding from the sun, but I found myself growing increasingly impatient and bored. Marcelle responded by buying an expensive laptop computer and encouraging me to write about our exploits. I would dress down and go to the café on the corner to drink cappuccinos and scribble. At the cafe, I was no longer Champagne, I was plain old Cynthia.

Jack made my cappuccinos and served them with a side of flirtation. Jack was early thirties, working-class muscular with a little beer belly, always in need of a shave. He slipped me his number countless times, and I always destroyed it before Marcelle could find it. It was more for Jack's protection than Marcelle's: Jack was a nice guy and I didn't want him to accidentally stumble into Marcelle's sticky spider web.

Jack invited me to his house for lunch one day, and I accepted out of curiosity. I knew that sex was going to happen, but that didn't worry me. He was not rich, he was not good looking.

Jack served grilled cheese sandwiches with potato salad, and we shared a bottle of cheap red wine. He showed me the films he'd made in art school, followed by an endearingly clumsy seduction on his threadbare sofa. But I was taken off guard when Jack gathered me in his muscular arms and picked me up.

"What are you doing!" I screamed, suspended in midair.

"What's wrong?" he asked, refusing to put me down.

"I weigh 190 pounds!" I declared, as if this revelation would suddenly turn my body to lead, forcing Jack to drop me.

"So?" he asked, and leaned forward to kiss me, then carried me off to his bedroom. Jack threw me down on the bed, pushed up my skirt, and yanked down my panties. Jack placed his hands on the insides of my knees and pressed my thighs against my belly so my shaved cunt was exposed. I squirmed as he paused between my thighs, lightly tracing the smooth pussy lips with his fingers. My wetness betrayed me as he slid his fingers inside of me, and a shudder of arousal ran through my entire body.

My heart was beating fast, and I had to admit I was turned on. No, more than turned on, I was *excited*. This was more exciting than anything I'd ever done with Marcelle, but why? I was no longer in control, I no longer had the upper hand. The feeling was terrifying, but I didn't want it to stop.

Jack fumbled with his belt buckle and pulled out his thick, uncircumcised cock, fully erect. He rubbed the head of his cock against my clit, and it felt so damn good. I was breathing hard, and the orgasm that overcame me as he rubbed against my clit was effortless and intense, even better as he replaced his cock head with his thumb and slid it into my wet cunt as I was still having contractions from my orgasm. I screamed as he thrust into me, bucking my hips to meet him, wrapping my thighs around his waist as he pounded me. He pulled out and came onto my tits and belly, then rubbed his come into my skin with his big strong hands. I was filthy with sweat and come, utterly glowing. No, this was not how it was with Marcelle.

Jack pulled me against him, sticky as I was, and murmured in my ear, "I've been thinking about this for months. And you looked just as beautiful as I imagined you would."

Something in the tenderness of his words caused something to break inside of me, and my eyes were overflowing with tears. *Money and cock, nothing more, nothing less,* Marcelle's voice chanted in my head. I squirmed free of Jack's embrace, feeling suddenly suffocated. I needed to leave as quickly as possible, before he saw me cry, before I got any closer to emotional attachment.

"What's wrong?" Jack asked, looking concerned as I struggled into my skirt and sweater, wiping my wet eyes on the sleeve.

"Nothing. I have to go somewhere."

"Don't you want to take a shower first?"

"I'll be fine" I replied, bolting for the door.

But I wasn't fine. I burst into sobs the minute I hit the street. I went swimming at the fitness center, where the smell of sex would be purged by the chemically treated water, and I could blame my red eyes on the chlorine.

My hair was still wet when I came home.

"You're late," Marcelle chided, standing before me in her chintzy aqua nightgown and maribou mules, caressing my damp hair. I could see the outline of her body through the transparent fabric, and suddenly I was overcome by the desire to fuck her the way Jack had fucked me.

"I went swimming," I told her, before grabbing her ass in both hands, and pulling her towards me for a kiss.

We stayed in that night. I bent Marcelle over the couch and fucked her from behind, using the biggest dildo we owned. I watched her tight red cunt lips stretch to accept my girth. I was not gentle with her; I pinched her nipples, I pulled her hair, I slapped her ass. I rubbed her clit as I slammed her from behind, and brought her to a screaming orgasm.

Afterward, we lay in each other's arms and she told me about Darling, the one who came before me.

"Darling was the most beautiful woman in the room, and she didn't realize it. Not until she met me."

"I suppose Darling was another beautiful woman with one perfect flaw?"

"Well, technically Darling was a beautiful man with a perfect flaw. And what a beautiful flaw it was." Marcelle said, closing her eyes and smiling like a contented cat.

"What ever happened to Darling?" I asked.

Marcelle's face turned cold and hard. "She made a mistake that made me very, very angry. And so I beat her with my prosthetic arm."

I felt my blood freeze with unspeakable guilt. "I didn't know you had a prosthetic arm," I said.

The smile returned to Marcelle's lips. "I only wear it on special occasions." I couldn't help but wonder if she meant the story as a warning.

I wanted to forget about Jack, but his memory would catch me off guard, causing my eyes to tear and my cunt to tingle. I avoided his café and started going to a chain where the coffee was bad and the perky teenage clerks posed no threat to my relationship with Marcelle. But one night Marcelle went home with a wealthy playboy who had rejected the offer of a threesome, abandoning me at the country club. Feeling vengeful, I took a cab to Jack's house, where he was watching TV in his underwear. We had slow anal sex in the shower, legs spread, tits pressed against the smooth tiles. Jack murmured filthy nothings while stroking my clit. I couldn't deny that sex with Jack had something that sex with Marcelle was missing: a sense of vulnerability.

I waited until Jack fell asleep to leave. I took a cab to the apartment, but Marcelle wasn't at home. When Marcelle still hadn't returned when I woke up, I went to Jack's café and gave him a blowjob in the bathroom during his break.

I began sneaking sex with Jack as often as possible. I got sloppy about it, coming home with disheveled hair, come stains on my skirt. Marcelle must have suspected, but she never said a thing.

After having sex in an abandoned factory on his day off, Jack asked me, "Why don't we ever go to your place? Why don't you ever spend the night? I could get some time off of work and we could go somewhere together . . ."

I paused for a moment. "I'm sorry Jack. I have a lesbian lover who is very jealous. She supports me, and if she were to find out I had a male lover, she'd kick me out." It was close enough to the truth.

Jack's face became stony. "I see," was all he said, before putting his clothes back on. He was silent on the entire drive back into town.

"Are you angry?" I asked him as he dropped me off in front of the café, a safe distance from the apartment.

"I don't think I can see you anymore, Cynthia," he said. "I'm sorry."

I didn't cry. I couldn't muster the emotion. I opened the door to our apartment. Marcelle was curled up on the couch, eating strawberries and watching TV. I bent forward to kiss her, and she kept her eyes on the television screen.

"You smell like sex," she remarked.

"I had to take the car to the mechanic to check under the hood," I said jokingly, but Marcelle didn't laugh.

"What do you want for dinner?" she asked.

"I'm not very hungry."

"You ruined your appetite."

"I need a vacation. I was thinking about going home to see my family, just for a few days."

"Are you bored with me already?" Marcelle asked, sounding annoyed.

"No, of course not, kitten," I said, sitting next to her on the couch and taking her in my arms.

She looked up at me with her perfect face, strawberry stained lips. "I'll miss you. I get lonely when you're not around."

"Just three days, Marcelle. I'll bring you back the biggest lobster I can find."

I got up from the couch and went into the bedroom to pack a bag. I reached into the closet to find the suitcase I'd stashed, and something else came crashing down: a scuffed, dirty prosthetic arm made from flesh-colored plastic. I recoiled as if burnt, afraid of finding dried blood on it.

"Does it disgust you?" Marcelle asked. I turned around. She was standing in the doorway, smoking a cigarette.

"What?"

"My arm."

"No, of course not. I was just taken off guard."

"You're not coming back, are you?" Marcelle accused me, her face shadowy.

"For chrissakes, Marcelle, why is it such a big deal if I want to see my family for a few days?"

"Do what you want," she said, going back to the TV.

I returned on Wednesday night, quietly letting myself into our apartment, a plastic bag full of live lobsters with rubber-banded claws in tow. I had planned to surprise Marcelle by coming home early and serving her a lobster dinner, but my plan had worked too well: I heard loud sex noises coming from the kitchen.

Marcelle was lying naked on the kitchen counter, the tiles making square-shaped imprints on her creamy flesh. She was being fucked by a drag queen who looked like a tall, muscular version of Betty Page: long black hair, vintage lingerie, and thigh high black vinyl boots. Marcelle was wearing the same boots in red, legs wrapped around the waist of her gender-bending paramour as she moaned in pleasure.

I stood in the doorway, feeling a little awkward with my squirming bag of live seafood. Marcelle's eyes fluttered open, and she smiled. "Hello Champagne," she said, as if she knew I'd been standing there all along.

The drag queen's heavily made-up eyes popped open, his erection slid out of Marcelle, and he held his gloved hands over his exposed crotch like a criminal. "Oh my god, Cynthia! What are you doing here?"

"Do I know you?" I asked, and after a moment had passed, I realized I did. Although the rest of him was unrecognizable, the voice was unmistakably Jack's.

"Champagne, meet Darling. Though it appears that you have already."

I looked from Marcelle to Jack. "*You're* Darling?" I asked with disbelief. I had imagined Darling as a beautiful boy with delicate features, not a big clumsy brute like Jack. It was a testament to Marcelle's powers that she was capable of transforming rough-hewn Jack into a beautiful woman.

"Oh goody, you brought lobsters!" Marcelle declared, hopping off of the counter and walking toward me. Her body smelled like sperm and pancake makeup.

"I think I should leave," Jack said, his erection wilting as he picked a pair of panties up off the floor.

"Marcelle," I whispered, still in shock. "I thought you and Darling had a falling out. What really happened?"

A smile crept onto Marcelle's lips. "Well, I loved Darling, but she was fucking around behind my back. You might even say she fell in love with someone else—a man."

A chill ran through my blood. I got the impression she wasn't talking about Jack anymore.

"So you beat her with your arm—"

"Well, I made up that part of the story for dramatic flair. No, baby, what really happened was this man came around the house looking for you, and I decided to have some fun of my own."

"So Darling never really existed?"

"She's standing right over there. Do you think we should invite her to stay for dinner? I've taken a liking to her."

I gulped and nodded. Maybe it was possible for me to have my cake and eat it too?

Marcelle turned around to face Jack. "Darling, leave your panties off. There's enough lobster here for everyone."

The Secret Life of Mr. Clean

Lori Selke

*M*R. CLEAN DOESN'T actually polish his bald head. Fresh from the shower each morning, he merely pats it dry before the mirror.

Mr. Clean always flosses after he brushes his teeth. Even the back teeth. Afterward, he rinses with antibacterial mouthwash. Then he washes his hands.

> *Brush Your Sink: Toothpaste can do wonders for your sink. Just rub it on, rinse if off, and shield your eyes from the bright shine.*

Mr. Clean doesn't like to cook. Too messy. But he's always willing to help out afterward, clearing the table, loading the dishwasher without protest. He knows the most efficient way to arrange the dishes in the racks. Knows the best detergent, the most effective rinsing agent.

His advice is always nonthreatening, always appreciated.

> *Could Your Garbage Disposal Use a Breath Mint? To refresh from nasty odors, add baking soda and sliced citrus peels, and grind away.*

Most of Mr. Clean's friends are women. They like to invite him to brunch, to tea. He takes in their gossip with a small smile on his face. They touch him on the shoulder, just beneath the hoop of his earring.

"You're such a good listener!" they say. He smiles. He hardly ever speaks to the women, but when he does, it's always the right thing to say.

Easy Party Clean-Up: To clean your blender after a party, add hot water and dish soap and—blend!

Mr. Clean had a great love, once. He fell hard for one of the Scrubbing Bubbles—the one with the moustache. Mr. Clean liked the bristly feel of facial hair against his groin. Hair he knew to be free of germs, spic and span. But this affair, too, was doomed not to last. They were from competing companies. There was a non-fraternization policy. They had to meet in secret.

"We should run off together," Mr. Clean said. "Someplace where we can be together."

"You wouldn't be happy," the Scrubbing Bubble replied. "You live to clean."

Later, the accusations turned acrimonious. "You don't love me anymore!" the Scrubbing Bubble accused one night. "You prefer your little tricks, your works in progress. I'm too clean for you, I can never satisfy your needs."

Mr. Clean had not contradicted him.

Give the Shower a Shower: Running the hot water for five minutes before scrubbing the shower or tub will loosen up the dirt and grime.

"Do you know how many germs there are in a teaspoon of saliva?" Mr. Clean asks the boy kneeling between his legs. The boy does not answer. Mr. Clean runs his fingers, the nails perfectly filed and manicured, through the boy's greasy hair.

These days, there's always some young fellow sleeping on Mr. Clean's couch. They never last for long, though. He tries to teach them a little grooming, a little hygiene, a little manners, before they leave.

They always leave. They always break his heart.

Mr. Clean wants to touch every grimy boy he sees. The ones on the street, the ones who call to him as he walks by. He longs to brush the dirt from their faces. To iron and fold their freshly-laundered clothes. He dreams of opening a Home for Wayward Boys. He would teach them to scrub, to listen to women's secrets, to wipe, to rinse, to shine.

Overheard

M. M. De Voe

——*I'M DRUNK*. Gym-warmed gluteus shrinkwrapped in designer leather screeches the air-conditioned vinyl, like the shiny chrome tailpipe of a classic car dragging on asphalt.

Peaks and valleys travel through the air and coil themselves in a snail-like cochlea. His.

—*That had to hurt. You've only had three.*

—*I'm drunk. Listen, I've got to tell you something.* Secrets hollered in the improved silence of too much sound. Still, the tipple of glass against polyurethaned ebony resounds. A halogen circle illuminates the girl-on-girl action like a spotlight. He participates uninvited.

—*You're not in love with me, are you?*

Frosted tips jut over the sleek banquette, upturned at the end, like tiny smiles.

—*Very funny. But you're on the right track.* Auburn leans closer to erstwhile brunette.

—*Oh shit. You're not having an affair.*

—*No.*— Complete with colored dancing lion and supple acrobats, an imaginary Chinese New Year parade marches through the pause. —*Well. Not exactly.*

—*But ten years. Mandy!*

—*Eleven. And it's not what you think.* Square nails even to the millimeter, painstakingly painted nude by credit card, rake through the bleached ruin of happy hair. Auburn lawn nods, encouraging.

—*Who is it?*

Five perfect clusters of dead follicles flick into the air. —*Don't know.*

—*You what?* Screaming horror replaces ambient screaming guitar.

—*I don't know who it was.*

—*What? Who was it?* Soundwaves screen all but moving lips. Lungs absorb secondhand carcinogens, return carbon dioxide to atmosphere. Restaurant ferns window-planted for seclusion temporarily thrive, chlorophyll working overtime.

—*I need another drink.*

White crescents scissor. —*Make it two.* Worn leather scuffs across the floor. The black arcs lead to the owner-run ranks of bottles, a glass chorus of frozen Mardi Gras celebrants. —*So?*

—*So, for my fortieth, Chad got me a massage.*

Bare shoulder rolls in imitation Fosse. —*Okay. That's nice.*

—*It was nice. I've been there before, you know that spa on Broadway?* Mind sheltered by reddish locks races through Zagat of hedonistic holidays, returns holding faded memory, as a scavenger hunt at home might turn up Aunty Yu's wedding photograph fresh from the empty nail on the wall.

—*The one with the dried roses in the window?* Victory salute. Two-legged hands, wobbly from alcoholic blood.

Worn leather halts tableside. Aging Crest kids do their gig. Several off-color portraits of the first president vanish into a fabric belt. Scuffled retreat sans gratitude. Condensation trickles into the spongy coasters. —*That's the one.*

—*Sure. Cute place. Expensive. Sucks when there's a bachelorette party.*

—*Everything sucks with tourists.*

—*Amen, sister.*— Quick exhalations rattle the costly dental work on both sides of the café table. Auburn locks sweep forward.

—So?

Mutual tastebud annihilation. *—So I went in for my massage.* Lime green liquid sloshes over the lip of a martini glass like a freed fish.

A reincarnation of trees dabs alcohol content from plummy protuberances. *—And you got molested?* This, while swabbing!

—Well . . . Fronds of mascara dart side, side, side. A nervous iris.

—Shit! Was it a woman or a man? Saliva coats these words.

—Man.

Palms slam table as if it were an offending portal, heedless of the fragility of French-manicured extremities. *—You have to turn him in! That's so wrong!*

—But, just wait. You haven't heard the whole story yet.

He blushes. Proud.

Lips parted, breath comes porn film staccato. *—So tell!*

Orbs glazed by sour elixir jump to life like newly cleaned plugs. *—Well, you remember all the complaining I have been doing about the spark going out of my marriage?*

—You mean the sex going out of your marriage.

—Yeah, well. That. Radius and ulna meet their twins; poise leaks from married side of table like spilled Bordeaux. Fourth finger shackled into compliant capture; opposite, the free agent bends a smug smile.

—Of course. Thick auburn strand brushes over naked shoulder as if painting it with coolness.

—Well, I blew out the candles on my bran muffin. Chad and I always put candles on breakfast food for birthdays; don't ask, it's just a thing. Swizzle straw becomes substitute thumb. Perky 36C beneath the cashmere. Gym membership $1000. Retinol every night, and dermabrasion weekends. Married forty looks maybe twenty-eight, -nine.

—Okay, so? This side, even better preserved, boasts weekly delivery of lustrous tuna steaks—one for her, one to feed the feline pair, Asta and Lavista. Rich and lonely some say, who have

never seen the week of wadded rubber suffocated into Glad bags on the curb. Red, orange, ribbed, lubricated for sensual pleasure, lamb thin or thick for extended pleasure. Not a one wasted.

—*So I wished for an orgasm for my birthday.*

—*You wished—?*

—*You heard me.*— Twinned escapes to the sanctuary of drink. A flurry of waitron activity. Legs shift in pretense of choreography. —*A luxurious orgasm, no less.* Chronometers throughout the city continue to jerk from black dot to black dot and at last to numeral. Girls miss curfew. Dogs are walked. VCRs spring to life or death. This news digests, and elbow loofahed to smoothness protrudes like flamingo beak as hand covers stomach. He leans in, waiting.

—*Well I assume you meant from Chad, not from some hairy masseuse.*

—*Masseur. And he wasn't hairy.* Forgiveness is a state of friendship where real evils evaporate like day-old milk, leaving stains no one mentions. The unconsciously arched neck reveals a raw strawberry memento on throat, mark of husband's property, delivered during the new moon before a late-night *Cinematherapy* in denial of sexual dysfunction. Bogey and Bacall in direct competition with winestung Mandy and Chad. Could it speak, the lovebite would say: *see? nothing wrong with this marriage.* (It would be prevaricating, toothless.)

—*Whatever.*

—*As I recall, he was Asian.*

—*Just because he was Asian doesn't mean he wasn't hairy.*

—*Doesn't it?*

—*Jesus, Mandy!* Correct response to racial slur, politically speaking, punctuated by squeal of vinyl against back of juicy thigh. Emerald silk skirt already too short rides higher, revealing fully the featherless chicken parts, glimpse of a nestled black thong.

—*What?* Substitute of bliss, performed without need of curtains.

—*You didn't mean you wanted to randomly fuck some guy, right? When you made your wish?* Crass. Crass. All women become crass when drinking alcohol. Men too. Dehydrated curse words lurk at the bottom of their souls, waiting for party atmosphere.

—*Well of course I didn't! But the point is, I didn't specify.* Glossy, glassy enamel taps rim of inverted cone, ringing tone ensues, audible over ambient medley of music/caterwauling/shouted introductions of one-night stands that will end this evening no longer STD-free.

Cellphone burbles. —*Didn't specify what?* Burbles again. Hips shift, skirt rides down again, thong or whatever curtained to backstage activity only. Show over. Audience does not applaud.

Deft fingerprint. Silence in bowels of Kate Spade. —*I didn't specify from whom I wanted the orgasm!*

—*Just who the fuck did you think was listening? God?*— Cackle of the born-again atheist. Soulless. Guiltless. Full of other men's semen and sticky desolation. —*Shit. You didn't say it out loud? Did Chad hear you?* Sometimes the sharp slaps of these size 7 Kenneth Coles echo through an apse of church, just one: St. Christopher's. Not for Godless self, no, for those cats, that they might end their ninth in peace and eternal tuna steaks, Lavista being mortally leukemiaed.

—*No! But someone heard. Whoever, whatever grants birthday wishes.* Birthday Bunny. Birthday Fairy. Birthday Claus. Twenty-first century Hallmark-Americans have failed to invent a birthday creature; it is a startling omission.

—*You're insane. You have to turn this guy in! Jesus. A random Asian. What happened?* Her mind has to be hovering on a late-night food delivery just two weeks ago. The anonymous delivery boy. His smooth, hard phallus in her mouth. Does she remember the red baseball cap? Music level rises at the flick of a manager's expert remote control. In concert speaking voices rise as well. A man in his late thirties passes the plate glass window with starved eyes that say *what a fun, happening place!* and yet his feet drag on toward the 24/7 to split his wallet on a quest for aspirin or milk or diapers, the open wallet a dry vulva.

—*Well, I went in for my massage.*

—*So far so good.* Under the canopy of shadow, an ankle twists, a banner proclaiming boredom. Or perhaps its owner requires a lavatory.

—*Chad was there. He gave me a kiss, told me to enjoy myself.* The kiss like fine wine: *secco* and costing the husband great effort; there the comparison ends. Osculation without hands, without tongue. Dutiful pecks. Those seablue eyes crave more from his wife, but have nothing to offer in exchange apart from the occasional public denigration he calls humor. He scoots from the front step eager to buy back her passion, runs through the heat to shop after shop, expecting advertisements to ensnare him and transform his marriage into ardor. The long legs a man wants to, but may never, spread with wildflower honey and lick clean despite the prickles of razor regrowth, the rasp of it on his tongue as exciting as the smoothness would have been the day before, to lick like a cat cleans its young, toe to pubis, lingering over the fishy parts, these vanish into the dark lavender-scented maw of the spa, safe from his lustful and impotent mind.

—*Eew. He said that?* Four matching moons rake pink trails across the naked shoulder. Return to rake again, and now there are four pink Xs marking the spots that had itched. Here. Here. Here. Here.

—*Well, what the hell else do you say? He bought me a massage!* Defensive temper raises volume surely as it raises blood pressure. Thudding heartbeat inaudible or lost to the soundtrack of the noisy bar.

Refuge in refreshment. Nylon sheathed ankles uncross, daisyspotted heel catches expensively on table support. —*Okay. So. Get back to the fucking story, will you? I have to pee and my edamame are getting cold.* Knees together. Knees together.

—*But edamame are supp . . . oh, okay I get it.*

—*You are drunk. Slow, too.*

—*Thanks. Go pee.* Body aligns itself perpendicular to the floor. Skirt falls to the spot where cellulite begins to gather, the union leader of old age. Black knockout slings sporting fresh gash on mudspattered heel force a curve in the well-known calf, a familiar dimple below the knee. Long thin arms brush invisible crumbs from waist, smooth blouse taut; accidentally profiling breasts small enough to cup in each hand. Away, away into the standing mobs of reservation-holding date-disappointers.

He orders another gin. No rush.

And back again. Less urgently. More sway in the hip. Clutching pert knockoff handbag containing Lipfinity (Sensual Plum), blue pen stolen from last hotel room, tiny coin purse in the shape of a frog, thin leather calendar with names and numbers inked in various colors beneath corresponding dates, eelskin wallet as soft as the skin of a throat (concealing cheater's hand of credit cards some with pictures, five twenties ironed by a cash machine, two singles that feel washed, a photograph of the cats taken six Christmases ago by a OneStep camera, receipts from three uninspired lunches), comb so small as to be useless, blue hair scrunchy in case of humidity, wireframe sunglasses in copper case, forgotten pair of faux diamond studs removed for quickie with hipster, cell phone, and an emergency Playtex tampon six months old. Hips slip snakelike over the vinyl banquette toward patient Eve. Curled back into a position of attentive listening, whiteness of scalp now illuminated beneath the glint of auburn by the halogen spotlight. Someone might want this woman. Might want them both. Climbing over each other, red and white hair tumbling together, moaning in harmony as he licks, thrusts, pulls, twists them the way he likes. Leaves them wet and wanting more—perhaps they will discover each other then, and he can watch: their master. Their lion. Oh the redhead will be the first, yes, she will take the blonde one's hand, lead her to the slippery shower to soap and find the blonde already wet. Wet skin. Wet cunt. Wet eyes, the tears salty as he licks them from her face. He trembles at the fear that the conversation would end, that their intimacies would cease and instead, dull talk of Oprah might surface where voluptuous secrets had recently swum in the nude.

—*So what happened after you reverted to an eight-year-old?*
Relieved gratitude silently surfs the soundwaves. The lamps lighting the household of three (one hidden) are made in France by a company with an unpronounceable V-name. Inside the inverted egg in miniscule type are the *bon mots*: "minor irregularities further enhance uniqueness." The cobalt glass is round as a tulip bulb, round as a pendulous breast. The glass is hot!

He puts fingers in his mouth. Sucks.

—*Shut up. I put on the robe, put on the nubby rubber flipflops.*

—*Don't tell me some freaky eighth grade shower story, okay?*

—*Matter of fact, they reminded me of the public pool.*

—*Don't go there. Stick to the story.*

—*Fine,*— Wrinkled pants pause tableside, obfuscate. — *Another margarita. Strawberry.*

—*Mmm. Two.*— Cursed wrinkled pants resume their orbit of the seven table station. —*So?*

—*So then I went into the public lounge. Scented candles, dim lights, white furniture, luxurious glossies, you know the sort of place. Some woman brought me deseeded watermelon cut into star shapes and a glass of sparkling water in a champagne flute.*

His dry mouth slaked with melted remnants of ice, alcohol content long since imbibed or evaporated to join the gaseous forms of tobacco clustered near the twenty-foot ceiling.

—*Are you going to tell me every fucking detail?* Impatience at lack of liquor. Shared by undetected stranger.

—*You asked.* The sulk, accompanied by downcast face. Precious. Often used to wheedle pricey dinners from overtired husband. Ineffective when begging for sex. From husband.

—*Fine. Just tell the story.* Superhero bartender blends ice faster than the eye can see. Tequila shots disguised as Slurpees materialize and cool the air. Oil the tongue. Loosen skeletons. US funds, trusted though unfaithful, transfer ownership.

—*So I get called into the room. The guy has my name on a piece of paper. I lie down, face in the hole.*

—*Wait! What does the guy look like?*

Blonde tips quiver within the realm of the allotted hairstyle's parameters. —*I told you, he's Asian.* Invisibility of service people well-documented in recent horror films: cable guy, photo guy, landscaper, temp. The most invisible person in the world is not one we see every day, but one we occasionally need. Interchangeable necessity, stripped of identifying details.

—*Jesus, Mandy. What the fuck does that mean? Is he tall, Chinese, fat? Korean? Big face? Small eyes? What's the matter with you?* The fifth drink toxifies them. Personality flaws float to the surface like dead perch in a contaminated pond. The one inclined to shyness gets abusive. The one inclined to wildness grows sullen. Both inclined to unfulfilled desires, they flutter and turn as if discovered littered in a secluded copse of trees.

—*I didn't look at him. Honestly. He was just the masseur you know? I mean, do you look at the guys who give you massages?* Wrists twist helplessly, broken bamboo in a storm.

—*I always request women.*

—*Yeah, okay, me too. From now on.* Possible bark of laughter, both heads turn towards the foliage—laughter turns to unconvincing coughing fit: a shroud of intimacy reflung over the dynamic duo.

Five toes wriggle free of confinement under cover of table, kick at their formerly overcrowded cell. —*No seriously, I do of course look at them. They're going to see me naked. Touch me. I want to know who I'm giving permission to.* Double faceplant into round four of adult-flavored ice. Gasp of cold summer shock as if post-handheld-jump into deep and lonely mountain quarry.

—*Well, that's very big of you. I didn't.*

—*Didn't what?* Second toe longer than first toe as per wives' tales indicates that this child will outperform its parents, monetarily speaking. It says nothing about sexuality, preference, or contentment.

—*Didn't look. I mean. He was short. I remember that. And not fat. Just average. Probably twenty-some years old. I have no idea, honestly. I didn't really look that hard. He was wearing a red*

*baseball cap. That's all I can tell you. I don't even know if he had
it on forward or backward or if there was a logo. I just know,
short Asian guy, red cap. I remember thinking how weird: a baseball cap in a posh spa, but you know, what the fuck. Everything's so casual these days, right?*

Four little piggies hold their pedicures of slutty red. One leaves
much to be desired, having been chipped away manually, while a
Lifetime Original bored the attached mind and the one healthy cat
circled restlessly. She dreamed of a man whose eyes alone would
bring her to climax. Unawares, she wrote a personal ad she could
fill from the selection of males who would visit the bar in the next
fifteen minutes. The stranger slugs dregs of juniper, shreds a two
inch square of napkin into hamster nest. He's getting bored.

—*Okay, okay. You didn't know what was going to happen.*

—*That's right I didn't.* No clandestine liberation of toes on this
side of the undertable. The married decade of professionally nude
metatarsals stay obediently enslaved by shoes and nylons. He
thinks about ripping them, cutting them with scissors.

—*So what happened? Naked heel touches cold linoleum.*

—*So. I lay facedown, like he'd asked. But here's the weird
thing: he didn't leave the room.* Fake natural nails tug at false natural highlights, as if to drag truth from a lie.

—*He didn't?*

—*No. He held up a towel. That's how I know he was short.
The towel was over his head height, but I could still see the top
of his cap.*

—*Weird.* Fronds of potted fern rustle as if someone is playing
Dr. Livingston.

—*Yeah. I thought so too. But whatever, I figured it was just easier that way, all the knocking and muffled "are you ready"s
always bugged me while I was getting a massage, I mean, because
they're going to totally see you naked anyway, so what's the
point?* Naked, she has a mole between her breasts. It is the size
of a pencil eraser and she examines it in the mirror on the occasional Wednesday to see if it has grown or changed colors, pinches

it to see if it hurts like a cancer. Melanoma, megalomania, melisma, Melinda, Mandy.

—*I agree.*

—*So, that was my first clue.* Phalanges starfish out, halogen slams brilliant facet.

—*I can see why it didn't really alarm you.*

—*It was totally normal, just weird.* Blonde breakfast ritual was eerily skipped in lieu of Starbucks this morning, no Pop-Tart was broken in half, no cherry filling licked out. No twenty minute endorphine-raising Nordic jog, breasts flying, sweat graying the cotton into maps of new worlds, no wasted hours of green eyes searching the windowpane for streaks, the sky for developing clouds, the past for clues. Today, the subway digests her and expels the carcass of the dead marriage before a window display of desiccated horticulture. A clandestine recurrence. A morning nightcap, a recap. His throat is dry, standing is impossible due to impending plot twists.

—*Okay. So what then?*

—*Then, he started the massage. Long strokes down the back. Nothing weird there. Only thing was, after about five minutes, he rubbed more quickly, touching the spine—and he seemed to be only doing it with one hand.* Music, loud as ever, has retreated to the background, as explosion whites out the sun.

—*No!*

—*Yeah. In retrospect, I'm guessing he was.*

—*Oh shit. No way.*

—*I think, maybe.*

—*Wow. And you didn't say anything?* Screaming guitar makes way for bluesy melancholy. Votive candle flickers like an appreciative Bic tribute to this slightly subordinate decibel level.

—*I was trying not to think too much. You know. It was my fortieth birthday. Four Oh. I was thinking about my life and what a shithole the last year has been, with Chad being all weird about having sex. Truth be told, though, he was always a little, I don't know, clammy in bed.*

—*Clammy?*

—*Well, you know. He can't let himself really go.* An itch gathers between shoulder blades, where the self cannot reach. There is no one to blame for this.

—*Ten years, Mandy?*

—*Eleven.*

—*That's a damn long time.*

—*I know it. I kept hoping it would get better. Sometimes, you know, it wasn't too bad.* A bracelet, glittering with rich recycled carbon skitters like a caterpillar from wrist bone to mid-ulna.

—*You don't sound too happy.*

—*But I am, really. Chad is my best friend.* This bracelet, a tenth anniversary gift, accompanied by a chaste kiss and a warm hug. The box was the color of dying lupine. The ribbon, white as a bridal gown. There was no wrapping paper, nothing to tear. The box fell open like her legs wanted to. The clasp, spotted with colorless carbon, shackled her to the man who loved her with the passion of leaking tap water.

—*Hey, I thought I was.* Naked feet fondle unoccupied slings, try to worm their way back in. Impossible without the help of hands.

—*Different thing.*

—*I'm just kidding.*

—*Well, don't.*

—*Sorry.*— Bent in half, long finger slips under strap, snaps everything back into place, shipshape. —*So Chad sucks in bed?*

—*He doesn't suck. He's just . . . disinterested. Okay, that's not the right word, it makes him sound gay.*

—*Is he gay?* Brief reek of Camembert and overripe fruit as hors d'oeuvre platter soars like French hovercraft over tête-à-tête to adjacently famished fourtop.

—*I don't think so.*

Stem of glass holds itself together despite its forced collision with the table's watercircled carapace. —*You don't think—?!*

—*We've talked about it, and he says no.* Follicles held fast by expensive salon product fail to stir though shaken.

—Holy shit on a stick! You talked about it? With Chad? He didn't kill you? Six years ago, Mandy, held by each shoulder as if in an embrace, was flung onto the sofa in an impotent ejaculation of violence. She was not hurt, but the relationship was irrevocably marred, as if the silver had been scored across the back of its smoke and mirror by the retractable talons of an invisible Asian tiger. Her first secret. The one that fastened this friendship.

—No. He was really good about it actually. We were talking about our sex life and how we haven't really cut loose in the last six years, and—

—Six?

—About six. Yeah.

—And you haven't told me? Twice, in this very bar, Mandy had held the confession on her lips, like a butterscotch that broke a diet. Twice, she had been forced to swallow the large oversweet lump because the subject had changed prematurely. Mandy was not raised to demand release. Not raised to demand at all: she preferred to be coaxed to orgasm both verbally and physically. He knows.

—I'd never had enough to drink before.— A year ago, Mandy stood before her bedroom mirror and counted her moles. She discovered fifteen. She missed two: one on her lower back, out of eyesight, and one just below her right earlobe, where she didn't think to look. *—Seriously. I wasn't interested in leaving him. I do love the poor fool. And like I said, sex isn't awful. It's just not anything to cheer about. It used to be. Just over the years, you know.* That red lace bustier thrust back into the pink and white striped bag after Chad announced at the sight of her that he was sorry he was so tired. His requesting a rain check as if she'd been marked down. Should have grabbed her before she was discontinued.

—I don't. My sex life rocks. Fourposter bed beating against plasterboard walls in tune to various tastes in music, none her own. Eggs scrambled for wolfish men who eye the door. The taste of her own *call me* spiraled in the seashell of a male ear, as if there were hope.

—*Well, you've been married twice and you've had boyfriends besides. You haven't had time to get bored.*

—*Jealous?*

—You becha. They could comfort each other, these two. Swaddle their antonym complaints in Egyptian cotton. Kiss the hurt. Oh. Yes. The thought trembles through the air and a napkin slips to the floor, unnoticed.

—*God, Mandy. I'm so sorry.*

—*I'm just kidding. I wouldn't trade Chad for casual sex. I just sometimes want to have my brains fucked out. It's not anything really big.* Thumb and index twist white platinum as if spellcasting.

—*Speaking of. Get back to this massage.* French-manicured fingers grope for fluid-filled sculpture.

—*Right! So, okay, there I am, and he does my back, and I'm thinking, gee, this guy isn't really a very good masseur. I mean, he lingered over my shoulder on one side, but moved quickly over the other. No symmetry, you know? And plus, I was distracted by the music, which was a tune I used to play on the flute in high school.*

—*Mandy. No fucking flashbacks. Just tell the story.*

—*Fine. So, then he whispers, "Mandy, turn over." And I do, and he covers me with the sheet, just like any normal massage.* There is a wedding rut on her left hand, made by the incessant spin of metal.

—*Okay.*— Feet emerge again to dance naked on the metal table leg. —*Does he have an accent?*

—*I didn't notice. Maybe. He said my name right.*

—*Go on.* The table must have an erection after all the footsie. A rock-hard boner, taut as clenched teeth, straining under the upanddown of that naked foot. The table's erection holds up their drinks, thrusts itself into the air, an invisible centerpiece, a fountain of smooth cascading over blonde over auburn, and into their glossy laughing mouths.

—*So, then he's massaging my right leg. And massaging. And*

massaging. And after about five minutes of him rubbing my inner thigh, and me getting hotter and hotter and—this is gross but, shit, I don't think I've ever been so wet in my life—I start thinking, holy crap, just fuck me already. I'm on my back, on a table, naked. My eyes are closed. You have already seen everything there is to see. Fucking do it. Touch me.

—*Did he touch you?*

—*He stayed put, about two centimeters from the good stuff. I was going nuts!* Manifestly, an unknown man strolls past the touching foreheads, the better to smell their scents together. A wall of privacy shuts him out.

—*And?*

—*Did I ever tell you that one of my most powerful sexual fantasies is to have a stranger touch me because he found me irresistible?* A gasp from the stranger swivels both faces, like twin sunflowers that must follow the orbit of the sun. As quickly, they close to him, shut him icily from their meaningfulness. As punishment, he mutters *suck me*, his breathy voice an unrecognizable pattern in the cacophony.

—*Really? Like rape?*

—*No, fuck no, not a rape fantasy. More like, well, more like I was getting a massage and the masseur found me so hot that he couldn't help himself, he had to touch me.*

—*I knew it.*

—*I know. It probably means I'm totally psycho.*

—*Probably.*

—*Very funny. But anyway, there it was, my sexual fantasy seemed like it was about to come true.* Openly staring, throat slaked with burning juniper juice, he giggles, transparent as their empty margarita glasses. Powerful. Undefeatable as a god.

—*So what did you do?*

—*What could I do? I sort of arched into it.*

—*No way.*

—*Way.*— They never see him. —*And once he'd actually touched me. God. I thought I was going to explode.*

—*Did you?*

—*Twice.* —No one has seen him for years. —*And once more when he went down on me.*

—*Holy fucking shit, Mandy! You let him go down on you?*

—*Fucking right I did. Red cap and all.*

—*Jesus! How did it end? Did he fuck you?* He knows everything about them: the gourmet smells of the blonde, the lively contortions of the other. Her cats' scattered gravel beneath his bare feet.

—*No! I have some respect for Chad, you know. It was a massage. Just a massage. It ended like any massage. Time was up. He thanked me. Told me to take my time. And left.*

—*Just like that.*

—*Just like that.*

—*And you watched him do this?*

—*No. I had my eyes closed.*— Her eyes are always closed when Chad rubs her back. —*I always keep my eyes closed during a massage. And once he started getting all, you know—well, I was afraid if I opened my eyes he'd stop! Anyway, at one point while he was, well, while he was down there, I peeked.* She is so innocent of herself that she can not say the words eating pussy. Even though she smiled—smiled!—with her eyes closed tight, while a stranger's tongue dipped into her.

—*And?*

—*Red cap. For a second I thought it was actually Chad—that he'd paid someone off to allow him to sub in as my masseur. Now THAT would have been a hot thing to do.* Her fantasies belie her innocence. She wants someone to show her how to fuck again. To desire her.

—*But it wasn't Chad.*

—*No. It wasn't Chad.*

—*You sure?*

—*Unfortunately, yes.*

—*Mandy. Wow. You had an affair.* The dark laughing lashes cloak a different set of fantasies: this one wants someone to fuck her and return for more. Knowledge of their minds swelltests the zipper over his groin.

—*I don't know quite how to think of it.*

—*You had an affair. With a total stranger!*

—*But I didn't. I was imagining Chad.*

—*Were you really?*

—*I really was.* Close at hand, a sound of blistered shock pops unnoticed. —*I mean, I knew it wasn't him, but I sort of wished myself into a place where I believed it might be. And then when I was positive it wasn't him, I actually thought that maybe he had paid this guy to, you know, give me a thrill. I mean, it's not like he doesn't know my fantasies.*

—*Do you think he did?*

—*Come on. You know Chad. Once I saw his pressed khakis out in the lobby—? He was waiting for me, sweet as can be, holding out a box of Godiva truffles. There is no way my loyal pup would ever EVER consider paying for sex for me. He's not into even the smallest hint of weirdness, no matter how much it turns me on.* Chad took her Kama Sutra pillowcases and turned them over to avoid the pictures. Chad kept the chocolate bodypaint in the bathroom until the jar dried shut. Chad put the tiny anal plug—aah!—into the bottom of his lockbox. Chad definitely did not know about the very extensive body massage he had purchased for his wife. And he doesn't know that his Chinese handyman sometimes moonlights as a masseur. And delivers food on the weekends for his cousin's Sichuan restaurant. A tongue licks a distant memory of capers and lime chicken from a bare upper lip.

—*So he paid.*

—*He did. I didn't have the heart to ask him whether he left a good tip.*

—*Mandy!*

—*Well. It's important.* Fifteen percent. More than adequate, considering.

—*Are you going to tell him? Chad, I mean?*

—*Never.*

—*Will you go back there?* A troubled tremor runs through these vocal cords, as if of envy.

—*Under no circumstances. I feel like I was granted a birthday wish and that's that.* He smiles at the lie. The little cunt is so precious, she can't even tell her best friend. He's already had her again. She keeps her eyes shut, moans prettily and quietly. He lives for women's habits. The ferns rustle under his hands.

—*Let me get the check.*

—*We'll split it.*

—*Fine.* The scent of the auburn hair, like scissored weeds. The click of gum in the blonde's mouth. Both. Together. Perhaps a stranger will follow them at a discreet distance. They live perilously close to each other, yet see each other so rarely. They are such intimate friends, yet they withhold certain shameful secrets: a surreptitious return to the massage table, a delivery-boy fuck-buddy whose name is still unlearned—the sweet, cold touch of duck sauce on nipples before they are sucked clean. Oh, to dance the sheets *à trois*. Patient as a saltwater crocodile, the stranger licks the rim of his glass, vows to layer their salty tastes and coat the whole with gin and tonic. They rise, laughing like girls. He does not move.

The city is a place where hundreds of strangers see thousands of personal acts every day. Bedrooms face offices where hourly workers grind on one side of the glass, and across the street, bodies. People-watching is a sport, an art form, a life substitute, an addiction. Two atoms of oxygen bound to their hydrogen slither with millions, billions of their molecular kind down a surface smooth to the eye, smooth to the finger, but porous as lies to something so small as they are.

Rape Fantasies

Margaret Atwood

*T*HE WAY THEY'RE going on about it in the magazines you'd think it was just invented, and not only that but it's something terrific, like a vaccine for cancer. They put it in capital letters on the front cover, and inside they have these questionnaires like the ones they used to have about whether you were a good enough wife or an endomorph or an ectomorph, remember that? with the scoring upside down on page 73, and then these numbered do-it-yourself dealies, you know? RAPE, TEN THINGS TO DO ABOUT IT, like it was ten new hairdos or something. I mean, what's so new about it?

So at work they all have to talk about it because no matter what magazine you open, there it is, staring you right between the eyes, and they're beginning to have it on the television, too. Personally I'd prefer a June Allyson movie anytime but they don't make them any more and they don't even have them that much on the *Late Show*. For instance, day before yesterday, that would be Wednesday, thank god it's Friday as they say, we were sitting around in the women's lunch room—the *lunch* room, I mean you'd think you could get some peace and quiet in there—and Chrissy closes up the magazine she's been reading and says, "How about it, girls, do you have rape fantasies?"

The four of us were having our game of bridge the way we always do, and I had a bare twelve points counting the singleton with not that much of a bid in anything. So I said one club, hoping Sondra would remember about the one club convention, because the time before when I used that she thought I really meant clubs and she bid us up to three, and all I had was four little ones with nothing higher than a six, and we went down two and on top of that we were vulnerable. She is not the world's best bridge player. I mean, neither am I but there's a limit.

Darlene passed but the damage was done. Sondra's head went round like it was on ball bearings and she said, "*What* fantasies?"

"Rape fantasies," Chrissy said. She's a receptionist and she looks like one; she's pretty but cool as a cucumber, like she's been painted all over with nail polish, if you know what I mean. Varnished. "It says here all women have rape fantasies."

"For Chrissake, I'm eating an egg sandwich," I said, "and I bid one club and Darlene passed."

"You mean, like some guy jumping you in an alley or something," Sondra said. She was eating her lunch, we all eat our lunches during the game, and she bit into a piece of that celery she always brings and started to chew away on it with this thoughtful expression in her eyes and I knew we might as well pack it in as far as the game was concerned.

"Yeah, sort of like that," Chrissy said. She was blushing a little, you could see it even under her makeup.

"I don't think you should go out alone at night," Darlene said, "you put yourself in a position," and I may have been mistaken but she was looking at me. She's the oldest, she's forty-one though you wouldn't know it and neither does she, but I looked it up in the employees' file. I like to guess a person's age and then look it up to see if I'm right. I let myself have an extra pack of cigarettes if I am, though I'm trying to cut down. I figure it's harmless as long as you don't tell. I mean, not everyone has access to that file, it's more or less confidential. But it's all right if I tell you,

I don't expect you'll ever meet her, though you never know, it's a small world. Anyway.

"For *heaven's* sake, it's only *Toronto*," Greta said. She worked in Detroit for three years and she never lets you forget it, it's like she thinks she's a war hero or something, we should all admire her just for the fact that she's still walking this earth, though she was really living in Windsor the whole time, she just worked in Detroit. Which for me doesn't really count. It's where you sleep, right?

"Well, do you?" Chrissy said. She was obviously trying to tell us about hers but she wasn't about to go first, she's cautious, that one.

"I certainly don't," Darlene said, and she wrinkled up her nose, like this, and I had to laugh. "I think it's disgusting." She's divorced, I read that in the file too, she never talks about it. It must've been years ago anyway. She got up and went over to the coffee machine and turned her back on us as though she wasn't going to have anything more to do with it.

"Well," Greta said. I could see it was going to be between her and Chrissy. They're both blondes, I don't mean that in a bitchy way but they do try to outdress each other. Greta would like to get out of Filing, she'd like to be a receptionist too so she could meet more people. You don't meet much of anyone in Filing except other people in Filing. Me, I don't mind it so much, I have outside interests.

"Well," Greta said, "I sometimes think about, you know my apartment? It's got this little balcony, I like to sit out there in the summer and I have a few plants out there. I never bother that much about locking the door to the balcony, it's one of those sliding glass ones, I'm on the eighteenth floor for heaven's sake, I've got a good view of the lake and the CN Tower and all. But I'm sitting around one night in my housecoat, watching TV with my shoes off, you know how you do, and I see this guy's feet, coming down past the window, and the next thing you know he's standing on the balcony, he's let himself down by a rope with a hook on the end of it from the floor above, that's the nineteenth, and before I can even get up off the chesterfield he's inside the apartment. He's all dressed in black with black gloves on"—I knew right away what show she got the black gloves off because I saw the same one—"and then he, well, you know."

"You know what?" Chrissy said, but Greta said, "And afterwards he tells me that he goes all over the outside of the apartment building like that, from one floor to another, with his rope and his hook . . . And then he goes out to the balcony and tosses his rope, and he climbs up it and disappears."

"Just like Tarzan," I said, but nobody laughed.

"Is that all?" Chrissy said. "Don't you ever think about, well, I think about being in the bathtub, with no clothes on . . ."

"So who takes a bath in their clothes?" I said, you have to admit it's stupid when you come to think of it, but she just went on, ". . . with lots of bubbles, what I use is Vitabath, it's more expensive but it's so relaxing, and my hair pinned up, and the door opens and this fellow's standing there. . . ."

"How'd he get in?" Greta said.

"Oh, I don't know, through a window or something. Well, I can't very well get out of the bathtub, the bathroom's too small and besides he's blocking the doorway, so I just lie there, and he starts to very slowly take his own clothes off, and then he gets into the bathtub with me."

"Don't you scream or anything?" said Darlene. She'd come back with her cup of coffee, she was getting really interested. "I'd scream like bloody murder."

"Who'd hear me?" Chrissy said. "Besides, all the articles say it's better not to resist, that way you don't get hurt."

"Anyway you might get bubbles up your nose," I said, "from the deep breathing," and I swear all four of them looked at me like I was in bad taste, like I'd insulted the Virgin Mary or something. I mean, I don't see what's wrong with a little joke now and then. Life's too short, right?

"Listen," I said, "those aren't *rape* fantasies. I mean, you aren't getting *raped*, it's just some guy you haven't met formally who happens to be more attractive than Derek Cummins"—he's the Assistant Manager, he wears elevator shoes or at any rate they have these thick soles and he has this funny way of talking, we call him Derek Duck—"and you have a good time. Rape is when they've got a knife or something and you don't want to."

"So what about you, Estelle," Chrissy said, she was miffed because I laughed at her fantasy, she thought I was putting her down. Sondra was miffed too, by this time she'd finished her celery and she wanted to tell about hers, but she hadn't got in fast enough.

"All right, let me tell you one," I said. "I'm walking down this dark street at night and this fellow comes up and grabs my arm. Now it so happens that I have a plastic lemon in my purse, you know how it always says you should carry a plastic lemon in your purse? I don't really do it, I tried it once but the darn thing leaked all over my chequebook, but in this fantasy I have one, and I say to him, 'You're intending to rape me, right?' and he nods, so I open my purse to get the plastic lemon, and I can't find it! My purse is full of all this junk, Kleenex and cigarettes and my change purse and my lipstick and my driver's licence, you know the kind of stuff; so I ask him to hold out his hands, like this, and I pile all this junk into them and down at the bottom there's the plastic lemon, and I can't get the top off. So I hand it to him and he's very obliging, he twists the top off and hands it back to me, and I squirt him in the eye."

I hope you don't think that's too vicious. Come to think of it, it is a bit mean, especially when he was so polite and all.

"*That's* your rape fantasy?" Chrissy says. "I don't believe it."

"She's a card," Darlene says, she and I are the ones that've been here the longest and she never will forget the time I got drunk at the office party and insisted I was going to dance under the table instead of on top of it, I did a sort of Cossack number but then

I hit my head on the bottom of the table—actually it was a desk—when I went to get up, and I knocked myself out cold. She's decided that's the mark of an original mind and she tells everyone new about it and I'm not sure that's fair. Though I did do it.

"I'm being totally honest," I say. I always am and they know it. There's no point in being anything else, is the way I look at it, and sooner or later the truth will out so you might as well not waste the time, right? "You should hear the one about the Easy-Off Oven Cleaner."

But that was the end of the lunch hour, with one bridge game shot to hell, and the next day we spent most of the time arguing over whether to start a new game or play out the hands we had left over from the day before, so Sondra never did get a chance to tell about her rape fantasy.

It started me thinking though, about my own rape fantasies. Maybe I'm abnormal or something, I mean I have fantasies about handsome strangers coming in through the window too, like Mr. Clean, I wish one would, please god somebody without flat feet and big sweat marks on his shirt, and over five feet five, believe me being tall is a handicap though it's getting better, tall guys are starting to like someone whose nose reaches higher than their belly button. But if you're being totally honest you can't count those as rape fantasies. In a real rape fantasy, what you should feel is this anxiety, like when you think about your apartment building catching on fire and whether you should use the elevator or the stairs or maybe just stick your head under a wet towel, and you try to remember everything you've read about what to do but you can't decide.

For instance, I'm walking along this dark street at night and this short, ugly fellow comes up and grabs my arm, and not only is he ugly, you know, with a sort of puny nothing face, like those fellows you have to talk to in the bank when your account's overdrawn—of course I don't mean they're all like that—but he's absolutely covered in pimples. So he gets me pinned against the wall, he's short but he's heavy, and he starts to undo himself and the zipper gets stuck. I mean, one of the most significant moments in a girl's life, it's almost like getting married or having a baby or something, and he sticks the zipper.

So I say, kind of disgusted, "Oh for Chrissake," and he starts to cry. He tells me he's never been able to get anything right in his entire life, and this is the last straw, he's going to go jump off a bridge.

"Look," I say, I feel so sorry for him, in my rape fantasies I always end up feeling sorry for the guy, I mean there has to be something *wrong* with them, if it was Clint Eastwood it'd be different but worse luck it never is. I was the kind of little girl who buried dead robins, know what I mean? It used to drive my mother nuts, she didn't like me touching them, because of the germs I guess. So I say, "Listen, I know how you feel. You really should do something about those pimples, if you got rid of them you'd be quite good looking, honest; then you wouldn't have to go around doing stuff like this. I had them myself once," I say, to comfort him, but in fact I did, and it ends up I give him the name of my old dermatologist, the one I had in high school, that was back in Leamington, except I used to go to St. Catharine's for the dermatologist. I'm telling you, I was really lonely when I first came here; I thought it was going to be such a big adventure and all, but it's a lot harder to meet people in a city. But I guess it's different for a guy.

Or I'm lying in bed with this terrible cold, my face is all swollen up, my eyes are red and my nose is dripping like a leaky tap, and this fellow comes in through the window and he has a terrible cold too, it's a new kind of flu that's been going around. So he says, "I'b goig do rabe you"—I hope you don't mind me holding my nose like this but that's the way I imagine it—and he lets out this terrific sneeze, which slows him down a bit, also I'm no object of beauty myself, you'd have to be some kind of pervert to want to rape someone with a cold like mine, it'd be like raping a bottle of LePages mucilage the way my nose is running. He's looking wildly around the room, and I realize it's because he doesn't have a piece of Kleenex! "Id's ride here," I say, and I pass him the Kleenex, god knows why he even bothered to get out of bed, you'd think if you were going to go around climbing in windows you'd wait till you were healthier, right? I mean, that takes a certain amount of energy. So I ask him why doesn't he let me fix him a NeoCitran and scotch, that's what I always take, you still have the cold but you don't feel it, so I do and we end up watching the *Late Show* together. I mean, they aren't all sex maniacs, the rest of the time they must lead a normal life. I figure they enjoy watching the *Late Show* just like anybody else.

I do have a scarier one though . . . where the fellow says he's hearing angel voices that're telling him he's got to kill me, you know, you read about things like that all the time in the papers. In this one I'm not in the apartment where I live now, I'm back in my Mother's house in Leamington and the fellow's been hiding in the cellar, he grabs my arm when I go downstairs to get a jar of jam and he's got hold of the axe too, out of the garage, that one is really scary. I mean, what do you say to a nut like that?

So I start to shake but after a minute I get control of myself and I say, is he sure the angel voices have got the right person, because I hear the same angel voices and they've been telling me for some time that I'm going to give birth to the reincarnation of St. Anne who in turn has the Virgin Mary and right after that comes Jesus Christ and the end of the world, and he wouldn't want to interfere with that, would he? So he gets confused and listens some more, and then he asks for a sign and I show him my vaccination mark, you can see it's sort of an odd-shaped one, it got infected because I scratched the top off, and that does it, he apologizes and climbs out the coal chute again, which is how he got in in the first place, and I say to myself there's some advantage in having been brought up a Catholic even though I haven't been to church since they changed the service into English, it just isn't the same, you might as well be a Protestant. I must write to Mother and tell her to nail up that coal chute, it always has bothered me. Funny, I couldn't tell you at all what this man looks like but I know exactly what kind of shoes he's wearing, because that's the last I see of him, his shoes going up the coal chute, and they're the old-fashioned kind that lace up the ankles, even though he's a young fellow. That's strange, isn't it?

Let me tell you though I really sweat until I see him safely out of there and I go upstairs right away and make myself a cup of tea. I don't think about that one much. My mother always said you shouldn't dwell on unpleasant things and I generally agree with that, I mean, dwelling on them doesn't make them go away. Though not dwelling on them doesn't make them go away either, when you come to think of it.

Sometimes I have these short ones where the fellow grabs my arm but I'm really a Kung-Fu expert, can you believe it, in real life I'm sure it would just be a conk on the head and that's that, like getting your tonsils out, you'd wake up and it would be all over except for the sore places, and you'd be lucky if your neck wasn't broken or something, I could never even hit the volleyball in gym and a volleyball is fairly large, you know?—and I just go zap, with my fingers into his eyes and that's it, he falls over, or I flip him against a wall or something. But I could never really stick my fingers in anyone's eyes, could you? It would feel like hot Jell-O and I don't even like cold Jell-O, just thinking about it gives me the creeps. I feel a bit guilty about that one, I mean how would you like walking around knowing someone's been blinded for life because of you?

But maybe it's different for a guy.

The most touching one I have is when the fellow grabs my arm and I say, sad and kind of dignified, "You'd be raping a corpse." That pulls him up short and I explain that I've just found out I have leukaemia and the doctors have only given me a few months to live. That's why I'm out pacing the streets alone at night, I need to think, you know, come to terms with myself. I don't really have leukaemia but in the fantasy I do, I guess I chose that particular disease because a girl in my grade four class died of it, the whole class sent her flowers when she was in the hospital. I didn't understand then that she was going to die and I wanted to have leukaemia too so I could get flowers. Kids are funny, aren't they? Well, it turns out that he has leukaemia himself, and *he* only has a few months to live, that's why he's going around raping people, he's very bitter because he's so young and his life is being taken from him before he's really lived it. So we walk along gently under the street lights, it's spring and sort of misty, and we end up going for coffee, we're happy we've found the only other person in the world who can understand what we're going through, it's almost like fate, and after a while we just sort of look at each other and our hands touch, and he comes back with me and moves into my apartment and we spend our last months together before we die, we just sort of don't wake up in the morning, though I've never decided which one of us gets to die first. If it's him I have to go on and fantasize about the funeral, if it's me I don't have to worry about that, so it just about depends on how tired I am at the time. You may not believe this but sometimes I even start crying. I cry at the ends of movies, even the ones that aren't all that sad, so I guess it's the same thing. My mother's like that too.

The funny thing about these fantasies is that the man is always someone I don't know, and the statistics in the magazines, well, most of them anyway, they say it's often someone you do know, at least a little bit, like your boss or something—I mean, it wouldn't be *my* boss, he's over sixty and I'm sure he couldn't rape his way out of a paper bag, poor old thing, but it might be someone like Derek Duck, in his elevator shoes, perish the thought—or someone you just met, who invites you up for a drink, it's getting so you can hardly be sociable any more, and how are you supposed to meet people if you can't trust them even that basic amount? You can't spend your whole life in the Filing Department or cooped up in your own apartment with all the doors and windows locked and the shades down. I'm not what you would call a drinker but I like to go out now and then for a drink or two in a nice place, even if I am by myself, I'm with Women's Lib on that even though I can't agree with a lot of the other things they say. Like here for instance, the waiters all know me and if anyone, you know, bothers me. . . . I don't know why I'm telling you all this, except I think it helps you get to know a person, especially at first, hearing some of the things they think about. At work they call me the office worry wart, but it isn't so much like worrying, it's more like figuring out what you should do in an emergency, like I said before.

Anyway, another thing about it is that there's a lot of conversation, in fact I spend most of my time, in the fantasy that is, wondering what I'm going to say and what he's going to say, I think it would be better if you could get a conversation going. Like, how could a fellow do that to a person he's just had a long conversation with, once you let them know you're human, you have a life too, I don't see how they could go ahead with it, right? I mean, I know it happens but I just don't understand it, that's the part I really don't understand.

Darrell Finch

Savannah Stephens Smith

AFTERNOON AND ALMOST summer in a stuffy classroom. Small rustlings, occasional coughs, and sniffles break the silence. There is the sound of papers shuffling and the exasperated sighs of the hopeless and those who haven't studied. The radiator along the far wall ticks randomly despite the warm weather. A plane drones overhead and a pair of girls chatter down the hall, the sound fading as they move away. Another class's muffled laughter leaks through the walls, too boisterous for the drowsy hour. Not heard are the sneaking glances and mouthed pleas, for the test is hard and the teacher isn't known for mercy or even humor.

High school. An unremarkable classroom in a plain building, a middle-aged man sitting at a desk as his students finish an exam. From the seats, he appears indifferent to suffering, theirs or anyone's. Budget cuts and boredom show in the marked walls and broken fixtures of an unloved place where people go because they have to, not because they want to. The classroom is clean, the teacher dutifully pins up articles of interest to encourage learning, and posters brighten the walls. The posters have hung there for years, and the teacher would be shocked if a student ever read the articles he tacks to the bulletin board. The man sitting at the desk is also worn. Supposedly grading papers, in reality he is counting down the minutes until he can duck into the men's room and surreptitiously take a long swallow from his flask, a burning, brutal three o'clock ration of relief.

Darrell Finch. He fits the school where he teaches, worse for the years he's seen. He's gone stale, like a jacket or shirt worn one time too many before it went into the wash. Chalk dust seems to cling to him, along with the miasma of defeat. There is a flat, wary, weary look in his eyes. Overheard words stayed with him a long time: *what a loser*. Scorn doesn't lower its voice.

A loser. Even the kids think so, when they think about him. Most don't. Neither hated nor beloved as teachers can be, he is solidly in the middle, among the vast forgettable, washed away with the end of each June. Ordinary as chalk, blank as paper, he's just another fixture in the school. Over forty and thickening, wearing khaki pants and a jacket, he's a study in browns: hair, belt. Eyes, shoes. He drives a rust-flecked Toyota that needs a tune-up, but the cassette player works intermittently. Some of the students laboring through his European history exam drive BMWs.

Beer Barrel Bird Brain, they'd taunted him when he was in school, a pudgy kid who didn't fit in, his solace found in books and grandiose dreams and ambitions. Twenty-five years went by in two blinks and a turn of the head, and here he is on the other side, teaching history and English to high school kids who couldn't care less. He doesn't care either, and stops in at a bar on his way home. Semi-regular among the irregulars, he drinks two beers and talks little, wetting his dusty throat. He's tired of words, speaking to indifferent eyes, and tired of the sound of his own voice.

Home is a ground-level apartment in a dirty cream-colored building. He drops the mail (a credit card offer, a grocery flyer, the Hydro bill, and a pizza menu) on the kitchen counter, stripping his jacket off. The unstirred air is stale and warm. He retrieves the pizza ad, vaguely thinking of dinner, and opens the dirty glass doors onto the square of concrete referred to as a "garden patio" as he tugs his tie off. The tie and flyer are abandoned on the couch as he moves out of the room.

Later, Darrell Finch lies on his bed, still dressed. In the living room, the television plays the evening news to a drooping ficus. On the bed, he eases his zipper down. The woman had come by, her breath deepened with need. Perfumed and seductive, how could he resist? Braless, with full breasts he craves. A richness of flesh. Blonde, blooming cherry in her lips and nipples, she grins and lowers herself onto his erection. She spreads herself wide, showing *all* the pink, and sinks onto his penis. Her tight heat squeezes the despair out of him. He stands behind her, the globes of her generous bottom pale and illicit as he bucks his erect cock into her, reaching forward for her breasts, fingers clutching another's skin as if it were his own.

It is his own. Darrell Finch falls asleep, penis softening, unable to even hold his own attention with his fantasies. His dreams shift and change, a movie he never got to choose playing behind his eyes.

HE WAKES IN the darkness, dick in hand, palms rustling outside his window. Something stirs him from sleep, noise or just the insistence of his bladder. His mouth is sour and his head feels thick. He rises, slow, and drifts to the window instead of the bathroom, wondering what jarred his slumber. The middle of the night. Not morning, not even close. He stands by the window, open to let cooler night mingle with the stale air of his apartment, trousers loosened and penis hanging soft again. Darkness and the window ledge save him from an accusation of exhibitionism. He blinks. The night is quiet, breezeless and still. And there is a girl under the streetlight. Her hair is long and her clothes are minimal. He stares at her standing beneath the light, bright and focused as a spotlight. She's pretty. She leans his way, and his eyes linger where his hands want to.

She turns under the spotlight, three-quarters toward him, showing off. Her hips sway. In silence, she struts and turns under the spotlight, then begins to strip. Breasts cupped by flimsy enticements, too scarce to be called clothes, more a costume. Illuminated, she slides something skimpy off and bares her breasts to him, a centerfold minus the staple, as he stands there, motionless. She is all ripe roundness, circles and curves, not a straight line anywhere. A skirt brief as a wink, long legs, black boots with high heels—

Darrell Finch is lying in bed, and he is erect, his penis jutting up from his trousers like a fist at the end of an arm. Snakes slide through the grass. Lust and the hot ache to piss conspire to make him iron hard. A dream. It is not a spotlight outside his window, just an ordinary streetlight, shining on nothing but a blank patch of sidewalk. There is no girl, just his imagination and the tease of uncertain memory. The street is empty and the night is quiet, but then a car rolls down the next block over, its engine rough, bass throbbing to intimidate.

Sweaty, he strips, pisses a river and wanders the four rooms of his apartment. The night is too quiet, and it makes him uneasy. It is not the same day he fell asleep and not yet the next: he is in limbo. Television is too loud and banal, and the radio stations are all oldies or nothing he recognizes. Talk radio's worse. He won't sleep now, and he knows it. On the coffee table, a crumpled pack tells him he's smoked the last of his cigarettes. *Shit*, he says aloud. There are no cigarettes to be found in his kitchen; the cupboard mocks him with instant coffee and instant soup and instant gratification. Bottles stand guard over crumbs on the kitchen counter. He keeps meaning to return the empties.

Sleep won't come before dawn. It's not the first three-in-the-morning that Darrell has spent alone and awake. He'll fire up his computer and waste his night time hours with idle reading in the screen's cold glow, with a drink or three, and a cigarette or ten. But he's out. Fuck. Now, or in the morning? Now. The night's too long to go without, and what's a weakness without indulging it? He pulls on jeans, sans shorts, and a T-shirt. He runs his hand along a bristly jaw, and gives a ferocious grin to the man in the dirty mirror. That man is a loser. He doesn't care.

Darrell Finch drives through the night, his throat aching for a smoke. There is nothing but stale butts in the ashtray and the old, dirty smell of cigarettes past in his car. The seat is stained with spilled coffee. Ketchup packets ride the floorboards beside stir sticks, cardboard cups, and grit. Darrell knows all the drive-through on the way home. The windshield has a pit he no longer sees, a glass spider creeping outward. He drives in silence, using his turn signal though there's no one behind him, stopping at stop signs and red lights, obeying the law, even at—

Three in the morning, and he's driving aimlessly through town like a cop, a cabbie, a criminal. Like a killer, a stalker in the dark, some thing apart. His imagination is running, taking him with it. Christ. Good thing it's a Friday night. Morning's going to be ugly.

A convenience store glows to the left off Oakwood. The night remains still, the sound of his car door *thunking* in the quiet like an announcement. No one seems to be around, odd for a Friday night. But then it's late, long late. There's an enervating heat lying over the city. Then why can't he sleep? The door jingles when he walks in, blinking at the brightness, the colors clamoring, and the sudden chill of air-conditioning.

Something smells slightly sour, but he can't name it, his eyes narrowed against the strident array of junk food and magazines, cigarettes and lottery tickets.

He may as well get something to eat since he's here. Darrell drifts down the aisle, the speakers oozing something saccharine, likely not the choice of the clerk in the polyester orange, blue and brown tunic, a morose jester with acne. Another loser, clerking on the graveyard shift. Bread and milk and juice. Fish sticks or cheap berry pie? Milk. Cigarettes and milk. There's a girl there by the coolers, not his type. What is his type? Men like him can't be choosy. He picks up cookies and something salty to go with his drinks, imagining the cool crunch of ice and the heat of scotch. A nod to nutrition and morning cereal means milk. But the girl's in his way.

He's in no hurry, so he waits, watching her.

She's wearing something, but not much. A black tank, cropped and gray from washing. Jeans, faded and riding low, showing off her flat belly. His gaze travels up. No bra. That's always good. She's leaning forward, her nipples raised by the chill from the milk cooler. The stark fluorescent lights, coldly bright, buzz and hum overhead and show him every detail. Hair too black brushes against cheeks too pale for a sunny oceanside town. She's pretty trying to be ugly. It would make him laugh if it wasn't so sad, as if he didn't see all the ugly girls trying so hard not to show how it hurts. And here she is, lovely, trying to be ugly. It's not working. The black top, like her hair, is the wrong color for her, but her back is smooth and flawless and her skin looks like spilt milk. She's reaching into the cooler, fingering the milk and cream, and Darrell Finch sees her skin disappear beneath loose clothes that seem to ask him to slide them off. He's got a hard-on, thinking of milk and cream, oh, yes, he needs some cream.

She turns quickly and grins at him. Her eyes say *gotcha*.

He's caught with his hard-on and his eyes easing under her clothes. He's caught: the reflection of the impassive cooler showed her the middle-aged man standing there gawking at her tits, small and up-tilted, nipples evident, ring glittering in her navel. The narrow lines of a tattoo cross one slim shoulder, and he didn't get a chance to see what symbol she chose for herself. He colors, heat flooding back in, feeling like a pervert, an old man. He's probably her father's age, good God . . .

Her neck is slender, and the chains she wears look too heavy for it.

He mutters something, probably *sorry*, grabs his milk, and ducks out of the aisle. He pays for his small assortment of groceries and stands outside the front doors of the store, concrete speckled with a hundred flat black globs of chewing gum. Litter like confetti thrown in grief has drifted where asphalt meets concrete. Chipped planters are filled with crumpled Marlboro packages and empty drink cups. Everything's utilitarian. The gray of old pavement eats all color, the trees leached of green under the burnt orange of sodium lights. The air smells like exhaust. He rips the cellophane to get at his cigarettes, and lights up, standing there in the hot, still night. Scattered trash should be blowing in an insinuating wind, but there's no breeze. Hot smoke fills his lungs, makes his head float.

"Got a cigarette?"

He starts when she speaks, and turns, despite himself. The girl from the store is beside him. Milk cooler girl. The teacher in him says *you're too young to smoke*; the man shrugs and offers her a cigarette. She takes it but doesn't light it. Instead, she stands beside him as if expecting something more. She has to ask if he's got a light. Under the green awning, the light reminds him of his dream, and he's still horny like he's tripped and slipped back into seventeen again, and his feet aren't walking him to his car. He's in no hurry to go home, feeling like he could move through this night as if it were still a dream, as if there would be no consequences to the other Darrell Finch, the one of the ordinary hours.

He notices that the girl has a circle of silver punctuating one eyebrow. She catches him staring again. She grins and sticks her tongue out at him, and it's pierced, and he wonders if it's true, if . . . And what would it feel like to have that kitten pink tongue flicker down the shaft of his penis, to feel the jeweled ball sliding along his taut skin?

They are at her place. How he arrived there, he isn't quite sure. There was something about the late hour, offering her a ride home, the danger in the night. A half-hopeful, feeble reference to the risks she'd take walking, a silvery, supple lure, all one hundred pounds of lithe girl. She laughed at that, seeing his invitation as the cliché it was. But she climbed inside his wretched car anyway. Unafraid of strangers, for he could be anybody: rapist or killer or both, the monster that lives by night and fear and blood. Somehow, she knows he's harmless.

Her apartment is smaller than his, but nowhere near as dismal. Someone lives here, crafted a home from small rooms. Bright posters of Greece, singing blue and white, and Paris in gentle gray, posters like the ones that he hung in his classroom back when he had hope. Mexican pottery in deep blues, golds, and reds. Thriving plants reach for the low, slanting ceiling. Books and CDs are jumbled up on shelves. She isn't stupid, he knows that at once from the surroundings, blinking and still bemused at how he found himself in her apartment. He checks his watch, but his wrist is bare. She clucks at a cat as it slinks away and pretends to offer him coffee. He declines, wondering what she'll offer him next. Hope and excitement mingle in his belly, then move lower.

Their fucking is just that. There is nothing tender, the only slowness is his tentativeness, his uncertainty about where to touch her first and how, if he's sucking too hard or too long. His hesitation is at the strangeness of another. Her cautious touches, gripping his penis too hard then too lightly, edging into an unwelcome tickle, drive him crazy anyway.

Impatient, she had kissed him first. She took his hands and brought them to her slight chest, husky voice suddenly twenty years older, saying: *you were looking, I know you were.* Sliding the black top up, and there her small breasts are, and his mouth is dry. Unencumbered by shorts, he is instantly hard. Her tongue flickers across his, and he is helpless. Still surging in his jeans, pressing urgent against denim. They kiss again, tentative and fumbling, and he feels a velvet thrill as his tongue slips wetly over hers and finds the stud. It makes him shudder, a slow dark pulse along the length of his cock.

He's harder than he's been in years. He can't stop touching her. His prick surges upward. Blood rushes everywhere, waking him from a twenty-year sleep. Her skin is so soft he could die for it, but first he'll do this one thing. He knows he shouldn't be there, feeling her fingers unzip his jeans. She's too young. She's a stranger. But her breasts are small and flawless. She doesn't need a bra, maybe never will. Delicate nipples, the color of pink lemonade, top soft mounds of skin, and his palms find them miracles. Touching her still, she laughs at his desperation. He doesn't mind. His erection would allow any mockery to get what he needs.

They are inexpert lovers in the insomniac hours, but her youth and her novelty are more than enough to arouse him. There is the twisted curiosity of fucking a girl who doesn't look anything like the lush women who please him in his dreams and taunt him in waking hours. Those women are peaches and cream, simple and pretty. Here he is, rolling over a girl too skinny, too pale, and far too young. She evokes a ghost, but she's warm and real and wicked in the night. No specter was ever so corporeal, so carnal. She takes him in her mouth, and it's all he can do to not come against the silver ball on her tongue.

It's not cold. For some reason, he thought the metal would be cold.

She twists beneath him, a writhing girl-woman, all slippery skin and quick touch, for they're both panting and sweaty, the fan not doing more than making the dead warmth move. There's nothing between them, no air, nothing but sweat, and his swollen prick finds the deeper heat of her cleft, finds the hot wet hollow, and pushes in. He doesn't have time to think about *condom pill AIDS*, he's already fucking her. Hip bones sharp, but her skin so soft and smooth. How could she pierce this skin? Tattoo this perfect skin? Youth is too good for the young.

But he is driving himself into her, his mind swirling a broken collage of half-thoughts and images, frantic and surreal. It's 4 a.m. and he was in his own bed in his own apartment not two hours ago and now he's fucking a stranger, lithe and scornful and as greedy as he. A girl who provoked him. She's beneath him, lifting to drive herself onto his penis, gasping and moaning.

It's gotta be another dream.

He'll wake again with a hard-on and the need to piss. Wake again, in his own four walls, three of which badly need painting and the fourth he never looks at anyway. So forget thought. Let there be just sensation, only now, the present moment. She is clenching his ass, urging him into her deeper, knees gripping him, small breasts jiggling deliciously. He thrusts hard into her and she moans. She's no virgin. She likes what he's doing to her. She's hot and ravenous and unafraid to touch him in places that make his eyes widen and his cock throb.

He drives in deeper. Hot urgency possesses him. With a bellow, he surges, and can't hold back. Sweaty, in a stranger's bed, hips driving, buttocks clenching, he rides her. It sweeps him up in a dark whirlwind. His ejaculate is hot, his pleasure sharp and slow and somehow pure. Darrell Finch comes inside her slippery clasp.

He's done, still flooded, panting, the hot waves of his orgasm ebbing. But she's fierce and frenzied beneath him, and he finally understands she needs more. Out of breath, he pumps for her, his need gone, but she's swelling beneath him like she's riding red waves. It'll drown them both. She bites him, the little bitch *bites* his shoulder, whimpering, and he understands. She's coming. He's making her come. Darrell grins, and the loser is a sudden wolf.

He fucks harder. He feels a drop of sweat fall to her breast and knows it's his. He's marking her everywhere with his body. She mews like an abandoned kitten, rolls like she's made of snakes, like she's dying, and he feels her coming. She throbs tight around his penis, and it's an unexpected gift that awes him briefly. He feels powerful, witness to roiling need and need's fulfillment.

It's done.

She pants beneath him, still at last. He pulls out, arms sore, and collapses on her sheets. His head is expanding and shrinking, pulsing like his penis did, and the ceiling blurs. He closes his eyes. He hears nothing but the fan in the corner and the sound of his blood rushing through his veins in an endless, pointless circuit. He wants to drift, but resists sleep, wary and exhausted. They lie there in the newness of what they've made. His heartbeat slows. She laughs. "I always wanted to do that."

"Do what?" he asks, not caring about the answer. It could be anything. Pick up a strange man, be impulsive, have a one-night stand with any old guy who leers by the milk cooler.

"Fuck you."

"Huh?" He doesn't understand, thinks it is just hostility. He's come to expect that from women. And as a high school teacher, he's heard *fuck you* a thousand times or more: muttered, screamed, drawn in chalk, or carved viciously into the desk and the driver's side of his car. Sometimes they even spell it right.

"To fuck you." Milk turns to cream in the slow satisfaction of her voice.

"Me." He is stupid, but none of it makes sense. Tonight doesn't make sense. It's four in the morning and he's just spread some girl open on sheets that will sprinkle daisies into his dreams forever and pumped a hollow lifetime's worth of desperation and desire into her. It was pleasure so hot it must have scalded him.

She sits up, clutching the rumpled sheets around her, the brash cockiness gone. She squints at him. "You don't remember me, do you?"

No. He's let a woman down again. There's hurt in her voice underneath the veneer of contempt. Then there is a new sick feeling gathering in his belly. Her age. He can put two and two together. He just wanted to lie back and feel good, to feel fucked in the right way for the first time in eons, drained and complete. But nothing lasts. Darrell Finch is a loser.

He knows what she's going to say just before she says it, like a curtain falling, like a blow about to land and put him into darkness. "I don't remember you," he says, and he is beginning to see the outlines of his dread. What else could it be? "I taught you," he says, hearing the irony in his voice. What did he teach her? He once tried to remember them all, tried to make a difference. But there were so many faces over the years.

"Yeah."

"I'm sorry."

Brittle laughter. "Don't be." She is scampering off the sheets, all pale legs and the curve of her spine like a sonnet. He still can't make out what her tattoo depicts. Her hair is too black and he's dizzy from no sleep. She dabs at the smudge of her sex with tissue, then silently offers him the box. The hostess was lovely, he thinks, and cleans himself off. The smell of what they made together is thick in the air.

He digs through his clothes for the cigarettes. He finds the pack and lights one, not asking. He's slept with a student. *Former* student. Does it matter? She holds out her hand and he surrenders another cigarette and shares the lighter. Smoke rises in her bedroom. She squints and scowls through an indigo haze. Light slants between the blinds at the window. She looks like she's behind horizontal prison bars, then she moves, and the illusion is gone. She finds an ashtray in the shape of an open hand and puts it between them. They smoke, not talking, his limp penis curling back into damp pubic hair like a fetus—

"How old are you?" he asks, dreading the answer, braced to hear two syllables that end in *teen*.

"Twenty-one."

Relief. She's of age, then. Redemption. Twenty-one. It's another decade altogether. He can't even remember twenty-one. Christ, he thinks, and watches the glow of their cigarettes in the dark. He only went out for cigarettes. Just smokes.

Twenty. Not last year, then, or even the year before. "What are you doing now?" he asks, polite. The conversation is ridiculous. He'd gone between her thighs, got his nose wet, thrust his tongue into her slick folds, and now he's enquiring about what she does for a living?

A barista. "A what?"

"Barista." A pause. "Coffee." He can hear the impatience in her voice, and feels old again. It's bizarre, having this polite conversation, the song in his head is *getting to know you, getting to know all about you* . . . With the scent of her on his fingertips and his upper lip, and the taste of her thick on his tongue. He smokes another cigarette, one more lighter flare closer to death, sitting in her bed, wondering how he can get out of there. He wants a drink very, very badly now. The lame conversation ends in silence, formality undermined by their nakedness. His body and hers, he thinks, are so entirely different, they should be two separate species, never mind just different genders. Man and woman. Man and girl.

He blinks in the sudden bright warmth of the lamp. She rises, graceful, and bends, her ass perfect despite her slenderness. She is supple. And lethal. Look how quickly she snared him. Laid him open, laid him, had him in a frenzy to lose himself inside her. There isn't a mark on her anywhere but for the ones she chose, where she's pierced and tattooed. Seeing the etchings and the rings makes him unaccountably sad. She picks up something from the floor, slips it over her head, and becomes small in a long white tee that reads *nobody*. The mark on her shoulder is an enigma.

He's still naked. His limp penis and the smell of semen. Her bedroom is a friendly jumble of books and clothes, candles and spilled jewelry. He feels like an intruder, too big, too old. She's not his type. She's pierced and tattooed, and he's screwed and blued, and he just slept with . . .

He asks for that drink, does she have something cold, knowing he can't leave just yet, and stripped of the pretense that he doesn't need one. After all, he was going to have a drink while waiting for oblivion or dreamless sleep. He wants—he needs—a drink, but doesn't want to get drunk in front of her. He's already turned himself inside out inside her. But Darrell wants very badly to get drunk.

She leaves him alone in her bedroom then returns with beer. The bottles are old friends and his throat is sand. They drink in silence, awkward for the first time. He places the beer down. "Look, I gotta go. I'm sorry."

"Where?"

Where, indeed. "Home."

"Back to the wife and kids?" A scowl, as fierce as his grin.

"No wife. No kids."

"Why not?"

"'Cause I'm a loser." He smiles, not minding anymore. Edging from her bed and into his jeans, the smell of their sex sharp again in his nose. What's he supposed to say? Play devil may care. "Thanks, hon."

She laughed, a short, ugly sound of contempt. "Yeah."

His honesty is bought by nothing to lose. "I'm sorry. I thought that's what I was supposed to say." There is nothing more to say.

He leaves, still not quite sure what happened. Darrell drives home, whistling. The edge of dawn is slicing the night sky in the east, breaking the deep blue. He left his cigarettes at her place. He laughs, until he can barely keep the car on the road.

He stops at a gas station. No more midnight rides. Christ.

COFFEE WITH HENDERSON in a place that oozes trendy, all shiny surfaces and dark colors, expensive fixtures and prints on the walls. Henderson's a lawyer, in private practice with his kids in private school. He isn't a loser. The slim dark-haired girl behind the counter reminds Darrell of something, and memory gathers like thunderclouds. A dream forgotten until now. She moves, brisk and slow behind the jars of fancy teas, the display of overpriced baked goods, and hissing stainless cappuccino machines. A careful arrangement of twenty-dollar coffee and fifteen-dollars mugs, things that make froth and foam, things that make coffee expensive, an experience. The line of her neck is achingly familiar. She turns around, boredom surly in her jaw. The silver rings shine in the bright lights that hang down, spotlighting her. Shadows and light mingle. The past and the present collide.

Christ. Her mocking smile greets his slack shock. The smile grows wider as he stutters an order, broken pieces sliding together, the picture changing again. "That a new tongue?" she asks him, smirking. Colors shimmer on her eyelids, her mouth's painted a dark berry red. She's still pretty.

A hot flush. He'd used his tongue on her nipples, her belly, and between her labia, on the slick pink cleft that glistened. His tongue remembers the bump of her clitoris, how she squirmed. She had the cutest set of little tits. How could he forget them? Or her tongue, pierced and supple, on his straining penis? Or . . .

Christ. She looks sixteen in the day, eighteen, tops. In the light of a cheerful, normal Saturday, family day. Henderson is watching their interplay, bright-eyed and curious, the raptor rapt.

Darrell mumbles something, hot as the coffee, and evades his friend's questions. They sit outside so he can smoke, and talk of the stock markets and elections. He wonders if she's watching him from inside.

He comes back to the coffee bar three hours later, dull need moving him. He waits, reading the incomprehensible menu calligraphied in colored chalk above her, the poetry of the bean and grind and roast. This time, his tongue works. "I'm sorry," Darrell says, and he's always apologizing. "I'm sorry," he repeats, and turns around to go, having given his penance. One last humiliation.

"Wait."

And he is there again. He drank too much coffee waiting for her to finish her shift, sitting in the corner like a surly poet twenty years late, watching her from the shadows. He drove her home, buzzed from caffeine and twitching with wanting her again. Too skinny, too pale, and he's burning for her.

In her bed, his erect penis presses cotton sheets, and he crawls between her spread thighs, craving the taste of her sea-slick wetness against his dry tongue. The taste of her makes him hard, and moving up, unexpected lace along her hip fills him with deeper desire. He shivers in the heat as she wraps her hand around his cock, squeezes him, and then licks his tight skin, sending that shiver down to his toes. She laps his testicles as he cups one breast and begs her for more. The fan blows hot air over them as they dance on her unmade bed, and find their way to the ancient sway, man over woman, thrusting and thrusting.

⁓

WHY DOES HE let it go on? Because of the way when he's fucking her, it feels like he has a second chance. Because she likes it, likes her body along his. The way the metal jewelry makes her skin look fragile, and he feels a suspect tenderness toward her. The way she seems to hate him, even as she sucks his cock, then kneels and invites him to fuck her. The way she seems contemptuous of him, even when she asks him to come inside her. When she hisses in his ear as she crumples into orgasm.

~

ONE AFTERNOON HE comes home and she is waiting. The empty inside isn't changed by her presence. Unaware, in a four-thirty stupor, he unlocks his door, dumps the mail, and strips off his jacket. Summer now, summer school for the surly and the futureless, he unbuttons his shirt, walks across the dirty beige carpet to open the glass doors, and—

She is out on his patio, facing the street, smoking. From behind, she looks like a girl. She is a girl. She's hunched into herself, curved slightly inward like a shell, still wearing black. In concession to summer, much of her skin is bare. A short gauzy skirt in black and gold and a black shirt small enough for a boy. The shirt rides up in the back and he can see the bumps of her spine traveling up like a chain, until they disappear beneath the fabric.

He wonders if he were to step backward very slowly and very quietly, would she ever notice he was home? He could leave as quietly as he'd come in, drive around for a bit, get an early dinner, then do something until night fell. By the time the ochre sunset urged the streetlights on, she'd be gone.

He opens the glass doors.

She stalks around his apartment, looking at everything, finding little to comment on. There is little to comment on. He waits, watching her assess his apartment, assess him. He dare not leave her alone, she'd steal . . .

No, she wouldn't. There is nothing to steal, nothing she'd want. He leaves her in the living room, walks around the wall that divides his rooms from each other, and gets beer from the fridge. He gives her one. He sits on the couch, surrendering to the inevitability of her presence.

Two beers later, she's on her knees, his hard penis in her mouth. She sucks him, slowly, assuredly, and she knows what she's doing. She knows how to please a man, how to make him surge and spill.

How many men have been in her mouth for her to get so good? He closes his eyes, with no need for movies in his head now, only the sensation of her warm mouth tight around his straining cock, sliding up and down, relentlessly increasing his pleasure. He comes with a groan, and she doesn't surrender a drop.

She rises catlike to her feet. He sits there, pants undone, prick diminishing. She finishes his beer, as if she can't stand the taste of him on her tongue, and laughs when he fumbles the offer to make her come, too. She saunters out of his door, and that is the last time he sees her.

DARRELL FINCH DRIVES downtown. November's leaves skitter in the gutters. He tells himself he's going to the liquor store, the one downtown just because it's near the bookstore he hasn't been to in a while. He forgets that he hasn't had a drink in three months. He stops into a small shop in a grim two-block area where he doesn't usually linger. He doesn't like this section of rough streets.

Bleeding Rose. The lettering reminds him of her. Maybe she's there, getting another silver ring, getting another mark. He pushes the door open. The noise of industrial music batters his ears. If real, the snickers are inaudible, the piercer and clientele playing too jaded to even bother mocking him. The edge moves to mainstream eventually. Still, he is out of place and knows it. And too stubborn to leave before he gets it done. He wants to feel something. He wants to be marked, too.

"Pierce it," he says to the boy with the shaved head and flat eyes. "Make it hurt."

It does.

Neroli

Susie Hara

*T*HE SMELL OF manure hit her right away.

"Shit," Rose said under her breath. She closed the gate behind her and latched it. "Stupid-ass fanatic gardening housemates."

She walked up the path, through the garden and alongside the patio. She looked at the table, with its red-and-yellow-striped umbrella, the white plastic chairs, each with a little pool of water in its seat, and the chaise lounge, a reminder of warmer mornings. Or is it chaise longue? she thought to herself, is that what it's called, from a French word? She shook her head. "Garden furniture. Christ."

She stopped in her tracks. She smelled something else— something divine. What was it? Was it the orange tree? She moved closer to it. It was the orange blossoms! She moved in close, stuck her nose deep into the blossomed branches and inhaled the scent. It was intoxicating. *Neroli*, that was the word, she thought. The name for the oil made from orange blossoms.

She went into the house. It seemed quiet, but you never knew. "Anyone home?" No answer. At least there was this comfort. The comfort of solitude. She walked up the stairs. The door to Juan's room was almost closed—but not quite latched. She could smell incense. Did that mean he was here? Damn. She listened for a sound of movement. Nothing. But then he was always so quiet.

She went into her room and closed the door. Home at last. She took off her shoes and sat down on her bed, letting herself feel how tired she was. Finally. These night shifts were killing her. She rubbed her feet. The only good thing about it was she had the house to herself during the day. Usually. She pulled down the opaque shades. The room, in artificial darkness, was soothing to her. She took off her scrubs and got into bed. She closed her eyes and put one hand on her chest and the other on her belly. She was bone tired.

She was already drifting when she heard something. A—a vibration. What was that? Why oh why did she have to be so sensitive, so—ugh. She sat up. It was *definitely* coming from Juan's room. The soundproofing was pretty good—the house was built in the early 1900s, but still, she could feel it. That was it—she could feel it. It was a feeling, not a sound. It was a kind of a hum, not a sound-hum, but a feeling-hum.

"God!" She collapsed back down on her bed. She had four housemates—if only his room wasn't the one right next to hers! She got up, put on her robe, and went out in the hallway.

"Juan?"

"Sí."

"Oh. Just wondering if you were—here."

"I am here, Rosa." Juan had moved in only a month ago, and from the beginning he had always called her Rosa, even though her name was Rose. It was kind of annoying in a way but really she liked it. She liked the way he said it, with the soft *sss*, like he was caressing her with the silky sound. She and Juan had a kind of alliance in that they were the only ones in the house who refused to get caught up in the gardening craze.

She stood in the hallway. How could she ask about the vibration without seeming nosy at best or crazy at worst? She went back in her room and shut the door. Now she didn't feel sleepy anymore. She thought about those oblique looks he'd been giving her lately when they passed in the hallway or the kitchen. And the smell of him, kind of a mixture of soap and sweat and something else, what was it. *Eau de masculine*, if they could bottle that stuff they could make a mint off it, she thought. Oh. It had just been so long, she thought, as she sat down on her bed. But—a housemate. No-no-no. No bonking a housemate. Too messy. And no one at the hospital, either, she reminded herself. It was a hotbed of intrigue, and she already had people gossiping about her, and she didn't want any more of that shit. Absolutely not. On the other hand, where exactly was she supposed to meet men?

She picked up her hairbrush. This always relaxed her. She undid her braid and ran her fingers through the length of her hair. *One, two, three, four, five.* In her childhood, it was commonly known that brushing your hair was what gave you beautiful, shining locks. But no one seemed to brush their hair anymore. It would ruin that fashionable messy hair look, she thought. But she loved to brush her hair, it was so comforting. *Twenty-four, twenty-five, twenty-six.*

She stopped in mid-stroke. Her breath caught. She heard—something. Breathing. Heavy, rhythmic, breathing. Is it possible? Could he be jerking off in the next room? Knowing I am here? How—how—creepy, she thought at first. But then a sudden sweeping motion in her belly rushed down between her legs and into every crevice of her hot spot and back around again. Oh. How *hot*, she thought. She let her robe fall open, put her fingers around her nipple and pinched it, hard. She put her other hand between her legs. She laid back on the bed. She tried to go slowly, slowly. Her breathing was ragged. Let him hear me, she thought, I don't care. A soft sigh escaped her. Oh no. What if he heard that. So what, what if he does. She put one finger inside and picked up the pace. She turned over onto her stomach and moved on top of him, his finger, his cock, his mouth. Her face was hot. She wasn't close, not yet. She heard something else from the next room, a whispering, a murmuring almost. This was too much.

Was he calling to her, was he saying her name? This sent her onto the next plateau, she could feel it, she was getting closer, so close, and then she slipped over the edge, moaning into the pillow.

Rose's heart was beating hard, and a wave of warmth spread all through her pelvis and down her legs, to her toes. A loud silence stretched between the rooms. She pulled the covers up around her.

She listened. She heard nothing. Almost—it almost sounded like a slight tapping. Was she imagining it? But she was already starting to feel herself unwinding, from working a ten-hour shift, from dealing with sad patients, angry patients, crazy patients, from trying not to feel so much. She was beginning to relax, gradually, feeling like she was heading slowly toward sleep.

She heard a knock. And then a pause—and two more knocks on her door. "Rosa?"

"Just a second!" She put on her robe and opened the door. Juan was standing there, fully dressed, looking . . . looking like he always did . . . perfectly groomed, even in jeans and a T-shirt. She felt herself blush. Did he know? Had he heard her?

"I was wondering," he said, and he looked so embarrassed, she was at once excited and terrified that he might finally be coming on to her, after all her fantasies. "I was wondering if you could . . . you know . . . help me with the computer. You seemed to know so much last time. Last time you showed me. Things. Oh . . . I . . . are you sleeping? I'm sorry. You just came home from work, probably. You need to sleep. I wasn't thinking. Never mind. Never mind. You go back to sleep, I won't bother you."

"No, that's okay . . . I was just . . . resting. I'll go to sleep . . . later. It always takes a while to unwind."

"Yes," he said. She looked at him. He seemed . . . nervous. Was it possible? Nervous about talking to her? No, probably not.

"I can help you, no problem." She followed him into his room. It was, as always, neat as a pin. She glanced quickly at his bed— perfectly made, no wrinkles. Had she imagined the whole thing?

"I was just . . . just now trying to do something and it stopped. It won't do anything, no matter what I try, it's stuck," he said.

She moved toward his chair. It was an office chair, the kind that twirls around. She sat down on it and scooted in closer to his desk.

She tapped at the keys. "It's just frozen, that's all. It happens. No big deal."

"So what do I do when that happens?"

"You just press these keys, see, the Control key and then the Alt key, and the Delete key. All at once. Control-Alt-Delete. And it shuts down the computer. And then you turn the computer back on and start all over."

Juan leaned in close, watching her as she tapped the keys. She could smell him again, and she thought . . . was it possible? She thought she detected a faint smell of sperm.

"So easy," he said.

"Yes," she said. *It would be so easy for us to touch.*

Juan smiled at her, then, a slow, sweet smile that made her temporarily lose her mind. "Thank you, Rosa."

"Oh, no problem! Well." She stood up. "Guess I better get some sleep."

"I am so sorry that I woke you up. Did I?"

"No, no you didn't. I always like to help you, Juan." He didn't say anything, just stood there, looking at her. "See you later," she said.

Juan closed the door behind her and leaned against it for a few moments. He smiled as he reached under the bed to get his book, *Programming in HTML and Java Script.*

He set his book on the desk, knelt down beside the chair, and took a deep breath. He smelled something—was it her? A fragrance that always reminded him of orange blossoms. He laid his head down on the chair, his cheek on the seat where she was sitting only a few moments ago. He stayed there, resting his head, for a long, long time.

Fever Blisters

Joyce Carol Oates

"*W*HY AM I here?"—on foot, in absurdly high-heeled sandals, in a tight-fitting red polka-dot halter-top dress that showed the tops of her breasts, in Miami. In waves of blinding, brilliant, suffocating heat. Not Miami Beach, which, to a degree, though she had not visited it in years, she knew, but Miami, the city, the inner city, which she did not know at all. And she had no car, she must have parked her car somewhere and forgotten the location, or had someone stolen it?—there were so many scruffy-looking people on the street here, and the majority of them black, Hispanic, Asian, strangers who glanced at her with contemptuous curiosity, or looked through her as if she did not exist. She could not remember where she'd come from, or how she'd gotten here, dazed with the terrifying tropical heat which was like no heat she had ever experienced in North America. Carless, in Miami!—she, who had not been without a car at her disposal since girlhood, and, in the affluent residential suburb of the northerly city in which she lived, a young widow whose children were grown and gone, famous among her friends for driving distances no longer than a block, and often shorter.

It was a nightmare, yet so fiery was the air, so swollen the sun in the sky, like a red-flushed goiter, she understood that she was not asleep but hideously awake—"For the first time in my life." On all sides people were passing her, pointedly making their way around her as she walked nearly staggering in the high-heeled sandals, forced frequently to stop and lean against a building, to catch her breath. The mere touch of the buildings burnt her fingers—the sidewalks, glittering with mica, must have been blisteringly hot.

The wide avenue was clotted with slow-moving traffic and flashes of blinding light shot at her from glaring windshields and strips of chrome; she had to shield her eyes with her fingers. How was it possible, she'd come to Miami without her dark glasses?

Had the sun become unmoored?—the temperature was surely above 120 degrees Fahrenheit. The air was thick and stagnant, she had to propel herself through it like a clumsy swimmer. Overhead, a flying pigeon, stricken with the heat, suddenly fell dead to the pavement; she saw, horrified, in the gutter and on the littered side-walks, the bodies of other birds shoveled in casual heaps. In doorways of buildings derelicts lay unmoving as death, ignored by pedestrians. Everywhere there was a stench as of garbage, raw sewage, an open grave.

Hazy in the distance, luminous with blue, was Miami Beach—causeways, high-rise buildings silhouetted against the fiery sky. She knew the ocean was beyond those buildings but she could not see it. She sobbed with frustration—"So far!" The beautiful city unreachable by her, separated from her by miles of heat, as if the very molecules of the air were ablaze.

She was lost, yet at the same time knew her destination: that dilapidated hotel across a littered, sun-blazing square: *The Paradisio*. This was the hotel, or a derelict version of it, that had once been on the ocean, on Arthur Godfrey Boulevard. Its stucco facade, painted a garish flamingo-pink, with mildewed white awnings, had a foreshortened, stubby look; a limp American flag hung motionless over the portico. How changed *The Paradisio* was, yet unmistakable!—she could have wept, seeing it. For she was to meet her lover there, as they'd done, years ago, in secret.

And she seemed to know, with a thrill of despair, that *The Paradisio* would have no air-conditioning.

⁓

"AND IF HE doesn't come?—what will happen to me, then?"

The lobby of *The Paradisio* was so dim-lit, after the dazzling sunshine, she could barely see at first.

Except to note, nervously, lifting her arms so as to hide her over-exposed bosom, that several men, all strangers, were staring at *her*.

She looked away, shivering. The lobby was hot, humid, its air impacted as the interior of a greenhouse, yet she felt chill. Was her lover supposed to meet her here in the lobby, or in the cocktail lounge; or was he waiting for her up in the room? And which name, of the numerous names they'd used over the years, would he have used?

She could not recall clearly that first assignation, here in *The Paradisio*. That is—*The Paradisio* that was.

How shabbily romantic the lobby was, and how much smaller than she would have imagined! Frayed crimson velvet draperies, absurdly ornate gilt-framed mirrors, enormous drooping rubber plants with dying leaves; underfoot a grimy fake-marble floor. Her nostrils pinched with the commingled odors of disinfectant, insecticide, and a lilac-scented air freshener. A uniformed bellboy—hardly a boy: an aged black man with a face creased as a prune, and rheumy eyes—walked past her very slowly, carrying luggage in both hands, but taking no notice of her. As if she did not exist. Yet the men elsewhere in the lobby continued to stare rudely at her: one of them was a red-faced white-haired Texas-looking man in a dinner jacket, another was a portly fellow with an embarrassed face, in a wilted sports shirt and Bermuda shorts; another was a stocky silvery-blond gentleman of late middle age in a candy-striped seersucker suit, white shoes with tassels. This man, obviously suffering from the heat, wiped his flushed face with a tissue, yet peered at her shyly, even hopefully—"But I don't know *him*."

The shame of it washed over her, that she, who had prided herself upon the exclusivity of her taste in men, she, who in even the worst years of her marriage had never been so much as mildly promiscuous, should have to have her assignation with a stranger: how sordid, how demeaning!

"Unless that is my punishment, in itself?"

After some awkward minutes, during which time she tried unsuccessfully to examine her reflection in one of the lobby mirrors, but found her reflection cloudy, like something dissolving in water or radiant waves of heat, the gentleman in the candy-striped seersucker suit disengaged himself from the others at the rear of the lobby, and made his way to her. When their eyes met, he took a quick step forward, smiling—"Ginny, is it *you?*"

She stared in amazement, trying not to show her surprise. She too smiled, shyly—"Douglas, is it *you?*"

They clasped hands. But for the heat, and the envious stares of the others, they would have embraced. She wiped tears from her eyes and saw that her lover was wiping tears from his eyes, too.

⌒

ON THE FIFTH floor of the hotel they wandered looking for their room, still clasping hands, and whispering together; the hotel was one of those old-fashioned hotels in which corridors lead off in all directions and numerals run both forward and backward. Several maids pushing carts heaped with soiled linen, damp towels, aerosol spray cans of insecticide and room freshener, and supplies of miniature soaps and other toiletries regarded them with barely disguised smiles of contempt. The maids were Puerto Rican, Jamaican, Cuban—Haitian? The youngest was an attractive, busty Hispanic woman who laughed openly at the lovers, took pity on them, and led them to their room at the far end of a corridor rippling with heat. In her torrent of amused Spanish they could recognize only the words, "señor, señora!—this way, eh?" For it seemed that she too was headed for room 555 with her cleaning implements.

The maid's boisterous presence in the room was a distraction and an embarrassment to the lovers, but there was nothing to be done. Out of consideration for their predicament, she began in the bathroom.

Virginia and Douglas clutched hands, whispered.

"*Can* we? Here?"

"We *must*."

But how unromantic, their room—meagerly furnished, with a sagging double bed covered in a stained, scorch-marked bronze satin spread; an imitation-mahogany bureau with a cloudy mirror; a squat, old-fashioned television set which the maid had switched on mechanically to an afternoon game show. The room's single window had no blind and looked out upon a glaring, smoggy, featureless sky; the ceiling was strangely high, as if set precariously in place, dissolving in an ambiguity of hazy light. And pervading all was the odor of stale cigarette smoke, human perspiration, insecticide and room freshener. Ginny wanted to cry—"It's so cruel, after so many years!"

She scanned her lover's face anxiously, even as he scanned hers.

Of course, she recognized him now: Douglas's younger, handsome face was clearly visible in this face: only lined, flushed, a bit jowly, creases beneath the eyes. His hair had gone silver, and thinned, but it was his hair, with its singular wave, and there were his gray-blue eyes, crinkled at the corners, unmistakable.

"Ginny, darling, you *did* love me? Didn't you? Those years—"

"Douglas, of course. Yes—"

Virginia's voice faltered as, in the bathroom, the maid rapped sharply on the partly opened door, and called out to them in Spanish.

Douglas whispered, "I think she wants us to hurry."

"Oh yes. My God."

They embraced, and kissed, tentatively; but their lips were so hot and parched, Virginia flinched away—"Oh!" A tiny fever blister began to form instantaneously on her upper lip.

Douglas stared at her, appalled. "Ginny, I'm *sorry*."

"It wasn't your fault."

It was the heat, and the dazzling light. And no shelter from it.

Yet there was the need to continue, so, stricken with self-consciousness the lovers turned aside to undress, with a hope that the maid would not interrupt further. The game show ended amid rowdy applause, and a sequence of gaily animated commercials followed.

How much longer it took to undress, than ever in the past! Arms bent up awkwardly behind her, Virginia fumbled with the zipper of her tight-fitting dress. She had not worn so low-cut and uncomfortable a dress for a decade, what had possessed her to wear it today? The ribbed bodice, supported from inside, had cut into her tender flesh—"Damn it!" At least, in this heat, she was not wearing a slip; only a pair of scarlet silk panties, tight too, which she kicked off in relief, along with the high-heeled shoes. Her hair, which she'd thought she had had cut recently, was in fact glamorously long, a thick glossy pageboy that fell heavily on her shoulders; the nape of her neck was slick with sweat. She did not dare sniff at her armpits for fear of what she might detect. And no deodorant! And no makeup! She dreaded to think what the heat had already done to her carefully applied makeup: the pitiless overhead light would expose every flaw in her face.

Fortunately, the bureau mirror was too cloudy to show anything more precise than wavering fleshy forms, like mollusks out of their shells, where she and her lover stood.

She could hear the man murmuring to himself, half a sigh, half a sob—"Hurry, hurry!"

At last, they turned shyly to each other. Virginia saw, with an intake of breath, that her lover had gained perhaps thirty pounds since she'd last seem him in such intimacy: the flesh bracketing his waist was flaccid and raddled, and he had a distinct potbelly. He, of all men, so vain of his body!—"It doesn't seem possible." Among their circle of friends Douglas had been the most competitive tennis player, the most energetic yachtsman; the most generally admired of the men. (Virginia's husband, years older, had been the richest.) Now, though she was making a womanly effort to smile encouragingly, she could not keep a look of dismay out of her face: Douglas's chest and pubic hair were so silvery as to resemble Christmas tinsel, and his legs, even his thighs, once so solid with muscle, were now strangely lank and thin. There was an eerie disconnectedness to the parts of his body she had never seen before.

Nor was his penis erect, yet. This too was an anomaly.

In turn, Douglas was staring at her in—amazement? apprehension? dread? *desire?* Self-conscious as a girl, Virginia made a vague effort to hide her breasts, which were still rather full, beautifully shaped, and her belly, where a faint incision showed, curving gently upward like an unbent question mark.

"*You*—you're beautiful!"—the exclamation, passionate as if it were the truth, seemed snatched from him, like a sob.

On the television, an evangelist named Reverend Steel was shouting a sermon about Jesus Christ and alms.

Slowly, Virginia drew the bronze bedspread back, dreading what she might see; and yes, she saw it. So humiliating! demeaning!—"The sheets haven't been changed, since God knows when."

Douglas, close beside her, looking, winced. Murmuring, in husbandly fashion, "Well, I don't think, Ginny, we have any choice."

Yes. She knew.

Yet—"If only we could draw a shade!" The room was as bright, she couldn't help thinking, as an operating room. But the window was raw, open, perhaps it did not even have any glass, a great gaping hole in the wall; and outside, a smoggy haze. Where was the city of Miami? Had it been forgotten, or erased? And if Miami was gone, how would she return to her life?—*to where would she return?*

Her lover, reading her thoughts, asked, in a low, worried voice, "*Why* are we here, Ginny, do you know?"

"I don't! I don't know!"

At this, the Hispanic maid leaned out of the bathroom to call out something to them, part Spanish part English; her tone was admonitory and jeering. Douglas winced again, urging Ginny to lie down on the bed. "She says, 'To do it right, this time.'"

"What?"

"'To do it right, this time.'"

Where in the past lying in bed with Douglas had been the extinguishing of consciousness, ecstatic and voluptuous as slipping into warm dark water of sleep, or of oblivion, this afternoon the experience was one of full hideous wakefulness. Shutting her eyes tight did no good, for the harsh sunshine was empowered to penetrate her eyelids; burying her face with erotic abandon in Douglas's neck did no good, for his skin was so slick with sweat it felt clammy. Virginia could have wept—"How are we to make love, in such circumstances!" The fever blister on her lip throbbed like a bee sting.

Douglas, gamely stroking her hair, did not seem to hear. He was speaking with the eager hopefulness of a man intent upon explaining the inexplicable; as a successful corporation attorney, it was his habit to fall back upon words as a means of defense. "—I think when we—that time—that first time, in Miami Beach?—when we first became lovers, Ginny?" pausing as if the memory in fact eluded him, so that Virginia nudged him to continue, gravely, "—we set so much in motion we could not have anticipated. My wife, and my daughter Janey; *your* husband and children. We were selfish, unthinking—"

At this, before Virginia could reply, or even collect her thoughts sufficiently to know whether she agreed, or disagreed, there came a loud rapping from the bathroom doorway: the Hispanic maid interrupted again, to shout a vehement corrective. Virginia, cringing in Douglas's arms, the two of them pathetically naked, exposed, could comprehend only a cluster of words here and there.

Fortunately, Douglas knew a little Spanish. Humbled, he whispered in Virginia's ear, "She was the maid for the room, she says. And we forgot to leave her a tip."

Virginia's eyes flew open, astonished. "What? Is that it? Is that all?"

In her fever state, she began to laugh. Douglas joined her, in a helpless spasm. Peals of laughter mingling with ecstatic shrieks and groans from the television set where Reverend Steel was exhorting the faithful in his studio audience to surrender themselves to Our Savior.

"Is that all? A *tip*?"

⁓

How hot, how prickly-hot, their skin!—their skins! In dread fascination, determined not to wince, or to cry out in pain or distaste, Virginia helped her lover lower himself upon her, and try to insert his only partly erect member into her; she wished he would not keep muttering *Sorry! sorry!*—"It isn't romantic at all." Where they pressed together, the length of her spread-eagled body, her flesh felt as if it were being assailed by hundreds of tiny stinging ants.

Now too the maid was running water loudly in the bathroom, flushing the toilet repeatedly. How inconsiderate!

Virginia could have wept—"It isn't romantic at *all*."

Yet she and Douglas gamely persevered. For, in *The Paradisio*, there is no turning back.

Lovemaking after so many years is inevitably awkward. Calculation has replaced blind passion. This had an air of the clinical, for Douglas had gained that weight in the torso and stomach, and Virginia, dehydrated from fever, was thinner than she'd been during the five years of their affair. She shut her eyes, trying to recall her fever in that other life. That life out of which she had stepped, into *The Paradisio*. Or had she died? Stricken in the Yucatn, collapsing in a seething pool of sunshine. Luscious bougainvillea flowers reeling overhead. Or was it in the hospital? the glaring lights, and the infection that followed? But, no, for God's sake stop—"*It isn't romantic at all.*"

And poor Douglas needed her help, he was whispering to her in desperate appeal, so, sighing, Virginia reached down to caress his poor damply-limp organ, recalling how, once, she'd been so in awe of it, and of him; of how, when *The Paradisio* had been a sumptuous luxury hotel overlooking the Atlantic Ocean, they'd made love passionately, blindly, unthinkingly . . . not once, but several times. And afterward, dazed with love, and with the violence of their erotic experience, they had been reluctant to leave the privacy of the hotel room and return to their spouses: Douglas had gripped Virginia's shoulders hard, declaring, "I will never want anything again!" and Virginia had laughed, it was such an extravagant statement. Yet, hadn't she felt the same way?

"My God."

Virginia opened her eyes, and saw what Douglas meant—several boil-sized blisters had formed on their chests! Virginia pinched one just above Douglas's left nipple, and a watery warm liquid ran out.

"Oh, sorry! Did it hurt?"

Douglas grimaced stoically. His face was a shimmering mask of sweat. "No. Not much."

Impatient with the lovers, the Hispanic maid had begun vacuuming the room, and the roaring pelted them from all sides. "So rude!"—in other circumstances, Virginia would have complained angrily to the front desk; here, at least, the noise drowned out the television evangelist.

Gamely, Virginia resumed massaging Douglas, as provocatively and as sympathetically as she could; for theirs was a bonded plight. She decided not to worry about the fever blisters, but kissed him full on the mouth. "My love! Yes!" Quickly, Douglas became hard, and, like a man rushing with a glass of water filled to the very brim, desperate to spill not a drop, very quickly he pushed himself into her, where she was rather dry, and parched, and feverish, but ready for him—"Oh yes!"

How long then they labored together, like drowning swimmers, the roaring of the vacuum cleaner pervading the room, and the shabby bed nearly collapsing beneath their exertions, neither might have said. Virginia stared open-eyed past her lover's contorted face, where droplets of sweat gathered like tears, seeing that the ceiling seemed to be lifting—floating. *Set so much in motion.*

Could not anticipate. Selfish, unthinking. Was it so? Had their attraction for each other blinded them to others? Douglas's unhappy wife, her drinking, dependence upon a succession of therapists; the pretty daughter who dropped out of Bennington to live in a rural commune in Baja California where the principal crop was marijuana. Virginia's husband never knew that she'd been unfaithful to him for years with one of his most trusted friends, yet, shortly before his death (but what a triumphant death: on the golf course, having sunk a diabolically tricky putt, to the envy and admiration of three companions) he had accused her of being a "promiscuous" woman—"So unfairly!" In fact, Virginia had had few lovers in her life and of those Douglas had been the sweetest, the kindest, even as he'd been the first; certainly he'd been the one Virginia had most cared for.

The bed was jiggling so violently, Virginia didn't know if Douglas's accelerating pumping was causing it; or the damned maid, inconsiderately banging the bed with the vacuum cleaner nozzle. Maybe, when all this was over, Virginia *would* complain.

To encourage her lover, she began to moan softly. In pleasure, or in the anticipation of pleasure. Or in a fever-delirium?

Seeing then, vividly as if the girl were sitting at her bedside, her own daughter, a petulant smirky high school girl of some years ago who had astonished Virginia by asking, suddenly, with no warning, one day when Virginia was driving her to a shopping mall, "You and Mr. Mosser—*did* you? When I was in grade school?" and Virginia blushed hotly, and stammered a denial, and her daughter interrupted her carelessly, saying, "Oh hell, Mother!—as if any of that matters *now*."

Virginia wanted to protest, But doesn't everything matter?

She opened her eyes to see her lover's sweaty beet-red face contorted above hers, veins prominent in his forehead, eyes narrowed to slits. His breath was so wheezing and labored, a dread thought came to Virginia: had Douglas died, too?

"No. It isn't possible."

She shut her eyes quickly to dispel the thought, and saw, at once, the most unexpected, and the most beautiful, of visions: Douglas Mosser, aged thirty-five, in white T-shirt, shorts, sandals, leaning to her to extend a hand to her, Virginia, his friend's wife, to help her climb aboard his yacht; smiling so happily at her, his eyes shining; squeezing her fingers with such emphasis, she felt the shock in the pit of her belly. And she cried aloud, now, in room 555 of *The Paradisio*—"I did love you! I still do! It was worth it!"

A fiery sensation immediately welled up in her loins, that part of her body that had felt nothing for so long; and shattered, yet continued to rise; and yet continued. Virginia clutched at her lover's sweat-slick body, weeping and helpless. As he groaned into her neck, "Ginny! Darling! I love you too!"

The bed jiggled, sagged, clanged in a final shuddering spasm.

〜

How EMBARRASSING, THEIR pooled resources came to only $44.67—which they offered to the Hispanic maid, with trembling fingers; and which she contemplated, with suspenseful deliberation, weighing the bills and change in the palm of her hand.

Anxiously the lovers awaited her judgment. Was that bemused contempt in her face, or malice, or a wry grudging sympathy; was it pity; was it, simply, a look of finality—as if she too were eager to leave, after a long grueling day at *The Paradisio*?

Until at last to their infinite relief she smiled, flashed a true smile, saying, shrugging, "*Eh, gracias!*" and closed her fist around the modest tip, and shoved it into her pocket.

History and Physical

Holly Farris

"*I*F YOU'RE A doctor, why are you at the beach on a Thursday?" Jeff says.

"If you're straight, why do you care?"

Jeff and Che Juan stand an arm's length apart in ankle-deep water at the beach. Their oiled bodies might have melted, clean, into the baby ripples, magically bypassing the Caribe Hilton's sugar sand. The year is 1980, and the men's story begins off the Avenida Ashford, San Juan's avenue linking tourism to the old city.

To one side of the hotel, ancient San Juan is a maze of narrow serpentine streets. Stucco facades rise from the alley coils, offering residents some protection against the noise and dirt of the chaos below. Tiny balconies flash geraniums blooming in window boxes or in terra-cotta pots on ceramic tile floors. Ornamental wrought-iron railings and enclosures outline deeply-recessed windows.

On the other side of the hotel complex where the men stand, a place where locals swim, the beach rims a lagoon, its water brackish and cut off from the drama of the open Caribbean. Minus business suit and other identifiers, Jeff prowls here. The whole sprawl is Jeff's playground, not simply where he has hotel reservations. As an executive on frequent corporate assignments in Puerto Rico, he straddles the line between what tourists want and what a resident requires. The Caribe Hilton, where his pharmaceutical company entertains investors, has brochures advertising outdoor bars and breezy verandas, decadent swimming pools, and rooms furnished with rattan. Raucous hibiscus flowers on upholstered chaises front the calm sea.

Exactly at the time and place the men stand, it is the first birthday of AIDS in America, though the threat is not yet recognized in the vacation paradise. Fair children's bright heads bob in the water near the two men. The sky overhead and the ocean are the burnt-charcoal gray of cooling grills, but the hotel children have wet hair the color of lighter fluid's first lick by a flame.

Jeff sees red, orange, yellow, and blue dunk. No, that last must be his balls aching inside baggy swimming trunks, so long he's been ogling Che Juan.

Since this morning, when they eyed one another from distant beach towels, Jeff has wanted to get him into the water, turn away from the nosy raft-riding boys and squealing pigtailed girls, show him he can do more than imagine it. Che Juan had trousers and street shoes lined up beside him on the towel, so he has somewhere to be. Jeff, not yet knowing the other man's name, passes as a geeky tourist.

~

JEFF IS SPECIFIC ABOUT his desires. Indeed, he has never felt so free as he does in Puerto Rico. He trolls the city's open air *cafeterías* late at night, killing time toying with an uneaten Cuban sandwich and sweaty canned pineapple soda. He taps a chip from the hotel casino on the table, holding the token between his thumb and forefinger, and spots a man who is curious about him. Assuming he is a tourist down on his luck, Latino locals offer Jeff what he really wants. There's a glance, perhaps a melodramatic kiss into the air in his direction. Smooching noises, a form of wolf whistle, emanate from island boys searching for either girls or boys.

Jeff inevitably follows a trail of cologne, dark head hair, and bearded jaw. Gold chains around a stranger's neck or wrist glitter under street lights. At the man's beachside efficiency, they slip inside the grillwork, the unchained *rejas*. The man bulges under his zipper, though he may never have spoken to Jeff, the *gringo*, following him. Jeff drops to his khaki knees as soon as he's admitted to the outdoor patio. He slurps the cock that's offered, from thick base to leaking tip. He adores the ridge where the prepuce folds on itself to reveal the glans. His tongue polishes the uncut trophy, and his hands work to caress the scrotum. He cradles each ball, separately and then together, lingering over the cool sack until he feels the testicles tighten.

On his first memorable night during this visit, Jeff licked and sucked, no surprises. One dry index finger probed the man's anus. The balls drew close to the perineum, the man's groin quaked, and Jeff cranked his neck to gulp another millimeter. At the last second, the man pulled out, mashing Jeff's chin against his coarse pubic fuzz. He shot his load into the tropical foliage fringing the patio, grunting.

"*Mira, 'manos!*" the man said in Spanish as he came, which Jeff heard as "Look!" and then what he thought was "hands." Pleased with his performance, Jeff believed the man had appreciated the ass play. To his delight, three erect cocks poked through the *rejas* above the waist-high concrete wall, an excess that nearly overwhelmed him. The meat belonged to a houseful of Cuban exiles who had watched in the darkness. Called to the scene by "Look!" and then a shortened "*hermanos*" or "brothers," the men who had dodged sharks while escaping Havana Harbor took turns bucking in Jeff's throat.

⁓

STEPPING AWAY FROM the shore at the lagoon, as though he knows how it's done, Jeff throws an occasional back or shoulder or elbow between himself and Che Juan so the two masquerade as strangers, and that's what they are, having just exchanged names. Jeff believes Che Juan is an alias, and why didn't he think of one, quick. While the doctor wades ahead into deeper water,

Jeff gapes as Che Juan thumbs his tiny Speedo, popping his cock into brief salt air view.

The uncircumcised tip sports a shield of foreskin. This small hood, absent on his own pale member, first annoyed Jeff when he began cruising Latinos. Now he tests himself, leering at Che Juan's thin membrane until the purple head blooms from beneath, wet with pre-come in anticipation. Jeff loves how the ridge thickens with the retracted foreskin, its dart on the under surface, the frenulum, pulsing.

Che Juan glides, buoyant in the water as he steps, his inflated cock one water wing among dozens the children wear, an arrow pointing his pelvis out to sea. When he's deeper than his height, and has splashed off to the side, smacking the tanned tops of his feet like surfaced scuba fins to divert attention, Jeff discerns a signal and dives. He aims straight for the man's crotch, grabbing for the brilliant reef fish he admires. His head pointing toward the sandy bottom, Jeff locks his arms around Che Juan just below his genitals, feeling the flare of Che Juan's pelvic crests across his hairless torso. Once he is upside down on the man, and hoping their combined weight will not float in the salt water, Jeff bites the upper thighs, ending with gobbling everything he can.

Untrained at holding his breath, an ungainly amateur, Jeff finally goes topside to gulp air, having devoured Che Juan and wanked himself as long as he dares. Pleased at having gone unnoticed by the families, as much as the release of orgasm, he chops the heel of his hand at the jism slick engulfing their toned butts.

"Tourist fuck," Che Juan says within earshot of the nearest four-year-old, jeering Jeff's best effort. He dives, his great brown head gouging hunks out of the water as he moves. He swims smoothly, leaving Jeff among the children and occasional daddies, slipping away from shore.

~

THEY'RE IN CHE Juan's car's freezing air, driving to their first overnight. The sun stands straight overhead and the humidity outside the car is close to 90 percent. It's barely noon, but they've made a pattern, if two days can be, of late-morning sex.

By custom during the forty-eight hours, Jeff sits against the headboard where pillows should be on the single bed at his condo. Che Juan, taking up all the rest of the narrow space, lies facedown, obscuring his own erection. He eats Jeff's thin and twitching member as if it were a toothpick, without any particular vigor. He lies quietly, receptive to a sun lotion back rub Jeff performs standing beside the bed. Even when he rolls over, Jeff strokes under his cock, avoiding the purple rod. "Martini with two olives," Che Juan had said about his pouch the first time. The testicles feel athletic, tightly wound, with barely enough skin to conceal the machinery of cream delivery. As Che Juan nears orgasm, especially if Jeff rims his man-cunt between the beautiful butt globes, these ball jewels harden. They become polished stones, their hair is that dark and slick.

"Am not a tourist," Jeff says in the car.

"Oh yeah?" Che Juan sounds playful, the first of what Jeff hopes is delicious teasing. "Well, if you live here, on the *isla*, you'll know where we're going."

"No," Jeff says. "Never heard of it. That kind of hotel in Bayamon?" His job is transferring him back to Boston, deleting the condo the company rents for him. He's had more than corporate affairs on his mind on these stints, though if corporate comes from *corpus*, which means body . . . ?

Wondering why he's been so reckless, picking up men off their beach towels or café stools along the Condado strip, Jeff vows to quit several weeks before his flight home, then realizes it's too late for that resolution. His girlfriend will be seated, pastel cardigan draped over her booth-tanned arms, near his arrival gate in Logan Airport in exactly three days. He'll kiss her on a pearly cheek, wait for her to bring the car curbside, then ask her to drop him off downtown at the office. He'll ring the Massachusetts doctor to have a complete physical as soon as he's checked his messages, make sure he can't pass on any island souvenirs. Jeff will be completely candid when this doctor asks questions, updating Jeff's medical history in his bulging chart. H & P is this record, what doctors call the patient's medical history and physical exam. The doctor will record as well Jeff's heartfelt promise to modify his sexual misdeeds, his randy Puerto Rican romps. Jeff is happy he chose this urologist to absolve him.

As soon as Jeff has squeaked out the question about the hotel, Che Juan is turning in. Jeff can't see the road in front of the car, the motor straining to make the grade and deliver all the air-conditioning they require. He can see the roadside's thick brush hides the car from the main traffic.

They stop in front of what looks to be a self-storage unit. Jeff scans for the *oficina*, where they'll register, but Che Juan closes the gap between the driver-side window and the door marked number one. When the decorative grillwork opens outward, all Jeff sees is a fist holding a key. Che Juan's palm connects with the metal, the pale back of his hand making Jeff think the professional must be too sedentary for this precise relay. What he really wonders is how often Number 1, the guy inside the first cubicle, expects Che Juan. When the two men's fingertips linger for a moment, Jeff interprets that Che Juan hasn't been here for a while. He is mesmerized by the doctor's hands.

Jeff relishes the moment when Che Juan, having pulled the car totally inside a private garage with a seamed overhead door, turns off the ignition and hooks both their suit jackets from the back seat. He grins widely, though sideways, at Jeff for possibly the first time. He palms the key (as would a magician drawing circles) in the frosty air: now you see it, now you don't.

Jeff thinks of Che Juan's cock, how the doctor flaunts and is subtle at the same time. He'll make him talk nasty in Spanish, lose himself, pound between Jeff's creamy buns. Despite the fantasy, neither man has a second's sweat under his dress collar by the time they traverse the tiny attached garage, and step inside the room.

Jeff, reasonably certain they're here for acts they can't perform in public, has never seen a sex hotel. His first thought is how clinically the so-called furnishings gleam. There's the door, no windows, therefore no neon to flicker across a lover's sweaty chest to inspire, bore behind an insomniac's thin eyelids. Only an interior set of grillwork that Che Juan screeches closed marks the exit. Jeff winces, slightly claustrophobic, and thinks of himself as a child wanting the bedroom door left open by his parents to repel monsters. Or to light his escape from them.

A prominent sink hangs off the wall on one side, and Jeff thinks of a cell, no privacy for washing up. The bed blooms, a pedestal of sorts, tiled in ceramic from the floor up to the frame supporting the mattress. He's sure the thin coverlet is a waterproof sheet because his shaving case actually skids off the edge, a hockey puck on ice, when he tosses it on the bed. Che Juan flips down the jackets and walks directly into the bathroom, closing the door separating the sleeping from bathing areas. Jeff hears the feeble shower trickle instead of squirt and decides to strip.

"Come to bed," Jeff says coyly when Che Juan steps onto the bedroom's colorful tile. He's stupendous naked, a real block of a man, though Jeff thinks, because he wants to believe, that Che Juan takes all his exercise in a clinic. Jeff pats the sad coverlet lying in limp waves over his prone legs, sees a woman's long black hair on the pillow he's fluffed for Che Juan. From this point forward, every physical thrill derives from Che Juan's medical play.

The doctor, if he is one, digs his own shaving kit's leather tooled face from beneath their jackets he's dropped onto the single vinyl chair. On one twin bedside table flanking the headboard, he cracks open the case at its spine and lays it flat like a book. Nothing Jeff has read or imagined is so arousing as this moment with the doctor, watching him set up.

Che Juan's burly hands shuffle and deal tiny packets, rounded-tip applicators. Their labels are an assortment of hues and print nearly as vibrant as the busy pattern on the tiles. He actually aligns everything in rays out from the buttery case, then hops, a charming bear cub belly flopping upon Jeff's covered feet. If Jeff is ever convinced of Che Juan's lack of guile, it's when the doctor's pink soles flash the imprint of the jigsawed ceramic floor. Wanting a moment to be tender, Jeff reaches to trace the odd foot pictures but is interrupted when his cock tents the thin covers.

"*Listo?*" Che Juan says, Spanish for "ready." He licks his lips, nodding at the obvious erection, but Jeff swallows hard. He thinks of Che Juan tapping at exam room doors multiple times each day, surely excited by the surprise inside. But where is the emotion with him, the longing? The complacency is what gnaws Jeff since the beach. Nearly wild, he's so engorged between his legs he's unsure how to move, whether he should kneel.

Che Juan unkinks Jeff with a back rub, tickling one hand at all times across his fresh sunburn. He dips into his cache of lotions and creams on the table, then slips his strong hands to Jeff's thighs. Working upward, his fingertips glide, skate across hairy puddles he paints. Jeff has to turn on his side as his own cock molds a groove in his soft belly. He's so cold and slick and hot all at once he groans for Che Juan to be inside him. He's crazed, not having felt this before, demanding to be taught the pleasure.

Dedicated, infinitely patient, Che Juan takes forever, though his own cock prods like a third hand in the way. He punishes himself, roughly pawing his member until it subsides, becomes less insistent.

"It has to hurt," he says. Does he mean himself or Jeff?

Obsessed, he continues on virginal Jeff, who whines to be speared. When it finally happens, and Che Juan balances to invade, Jeff frosts his blond chest mat with his own come. He falls flat on the twisted sheets, leaving Che Juan to discharge between his thighs as if he were an underage girl. Sweat and semen weight the humid air, but it's essentially a dry hump. Che Juan bellows, not as gentle, and Jeff is afraid. He vows to beg more convincingly for the inevitable rough penetration second time around.

Che Juan, greased to his elbows and in a stripe down his sodden front, ducks away to the shower. Jeff punches the air conditioner with a pinky toe, wondering if Che Juan ever lingers. He fans all the bedclothes, though stain-resistant surfaces have channeled their fluids toward the lumpy bed's approximate center, a wet spot they must share. He takes his turn under the showerhead when Che Juan fiddles with his packets in order not to be in bed so obviously alone.

"Drink?" Che Juan says hospitably when Jeff is toweling off. The doctor, waving a furry hand toward the black rotary phone, lounges across vinyl that keeps gluing his smooth hips. He'll say something in Spanish, Jeff just knows, to Number 1, who'll laugh back about unpredictable initiations of *touristas*.

"You bet," Jeff gulps, willing to take his chances. It seems caring, even more gentle than before, when he'd been merely Che Juan's trollop, his lubricated slide to getting off. Jeff smarts, still the unreamed, hoping their rums don't arrive with cherries he can interpret as accusation for being, still, a back door virgin.

Before he hears a rustle, Che Juan is brandishing two drinks, meaning he had actually called while Jeff was in the shower. They clink glasses, order two more, and Jeff revels in being a date. Che Juan touches Jeff's arm, wrinkling his forehead in the direction of the pedestal bed, and Jeff calculates to take his time. The fresh drinks have appeared in a boxlike contraption on the wall that reminds Jeff of an indoor rabbit hutch. Panels on either side can open, though they are counterbalanced so that only one opens at a time. Privacy, Che Juan explains, nudity Number 1 can't see from his kitchen's bar on the other side. Jeff wants to cuddle, may try to doze, so he takes Che Juan's uncalloused hand and leads him to bed.

"Let's go," Che Juan says, and Jeff cheers the alcohol that will pace him this time. Jeff bats the covers, feeling fuzzy and cottoned, but Che Juan almost immediately stands beside the rutted mattress in dress slacks. Jeff stares stupidly, not liking the surprise.

"Out," Che Juan says. Jeff fears he's not using a Puerto Rican expression about their being a declared homosexual couple. "We have to leave."

"We're not staying the night?" Jeff says, risking a direct challenge to Che Juan's plan.

"It's not done," Che Juan says, an oddly formal etiquette lesson. Jeff coughs politely, though there's no reason, and drops a hand to the floor to feel for his underwear.

"What a dump!" Che Juan ridicules, only Jeff senses he's the target. "Do you know what some lovers," he snorts, "come here to do?" Jeff collates bodies in his mind, wondering what's left. He slaps at zipper and cuffs, unwilling to seduce his arms and legs back into the clothes he's so eagerly shucked off.

Most basically, Jeff the unwanted, the anonymous, condenses and mirrors another person's desire in order to fake self-esteem. He's like Puerto Rico's radio telescope in Arecibo, whose construction began in 1960: searching continuously for any signal, however faint.

"No, I don't know what couples do," Jeff says, actually wondering if he'll cry.

"Well, *Uno*, that guy," Che Juan says, pointing a finger at their door bolted on the inside, "he's had trouble. Men, though usually a man and a woman, overstay their two hours to fuck. They're always hiding, from wives or husbands. When their time ends, rather than go back to ordinary lives, they take an overdose or shoot themselves. *Locos* in love."

"Who could?" Jeff says later to Che Juan in the car. "Care enough to die with someone in that dirty hotel?" Che Juan dials up louder *salsa* on the radio.

⁓

ON THE FLIGHT home, though he's had two Ronrico rums—only tourists drink Bacardi—Jeff is especially sorry he missed having the goodbye he wanted from Che Juan. He's confident that imagining a physical coupling for great spans of time is more intense than the actual tumble, the risk of being caught not particularly additive to the thrill. There will be other trips, other partners, and he's in no rush. Besides, he doubts he would want the sex to continue, needing, as he does, a respite and some antibiotics.

However, in this cramped cabin he panics for tightness with

another person, to have him inside and around simultaneously, Jeff wrapped and pierced and strummed until he forgets to be selfish, relinquishing self to be with. It is the point of sex, after all, that small death from which one is resurrected, straining to flirt with suicide anew. If Jeff entices, he is also fundamentally solitary, and he begins to tremble. Powerful ghosts haunt sleazy sex hotels, those who cocoon two-by-two.

Waving away the flight attendant who winks toward more alcohol, although the stranger in the seat beside him pleats a ten-dollar bill, Jeff resolves to land at Logan Airport convincingly in love. So brazen as he's been alone, *uno*, his is an easy stretch to be half of an established couple. He will be attentive, sober, monogamous; the virtue ticker runs woozily inside his head.

Blankets are requested, paper pillows passed. His seatmate looks like another biotechie who has visited Eli Lilly, the pharmaceutical company near San Juan. The man must rarely wear vacation clothes, for he claws a sunburn ringing his pale blue collar. His eyelids are half-closed, bored, as if all the island has to offer can be found under fluorescent office lights. The woman in his life probably coordinates the abstract designs in his tie with a faint tick in the suit. Jeff feels very queer beside him, a debaucher in withdrawal.

Puerto Rico itself brought him out, for men's crotches carry the same heat, perfume, violence, and sugar of tropical nights. Latin *paquetes*, or sexual equipment, under linen or nylon, denim or tweed, are dense slabs in search of someone. How heavy a night can be, as well as the beauty of the Southern Cross stars in the sky, these thoughts flooded Jeff the first time his airline cabin opened to San Juan's midnight twinkling.

When Jeff tosses the blanket over both his and the man's laps, looking like a mistake, the stranger's leg rubs too hard to be an accident. Jeff, hurrying to open up as his cock stands, unzips to permit access within his dark blue trousers and blanket lint.

It's a race, like his island sex always is.

Swallowing men's organs fills him, sates him, though he has

always yearned to skewer himself with a new one. The balls, the puckered hole, are the only bits with which Jeff is generous, touching patiently until there is a sharp intake of breath, a moan, a *por favor*, please don't stop. Here in the plane, he allows himself to be owned, used, tossed out like last night's condom.

Because he is not the active one, and glowing in his novel spirit of fidelity, Jeff summons best wishes for Che Juan. He splays his legs as he pretends to sleep; the stranger's hand frees him. To keep himself soundless, Jeff seals his lips in one smashed kiss against the airlocked cloud-bright window and hopes Che Juan will see a doctor.

Viva Las Vegas

Catherine Lundoff

*I*T'S NOT EVERY night that you see Elvis, not even here in Vegas. But there he was, up on stage at the Starburst Lounge belting his heart out. For a few minutes, the King himself was here with us, hanging out in a gay bar that he wouldn't have been caught dead in when he was alive. I couldn't take my eyes off the singer: all slicked back DA, glittery jacket and long-nosed, darkly romantic face that was Elvis and Dean and every rebel America ever got wet or hard for.

Then he really let his hips go, giving them a twirl that said that this drag king watched the movies, too. I whooped and got a dirty look from a short woman in a sixties-style frock. "Ooh, you got competition, baby," Julio muttered over his beer.

I grinned back at him. "So what do you think?"

"Well she's not exactly my type, sugar. Nice action on them hips though. Maybe I'll reconsider. Heh. Just wanted to see the look. What the hell, sweetie, you're only in Vegas the first time once. Don't you wanna tell the folks back home that you did a dyke-Elvis at the Starburst Lounge?"

"Maybe, but a lady never kisses and tells. And I can always make it up whether anything happens or not." I decided to change topics. "How come you knew about this place?"

"My ex likes to hang out here. Says it's the essence of true camp." Julio gave me a savage grin in the bar's dim light.

I was momentarily sober and alert; nothing good ever happens with Julio's exes. Time to go. "Oh look, she's done. Well, I've had enough Elvis for one night. Let's go see if the pirate show has started up." I looked at him hopefully, hoping he wouldn't remember that I almost never had enough Elvis. But this was my post-breakup with Sue trip after all, and he'd talked me into it because he wanted to cheer me up. At least that's why I hoped we were here.

Julio tried melting me with the grin that drove us all wild back in college, even some of the girls who said that they'd never sleep with a guy. But I was pretty much immune. He reached across the table and grabbed my hand, making me jump. "Don't look now, but Elvis is heading this way and I don't think I'm the attraction." He patted my hand then sat back with a flip of the wrist that told the world he was my bestest boyfriend.

"You have got to stop playing me like this, bro. See, she's all over the Jackie Kennedy wannabe now. I'm just not a pillbox hat kind of gal. Now come on, I wanna see cannons and pirates and shit." I stood up and he joined me reluctantly, his eyes still fixed on every new guy who sauntered in.

"I can't see you in a pillbox either but I can't help but wonder what you'd look like in blue suede shoes." The speaker's soft drawl hit my ears and tickled them like Sue's tongue—oh never mind. Telling myself that my ex was history, I turned around to find Elvis herself standing behind me. Her eyes roamed over me like I was Ann Margaret. I squirmed at the unfamiliar attention and the wave of heat that came with it.

"Thought you already had a friend." I nodded at the woman giving me a bitter glance over one shoulder as she walked out.

"Looks like you have one, too," she nodded at Julio, who fluttered his eyelashes at her. "But so what? You visiting?"

I nodded, not having anything really clever to say.

"You know, you've got the Look, like a shadow of the King his-self. How about you try on one of my costumes and we hit the Strip together? I can show you the town and it'll be good for my show. I'm Chloe, by the way. Come on, whadda you say?"

Julio bent over giggling until I kicked his shin. "Ow! Oh come on, Pam. You gotta cut loose sometime, girl."

I didn't think I was that dull but seeing the way he was look-ing at me, I had to wonder. "I still wanna see the pirates." I said sulkily by way of agreement. It was the beer talking—I knew I should've skipped that last shot as well, but it was too late now.

"Done!" She had me dragged backstage before I could say any-thing else. Up close, I decided that I'd like to hear her croon some dippy love songs to me while we went waterskiing, just like in the movie. Except I was through with love. Fine, then, she could still sing them. Just as long as she didn't mean a word of it.

A few moments with Chloe and Priscilla herself would've given me a second look. It helped that I was about her size and I'd already had the mullet chopped off after Sue said she'd puke if she had to look at it one more day. What was left of my hair was slicked back and darkened with something out of a bottle. She touched up my brown lashes and worked her magic on my would-be smoldering gaze until the blue suede shoes looked just right. One blue glittery blazer and some tight black pants later and I was ready for anything. Just so long as no one wanted to hear me sing.

Julio smirked like an extra from the *Boys in the Band* when we came out to get him. The regulars all whooped and hollered until I took a bow and swiveled my hips a bit. Then they laughed. I laughed with them. Why not? We went out arm in arm, still giggling.

Once outside we hopped on the trolley bus and headed toward the distant lights and glowing fountains of the big places at the tourist end. I practiced my sneer until we climbed off the bus at Treasure Island to the great delight of the tourists. Chloe made me pose with her while a couple of obliging drag queens heading off to do their show at some other club shrieked. It was all good.

Mid-pout, I took a good look at Chloe. She gave me the full impact of the Look and blew me an air kiss. My stomach did a little flip just then so I didn't notice Julio taking off until it was too late. "I see something yummy, kids. I'll catch up with you later." He sashayed off with a focused look that reminded me of a cat stalking a bird. The sweet little college boy he was after wouldn't know what hit him. Oh well. Chloe dragged me across the street and onto the walkway in front of Treasure Island. I waved to a couple of people who yelled, "I see Elvis!" Probably thought there was a convention in town or something. The crowds were already getting thick when Chloe parked me in front of her by the rail. "I've seen it before. Watch your wallet. Things are gonna get kind of crazy."

The crowd filled in, packing the wooden sidewalk until I couldn't have gone anywhere if I'd wanted to. Chloe's lips were at my ear. "The Elvis look really suites you, Pam. You a fan of the King?" I nodded my head and tried not to shiver as she leaned a lot closer. Her thighs burned me through my jeans and she slipped an arm around me as if to hold onto the railing. The pirate show started up and as the ships maneuvered, her fingers found my nipple and pinched it hard. I bit my lip to keep from yelling and tried not to arch my back against her.

That was when I realized that she was packing. I could feel the solid flexible weight of the dildo pressed against my butt and got a lot wetter while I warmed up to the idea of sex with the King. Or as close as I wanted to get anyway. The crowd crushed us together until I thought I was going to melt all over her in a big molten pool. I could barely breath, especially when the cannons started firing and her hands got busy exploring. They roamed under my jacket and shirt, caressing my skin. Her breath was hot on my neck and I could see her lips curl in a sexy smile from the corner of my eye. I bit my own lips hard, smothering the moan that wanted to explode from them.

She maneuvered one denim-clad leg between my thighs and I spread them apart and tilted gingerly forward so I could grind myself against her. "Having fun?" Chloe murmured in my ear, her hand sliding down to the front of my jeans. I sent furtive, frantic glances to either side, watching the jubilant pirate-watching faces of happy tourists and wondered how long it would take them to notice two Elvises doing it in front of them.

I was worried for nothing. Between the difficulty in breathing and the noise of the battle, everyone's attention was pretty well occupied. Chloe's fingers found the front seam of my jeans and rubbed firmly. My clit sang its own version of any of the King's songs you'd care to name and my legs trembled with the effort of standing and grinding against her at the same time.

It felt liked I soaked my jeans all the way through but I still couldn't relax enough to come. I closed my eyes and gnawed on my lip, then forced my eyes open again so as not to look too obvious. That part was a mistake. Once I started looking around again, I got distracted. She could see it too and pulled back both her hand and her leg, settling instead for leaning against me in the crowd. I caught my breath and coughed in the clouds of smoke.

"I can think of a better place. It's nice and quiet and I won't have to compete with pirates. Whaddaya say?" The drawl purred in my ear until she had my full attention again, from my quickened breath to my wet jeans. I didn't trust myself to speak, just nodded my head and hoped that she meant her apartment or wherever Elvis wannabes go to rest their weary heads. Maybe that the place was called Graceland; after tonight, something told me I'd always think of it that way.

The show finally ground to a halt amid a final blaze of glory. I think the good guys won but by then I didn't care. The crowds broke up so slowly that I thought I'd be screaming or crying from frustration by the time we got out. Chloe just watched me, standing so close I could feel every breath, every movement. I was drunk on her, on the smoke filled air and knowing that I was about to do something with a stranger I'd never have done with Sue.

I turned my head and kissed her, my mouth fumbling against hers like it was the first time I'd ever kissed anyone. Her lips were warm and moist on mine and their touch sent a shock through me until I thought I'd fall over. "Oooh, baby," Chloe murmured. "Very nice." She caught my arm and started towing me upstream against the crowd's flow and some puzzled glances.

"Do 'Jailhouse Rock'!" One wit yelled and Chloe turned to grin at some two hundred pounds of hostile Midwestern beef. The kind who probably tortured school band members like me in high school. Some of his buddies took up the chant and soon we had a lot of not terribly friendly attention focused right on us. My skin crawled. Somehow, call me crazy, I'd never once dreamed of being gay bashed on the Strip while wearing Elvis drag.

"You know the Vegas anthem, right?"

"Ummm—sure," I volunteered, trying to sound like I had some idea of what she was talking about.

"Well, I've been saving this 'til later on tonight but since you boys are so enthusiastic, we'll just do it now." Chloe grinned at our audience while I tried not to pray out loud to anyone who would listen. "Just do what I do," she said and broke into "Viva Las Vegas" at the top of her lungs.

I picked up the tune at the first chorus and we sang our hearts out. I tried to remember how she moved her hips on stage and did my best imitation, always a few beats off. For a couple of glorious moments, we had a small crowd swaying along and even singing the chorus. Just a pair of dyke Elvises doing the King on the Strip in a city that never sleeps.

We got to the last verse and took our bows. A few people even tossed coins at us and the herd of bad news wandered off in search of other entertainment. Chloe grinned at me, "Sure you don't want to move here and do this every weekend?"

"Yep." I collapsed on the ropes and ran my shaking fingers through my slicked back hair. They were brown when I looked down at them. "Damn."

She laughed. "Come on, I told you we'd go somewhere better."

She dragged me to my feet and towed me along behind her. "You haven't really lived until you've done it on the monorail. And the roller coaster." Her grin was wicked in the bright lights.

"Why stop there? Why not the fountains at Bellagio?" I was trying my best to look like I did this all the time. Like she wasn't scaring the crap out of me.

"Spoken like the King hisself! Where have you been all my life?" She struck a pose for someone's video camera, then handed a business card to a passing group of women. One of them even batted her eyelashes while I tried not to roll my eyes.

"So what happened to going some place quieter?" Great, now I was whining at my Vegas fling. No wonder Sue dumped me.

"Oh we'll get there, hon. Don't you worry. I just like to make sure my friends are ready for a good time when we get there." She gave me the Look again, so much Elvis that the breath caught in my throat. The fountains were starting to look better by the second and that realization made me uncomfortable. Would I want Chloe as much if she weren't Elvis tonight? Then again, did it matter? It's not like we were getting married.

We kept walking, fighting our way through the crowds. She kept managing to bump into me, the touch of her body sending ripples through me until I hardly felt anything else. Except tired of being uptight, depressed Pam who just got dumped by her girlfriend. I was the King tonight, dammit, just like my clothes said I was. My doubts evaporated like the mist spray over the casino doors. I reached out to grab her arm and pulled her close. Then in a voice that was more Elvis than mine, I whispered "I'm ready now, friend," so close to her ear that my lips brushed her skin.

Chloe's eyelids dropped so that those big blue eyes looked half-asleep and I could see her lips part in what looked like a pant. My turn. I tugged her down a path and into some bushes in front of a casino I didn't recognize. A quick look around told me we were alone for the time being and probably out of sight. I fumbled with the zipper on her tight pants while I kissed her, my tongue sliding into her mouth like I did this all the time. The soft plastic of her dildo flopped into my hand and she gave a little moan.

That was all the invitation I needed. I dropped to my knees in the damp grass and closed my lips around the latex. I rocked my head back and forth for a moment, for all the world like it was a real dick and I could smell her, hot and moist with every motion I made. Her eyes were closed and she rolled her head back, loose and limp, but her fingers gripped my shoulders so tightly I knew she couldn't let go here anymore than I could in the crowd.

I wasn't so uptight after all and I grinned to myself as I pulled her hips forward and took the entire length of her dick into my mouth. Then I stuck my fingers inside her pants, hunting for a gap in the harness. I explored her wetness until she gave a choked moan that let me know that I was on the right track. Her fingers were in my hair, probably getting covered with brown dye. "Baby," she whispered between gasps, "let's go back to my place. C'mon, hon." She tried to pull back with the words and I grinned up at her.

"Your place? I thought we were going to do it in the fountains and the tram and everywhere else on the Strip. C'mon, Chloe, it's my first trip to Vegas. How can I leave before I've had Elvis all over this town?" I gave her my own version of the Look. It was good enough that she dragged me to my feet and kissed me hard.

"Hey, you two, break it up!" Casino security had finally showed up. Chloe had the dildo tucked in faster than I could have believed and was sprinting awkwardly away from the voice. I took off after her and we bolted down the path to throw ourselves into the river of Saturday night crowds. We got some very curious looks, especially since she was still trying to zip up and run at the same time. I started laughing and a few breaths later, she joined in. We fetched up on some benches outside one of the big places and howled until our ribs hurt.

It felt great. I hadn't laughed this hard since, well, I couldn't remember when. Julio was right. This trip was just what I needed. I wondered if he was having as much fun as I was, then decided that he could take care of himself. Chloe grabbed my hand. "Let's go check out that tram." Her eyes were glinting in the glow of the casinos and I was in love. Well, lust, anyway, at least for tonight. I wanted her so bad that everything below the waist was aching, wet and empty. To hell with the tram ride, I was making my move now.

I caught Chloe's arm to turn her around. Her makeup was smeared and her lips were full, pouting and begging to be kissed. Time to find out if tonight's electricity was more than good makeup. I gave her my sternest look and placed a hand on either side of her padded shoulders. "I've changed my mind about trams and fountains. I want you naked and I want you now." I managed not to let the grin inside make it to my lips. Sue always said I needed to be more assertive. If I couldn't do that as the King, it was never happening.

Chloe's kissable lips curved up in a sweet smile. "Oooh. We'll have to do something about that. Next block and we can catch the bus. Unless you want to volunteer your room. But I'm guessing that's being used." We shared amused smiles. After that, it was all a blur of stolen touches and kisses 'til we got to her apartment.

If her place was Graceland, I didn't ever want to see the real thing. Clothes all over the place, old pizza boxes and burned out light bulbs completed the décor. She locked the door behind us and pressed me up against the wall. This time, we kissed without fear of interruption, her tongue hot and burning in my mouth. My fingers found her nipple through her shirt under what felt like an Ace bandage. She moaned, momentarily drowning the sound of her neighbor's stereo through the paper-thin walls.

I tugged the glittery jacket off while she fumbled at my belt. I had her shirt unbuttoned by the time she had it all the way out of the loops and I was sucking on her tit through the elastic before she could get any further. By the time I found the end of the bandage and started working it free, she was gasping for air. Out of drag, she was lean and muscled like a greyhound. I wondered what she did besides impersonate the King but this wasn't the time to ask.

I yanked her pants down, almost taking the homemade harness with them. She scrambled to hang onto it like it was a security blanket or something. "I've got a better one inside." She jerked her head at what had to be the bedroom and grabbed my arm. I followed her, dropping the jacket and shirt over a chair as we went.

The bedroom looked better, like this was where she entertained. There was a life-size poster of Ann Margaret on one wall, Elvis on the other. No need to ask what she was putting in the CD player. The King's velvet voice filled the room and I got even wetter. Across the room, Chloe was lighting a candle and yanking a bundle of leather out of a drawer. I held out my hand. "I bet that's just my size." My voice didn't even quiver. She looked at me and I looked back, seeing the King in her eyes just like she could see him in mine.

"I bet it fits us both," she said at last, lips curling into a half-smile. She pulled out a dildo and some condoms and laid them all on the bed. I reached for her across the bed and pulled her down next to me. We kissed, tongues wrestling for control until I let her win. I had my hand on her zipper by then anyway and down her pants a minute later. She moaned into my mouth as I slid my fingers into her wet slit and shivered when I found her clit.

I pulled away from her mouth and pushed her down on the bed, running my tongue down between her breasts while I tugged off the harness she was still wearing. Her underpants went with it and I ran my tongue lightly over her bush, then down the damp skin of her thigh. She was gasping now, biting back little moans while I licked my way all up and down her legs, my tongue everywhere but where she wanted it most. I smiled as her hips bucked and wiggled to get closer to my mouth.

I yanked my jeans off and stuck my thigh between hers, thrusting against her. When I decided she'd had enough of that, I drove my fingers into her, feeling her body go rigid then shake with release. Feeling her fingers in my hair, her skin warm and sweaty against mine. I could almost come just from that. Almost. My free hand nudged the dildo and the harness and I gave a final thrust before I stood up to buckle myself in.

She watched me under half-closed lids, her eyes gleaming with anticipation. I rolled the condom on, trying to look like I did this every day then knelt between her legs. That was when she sat up. "That isn't where I want it, Mr. Presley." She twisted around until she was on her stomach and I was left looking at her ass, my heart racing. She pulled some lube and a glove from the drawer and put them on the bed next to me.

I noticed she wasn't meeting my eyes and wondered if she'd ever done this before either. Moment of truth time. I pulled a glove on with a snap that almost drowned out "Jailhouse Rock" and squeezed some lube onto my finger. What happened next was a blur of moans and missed openings, of fumbling and feeling our way until I was inside her, my hips rocking and rolling to the King's voice.

By then I wasn't just guessing. She was howling like a cat in heat and thrusting herself back against me until my thighs were sliding together in a mix of want and lube. I dug my fingers into her hips, wishing for a moment that the dildo was part of me, that I could feel her hot skin against mine. Her fingers reached for her clit and she wailed into the pillow as she rubbed herself off. I rode her faster, my thrusts rubbing me against the harness until I came with my silicone dick buried in Elvis's ass.

She came a moment later, shaking so hard I thought she'd pass out, especially since her face was buried in the pillow. I pulled out of her and tugged the condom off with as much style as I could manage. Elvis crooned his way to the end of the CD and she turned her head to watch me from the edge of one blue eye. "Viva Las Vegas," I offered as I lay down next to her and ran my fingertips up her back.

"I told you you'd be the spitting image of the King with a few pointers." She kissed me, her lips soft and lingering on mine.

"Can't sing worth a damn, though."

"Really? Maybe you just need incentive." Her fingers found the harness buckles and tugged them open. "I think I can help with that, too." I could see her grin in the flickering candlelight and the breath caught in my throat. What the hell, Julio would never believe I did any of this anyway. I could hear latex snap against silicone and skin and tried to stifle a moan. It sounded a lot like something about a hound dog.

Lips, Tits, Hips: A First Relationship

Solvej Schou

Lips:

A mixture of cigarette smoke and pomade, the smell of his hair both repelled and lured her in. She tried not to touch him at first, but the cab lurched forward, throwing her chest against his shoulder. Her hand landed on his arm and stayed there. For the rest of the ride she looked out the window and felt that particular prickly warmth through the sleeve of her sweater.

Houston, Bleecker, 10th Street, Broadway. Fresh piss, vomit, stale onion bagels, raw meat. Honking and catcalls, barking dogs, shrieking wheels. Wind banged against her window. And slowly, the sound of his breathing asserted itself over everything else. It beat against her neck, and imitated her own staccato breath.

When the cab jerked to a stop, he pulled away from her body, and stood outside the car door. The air seemed swollen and tight. His lips descended on her mouth, but missed. At the very last moment, she turned her head. The kiss landed, a wet surprise on her cheek, and she felt herself blush. Still, her smile met his stare, and he looked hopeful, yet confused. She mouthed the words, "I'll call you later," and the door closed.

As the cab pitched its way uptown, she tucked her tingling fingers between her legs, closed her eyes and thought about lips.

Tits:

Though she wasn't quite 19 years old, she had convinced herself that her breasts sagged like those of an old woman. The first time he touched them, reaching up underneath her thin T-shirt, she froze.

His back pressed against the mirror, while her hips pressed into his thighs. The small clip-on lamp on her desk cast a yellow stream of light on the glass. A blue shirt lay in the corner of the room, along with a gray wool cap, a belt, and a pair of shoes. His breath exhaled into her ear in a long and focused rhythm. Her toes scraped against the white linoleum of the floor.

When his fingers touched the sides of her chest, she imagined his hands retreating in horror. Instead, they squeezed her harder. Staring at the mirror, she tried not to remember the roundness of her stomach, or the pimples on the back of her neck, or the tiny black hairs on the tips of her breasts. In that moment, she knew she had a certain power.

The reflection of her face mirrored back eyes larger than she had ever seen them. And as her hands began to grip his waist, she closed her eyes. Feeling a close wetness curl around her nipple, she felt like a mother. A boy, a breast, a baby, a breast. Sliding her hands up to his head, she grabbed fistfuls of curly blonde hair. The wetness spread, and her body pressed against the dry warmth of his skin.

She smelled toothpaste, sweat, and tobacco. She wanted to sink into this, his chest, into the mirror, into this new taste, into herself.

Hips:

He had called it a "loft bed." It towered above the ground on rickety wooden supports in his apartment, a one-room sixth-floor walk-up overlooking a high school backyard in Chelsea. The ceiling, only two and a half feet above the mattress, and the floor was a dizzying distance below.

Earlier, he had warned her not to move too much. They would fall, he said. He had built it himself, and he was a little scared, but proud. She tried to remember this as the bed twitched back and forth, and a familiar sour stench and heat rose above their heads.

It was a muggy late summer day, and the air lay thick and damp between them. She hadn't seen him for a month and a half, and school was about to start in two days. Their clothes lay in a rumpled mess of baggy black pants, bra, underwear, and orange lace dress on the floor. The last red flicker of the sun shifted across the ceiling, and disappeared slowly.

She lay on top of him, looking down at his tightly screwed up face. The only sound in the room reminded her of a wet mop being slapped down on the floor over and over.

She wanted to break this silence between them, but he would tell her to be quiet. The neighbors would hear. The walls were thin. She wanted to move violently above him, to crush herself into his body, but he would warn her. The bed would come crashing down under both of them. So instead, she bit her lip.

With a deep sigh, he closed his eyes and shuddered abruptly. The rocking stopped. He lay still for a few seconds, then slid out from underneath her. Rolling the latex sack of fluid in a ball of tissue, he reached over her head and dropped it to the floor. Then he turned and faced the wall. She stared at his back before looking down.

The moonlight through the window made her hips appear paler than usual. Touching a moist spot between her legs, she felt coldness and warmth. She pressed down until the pain made her head throb. Her fingers stayed there the rest of the night.

Bitter Kiss

J. S. Jordan

*H*E LOVED JUST watching her move. The way she walked through her days with a deep core of joy that she seemed to express with every gesture, every gliding step. Sometimes he'd stand behind her and breathe deeply, taking her scent into every cell of his being. But he was denied the sense of her that he most wanted to fulfill.

He could never touch her. Every sense he had was saturated except that one. The one he longed for most.

To touch something, anything, was all he'd wanted since he came to be. To feel the supple velvet of a rose petal, the moist flesh of a peach. But to see everything his fingers caressed wither in his hands made a mockery of his desires. This existence brought a suffering to him worse than that of Sisyphus.

"A punishment worse than death," he said and smiled ironically to himself.

To touch what he wanted most would destroy it and instantly take it beyond his reach forever. It was a rather melodramatic predicament to be in as the result of straightforward need. He coped with it as best he could. Lately, by making due with stalking an inadvertent sensualist in the full flush of her youth. The gift of immortality seemed inane compared to walking in the sunshine with his hand entwined with hers.

Looking down at his hands, he could see that they looked like any other man's hands. His fingers long, the flesh pale, but warm. There had never been a speck of dirt under his nails or a tear in the skin. His physical existence remained whole and completely isolated.

Standing in the midst of the throng streaming around him, he had no need to move aside and no one ran into him as they went past. Their eyes saw him but their minds never registered the fact as their bodies avoided his in an unconscious act of preservation.

If they could discern him, they'd see a young man with dark, unruly hair and sharp cheekbones. His lips were full and curled in a subtle cupid's bow. As he walked, he moved with the careless grace of the unaffected.

He brought his eyes up to watch her move through the throng of people walking their dogs and dragging their children. She bent down to run her hands through the fur of a happy mutt and she beamed up at the man that kept the dog tethered. The man smiled shyly back at her as the mutt covered her face in kisses. As the sun glinted through her hair and kissed the skin on her face, Adriel's heart felt like it would burst and warmth flooded his body. His blood sang.

"Shit," he sighed and shook his head. "I didn't even know I had a heart until her."

She rose, laughed and said thank you as she turned back to her destination.

Trailing slowly behind her, Adriel smiled at the bounce in her step and the attention her lush curves were getting. And then the sun hid behind a cloud and he felt an intense cold envelope him. He stopped in his tracks and hung his head.

"Hey, Gabe."

"Adriel," the low baritone swallowed up every other sound around them. "You know we have a war going in the Middle East. Where the hell have you been?"

Of their own accord, Adriel's eyes followed the lithe form that kept moving farther away from him. Gabriel's eyes followed Adriel's and he shook his head.

"Man, what have I told you about that shit? Never get attached to them. You know better than that."

"Knowing and feeling are two different things."

"And doing your job and slacking off are, too." Gabriel put his hand on Adriel's shoulder and gave it a quick squeeze. "Come on, we've got souls to reap."

Adriel looked down the parkway at the girl who'd almost disappeared from view. Gabriel clucked his disapproval.

"Don't worry, Adi," Gabriel said and then sang out, "Her time is gonna co-ome." Then he threw his head back and laughed.

"Dammit, Gabe," Adriel shouted, "you know I despise gallows humor." Then he started to laugh, too. "And I could happily live without the constant Zeppelin references."

"They were a great band, man. I don't want to call anyone's number too soon, but I can't wait for those guys to get back together."

"Give me Coltrane any day, Gabe. Get him and Miles together and I'm in heaven," Adriel said and blew a mock horn.

"Hey! Don't even try to squeeze in on my horn action," Gabriel said. "You know I got a gig in New Orleans tonight, don't you? The Jazz Festival? Don't even tell me you forgot."

"I didn't forget," Adriel said and found himself pulled into conversation and away from the park. He knew he'd see Serena later. He'd watched her for so long her every routine had become his own. He'd watched when she'd moved through the ranks at the ad agency and as she'd moved in and out with two different boyfriends. He'd been racked with jealousy and hot desire at the same time. Watching her with them, he could see how her body reacted to a man's hands and lips—they couldn't touch and kiss enough of each other. Frantically they'd roamed each other's bodies. He'd watched as one had lowered her to the floor and attacked her clothes. Noticing the disparity, she'd told him it was hardly fair. The man tore his shirt off, stood and pulled his jeans off as if they'd offended him and threw both across the room. She'd laughed then pulled him down. His tongue was magical, she'd told him. Like the injured hummingbird she'd held to early spring hyacinth, he answered her by darting his tongue, fast and true, for her nectar. And as a flower at full bloom, she opened and her body wept with need for him. But this was not a poetic encounter and they were hardly making love. This was the purest fuck Adriel had ever witnessed, with no pretense of soft emotions. They would fuck in every corner and on every surface. She'd try to take control, to ride him as he rode her, but he would have none of it. He suckled her breast, then gently bit, playing with the nipple. Climbing down her abdomen, his hands would labor after his mouth, rubbing, stroking, and kneading any flesh that his mouth had overlooked. She'd reach up and grab the headboard, scraping along its expanse trying to gain purchase. His mouth would find her clitoris and, groaning, she'd grab for him instead. His tongue, moving fast and furious, explored and claimed her.

Too much. It was too much. Adriel would look away. His own pleasure and pain was so immense, he could barely stand it. Behind him, he would hear them moving off the bed. As she scooted across the carpet, her boyfriend would crawl every inch for her inch, until he was on top of her again. When he lowered himself this time, he would be gentle. He moved slowly with the surge held at bay. Kissing her lips sweetly, she would run her hands over his arms and back. She'd feel the tension in his muscles, the restraint of his passion.

He put his cheek to her cheek and sighed deeply, then inhaled. His lashes would sweep across her cheek like a wing in flight. Leaning back, he'd look in her eyes. Helpless. He looked helpless.

She always took pity on him.

Wrapping her legs around his waist, she'd pull him into her. Her body welcomed him and would close around his cock in an embrace. As her vagina tightened its hold he would groan and bury himself in her. She met him thrust for thrust with her hips, her lips feeling the pulse in his neck. It was a fast and furious fuck that left all three of them breathless. God, it was too much.

As Adriel knelt beside them, laughing and sweating in the aftermath, he would barely keep his hands from reaching to her, to bring death to her—to bring pleasure.

Coming out his of reverie, Adriel saw Gabe shaking his head in disgust.

"Like you've never loved one of them before," Adriel muttered, disgusted with himself.

"That's not love, Adi," Gabe chuckled, "that's pure lust."

"Fuck you."

"I wish you could, man," Gabe laughed. "That would save us both a lot of trouble."

Adriel smiled and blew a breath out to release all he'd held pent up inside at the memories.

"Why isn't there angel porn? I could just grab a magazine and head for the dark side of the moon for a while."

With a snort, Gabe clapped him on the back and they headed east.

Adriel knew it would be good not to feel so much for a while.

By midnight he stood beside her as she slept. Moonlight streamed through the window and painted her face with shades of blue. Adriel, hands inches from her, traced her body with his fingertips and leaned over to smell her hair. The sweet and clean smell of apples filled his nostrils. He sighed. Seven hours until she awoke. He would be waiting.

The alarm rang and Serena stretched her arms as her nose crinkled in displeasure. With a disgusted grunt, she heaved a pillow at the offending clock. It became readily apparent that that wouldn't work. She heaved herself out of bed and crossed the room to turn it off. Grabbing her robe, she headed for the shower.

The hot water relaxed her sore muscles. She could stay in the shower for hours. Slipping her hand between her legs, she circled her clitoris with languorous strokes. Her toes curled as a moan escaped her lips. She stroked harder then slipped a finger inside.

Sticky come coated her fingers as she gently explored herself. She groaned and felt her legs buckle.

Standing behind her, his clothes dry despite the water sluicing over them, Adriel moaned as his hands clenched and unclenched at the open air surrounding her. When she stepped out of the shower and wrapped a towel around herself, Adriel slid to the bottom of the tub and held his head in his hands. He wondered if angels could go crazy.

Leitmotifs

Debra Hyde

I KNOW WHEN she wants me. Sometimes, it's the gleam in her eyes and the sly turn of her smile that tell me. Sometimes, it's the firmness of her touch. Or that certain sigh that lingers on her lips. I like it best, though, when I hear it from afar, from across the stage. When Meg forms that tight, controlling embouchure, when she blows and beckons me, I go weak in the knees. The sound of her horn takes my breath away.

How Meg calls me is haunting. It's a motif from *Petrushka* that I hear, the one which symbolizes Petrushka's ghost, the spirit of a scorned, betrayed, and murdered clown made famous in ballet. Slow and piercing, it is the wail of the dead. But it brings me to life. As I work the contortion that is my instrument, it rises above the din of the orchestra like the ghost of Petrushka when it rose above the circus that had been its corporeal home. The specter motif seizes me and thrills me because I know she'll have me.

This time, the motif reaches me just as the concert master taps us into silence and signals the oboist to baseline us with an A. Only a few notes reach me before the silence descends but they're enough to follow me all through rehearsal. They become a pang in my awareness, a haunting distraction that I can ill afford. The tension between knowing and waiting tears at me, and throughout the

Brahms, the Ravel, and the Shostakovich, I cannot resist the knowledge that Meg wants me. I cannot help but obsess over how she'll deign to do me.

Now it's one thing to think of Meg at bedtime when I'm alone, when I can ease my urgency with a hurried finger between the sheets, but it's something else entirely when it disrupts my focus during rehearsal. I blow a passage and drop enough notes that the principal chair insists we review it afterward. It takes just under ten minutes of my time, but it's a ten minute scrutiny so judgmental that it would make a strict mother look gentle and kind. Motivated, I demonstrate my proficiency.

"Why didn't you do that earlier?" the first chair asks me.

"Brain fart," I answer.

"Eat Beano," he replies, dead serious and poker-faced. I get off easy; he doesn't read me the riot act. But I know not to take it for granted. Ruin enough passages and I'll be out on my ass before I can say "every good boy deserves fudge." Professional orchestra seats don't grow on trees and plenty of perfectly capable musicians go begging for jobs like mine.

Humbled, I scramble to make my escape and as I leave the concert hall, there's Meg, leaning against my car. The cool evening breeze lifts her hair and a long strand whips across her face. Indelicately, she pulls it aside and tucks it behind her ear. Her hair amazes me. Long, straight, and on the brown side of red, it's rich and womanly and a defiant contrast to the stocky dimensions of her body. Butch? Femme? It doesn't matter a whit to her and when our bodies locked together that first, frenzied time weeks ago, I discovered that it didn't matter to me either.

When she sees me, she straightens. "Toss me your keys," she says, cupping her hands to catch them. "I'll drive."

But first, she kisses me, long and deep. She probes, seeking my tongue, eager for my response. Hers is electric as it flits around in my mouth and I moan at what it promises. I almost melt when her hand goes to my breast. She squeezes it, kneads it, then tugs at my nipple.

She pulls away from our kiss and murmurs into my ear, "No bra. Good choice."

In my car, she turns the key, the engine ignites. She looks me in the eye and says, "Unbutton your blouse and open it up. Let me see those tits, girl."

When Meg talks like a trucker, it's thrilling. Embarrassing, but thrilling. So is exposing myself like this, in my car, in public, and no matter how deserted the parking lot might be or how dark it might be outside, I always feel one step away from discovery. It's risky and transgressive, and Meg likes it. And I comply because I ache to please Meg.

On the way to my condo, Meg drives so haphazardly that she hits every pothole along the way, making my breasts heave. It feels wanton and my nipples harden so much that arousal pulses through me, twisting me in delicious agony. It's more than I can stand and by the time we're on my couch, I'm wet and impatient.

⁓

I HAVE LONG loved Stravinsky's music, first when I learned that a bassoon solo opened his riotous ballet of fertility rites, *Le Sacre du Printemps*, later when I grew to understand and appreciate its modern complexities. As a music-geek teenager, I worshiped Stravinsky's genius and promoted the notion that he was to modern music what Picasso was to modern art. All of which became the first thing Meg learned about me.

By contrast, the first thing I learned about Meg was that she had it bad for me and she'd use anything to get to me. Even Stravinsky. She wooed me with his music and, like a virgin acolyte standing amid the pagan frenzy of the fertility dance, I followed her blindly into bed. Now, weeks later, it's my blind lust and my greed that have created our problem. Correction: *my* problem.

But I'm not thinking about that when I'm on the couch, secure in Meg's arms. I'm not thinking about that when I'm lost in her fierce kisses and crushing caresses. She's a sure lover, confident in her lust. I can't help but yield to her.

It doesn't take much tongue to make me imagine myself naked and getting fucked silly. But I'm not. I'm dressed, immersed in heated petting and seeping with readiness. I pull away from Meg's mouth, from her hands. "I can't stand this anymore," I tell her as I tear off my blouse, shimmy from my shorts and kick my sandals under the coffee table.

Naked, I lean back against the arm of the couch. My breasts spread in repose as I splay my legs, lay my head back, and close my eyes. As I run my hands from my thighs to my breasts, I can feel my labia separate and part. I hear them smack apart with a wet pucker and I pray Meg hears it, too.

"Please?" I coo.

I hope Meg can smell what she sees, that the wet rim of my cunt is all the enticement she needs to go down on me. I toy with my nipples, hoping to draw her nearer.

"That's not what I want," I hear her say.

Surprised, I raise up and open my eyes. Meg's smile is lurid and suggestive, and I know by the gleam in her eyes that she's about to reveal to me exactly what she does want.

She motions to me. "Come here, baby. I got something to show you."

Too perplexed by her mystery to realize that I've failed to seduce her, I sit up and slide across the couch to her side.

"It's not me going down on you that I want."

She points to her crotch. OK, I think as I fuss over her belt and zipper, she wants tongue. But she's got me by the nipple, pinching and pulling, and I'm thoroughly distracted as I fumble at her zipper. I struggle to spread wide her fly and when I succeed, I discover her secret. Stunned, I can only stare at it.

"Take it in your mouth," she insists. "Suck it the way you suck Ben."

Ben. The sound of his name makes my blind lust melt away. Ben, with whom I share my bed through the wee hours of the night and my life in the light of day. Who knows what I long for, Ben, who doesn't yet know I've compromised our bed and realized my desires with Meg. And who would understand and accept—if only he knew.

Meg's hand goes to the back of my head and pushes me insistently toward her counterfeit creation. Its manufactured smell assaults me as I near it. Instinctively, I want to reject it. I want to spit it out, refuse it and turn away in protest. But I can't. No matter how much I want Meg's smell, Meg's wetness, Meg's realness, I can't reject this fraud. Rejecting it means denying Meg and I'm too weak, too taken with her to ever do that.

I lick it once, twice, and take it in my mouth. Thick, it stretches my mouth and jaw, but its length isn't too much for me. It fits compactly into my mouth. I put lips and tongue and throat to work. I put a hand to it as well, stroking. I work Meg like she's a man, like she has the weaknesses of a man—the same tender spots to lick, the same tough, hard length to jerk off, the same desire to see a head bobbing up and down in her lap with only cock on its mind.

Except I cheat, just a little. With my spare hand, I snake a couple of fingers under the leather shield of her strap-on. I make a play for her clit, barely reaching the folds of her labia before she catches me.

"Oh no you don't!" She grabs my wrist and pulls my hand away, drawing it behind my back. She grabs my stroking hand and brings it behind my back as well, putting me at an angle that makes cocksucking instantly impossible. Without my arms to prop me up, I can only loll to one side, helpless, my head on Meg's belly, my mouth reduced to being a receptacle.

And Meg knows it, too.

"What? Can't suck me this way? You only good for a face fuck?"

Meg bucks her hips and pummels my face—and with a few curt words, she pummels my soul as well.

"Is this how Ben does it?"

The words sting me. They strike me dumb. Immobile, too stunned to answer, the receptacle that I've become cannot speak.

She pulls me off of her, pushes me off the couch and onto the floor. It seems all so swift and rough and before I can take it all in, she plows into me from behind. Meg's silicone simulacrum makes it all feel oh-so real, and as her punishing rhythm overwhelms me, Meg demands the answer to her question.

"Is this how Ben does it?" She slams me ferociously.

"Is it?" She pinches my nipple; pain ripples through my breast.

"Is it?" She lets go of my tit, grabs my hair and pulls my head back. The burning in my scalp, the crick in my neck, the thing in my cunt, they all make me want to scream.

But instead, I confess. "Yes!" I admit, "Yes!"

I cave to that which Meg has shoved into me and realize that the real insult isn't that it's phallic and fake. It lies in the fact that Meg used it to make me face a fact I'd rather ignore—and she's succeeded. I can no longer deny the duplicity of my two worlds, those of Meg, of Ben. Meg has fucked the denial and procrastination right out of me.

My admission given over, my surrender had, Meg pulls out and abandons me. I cry out as I'm voided but enticed when she drops her pants to her ankles and throws her equipment aside.

"You have to tell him," she tells me in no uncertain terms. "You promised me you would when we met."

She's right, of course, and no matter how much I want to pretend otherwise, I can't deny it. She's right; she's waited long enough for me to square things with Ben and she's not going to wait around much longer. My greed for her can no longer go unchallenged.

She sits and draws me into her lap, face first. "If he's half the polyamorist you say he is, he's not going to have a problem with this." She's right; he won't. I've always known this.

I scold myself as I put my tongue to her sweet, bold clit, silently acknowledging how long I've put off the truth. I feel Meg shudder at my touch on this, her all-too-willing spot and, as I lap at her, I think of him, of Ben. Meg's right—Ben won't have a problem with this. He'd welcome her, even if she's too dyke to so much as let him watch.

But the problem is, I want Meg all for myself. I covet our clandestine couplings; I'm greedy for them. I don't want the rest of the world to know about this, my sweet secret, even if the rest of the world is really just Ben.

I slip a finger into Meg's cunt and find an oasis there. I breathe deeply, drawing her sweet scent into me, wanting it all, now and forever. But Meg is right. It's time I relinquished this magic, this secret that, until now, has been mine alone.

It doesn't take long for Meg's breath to quicken, for her body to clench. As she comes, I watch her. I watch her body stiffen, her eyes squeeze tight, her lips part. I watch her shudder. I watch every inch of her slowly go slack. Entranced and fascinated, I worship her rapture and as her mewling and her throbbing slowly subside, I fear that giving up my secret will change all this, that I'll lose this sweet assignation of mine, that it'll never be the same once I voice its existence.

But Meg's ethics can't be a fuck buddy to my greed. Either I lose my cherished secret or I lose Meg. And so, as she quiets, as we grow soft in our satisfaction, I voice my promise.

"I'll tell him."

Yes, I'll tell him. Later, after I practice that Ravel passage I blew in rehearsal. Later, after he's home from his shift. Later, after sex, when we're sated, when he's limp and spent. I'll take his cock into my mouth and let him enjoy the luxury of my wet tenderness around his soft shaft. That's when I'll tell him.

Then, when next I'm near Meg, I'll assure her that I did the deed. My own motif of music will rise above the din and sing out its message to her. She'll recognize it. It's the one that's ripe with desire, the one that made me love Stravinsky in the first place. Yes, I'll beckon to Meg with an ode to fertility and sex and erotic mystery and when I ply those notes, Meg will cease to be my secret. The world will know. But she will always remain a wonder to me, and I will always long for her and lust after her. I will remain impatiently and urgently hers. Perhaps that can remain a secret, mine and mine alone. And that, I won't share with anyone.

Aural Sex

Alison Tyler

"*I* MIGHT JUST have to let you seduce me."

These were the strangest words a man ever said to me, and the last words I expected to hear from Nick.

"I might just have to let you slide over closer to me and press those pretty lips to my ear and whisper the naughtiest things you can think of."

Me. He was suggesting this concept to me. And he wasn't being coy, or sly, or even particularly quiet. In fact, the rock 'n' roll duo at the next booth had obviously heard every word Nick had said, because the long-haired blond man turned his head slowly to glance over his shoulder at me. When he saw my shocked expression, he grinned and nudged his dark-haired buddy who turned to look at me, as well.

"What do you mean?" I whispered to Nick, my cheeks scarlet.

"You heard me," he said.

"And so did those rockers." I knew the boys were musicians because they had the prerequisite black T-shirts and colorful tattoos, and because just about everyone at the Rainbow is a musician. The outfits and the fact that two guitars rested in the spots where their dates should have been clued me in. Since sleek-looking, dark featured Nick was a musician, too, he fit perfectly into the atmosphere. I was the odd-girl out, a writer instead of a player. So why was I struggling so hard for words? Easy enough to answer that one:

Nick left me speechless.

My crush didn't seem to care that the headbangers had heard him. He put one strong arm around my shoulder and pulled me even closer to his side. I could feel our hips press together, our legs align themselves with each other, and I basked in his heat and his closeness. Even though this was our first date, I felt comfortable in his presence, but that didn't make his request any easier. Not for a shy girl like me.

The truth is that I've always had a thing for listening. If a boyfriend says that he wants to kiss my neck, or strip me naked, or use a blindfold to cover my dark green eyes, I'm halfway to the finish before we even start. I love to hear dirty words whispered in a husky voice, but mostly, I like to star in X-rated make-believe worlds, described to me in delicious detail by a bawdy bedtime partner.

This is why I was sure Nick was my perfect man. He always had something to say. He was a singer and a deejay and I'd seen him work a crowd before a concert and give witty off-the-cuff interviews. There was no way he wouldn't be able to satisfy my desires. In fact, I had it all worked out in my head. During dinner, he'd lean in to tell me each and every action he planned on doing to me later in the evening. My panties would be sopping before we finished our meal.

Apparently, he had his own plans for the evening.

"You want to, Samantha," he said, "isn't that right? You want to tell me all the secret fantasies that fill your thoughts at night. The sexy things you think about when you touch yourself in bed."

Finally, I found my voice. "Yes."

The blond rocker looked over his shoulder at me again and said, "You're going to have to talk a bit louder than that for us to hear you, sweetheart. They've got the music cranked up too fucking loud tonight."

But that bit was just in my head. The tattooed musician did look my way, and this time he gave me an encouraging wink before nudging his friend again. Customers are like that at the Rainbow. Everyone wants to know everyone else's business, and the dark cherry-red leather booths are situated close enough for people to easily eavesdrop. I've been at the joint late enough when strangers actually share pizzas, passing slices over the booths and taking bites off other people's forks. "Trade you a slice of Hawaiian for a slice of pepperoni." Crazy. But that's L.A. for you. We may curse at each other when we're on the freeway, but we're all part of one big fucked-up family.

This scenario tonight was classic Hollywood, with Nick's roaming fingers running up and down my arm, and his hot breath against my neck as he continued to tell me how I was the one who was going to seduce him. His hand slid over my breasts and he squeezed each one gently, instantly making my nipples hard through the filmy material of my halter. This evening, I wore a skimpy petal pink top with my faded 501s, and I'd dusted blush between my breasts to deepen the valley and draw Nick's attention there. My trick had worked. Nick palmed both of my breasts, and I moaned out loud, loving how firmly he touched me. The sound surprised me, and I sat up straight, but I knew that nobody was concerned about the fact that we were canoodling in the booth. Waitresses have seen worse at the Rainbow.

Much, much worse.

I must say here that this scenario wasn't my style at all. Yes, I may have an extremely dirty mind. In fact, I might have already fucked Nick twelve thousand times before, all in my head, with my legs spread, fingers, dildo, or shower massager playing over my clit. But I hadn't told him that, and I didn't think I could. He had other ideas on the subject entirely. He seemed to believe that I was some sort of she-cat, able to stalk her prey . . . with words if not actions.

"You tell me," he said.

"Tell you what?"

The rocker leaned over the booth and said, "Tell him how you want to fuck him, doll baby. Tell him that you think about his steel-like cock parting your nether lips and sliding inside where you are all warm, and wet, and ready. Tell him that late at night, you envision him slipping a black velvet blindfold over your gorgeous green eyes and taking you from behind, doggy-style, so he can get in deep. That's how I'd fuck you, if you want to know the truth. That's how every man in this joint would fuck you. Because you like it doggy-style, don't you, kiddo? So a man can pull your hair and take charge of you. Yeah, I can tell. You have that look." But again, that part of the conversation occurred only in my imagination.

"Tell me everything," Nick suggested.

"Oh," I said. "Everything. That's easy enough. Just, you know, everything."

"You asked me here, Sam," Nick reminded me. "Right?"

That part was true. After months of crushing on this guy, I'd finally gotten up the nerve to ask him out for pizza. I'd thought that if he saw my interest in him, he'd do the rest. Apparently, my life wasn't going to work out like a B-movie plot on Lifetime Television for Women. I was going to have to do more than simply set the script in motion.

"All right," I said, feeling his warm fingers find the button fly of my jeans and slide in between the row of shiny gold buttons. He started to stroke me gently, as if I were his instrument, and I felt my body automatically respond. My thong was drenched in seconds, and if Nick's probing fingers fully split the fly of my jeans and probed southward, he'd have found that out for himself. "Sure, I'll seduce you," I said, using the most confident tone I could manage.

Immediately, I heard the rockers snicker, this noise not in my head at all. Maybe my statement was a little too matter-of-fact to be sexy. Maybe she-cats aren't supposed to announce their intentions to their prey in the style of a waitress stating, "I'm Brittney and I'll be your server tonight." But suddenly, there in the dimly lit Rainbow, surrounded by pictures of my musical idols, I found my sex appeal.

The way to seduce this man, I decided, was to come clean. To tell him everything I wanted, and to let him listen. I was going to give him a first-class aural experience—him and the rock 'n' rollers who had pressed themselves as close to our booth as they possibly could. They'd completely stopped their own conversation, not even pretending anymore that they weren't listening to us.

Nervously, I pushed my long dark hair away from my face and leaned in even tighter against Nick. My skin was sun-kissed from a day out at Malibu, and I could feel the heat still beating on my bare shoulders and at the hollow of my neck. "Here's the thing," I whispered. "I've been dreaming about you since I first saw you." No, that was all wrong. "I mean," I continued, "I've been dreaming about fucking you."

That won me a deep intake of breath from Mr. Blond Rocker, whose attitude let me know that he didn't think I had it in me to say a four-letter word. I looked too sweet, I supposed. Too nice and young and naive. But even sweet girls like to fuck every once in a while, or twice in a while. And this sweet girl in particular was very ready to fuck the man at her side, regardless of whether the musicians were listening in or not. This particular sweet girl was already desperately wet, shifting on the leather seat to gain a deeper connection to her date's fingertips. Nick let his finger graze over my panty-clad clit, and I almost cried out at the instant wave of pleasure that flared through me.

"Since that first time?" Nick prompted.

"Yeah," I nodded weakly. I thought of the offices at the alternative entertainment newspaper where I work, the courtyard below that houses a music agency. And I thought of catching a glimpse of Nick wandering into the agent's office, seeing his fine figure in the dark jeans and black T-shirt. Knowing, somehow, that it was his custom Harley parked out there on Westwood Boulevard. I'd grown accustomed to his visits, and I'd made myself known to him, as well.

We have upstairs and downstairs offices, and I began to run errands between the

two whenever I heard his bike pull up. I saw him watch me, and I watched him back, and then finally, I asked him to the Rainbow.

"Because," I told him now, "I want you to bend me over and fuck me."

"Here?" he seemed to find the idea charming.

"Here," I repeated, and the dark-haired rocker grinned at me and would not look away. If I was going to get fucked on this table, then he was going to have a front-row seat. He'd call out encouraging comments. Or maybe he'd get involved, his fingers reaching out to sweep my hair out of my eyes, or pinch my nipples or lean in to graze my ass. He might bite my bottom lip hard, or he might throw money on the table, as if we were putting on a show for his pleasure.

"On this table?"

"Yeah," I said, firmly. "On this table."

Nick chuckled, and I'm sure he saw the vision in his mind. I wanted him to. I wanted him to see me, stripped down and bent over, while he plunged into me from behind.

"Look, I know it won't happen at the Rainbow," I said softly. "But that's what I fantasize about."

"So tell me."

"So I am," I laughed, suddenly feeling more confident in the way his fingers continued their tantalizing caresses over my thighs and then back to my button-fly, teasing me once again by sliding in between the row of buttons to touch my naked skin.

"When I saw you that first day, I imagined you walking up the stairs, entering the office and stripping me naked. I saw it in my head, saw you putting me up in that picture window, fucking me from behind so that everyone could see. My hands flat on the pane of glass. My ass pressed against you. I imagined all the people on their commute along Westwood Boulevard getting the show of their lives. Watching the two of us fuck."

"That's what I thought, too," he admitted. "When I saw you, I thought, *just do her here. Mount her here. Now.*"

"And the next time," I told him, "when I saw you park your bike, I had a different X-rated vision entirely."

He nodded before I could say it. "You, bent over the seat. I'd pull your jeans down your thighs, and you wouldn't have any panties on underneath. I'd touch you to see if you were wet and my fingers would come away sopping."

Somehow, I realized we were now playing each other—both equal partners. Our

audience was clearly spellbound, not moving now in case they broke the enchantment. They were visibly having the best time listening, and I realized with a shock that I was having the best time performing for an audience of three.

"I'd never been on a Harley," I told him, "but I thought of you taking me up to Griffith Park and then fucking me over your bike."

"You like to say the word 'fuck.'"

"I like the action even more than the word."

"I thought writers were more inclined to use a variety of terms. You keep repeating that same one over and over."

"Because that's what I want," I told him. "I know all the euphemisms, but I don't want you to 'make love' to me. And I don't want you to 'do' me. Or 'take' me. Or 'ravish' me." I drew a deep breath before saying this last part slowly and emphatically: "I just want you to fuck me."

Confession time was over.

Nick pulled me to him and kissed me, his strong chest pressed against mine, hands sliding up and down my arms. "Yeah," he said softly as we parted. "Yeah, Sammy. That's what I'd like to do, too." I felt tremors run through me at his kiss, and I forgot to keep myself in check. I moaned louder as he moved his lips down in a line along my throat to the dip of my cleavage, and then I slid my own hand under the table to feel Nick's cock through his jeans.

He was hard. As hard as I'd hoped he'd be. Harder, even. I thought of his bike out back behind the Roxy, the club right next door where we were supposed to go after dinner. And I realized we weren't going to make the show, but that we might make a show of our own.

⌒

THE MUSICIANS STOOD up then and threw money down on their Formica table for the beautiful blonde waitress who has been a fixture at the Rainbow for at least twenty years.

"She did good, Nicky," the blond one said as he walked by the table. "She seduced you all right."

"And us, too," the dark-haired one added.

"What do you mean?" I stammered, startled by their boldness.

"Don't be embarrassed, sweetheart," the blonde told me with a wink, and then he put enough money on our table to cover our meal as well.

I stared after the rockers as they left the restaurant, and then turned to look at Nick, confused for a moment before I got it. They were his friends. Made perfect sense, didn't it? We were here, at the rock 'n' roll hangout in Hollywood, where everyone knows everybody else. These musicians would be going to the show next door to see their buddies play. The Rainbow is the natural stop for anyone who's in the mood for a bite before heading out to the strip.

"You knew they were listening, and you let me talk like that."

"You knew they were listening, too." He was right. I did. "And it turned you on, didn't it? All that dirty talking in front of a willing audience."

I nodded.

"But we don't need any audience anymore, do we?"

"No, Nick."

"And we don't need to play make-believe in this booth anymore either."

I shook my head as he took my hand and led me out to the parking lot, whispering to me as we walked. "But I don't want you to stop talking, baby," he said. "I want you to keep whispering those pretty little secrets to me—which is exactly what you've wanted to do all this time, isn't it?"

I'd been found out, a secret desire uncovered, which was far sexier than my original plan for the date of having Nick be the one to seduce me. As sexy as Nick driving up to the hills in Hollywood and spreading his battered leather jacket out on the ground and fucking me—not taking me, not doing me, not making love to me, just fucking me.

I felt the firm ground beneath me, felt the bed of grass under my ass and Nick's hard body on mine. I closed my eyes and thought of all the visions I'd had of him, the months spent fantasizing, and now here we were. Fucking for real. Nick brought his lips to my ear as he worked me. He took over, doing what I'd thought he would the whole time, telling me everything.

"You're so nice and tight," he crooned to me. "Squeeze me like that, baby." I did as he said, and he continued, "Oh, god, just like that."

I contracted on him, helplessly, as he lifted me up, changing positions so that he was on his back and I was astride him, my halter the only item of clothing left on my body, my nipples like pebbles beneath the filmy material. A cool night breeze stirred the leaves in the trees around us, but our bodies stayed warm from the heat of one another. As I moved myself on Nick's cock, I found that I couldn't stop talking, either.

"You knew they were there," I said, smiling. "You liked them hearing."

"I wanted to see how far you'd go."

"How far?"

"Just far enough," he said, and he slid a hand between us as I pumped my thighs, and his thumb found my clit and stroked it up and down, then in a circle, then just pressed hard, giving me exactly the contact I needed.

I could feel the silent shudders work through my body. Looking down at Nick, I felt my hips work faster, felt the passion take over, so that I wasn't thinking anymore, I was letting the sensations happen to me. We had that unbelievable connection, where everything clicks. How wet I was, how hard he was, how he knew to draw me down against him, so that my breasts were pressed against his chest, so that he could grip into me, bite into me with his teeth on my shoulder.

I cried out, so hungry, so happy, as I began coming on him. The world felt still around us. The stars were obscured by the lights of L.A. I heard the melody of traffic down below, the endless hustle that is never entirely stilled in Hollywood. But there was silence close around us, and noise further off, and then the almost indecipherable sound of our skin on skin, as we slid together. He whispered something under his breath as he came.

"Talk to me, baby. Talk to me."

And I did.

I'd been quiet for so long. His lesson in seduction had given me a voice.

The Pants Girl

Rachel Kramer Bussel

I USUALLY GO for girls in skirts, girls whose legs peek out from all manner of clingy fabrics, whose legs I can imagine sliding my hand up, up, up and meeting a hot, wet pussy that I can taste and twirl and play with to my heart's delight. Girls in skirts invite this kind of speculation, as they sashay down the street, a slight breeze all that stands between them and a peek at their lacy, pretty panties.

Girls in skirts are much more likely to be flirts, to try to get me going with a carefully placed twitch as they inch their skirt just enough for me to catch a glimpse of thigh. Skirt girls are teases, their mouths almost always lipsticked into some bright shade of pink or red, their eyes round and taunting. Skirt girls bring out my most aggressive side, and even though I'm one myself, I feel a flush of heat pass through my body when skirt girls, whether in thrift store dresses, clingy minis, or prim to-the-knee office numbers, pass me by. Skirt girls make me wish I were a boy, wish I were a butch, wish I could grab them and shove them up against the wall and find out exactly what's happening underneath their hems. But this story isn't about a skirt girl. It's about another kind of tease entirely—a pants girl.

Shana was wearing pants that were clearly not from this era, with a slight resemblance to bell-bottoms, which curved all along her tender ass. Her ass wasn't big, but it was perfectly rounded, not flat, which is all the rage but does nothing for me. These pants made me want to *wear* pants, to be a pants girl, made me realize that for all the allure of the skirt, pants could cling and tuck and bend in ways a skirt just couldn't do. In addition to her pants, Shana wore a '70s style shirt, a burnt orange color covered in white beads that clung to her breasts with tenacity. She looked like an extra from *Charlie's Angels*, a '70s hot mama ready to take me for a ride. I couldn't take my eyes off her legs, her ass, covered in those gorgeous pants as she danced to the music at the annual dyke rock festival, shaking her hips as her drink sloshed around in its big red plastic cup.

We were in that kind of crowd where the butches and the femmes pick their sides, but she was a free spirit, shaking her ass in the midst of a group of freaks who didn't care what the rest of the crowd was doing. She raised a hand in the air, trying to hold onto her cup, her ass jutting out. I'd been talking to some friends but had stopped abruptly when I noticed her, my eyes glued to the way her clothes clung to every feminine curve. Though she wasn't wearing a skirt or any makeup, she was clearly a femme, her hair flopping down around her in pigtails, her face sun-kissed and healthy with a perfectly earthy glow.

She looked over at me, a brief smile flashing across her lips, before she closed her eyes and threw her head back. I knew I'd have to be the pursuer if I wanted to start something, which I most definitely did.

I pushed my way through the crowd, clumping along in my black combat boots. Normally, I stood to the sides, watched the other dancers, never admitting to my deep-seated self-consciousness. But this time, I threw myself into it, matching her beat for beat, showing her that even though I was in a dress straight out of the closet of a '50s housewife, I was a truly modern girl.

I grabbed her a few times, gave her a twirl, copped the lightest of feels, the kind that would make her wonder whether it was her imagination, whether I meant it or was oblivious to her beauty.

She finished her drink and tossed her cup to the ground, closed her eyes and proceeded to ignore me, dancing up a storm to her own unique beat. I did the same, not caring what my friends thought, knowing that the only way to woo her was to match her individuality with my own. Finally, hours later, the music stopped, and she looked up at me, glowing with sweat and energy and sass. She leaned up and kissed me on the forehead, then I led her onto the street, onto my bike, and into my bed.

When I had her alone, I realized I had my hands full. Girls in skirts are generally easy to figure out, they'll grab my hand and slide it under their panties. But "pants girl," Shana, was harder to figure out. She straddled me, grinding her hips down, pushing against me until I was totally wet. I grabbed her hips and tried settling her onto my lap. She was hot, yet somehow I wanted her to keep her clothes on, those clothes that hugged every curve. She leaned close and kissed me, a full, juicy kiss that made me topple backward.

We tumbled around on the bed, laughing, turning over and over, until finally I landed on top. I wedged my knee between her legs, pushing it up hard against her cunt, and she instinctively brought her legs up onto my shoulders.

Her huge breasts were straining under her shirt and I had to taste them. "Lift up your shirt," I said, a shiver racing through me when she quickly did as I commanded. Her breasts were barely covered by her wispy bra, and though her breasts were big, they were clearly natural, full and round and perfect.

I planted my knees on her legs, keeping them pinned down as I pushed her luscious tits together and began attacking both nipples at once, peeling down the lacy edges of her bra with my teeth to take in the hard, pink nubs.

I licked them at first, my tongue darting out, tasting and teasing, before bringing my lips together to suck on them. I knew she'd be the kind of girl to go crazy if I so much as brushed against her nipples, and I was doing much more than that as I pressed my lips together tightly, kneading her nipples into dark red points before lashing them with my tongue.

"*Yessss,*" she hissed as I twisted them hard between my fingers, so hard I knew she'd feel it for days afterward, welcoming the pleasurable pain even as it made her tender buds stiffen under her shirt, letting anyone around her see them. I loved how she didn't flaunt her tits in public, didn't have them practically hanging out, an offering to any horny passerby, but instead kept them covered, the full, rich orbs practically obscured by her plain brown top, just waiting for the right lover to come along and unlock their secrets. The more I twisted, the more I licked and sucked and bit, the wilder she became, squirming all around, making a pretense of wanting me to stop but clearly desiring nothing of the sort.

Finally, I paused, reaching my hand between her legs, pulling her now-wet pants tight against her straining pussy. She was practically dripping; melting, so wet I knew she couldn't stand it, which is exactly where I wanted her. And I was wet, too; my panties were drenched from having my face buried between those juicy tits, now glowing a gorgeous red.

"Turn over," I barked at her, not certain whether she'd comply.

She did, too caught up in her erotic trance to care what I'd do next, as long as I touched her, somewhere, anywhere along her blazingly hot skin.

I reached underneath her and unbuttoned her pants. She lay passively and let me do it—like a child, even though she was 100 percent full-grown woman. I went slowly with those pants, playing with her pussy, pinching her ass as I went. I felt her shuddering beneath me, and when I finally eased those beguiling pants all the way down, I found only the flimsiest of panties, soaked through with her juices. I peeled those all the way off, too, and spread her legs, admiring the view of her pink pussy lips as she waited patiently for my next move. Holding the lips open with my fingers, I played with her wetness, stroking her, priming her. I slid a single finger up her and it practically melted inside her as she silently begged for more, her cunt tightening around me. I slid the finger out, trailing the wetness along her inner thigh. Then I leaned down and licked along her slit, plunging my tongue inside her. She was sweet and salty, ripe in the best possible way as she pushed herself against my mouth, slick and delicious. I squeezed her ass cheeks, giving them the occasional slap as I tasted her wildness.

Then I turned her over, needing to see her in every possible position. Her eyes were closed, her hands splayed out at her sides, her body totally serene as her pussy beckoned to me. Her hips arched involuntarily and I pushed three fingers inside her, pressing and twisting as her cunt again tightened around me.

I didn't know her, not as well as I would come to, but for now, this was all I needed to know; that she wanted me, was ready and willing and needy. If I'd thought those pants did her body justice, they were nothing compared to what her naked body did to me, leaving me breathless.

She reached for me, her fingers grasping for contact as she grabbed my arm, and I lay down alongside her, nibbling her lips, whispering sweet nothings into her ear as I pressed another finger into her.

"More, please," she said quietly, again like a child, but with an adult's manners and grace, her voice breaking as I quickly gave her exactly what she'd asked for. I pressed my thumb against her clit, pushing it deeply against her pubic bone, swirling it into ecstasy, before sliding that last digit inside. She took my whole hand like it was nothing, but we both knew it was much more than that. She clutched me tightly, her teeth clenched, eyes closed tight as she spasmed around me. I barely had to move, only ever so slightly, my knuckles grazing her most tender walls, brushing against her body's deepest secrets, making tears of joy form in her eyes. She let go of me and jerked backward, coming in a torrent of curses and contractions that left both of us speechless.

I held her afterward, cradling her in my arms as she curled up against me, gripping my thin cotton dress as if for dear life. I looked down at her, her shirt still rising above her jutting breasts, her bottom half pale and bare. After seeing her so stark and vulnerable, so graceful even as she let everything go, I knew I'd never look at her in quite the same way again. But no matter what, she'd always be my favorite pants girl.

Switch

Claire Thompson

I **WAS USED** to being on the wielding end of the whip. That's how I liked it; that's how my slave boys liked it. I thrilled to the power of possession. I loved to see the flash of fear in their eyes, mixed with raw lust and pure desire. I was rough on my boys, riding them to complete submission. Then I would kiss away their tears and ease their pain.

It was hard to find a decent selection of slaves until the Internet came along. And then how many wasted hours did I spend developing elaborate cyber-relationships with eager, desperate sub boys looking for a good, firm Mistress? I even went so far as to have drinks with a couple of guys who seemed like they might have potential. Alas, though they could type a good story, in real life they turned out to be about as exciting as a chainlink fence going to rust.

I did eventually find some submissive guys to use and abuse, but there was rarely a connection beyond the sexual. Things usually fizzled out after a few weeks or, at the most, a few months.

Then I met Andrew. He told me he was a switch who liked to sub and to Dom. I was intrigued. It turned out he was local, so we decided to meet in the flesh. Miraculously, he wasn't a total jerk and we started to go out.

Andrew liked to wear silky panties and stockings while I whipped him and tortured his cock and balls. I called him my little pussy boy, which always brought a pleasing flush to his cheeks. Things went along like that for a while until one evening after dinner I said, "Hey, Andy, I thought you were a switch?"

"Yeah, so? You want to submit? Is that what you're saying to me?"

It was weird. I was usually the one so in control of myself—so calm and cool about everything. I actually found myself blushing as I avoided his gaze and said, "Maybe."

He didn't need to be told what to do. He came toward me, his mouth an unfamiliar sneer. Grabbing hold of my T-shirt, he literally ripped it off my chest. Then he pulled out a little pocketknife and cut my bra cleanly between my breasts. I gasped at his sudden transformation.

With one hand he pushed me down to the floor until I was kneeling in front of him. Holding me by the hair, his free hand unzipped his fly. Then he rammed my face into his crotch.

Inexplicably, I was on fire as I took his cock. He held me tight and fucked my mouth until he came, pulling out to spurt all over my face and hair. Without saying a word, he pulled me to my feet and half dragged me over to the bed, where he threw me, messy face and all, down into the pillows. Grabbing a hairbrush, he started thwacking my ass through my blue jeans. Even with the denim between the hard plastic brush and my butt, it hurt like hell.

I yelled and tried to get up but he pushed me back down. "You asked for this, bitch, now take it!" Every time I tried to protect myself from the blows, he would hit my hands hard with the brush and I'd jerk them away.

"Stand up!" He barked at me. I was whimpering into the pillows and didn't respond. "I said, stand up!"

Andrew jerked me to my feet as he spoke. I felt a thrill of real fear—this was not my pussy slave boy. He was like a stranger to me now. And yet, at the same time, I was so excited I felt like I could come right then and there.

As if reading my mind, he pulled down my jeans and panties and forced my legs apart with one beefy hand. In pressed two fingers, hard; they slipped in easily because I was that aroused.

"Ah, you need this, don't you, slut? Mistress Dominatrix likes to have her butt smacked and her clothes ripped off. But can you really take it, slut? Can you take a beating like the kind you dish out?"

My eyes must have been as big as saucers. I realized the loud rasping sound I was hearing was my own out-of-control breathing. My heart thumped in my throat and my mouth felt dry.

"Cat got your tongue, eh?" Andrew laughed and then he leaned forward and whispered, "Prepare for your first whipping, slave girl."

God. Just the words *slave girl* sent shivers through me. He was tapping into some deep secret longing that I didn't even know I had. I licked my lips nervously as he got out the whip, the heavy braided one with twenty long tails waiting to bite my flesh.

"Kneel," he commanded in exactly the same imperious tone I used on him.

I knelt, trembling, my blood hot with a delicious mixture of desire and terror. "Now," said Andrew, "before I whip you, lick my asshole." Andrew bent over, dropping his pants. I hadn't allowed him underwear that very morning, so his ass was bare. Lewdly, he spread his own cheeks and waited.

I knew what was expected. I leaned forward, trying to comply. I couldn't. My will gave out even before my tongue got past my lips. I couldn't kiss his ass, I wouldn't. It went so against my grain.

"Well?" he demanded, sounding irritated. Still I didn't obey. Andrew whipped around then and slapped me, hard, across the face. Stunned, I gasped and my hand flew up to my burning cheek.

"What a piss poor excuse for a submissive you are, *Mistress*." He spat the words at me and they stung as much as his palm had. "Bend over, bitch. Get ready for the beating you have earned."

He set the whip to me right away—no tender, sensual warm-up. Just a beating, solid and steady. It didn't take long before my tears were flowing. After a while I didn't even try to stop the tears or the cries, or to block the blows. I just lay there, drifting in and out of pain and semi-consciousness.

I don't know when the whipping stopped but slowly I became aware that I wasn't being beaten anymore. There was his big ass again, right up in my face. This time I did it. All thoughts of protest had been removed by his relentless whip.

My tongue snaked out and up until I made contact with his asshole. It was clean, thank god, and tasted of salt and apple cider. He squatted down further, forcing my tongue up into the tight little opening. At last he was satisfied and turned around, jamming his now hugely erect cock into my mouth. I sucked and kissed him as if my life depended on it. He spurted huge gobs of semen into my throat. I'd never allowed him as slave boy to come in my mouth. When he was done he pulled out without a word, stood up and walked away. I heard the shower going but didn't have the strength to get up and join him.

Lying in a heap, covered in welts and my own drying sweat, I fell asleep there on the floor. At some point he must have lifted me onto the bed because when I awoke I was under the covers.

As I squinted one eye open, I saw that Andrew was kneeling next to the bed. His head was bowed and his chain collar was on.

"My turn," he said softly.

Well, they say nothing lasts forever. We tried after that, we really did. But in the end it came down to who got to be the slave and who would be the Master. I suppose it's really my fault. I mean, he entered the relationship to serve a Mistress and I turned the tables on him. Something between us was missing. I didn't understand at the time that it was love.

When Andrew left we barely said good-bye.

Some months later, having withdrawn from the "scene" and still licking my emotional wounds, I was wiping down the bar where I worked, thinking about nothing in particular when a tall man, his thick dark hair pulled back in a ponytail, sat down on a stool. Surreptitiously, I admired his long lean lines. He was wearing a faded blue T-shirt and well-worn jeans.

"A gimlet, please, neat," he said, smiling at me with white even teeth. I am a sucker for good teeth. I had stuff to do but instead of doing it, I wiped down the already clean bar and moved glasses from here to there so I could sneak a few more peeks at Mr. Handsome.

"I'm new in town," the man said suddenly, startling me. His voice was deep and slightly gravelly. I wanted to hear it again.

"Oh, where are you from?"

"Texas. Houston to be exact."

"Well, I hope you like it up here."

"My name is Nick. Nick Hightower." He gave me a lazy half-smile.

"Laura Wilson. Nice to meet you." I held out my hand and his grip was firm. Something seemed to flow through us, but maybe that was just my overactive libido kicking in. I glanced at him to see if he was feeling what I was and his intent gaze actually made me blush. I slid my eyes away and pulled my hand from his.

Unperturbed, Nick started to chat, asking me about the town, the sights, where to shop, where to eat—chamber of commerce type stuff. Harmless enough. I wasn't too busy and I enjoyed the sound of his voice.

He asked for a second drink and asked if he could get me one, too. "No, thanks. I don't drink on the job. I would get too sleepy."

"When do you get off, around 2:00?"

Why was he asking? I shivered a little inside, feeling suddenly like a high school kid waiting for some boy to ask her out. Nonchalantly I said, "Tonight we close at midnight. But I have to clean up and make sure things are ready for tomorrow. I should be done by 12:30 or so."

"Well, Laura, I have absolutely nowhere I have to be and absolutely nothing I have to do until Monday morning when I start the new job. If it's all right, I can't think of anything better than spending my evening right here in this bar with you." He smiled and his eyes crinkled up nicely at the corners.

"Sure, I'd love the company."

Though our talk remained light, his eyes were on me constantly. I felt exposed somehow—but in a delicious way. When my shift was over, we walked outside together. Normally, I walked to and from work. When he offered me a ride home, I accepted.

When he pulled up to my building, Nick asked quietly, "May I come in, Laura?"

"Yes," I said, sensing that something was going to happen. Something new.

Now, up until then I had a personal policy that I never slept with a man on the first date, but that night there was no question. He didn't ask, he took. Almost as soon as we were in the door he pressed me against the wall and began a long slow kiss that didn't end until he had somehow removed all of my clothing.

He actually carried me to my bedroom, making me feel small and dainty, no easy feat. He threw me on the bed and quickly pulled off his own clothes. Naked, he looked stronger than he'd seemed with his clothes on—all sinewy muscle with skin stretched taut like soft supple leather. He held me down, his mouth, his strong hands, his thighs against mine as he pressed me open.

He held my wrists high over my head as he plunged his stiff cock into me. He hadn't used chains or a whip and yet his domination had been sure and true. I lay in his arms deeply contented, drifting near sleep.

Nick stroked my hair, tucking a stray bit behind my ear in a gentle gesture. Quietly he said, "Laura, I know we've just met. But there is something between us, isn't there?" It wasn't so much a question as a statement of fact. I nodded yes.

"I want you, Laura. I don't mean I want to fuck you, though of course I do, you sexy, wonderful woman."

I grinned in the dark, loving every word.

"What I mean is, I want to possess you."

I became very still. This couldn't be happening. This wonderful, exciting man was a Dom too? Had I died and gone to heaven? Maybe I had misunderstood. I decided to stay quiet and see where he was going with this.

"You understand me, don't you?"

"I-I think so," I stammered, not daring to say more.

"You need a strong man. Someone who can tame that wild spirit of yours." Again he was stating facts, not asking. I felt overcome with gratitude and need. I buried my face in his chest and held on to him, feeling his strong arms slip protectively around me.

Nick never left. He moved in that evening and wound up canceling the temporary lease he had put on a place in town, moving his things into my roomy three bedroom apartment. He insisted on paying the rent, explaining that he would have had to pay it somewhere. He assured me that he was getting a hefty allowance from his company to cover rental expenses since he'd been transferred at their request.

At first we took it slow, the sex spicy and a little dangerous but not a true D/s relationship. We definitely had a lovely groove but it wasn't at the level that left me breathless. Then one evening when Nick came home and I hadn't left for my shift yet, he said, "Laura, I'd like you to consider quitting your job. I think the time has come to begin your slave training."

Slave training! Like some erotica novel! I was intrigued and excited. My pussy felt warm and tingling as he continued. "I don't want a part-time sex slave. I want a full commitment—24/7 arrangement. I want to own you completely. You won't leave the house without my permission; you won't eat, or go to sleep, or read a book, or pee in a toilet, unless I tell you first that you may. Do you want that kind of life, Laura? Think, think on it tonight. Don't answer now. Tell me in the morning. And listen, my sweet girl. If you decide that it isn't for you, I will completely accept that. I adore you however I can have you. But I will claim you in that way if you wish it."

I couldn't fall asleep that night. While I loved to play the sex slave, did I really want to commit to such a complete arrangement? Could I even do it? When Andrew had Dommed me the thrill was real but still I had been left incomplete somehow. Was the missing ingredient love? Was love essential in a D/s relationship, as in any abiding and meaningful connection? Did I dare risk the pain of loss again?

In the morning when I awoke, the other half of the bed was empty. After a moment, Nick came in from the shower, his body warm and damp, his long wet hair curling against his neck. From my vantage point in the bed, I openly admired his body. Kneeling next to the bed he took my hand in his like someone proposing marriage in an old movie. He whispered, "Do you want it, slave girl? Will you submit completely to me?"

"Yes, sir," I whispered, the breath suddenly knocked out of me. Until that moment I hadn't realized I had made up my mind. Now it was all I could think of.

⁓

"LAURA, PLACE THE whip in my hands." I arose from my kneeling position on the hallway carpet. In the mirrors that lined the walls, I could see the faint marks of purple and the pale lines of pink striped across my back and ass.

The whip, which I held in my teeth, was deposited into his waiting palm. With one hand on the back of my neck, Nick pressed me gently until I was again kneeling, my ass offered up, my forehead touching the ground.

I could hear him stripping, kicking away his shoes and dropping his clothes in a heap. I had to resist my impulse to look up and stare at his beautiful body. I knew better than to move out of position.

As I received my daily whipping, my skin quickly heated and my breathing became ragged. The lashes kissed my ass, caressed my back. Then harder, the delicious, sudden sting, then the dragging, sensuous feel of the leather. I was in a near-trance of submissive exaltation when the whip was withdrawn. It was replaced by his body, pressed up against mine. Without preamble he thrust his pulsing shaft into me, sending me shuddering and moaning in perfect ecstasy.

The English language isn't big enough to express the state of grace Nick has brought to me. At his first kiss in the morning, a cloak of desire settles over me, wrapping me in a submissive state of being as tangible as a net wrought of fine steel. I feel completely captive, and captivated, by his mastery over me and over the moment.

He possesses me completely and I wouldn't have it any other way. A connection that had eluded me all my life has finally become a part of what and who I am. There is never a false note between us when this dance begins. I guess you could call it the dance of love.

Matilda's Touch

Saskia Walker

*H*ER HANDS WORKING with the dough, that's how I always think of her. Her long, strong fingers coaxing the dough into life, giving it the ability to swell and blossom in the oven. The first time I saw her hands at work in the kitchen I knew, instinctively, that her touch would be firm and sensitive. Matilda's touch changed my life, but she led me to that touch slowly. She overcame my reluctance for human contact through an undemanding friendship, gentle and pure, and then she led me further.

It was 1961. I had just turned eighteen. My mother had sent me away from London to Fawcett-McLaughlin's—a finishing school for young ladies—after the trouble at home. She had taken sides against me with her latest boyfriend, Jack. He was one of several, since my father had left us when I was fourteen. She didn't really have time for a boyfriend—she was one of a rare breed in those days, a career woman.

Jack wasn't much older than me and acted even younger. He was wily and slick, with a nasty streak that he never showed when my mother was around. The trouble came when he started picking on me, teasing me for being such a tomboy and not having a boyfriend. I called him a spiv when he called me a scruffy tart. My mother walked into the kitchen just as I flicked a spoonful of porridge over his smarmy face, assumed I was having a tantrum for no good reason, and packed me off to the school for the summer.

Jack would soon be gone, I knew that, and I was bound for art college in the autumn, but my mother's actions hurt. It was my last summer at home and she had sent me away because she didn't know how else to deal with the predicament. I felt ugly, I felt betrayed. I traveled the length of the country in silence, sat in the taxi from the station and looked at the dreary gray school building feeling numb and indifferent toward it. I sighed and wondered why life had given me so many things that were beyond my control.

It wasn't a finishing school of the fancy type one might read about in Switzerland or on the French Riviera. It was on the northeast coast of Yorkshire, England's bracing coast. Bleak and desolate for the most part, often gusty even in summertime, but with an eerie, gaunt beauty nonetheless. Fawcett-McLaughlin's was named after the two prim proprietors, and was set in a decrepit old manor house with rambling gardens. Even in the early 1960s it had that dusty postwar feeling of make-do about it. Alas, the same could be said of the prevailing attitude.

The other girls were mostly middle class, their parents aspiring to make something special of their daughters. They sent them off for the summer to be taught how to act like a lady, how to run a home properly, and how to use a typewriter—the latter in case the requisite husband didn't appear and they had to support themselves. The 1960s had only just begun, but mercifully they were under way.

Arabella Fawcett, the senior tutor, soon realized my typing wasn't improving with any great haste. She called me to her room, where I had been deposited by the glum taxi driver two days earlier, and offered me some tea.

"Sally, dearest, are you settling in?" She gave a plump approving smile when I nodded. There seemed little point in saying otherwise or complaining about the lumpy dormitory bed.

"That's good, we like our girls to feel at home. But typing isn't really your strong point is it, Sally?" I struggled with the urge to respond with monosyllabic answers. I had barely uttered a complete sentence since I'd left Ealing.

"I gave it up for woodwork at school," I managed. She frowned, fingering the ruffle on her fuchsia blouse.

"They might let young ladies do things like that in London," she didn't look convinced, "but we don't, here at Fawcett-McLaughlin's."

I sighed. At least in the typing class I had avoided communicating with the other girls. They had divided into cliques and were well ahead of the new girl in the set exercises. I didn't mind feeling like an outsider; it seemed easiest. Truth be told, I was still smarting from my mother's rejection.

"Don't worry, pet." She leaned forward and patted my knee. "Typing isn't the most important thing in life." Well thank God for that, I thought. I hated it. I looked out the window behind Arabella's head. I wanted to be outside. I let my mind wander to some old war time posters Mum had kept, recruiting women into the factories and fields. Mum was an illustrator and had designed some of the most famous land worker images. Strong, proud women, working in the fields and mending tractors.

"Cookery is a much more important skill to learn," Arabella announced, and beamed at me, benevolently. My heart sank. I noticed then how violently her sticky coral lipstick clashed with the pink blouse.

"We have a very good cook here, from Norway, and she can teach you." Apparently there wasn't a lot I could do about it. I had never cooked, but I did enjoy food, not that my scrawny underdeveloped frame attested to it. I was resigned to go along with whatever others decided on my behalf; little did I know that my apathy was soon to be forgotten in the meeting that was to follow.

Arabella picked up her ornate telephone, asked her secretary to send Matilda up, and then munched her way through a round of Highland shortbread while we waited.

I looked at the girl with curiosity when she entered the room. She was probably only a year or two older than me, tall, with pale blonde hair tied at the back of her neck. She had clear blue eyes, broad cheekbones and a strong attractive face. She looked back, her eyes taking me in from head to foot, very quickly. It was a blatant appraisal and it triggered some strange yet delicious response inside me. Heat rose in my cheeks. She gave a slight smile but didn't say anything and then looked at Arabella for instructions.

"Sally is eager to join in with your baking, Matilda," she said, over the edge of her shallow bone china tea cup. The girl looked back at me, as if waiting for me to say something.

"Miss Fawcett recommends your class," I said, unsure what was required of me. The girl smiled, as if to herself, still staring at me. Arabella shuffled, crossing her legs at the ankles.

"Not so much of a class, as personal tutoring." Arabella was mistress of the euphemism—what she meant was that I would be helping out in the kitchens. As it turned out, I couldn't have been happier that my mother was paying for this privilege.

"Tilly is very quiet," Arabella added, lowering her voice and leaning forward conspiratorially. "She came from Norway for a few weeks and then stayed with us this past year." I realized she was still talking about the girl she called Matilda, though she had shortened her name and lowered her voice, as if the foreigner wouldn't understand what she was saying. Perhaps she didn't understand, I thought. I realized then that she hadn't spoken. I looked at the girl again and saw that she was waiting for me to make a move, so I stood up. Arabella nodded her good-byes. Matilda led the way from the room and I followed her down the big staircase to the ground floor, my curiosity already beginning to lift my woebegone spirits.

The kitchens were extensive and mazelike, with many disused anterooms where old pans and equipment cluttered the surfaces. They were in a distant wing, far from the main school rooms. Only the faint sounds of laughter, chatter, and badly played piano followed us. Matilda worked in a long, narrow room with a tall window at one end. It was painted creamy magnolia and a dull pale green. A huge range and two deep ceramic sinks were set into heavy wooden work surfaces down one wall. The opposite wall was lined with shelves of utensils that rattled and chimed when we walked up and down the narrow central aisle.

Matilda waved me in, smiling secretly. I assumed she didn't speak much English, or wasn't confident with it. She didn't seem to need it, though, for she spoke to me in other ways. She passed me dishes and indicated where I should set them up. I was immediately at ease in her company; she accepted me into her space without reserve, and began to involve me in wonderfully simple and fulfilling tasks. I soon realized that all the bread and pastries— pretty much the only edible thing on the school menu—were baked by Matilda.

She was beautiful, elegant, and proficient, and she intrigued me; my eyes followed her every move. She pointed up at a set of scales, and when I couldn't quite reach, she gave a quiet chuckle and stepped behind me, close against me as she reached up for the heavy brass contraption. Her body seemed to nestle mine; I closed my eyes when her presence all but totally embraced me. She smelled of baking and something else: lemon zest, fresh and tangy. When she exclaimed suddenly, I caught the eight-ounce weight that slid down in front of me, and joined in with her chuckles.

I watched mesmerized, as she lovingly gave the bread life. I felt warm and alive when I was with her. Her hands rode the dough back and forth, her fingers flexing as she pressed the ball of her hand into it. She altered her supple touch in response to the dough; it was her strong sensuality I was witnessing and absorbing then, only I did not realize that until years later. She hummed quietly when she worked, a half-smile hovering around her broad mouth as she glanced at me from under her eyelids. I liked being with her. She didn't seem to expect much of me, but at the same time she seemed to enjoy having me there.

When she looked up at the loaf tins that first day, I reached for them, trying to guess her needs. She nodded, smiling, and then grew serious when I rubbed briefly at the tension in my neck. She laid a floury hand against the knot of muscles at the base of my neck and pressed into my collarbone. I flinched; it was painful because so much tension had gathered there during the previous weeks at home. She gave a *tutting* sound against the roof of her mouth and gently kneaded the muscle, as if I were dough. It felt strange, but good. Just as a quiet groan escaped me, she stopped, and turned to roll the dough into the loaf tins. She rested them on top of the range, covering them with a gingham cloth. Then, dusting her hands off, she crooked her finger at me and led me from the kitchen.

She took me to a small attic room that housed a patchwork quilt–covered bed, a set of drawers, a chenille rug, a plain dressing screen, and little else. She turned to me as I shut the door behind us and lay her hand on the bed. I smiled, nervous, but also intensely curious. She guided me to sit on the edge of the bed. She seemed able to show me how to move without pushing or saying anything and I found her actions intriguing.

She touched my shoulders and then moved her fingers, indicating that she was going to massage me. As I lay out, face down, as directed, she undid the back of my dress and began to stroke and knead my back across the shoulder blades and up the column of my neck. I was distracted from the rather odd feeling of sudden and unexpected exposure, because I was immediately focused on her actions. Her hands moved to loosen a deep disharmony in my body, freeing me from the burden I carried. I remembered that Scandinavian people did things like this; I had seen pictures of their wooden sauna houses and steaming coals. I found myself imagining Matilda stepping out of one of those sauna houses into the snow, naked and laughing. I blushed into her pillow. With her hands on my body, so sure and confident, I felt suddenly weak and dizzy.

"It feels so good," I whispered, almost unconsciously. I had almost melted into her bed. She leaned forward and smiled at me over my shoulder, her cheeks rosy, pleased with my praise. When she had covered my entire back with the firm deep massage of her fingers, I thanked her, and sat up. I was tingling all over. I wondered if I was the only person in the school for whom she had done this. I wanted it to be so.

"Will you teach me this, too, as well as the cooking?"

She beamed, her cheeks warming, and nodded.

"I hope I can learn," I murmured. I suddenly realized that I had spoken without thinking, and that she had understood me.

Tilly picked up my hands and looked at them, squeezing the pads of my finger-tips. She slid her hands up to the slight muscle of my upper arm, circling it with her fingers as she felt its shape in her hand. The way she touched me, so firm and decisive, made me feel light and weightless, as if I would float away if I wasn't sitting down.

My dress was still open at the back, and it slid down as she moved around me. Her eyes glanced across my partially exposed breasts, spreading heat beneath my skin, and then she continued looking at my hands, feeling my knuckles. My eyes slid across the outline of her torso with curiosity, before she smiled again and gently pulled my dress into position. I felt a sense of disappointment when she covered me up, but wasn't sure why.

"You will be able to learn," she said, in a low, halting voice. I jumped, surprised to hear her speak. Her voice was deep but quiet, heavily accented. I blushed, embarrassed at my surprise.

"Oh, good," I said, feeling suddenly awkward and silly, and stood up. When we returned to the kitchens, she pulled back the gingham cloth that covered the loaf tins. The pale dough had begun to rise and swell and she let me look at its first transformation, before she put it into the oven to continue its development.

I WAS ISSUED a big cover-all apron, rather like a pinafore dress. Tilly had one too. They slipped over the head, tied at the sides and kept the mess off our clothes. Mine was a bit too large for me, so I gathered some of the material up on the shoulders into safety pins. I felt a bit like I had as a little girl, dressing up in my mother's clothes.

As the days passed, I settled into a routine. After dull morning classes on etiquette and conversational French I would pick up my things and hurry off to join Tilly. After lunch in the refectory with everyone else we would escape together and walk over the sand dunes to the wide shoreline. We stood there and joyously threw yesterday's bread out for the gulls, running back quickly, laughing, when they swooped down from the sky. When I close my eyes now, I can still see her flaxen hair fanning out against the roaring skies.

Exhilarated and alive we would return to the cozy kitchen or, equally cozy, to learn the skill of massage in her attic room. The two interchanged and overlapped. She showed me the massage techniques on the dough, and then we would go to her room to put them into practice. She would always turn and smile at me when I followed her through the door, as if secretly amused by the baggy pinafore that made me look like a little girl. Between massages she teasingly tweaked my skin, like the gentle twists on a plaited loaf, making me giggle and squirm.

"Sally, stop with this wiggle," she laughed, her pronunciation of my name softening the "S" into a "Z" and lengthening the "e" sound out into a long oral caress. Everything about her made me feel warm and alive.

When we were alone in the kitchens I told her stories of my friends in London, miming or pulling faces to explain what I meant if she did not understand a word or phrase I used. It was a time of many smiles. I learned slowly that her father was a diplomat and her parents were stationed in the Far East. She loved to read and wanted to write about places she had visited with her parents. She usually traveled with them, but it was a dangerous place they were in and that's why she had been sent to England. They wanted her to continue to learn and experience different cultures, as they had. And she *would* write about it: Matilda became a renowned travel writer.

When we walked in the gardens, she showed me a chestnut tree and stroked her hand over my hair. "Your hair is like the beautiful color from the nut of this tree," she said, stepping cautiously over her words. Affection flowed through me at her efforts to describe. I could not contain my smile; the way she looked at me then made me feel proud and vibrant.

When she was satisfied that I had memorized some of the massage techniques, she offered me her back to massage. I felt so nervous, trying to focus on the lean smooth stretch of her body when she lay down on her bed. Her body was beautiful; it reminded me of the wind-smoothed dunes at the outer shoreline, smooth and gently undulating. Her skin was soft and warm and my tentative fingers spread out against it, eager and yet afraid.

"Your strokes are too gentle, Sally."

I found it hard to press against her as firmly as I wanted to. Something made me resist. But Tilly patiently led my hands and worked my muscles until they began to respond naturally to the layered mysteries of the flesh.

That night I dreamed she lay over me on the sand dunes with the sun streaming behind her head as she smiled down at me. I awoke embarrassed, yet I could not ignore the heavy hot longing I felt inside. My fingers crept into the humidity between my thighs. I stroked the eager, damp swell there and let the dream continue.

⁓

AFTER LESS THAN four weeks I got a letter from Mother: she wanted me to come home. She missed me. I supposed she had finished with Jack. Although part of me missed my home and my friends, I felt quite happy as I was. I didn't want to rejoin the real world for a little while, and I didn't want to leave Tilly.

She watched me with thoughtful eyes. We were in her room. I was only half with her, half with my thoughts. Her stare gradually transgressed my detachment and she looked as if she were going to say something and disrupt our easy pattern of behavior somehow. In fact she was looking at me with a directness that set my pulse going faster. The atmosphere of suspense harnessed my attention. I wondered what she was going to say.

"You must go home soon, yes?"

My silence was confirmation enough. After an infinite moment, she walked toward me. She reached forward to touch the knotted material of my pinafore at the shoulder.

"It is my dress," she whispered. "It is from Oslo, too."

I smiled, realizing why it had always amused her when I had wandered in with those two clumps of material on my shoulders. Tilly chuckled as her fingers stroked the material at my shoulder. She seemed to be taking pleasure in the fact of her clothes against my body. The pinafore was hers. For some reason that was more arousing than if her hands had been on my naked body, the intimacy of her caress through that pinafore of hers. She did not meet my eyes, looking instead at her hand on the pinafore, but I felt her speaking to me within, asking if I wanted her to touch me more. The atmosphere was filled with anticipation. My heart was racing.

I wanted to respond, but wasn't sure what to do or say. Would I even have been able to, back then, had she been English? She must have sensed that I was unsure, because she became serious and gently let her fingers slide down to my breast, laying her hand gently on the material, as if in inquiry.

A huge blossom of desire spread out beneath her hand. I instinctively moved forward, wanting to feel the pressure of her touch more firmly against my breast. Tilly reached her free hand to my face, to slip a stray hair from my cheek and tuck it behind my ear. She bent down and tentatively touched her lips to mine. Physical longing rose up inside me, a reaction that made me suddenly move forward to cling to her, my mouth responding to hers, pressing my body close against her; I wanted to feel every inch of her body against mine.

She took my face into her hands and kissed me more deeply, her mouth a warm moist caress that made me melt with relinquishment, then chase after her for more when she moved her face away in between kisses. My hands began to explore her body, touching the outline of her waist, the swell of her breasts. My body leaned forward to meld and shift against her strong high hips, her thighs, and the jut of her pelvic bone.

Tilly smiled at my anxious movements against her body and whispered, "May I undress you, little one?"

I nodded, my body tingling with anticipation; I wanted to be seen, to be touched, to be loved by this girl with whom I had grown so close. She undressed me, her beautiful hands carefully laying the pinafore and my petticoat across the screen, and then she turned back to me. A little voice in the back of my mind reminded me of awkward fumblings with boys after school dances, but it went unheeded as my body followed hers in the sure path of reciprocated need. I was flushed with desire. This is what I wanted, and she wanted it, too.

Tilly began to unbutton her dress and I helped. Her breasts, full and heavy, buoyed up on the strong outline of her ribs and shoulders. As the dress slipped down to the floor I pressed forward, eager and jittery. I lay my face against the soft rise of her breast, my fingers fumbling on her nipples; I wanted so much to feel those nipples pressed against mine.

She drew me down to lie on her bed with her, her body against mine. The feeling of our breasts meeting was divine, soft, flesh on flesh. My juices began to melt onto my thighs. I couldn't help but give a moan of pleasure as Tilly lifted up on her arms to lie over me, and pressed our hips close together. I let my hands curve around her breasts, the weight and texture of them resting against my palms. Her body was strong and athletic, the muscles shaped and smoothed by her work, but her flesh was softened with beautiful curves.

Her nipples stiffened at my touch. The thrill of it sped through me. I found my thighs aching to part, to open, to be touched;

overcome with eagerness, I was unable to stop myself moving under my friend. The blood was pounding between my thighs. Her face was equally flushed with desire, mirroring my own, and she reached forward and slid her slim tongue into my open mouth, running it along the inner surface of my lips and along my tongue. I captured it with my lips, tugging gently at it as my body curled up against hers.

She slid her hand along my thigh and into the moist crevice of my sex. My flesh was palpitating against her fingers, suffused with heat. I leaned my pubis into her hand, while my mouth followed hers. She caressed my tongue with gentle embraces and my arms wrapped around her, caressing her body. She laid one finger gently over the rise of my clit. A loud moan escaped me with the excruciating pleasure it brought me. As she moved her fingers over my flesh I heard my voice echoing through the room, as if a calling bird was in flight above us.

When I felt I could bear no more tension, she inserted her finger inside me. The muscle of my sex gave a brief instinctive flinch, and then opened to her touch. She went gently, aware that I was anxious; I wanted this, but I still felt unsure.

She followed the first finger with another, the palm of her hand spreading open against my pubis. My flesh responded to the raindrops of sensation she teased from it. Great pangs of longing for more pressure swept over me, taking away my last bit of shyness. I spread my legs wide and tilted my hips up. As she moved her hand against me I felt her fingers flexing inside and the soft palm of her hand closing over the swell of my clitoris again.

It was such sweet, sweet rapture. The intricate binds of pleasure and the need for more tightened on me and I pressed myself closer, answering the rolling of her fingers with the movement of my hips. She looked so aroused, yet strangely collected, as if absorbing each sensation with a controlled appreciation. She nodded, watching me, her lips parted, encouraging me to move with her. She watched my face as the movement of her hand drew wave after wave of sensation up inside me, bringing me suddenly to orgasm. I moaned deeply as my hips rolled further apart with heat and density. My orgasm buoyed up, before washing over my whole body in hot release. It became so intense, it was almost painful.

Tilly stroked her hand across my hipbones, raising the delicious heat to the surface there, and then bent to touch that sensitive place nestled in my sex, gently kissing the tender folds and the nub of desire that throbbed, until my whole body hummed, the glow of my climax drawn out longer and longer. My limbs shivered gently. I felt strange and glorious with that weight floating away inside me.

Tilly looked down at me, eyes shining, her lips moist. She whispered words I didn't understand, but they felt close and intimate, and I slid my arm around her neck, drawing her closer. The musk of our bodies filled the air. My hand was already against her hip, tracing the curve and plane of it. I remembered her attention to my hips, how good it had felt, and leaned over to kiss a trail along the line under my fingers. Tilly sighed deeply, whispered quietly in her own tongue again, then rolled onto her back.

I moved across her stomach and trailed along the other hip, kissing the surface lightly with my lips, responding to the pleasurable sounds that she made. Her skin tasted of salt, and smelled of desire. I slid my mouth over to her navel and sucked deeply, pushing my tongue in and circling the crevice, exploring. Tilly moaned out and then chuckled.

"You have done this before?" she breathed. I lifted my head, my hands sliding to her breasts.

"No, but I am glad I'm doing it now, with you." I was rapt with pleasure. I climbed over her, straddling her. I looked down at the brush of pale hair on her groin. Between the soft down the hood of her clit puckered and exposed itself to me. I slid one finger into the slit of her sex, resting it over the nub of her clit. My legs moved around one of her thighs, as I moved down, pressing my wetness onto the hard surface of her knee. Then I pushed my finger inside her, and she opened her free leg wide, allowing me to slide my thumb against her clitoris and move my hand over her mound.

My fingers discovered the smooth slippery walls of Tilly's sex. I wanted to cover her body with mine, and straightened out to lie against her, keeping my hand deep inside her and propelling it with the thrust of my hips. Tilly bucked against my hand and hips and with a gentle cry, spread her arms in release. I was still grinding against her thigh, but the rich cream inside her beckoned to me and I slid down and embraced the stiffness of her clitoris in my lips, her moist flesh pulsating against my mouth. My fingers, damp from her, rubbed frantically against my sex to finish what had been started.

Tilly's thigh trembled beneath my breasts as a second climax rose up and seeped through her body. I was doing this: I was bringing her this pleasure. The thrill empowered me, and my mouth sought and begged her flesh to enjoy it even more. My mouth was hungry and desperate. I rubbed another pang of release from my lusting clit. Her hands went into my hair, tugging. She held my head in place when her body bucked and writhed. When she fell limp, my curious tongue stole inside her for a taste.

Warm and pungent, I took the precious nectar into my mouth. I bathed my cheeks in her moistness, intoxicated. Her skin tingled with vitality against my face. I turned to kiss the soft folds of her sex flesh, my own radiant sex still pressed against the flex of her foot. When I had licked the heavy sweetness from her, inside and out, I gently kissed a line up to my friend's mouth, to end with a deep mutual kiss. She stroked my hair and I looked at her in wonder. This language needed few words.

~

ARABELLA WALKED INTO the kitchen with the quick sharp steps that indicated her busyness. We were sitting over tea, admiring a tray of butterfly buns we had just finished icing. She gave Tilly a smile and a nod, and picked up one of the buns. In between delicate bites she told me my mother was coming to collect me the next day.

"We've enjoyed having you here, Sally. Mmm, delicious." There was a dusting of icing sugar among the heavy face powder on her cheek; it didn't look out of place. "If you want to come back next summer, we would be happy to welcome you again." She took another butterfly bun with her as she trotted out of the kitchen.

I let my eyes slide to Tilly, who stared at the table in front of her, moving her cup slowly round in her fingers, as if absorbed by its outline. We sat in silence for a few moments and then I walked over to stand behind her, my hands resting on her shoulders.

"Can I sleep with you, in your bed, tonight? I could sneak out from my dormitory."

Tilly covered my hands with hers, and leaned her head back against my body. "Oh yes, Sally, little one, yes you can." She pressed my hands firmly onto her shoulders. I bent to rest my cheek against hers.

⌒

WE WROTE, SPORADICALLY. We lost touch in our twenties, while she was traveling. I got drawn into the women's movement— found it wasn't only Norwegian women that made love to each other—and began a successful career in interior design. Then we found each other again, through a Fawcett-McLaughlin's newsletter, and visited one another across the North Sea. I even learned some Norwegian phrases, though English is our favorite tongue, bar one.

Later, our families met and mingled. Her eldest son and my daughter fell in love and made beautiful children together. We laughed and cried with joy over it. Now, at Christmastime in England and during summer holidays in Norway, our grandchildren play together while we take time away from the buzz of our everyday lives to bake together, again.

Matilda is still strong and beautiful, though her hair is touched with gray now, and I am still scruffy and scrawny, though my hair is touched with gray, too. And Matilda still has that magic touch and that secret smile that says more to me than all the languages she had gone on to learn could ever say.

An Exploration

Dorothy Allison

*F*OR YEARS I didn't really understand it—the way women would look at each other's hands across the bar, the way some women's glance would trail up from the fingers to the swell of the knuckles, past the wrist to the forearm, and then look away suddenly if they saw me watching them. I used to hang out at the only gay bar in Tallahassee, Florida, and watch women stare as the tall, slim-lipped bartender would lift four beer bottles together, their pupils reflecting the cable-like tightening of the muscles from her wrist to elbow. I watched the other women lick their lips, look away and inevitably look back again, and I knew by their manner that it was about sex.

I'd look back myself, admire the bartender's jaw, black eyes and the curling short hair on her neck. I loved the way her hips moved, the way her tongue would peek out between her lips when she was counting change, but I didn't really see the power of her hands. They were small, finely shaped, and the nails were trimmed down and filed, but then most lesbians wore their nails that way. It was nothing special as far as I could see. I would look back to see what all the women were watching, but I couldn't quite figure it out.

There was a whole language in the subtle movements of

women's hands on a shot glass, but for me it was like hearing someone speak French. Even what I thought I understood turned out to be mostly misunderstanding. A raised eyebrow, a direct glance, or a shy tongue appearing suddenly on a full lip were all obvious evidence of erotic interest, and I knew how to respond. But a woman who cracked her knuckles while looking into my eyes confused me. I suspected she might want something of me I might not want to give.

The older butchy women I liked best seemed to think that I would surely catch fire if they held me down and fucked me. I responded powerfully to being held down but not so well to fucking. Years of severe and persistent endometriosis had convinced me that nobody could possibly enjoy fucking. Well, one or two fingers perhaps, during that time of the month when you want to howl at the moon anyway, but not more than that, and certainly not with any kind of sudden or forceful movement. The kind of sustained and forceful fucking that made women with big powerful forearms so attractive was unimaginable to me. I was a master at coming by rocking on my partner's thigh or pulling my thigh muscles tighter and tighter while I sucked and tongued at my partner's clit. But fucking hurt me, and I'd only do it if my partner insisted, biting my lips and giving it up like a gift too costly to offer often. It wasn't until my mid 20s, well on in my life as a lesbian, that I finally had the surgery for what had plagued me since my adolescence.

Curing my endometriosis changed my life. After that, when the moon came on me, and a woman pushed three fingers into my wet and aching vagina, I got the shock of my life. There was no pain; there was a heated rush of desire. I wanted that hand. I wanted it hard. I wanted it fast. I wanted it as long as she could keep giving it to me. I remembered every bartender I had ever seen pick up a handful of cold bottles, and in the middle of an orgasm I laughed out loud. I had acquired the language.

"Speak to me," I told my lover. Without knowing what the hell I was talking about, she did just the right thing. She slipped another finger inside me and started all over again.

In the movie in my head, fisting is as savage as big cats rolling over each other in a jungle clearing. The instant of being entered is as abrupt and shuddering as a flying kick. In my bed, however, fisting is neither savage nor abrupt. It is slow, measured, enticed and enticing. My women take their time, sometimes to my great frustration. When I beg them to move faster and harder, they just go on taking their time, putting in only as many fingers as the drum-ring entrance to my vagina will allow. They work me up slow, making sure that I am as open and aroused as possible. It is slow, teasing work, getting a whole hand in my cunt. But if it were easy, I don't think I would enjoy it half so much. Part of the charge is the excess of the act.

If we have to work on it, then it's about submission. If it's easy, then it's more about the physical sensation. It's the overwhelming aspect of it, the being totally carried away, shouting demands, shrieking to be fucked. The fact that it's hard makes it better, more satisfying.

I don't react to fucking like a character in a jack-off manual. My women almost never get their fists going in and out the way it's described in cheap pornography. Once the fist is fully inside, the motion is a slow, sliding, back-and-forth movement with the wrist sometimes swiveling enough to turn the knuckles up, pushing toward that mythological G-spot where all the nerves leading to the clit seem to cross.

I don't spurt the way some women do. Push me hard there, though, and I might pee. That's excessive too, the idea that we are fucking so hard and so furiously that I will just pee all over us. I like that. I like the idea of being that far out of control. Even the moment when I am shocked and embarrassed has its enjoyable aspect. Just so long as we don't stop, and especially if I am told that she wants it, wants me to let myself go like that, the thought turns around and I'm proud of myself. We are bad girls together, enjoying ourselves.

The first woman I ever really fisted was a big butch girl—a tall muscly woman who left working on her motorcycle to polish my belt buckle, get me a cup of tea, and blush when I hooked my fingers in her belt. She had been flirting with me and my girlfriend, and we were both enjoying her enormously. It was my girlfriend who checked it out with her girlfriend and got us all together at a party later.

"What do you want?" I kept teasing that girl, enjoying the size of her, the stretch of her shoulders and the slow, gliding way she moved.

"What can you do?" she replied, looking down at us. We were both so much smaller than her. Well, what? I wondered, but my pride wouldn't let me show her any uncertainty. I squeezed her, pinched her, and ran my hands over her body as firmly as possible, enjoying every little sigh and quiver she made. I was looking forward to watching my girlfriend fuck her, but somehow when we had her lying back and her jeans off and her legs spread, it was my fingers that were teasing at her slippery labia. I slid my thumb inside her and felt around. It was smooth and open and welcoming. I pulled back and slipped two fingers in and looked up into her half-closed eyes. There was lots of room. I pulled back and went in again with three fingers, then four. Her next sigh was deeper, and she shuddered slightly in our arms.

I looked at my girlfriend. She was smiling and nodding, watching my fingers closely. I laughed and pulled back, cupping my fingers. I was going to push, slowly, feel my way tenderly, but the big girl had other ideas. It felt almost as if she reached for me with her whole body. My hand disappeared, sucked into the warm, enclosing glove of her. I gasped, and my girlfriend laughed. I wiggled my fingers and felt the walls of the surrounding vagina balloon out and in on my hand. I closed my hand inside her, and the big girl rocked on my wrist.

"Goddamn!" Everybody around me laughed. I had never felt anything so extraordinary in my life. I tried to remember everything anybody had ever done to me that I liked. All right, I told myself and started moving my hand, the motion flowing from my elbow while I watched her face. When she started moaning and rocking with excitement, I let the muscles in my upper arm go to work. I felt my whole arm working. I wanted to do it right. All of my senses came alive. I needed to feel every motion she made, smell her as she got hotter, hear her guttural cries and slow grunting "Please," I wanted to shout, but that would have distracted me. I tried instead to speak the language of her body. I felt a hot sweat break out all over me, and every time I looked to the side I saw a proud, happy smile on my girlfriend's face.

"This role reversal stuff," I told her, "I like it a lot."

"Uh-huh," she laughed back at me. "I can see that."

~

I KNOW REMARKABLY few women who enjoy anal fisting. But there was a time in my life when I became quite accomplished at it. Not that I listed being fisted up the ass as a goal—I just had lots of fantasies about anal sex, and I told a woman I was seeing at the time about those fantasies. Natalia was much older than me, and we had been playing schoolgirl and governess. When I was the governess, Natalia was my toddler who needed to be washed tenderly, powdered down, sometimes have her temperature taken—"Turn over, baby"—and invariably be nuzzled gently until she orgasmed in my arms. When I was the schoolgirl, I was a stubborn adolescent who accumulated countless demerits and had to be taught how to wash behind her ears and between her thighs. After weeks of this play and lots of talk about our mutual fantasies, Natalia decided she would like to play out one of hers and see if she couldn't train her schoolgirl to enjoy having her ass used.

"For me," she begged, feeding me warm baklava and cold dry wine. I didn't know if the butterflies in my tummy were from her suggestion or the snack, but I agreed. Thus began a period of about three months in which I spent at least two nights a week lying belly-down on her big oak bed stand while she whispered threatening enticements into my ears and slipped magic greasy fingers up my butt. She took her time getting me used to her manipulations and refused to tell me just how many fingers had done what at any one time. Regardless, it didn't seem to take very long until I was comfortable enough with what she was doing to climb up on my knees and start pushing back at her thrusts.

"That's my girl," Natalia would purr, and reward me with the fast, slippery swipes at my clit that always made me come.

Finally, one evening Natalia asked me to come early and have dinner. She served raw oysters, lots of wine, and a big salad, and after dinner sent me off to clean myself out and lie for a while in a hot bubble bath with a glass of cognac while she did some tidying up. When Natalia came for me later I was pink all over, giggly, and very tipsy. She was wearing her highest heels and the black jacket with the high collar and the tight-fitting sleeves. Without a word she wrapped me in a big towel, bundled me into the bedroom, and plopped me facedown on an enormous pillow on the floor. Before I could hiccup in confusion she had my wrists tied to a ring in the floor.

"Ma'am?" I tried, unsure which game we were going to play.

"Be still," she said sternly. "Don't think, just relax. I want something from you, and tonight I'm going to get it." She poured a pool of thick, creamy lotion into her palm and began to massage my ass, her blunt fingers pushing dollops of cream up into my butt. I hiccupped, giggled, and after a moment wiggled my ass at her. She laughed, slapped my thighs, and, leaning forward, placed a small, silver, bullet shaped object in my hand.

"Take a deep breath of that," she told me, still pushing at my ass. I did, and was rewarded with a slow spiral of pin lights that rose from the base of my nose up to my brain. The room got hot. I got dizzy, and a beehive started buzzing in my ears. I had never done poppers before, didn't know that was what I was doing. I just knew I was suddenly high and horny and desperate to push back at her pushing hands.

"Ma'am," I wailed, and she purred back at me, "That's my girl," while her hand worked its way steadily into my butt. She hurt me, and I screamed at her. She laughed at me, and I howled at her. But she'd had all that practice and knew every crevice, every rudimentary panic, every movement I would make in response to every movement of hers, and nothing I did or said or cried stopped her. After a while she wasn't hurting me, she was guiding me, whispering soft words while her fingers played tickle-touch so deep inside me I wanted to burp. I was gasping and begging and coming every little while as easily as a big sponge choo-choo train would fall off a cartoon trestle. Everything was slow-motion, overwhelming and marvelous.

"Fuck me, ma'am. Oh, fuck me," I kept begging her.

"Oh, I am," she kept telling me. "I am. I am. I am."

The sun was coming up when she slid her hand out of me finally and completely. I burst into tears and tried to grab her with my thighs. I wanted it back, that full, marvelous, scary, wonderful feeling. She had pulled the slipknot loose on my hands hours before, and I was free to be coaxed up into the bed to wrap around her and fall asleep, but groggy as I was, I didn't want to sleep. Even if I couldn't move, I wanted to do it again. I pulled her hand up, cradled it to my cheek, and ran my fingers along her forearm. I dreamed of bartenders; slow-eyed, grinning butch girls; and big cats rolling over the jungle floor—big cats with wide, wide mouths, great hanging wet labias, and muscly, tapered forepaws. That woman spoke my language; what she could do with those hands. Oh!

Perfect

Sharon Wachsler

My **MASTER IS** good to me. She arranges butterfly pillows under my knees and ankles so that my legs can be spread open— my feet high—all day, and my muscles stay loose. My calves do not cramp.

My Master believes in rope, in simple things she buys at the hardware store: slick, strong cords that won't splinter into my skin, chrome-plated pulleys, and thick eye bolts she screws into the walls after she tracks down the stud. She drums the mallet gently against the plaster, listens for the hollowness to become hard and sharp. I anticipate that sound, the stud. I know what it is to feel that hollow, to wait for my Master's hard, sharp hand to find me, fill me, faultless.

My Master's ropes are extensions of her arms: they wrap around my chest in a figure eight, pushing out my breasts so that my nipples lick up to taste each passing current. Her ropes sluice up my arms and tie my wrists over my head. But she places more pillows beneath my arms and hands, so I am pure and supple in my submission. I flush beneath the bindings.

My Master believes in thoroughness—in my legs, my breasts, my wrists being held motionless. I cannot squirm, and now, for us, the ropes are the cause. We make my bindings the reason I cannot disturb the perfect position she has set me in.

She brings me water and tea, cradling my head to set my lips against the cup. When she feeds me she cares about what is soft, what is hard: wedges of plum, fresh slivers of raw salmon, her nipples, her fingers, her dick. She is immaculate with the blender and magics my meals into frothy milkshakes. We know how to suck, each sharing the same straw, back and forth, so that when my tongue wraps around the tube, taking it from her, she sees what I can do. In this way she allows me to tease her, because my mouth is awake to every nuance of movement and texture and taste. My mouth is my most alive place. My tongue never tires of pleasing her. My mouth is the freedom we celebrate.

My Master already knows about the catheter. Before, it was for play; now it is for necessity. We use it so that I am always available to her desires and to my body's needs. This is another way in which my Master is perfect: her demands free me from my body's; my restriction becomes delicious. We enact my limitations as her will—vanquishing the power of doctors' diagnoses and of the frequent failure of my muscles and nerves to do my bidding. Our bodies' needs caress each other.

My Master adores my body with ritual. Every evening we bathe, anointing me with oil. She braids my clean hair so that it lies wet and heavy against my neck. She grabs my noose of hair and pulls my mouth against hers. I gasp. I gasp. I gasp.

My Master performs a sorcery of stirrups and cushions. I am open and yielding on the silver sheets, shivering in the heat. She stands with her hip against my jaw while she straps on her acrylic dick. It is rigid and cool. I try to lick the rippling head but she rocks back. I eat my Master's dick with my eyes.

My Master runs lube over her dick and against my swollen lips. I cry out when her fingertips brush my clit. It feels like it has been years since she has touched me, although it was just yesterday. Time stretches me in this bed. I beg for her fulfillment.

My Master lowers herself onto me—her ribbed white shirt pressing against my breasts—and plants her hands below my pillows, thrusting deep into me. So cleanly she slides the head of her cock, rolling it against the roof of my cunt until she owns me completely.

It is impossible to be still now with this wildness in my cunt, this confident intensity on my Master's face. Her dick rubs my spongy inner clit, making me want to yank at my bindings, to snatch at the small hairs at her nape—Goddammit!—to clasp my ankles around her waist. But I cannot. Thus I scream her name and bite her jaw. She rears back, pulls her cock to the outer edge of my cunt. I howl. My Master rams back in and against me, grabs my hair and forces her tongue to the back of my throat. My Master is so good to me. "Don't bite," she growls, "or I will stop fucking you." I hold still, because my Master is good and she wants me to come.

When my Master rocks against me, again and again, I feel my orgasm mounting, my true gift. We are raw now with sweat and slippery with lube and come. We ache against each other. Heat races to my center, radiating out from her cock, warmth pouring inside my belly and breasts, legs and toes. My Master is filling me with her complete demand and I scream out with giving it to her. I cannot afford to relinquish any pleasure.

Deliriously we stick to each other, unraveled, cooling. I kiss my Master's neck, her collar bone, her shoulder, the hollow at the base of her throat. She breathes against my ear, my cheek, kisses my hair, bites my lower lip until it is swollen.

We curl together. "You are perfect," she says. I am good to my Master.

Moving On

Bryn Colvin

$\mathscr{T}$HE STREET WAS crowded, and everywhere Cora looked she saw the desperate faces of poverty-stricken humans, blighted by an ongoing disaster of their own creation. Around her massed evidence of pain and anguish in bodies battered down by too many years of struggling. The gray faces of those who inhabited the borderlands between life and death were ever present around her. She had never become numb to this; never learned to tune out the misery, to turn off her horror and dismay, but then, that had always been the point. There was so much wrong that it overwhelmed her, sometimes, making any dream of improvement seem utterly deluded. She dreamed furiously and endlessly because it was the only way she knew of to survive.

He was a few feet away from her, no more, when they both stopped. Out of the desolate hordes came a face, startlingly real among all the rest. His hair and skin were caked with gray filth, but there was passion in his eyes, where so many around them were dull and lifeless—the people catatonic from poisons. They stared at each other, and it was one of those rare moments of connectedness and communion that made some of it, at least, seem worthwhile. Cora looked past the grime and saw only his eyes, dark and flashing from within the ash and muck covering his skin.

The filth in his hair made him look ancient, the gray of the ash gave him the pallor of a corpse, but the light of his eyes drew her, held her, and for a moment the sheer vitality of his presence enchanted her.

Moving out of the crowd, the stranger with the brilliant eyes approached her, perhaps sensing that she was also an outsider, not yet fully caught up in the destruction of mind and body that continued relentlessly around them. He stepped forward and kissed her, as easily as that. His mouth tasted of ashes and death, but his tongue was sweet. Cora touched the grease-laden hair at his temples, but he slipped away and was gone, lost among the other gray faces.

Having lived among delusions and death for many years, Cora had started to think she was beyond being surprised but, even so, the memory of his kiss stayed with her, lingering on her skin and awakening senses that had lain dormant for years. From time to time, afterward, she would find herself remembering his lips—soft and warm beneath his mask of grime.

Sitting in the drafty privacy of her small pad, in what had once been a station of some description, Cora allowed her mind to wander; a luxury she seldom dared to indulge. She had almost forgotten what gentle, sensual contact could do to her, and a lost, forgotten part of her psyche was awakening once more. In this world of filth and decay, there had seemed little scope for joy or pleasure. The people she encountered were too ground down, too far beyond hope for anything and her sentence weighed heavily upon her. Her old life, the life of a few years previously, seemed like a distant dream. It was almost impossible to remember the feeling of truly clean skin, or the taste of pure, clean air. She supposed she would remain here until the pollution killed her, as it seemed to be killing everyone else. Her lips felt warm as they had not done in a long time, and she was conscious of them as though his touch had somehow lingered there: still pressing against her hours later.

The place of her exile was a world she knew nothing about— some far-flung industrialized mess that had yet to make formal contact with the rest of civilization. Their history was unknown to her, their habits unfamiliar. However, their language contained considerable elements of Original-B, a theoretical guess at an ancient intergalactic tongue hypothesized from the coincidental similarities of communication existent between far-flung races. Having studied it during her youth she had not struggled to learn their modes of verbal expression. Thus far she had survived, but it had not been easy.

That week she found a new job. It was nothing special but better than most. It meant relief from having to steal and from the fear of getting caught. What little she had learned thus far taught her that punishments were cruel here; the loss of a limb for a petty crime was not unusual. When she first arrived, she had only the clothes on her back, and no sense of where she had been sent. She lived as a beggar and an outcast, learning from observation that the airborne ash was toxic, that half the people around her were slowly dying and that above them in the great towering city, was a whole world of privilege and careless indulgence that cared nothing for the destruction it wrought. She learned that there was no hope, and it was a hard lesson indeed. Gradually she acquired useful things; a knife, a blanket, something to wrap her face in and a grasp on how to talk. It did not take her long to realize that with her considerable wit and knowledge, she could survive far better than those around her. Gradually, however, her ruthless self-preservation had melted into compassion for those innumerable blighted lives around her; something she would never have thought herself capable of feeling.

The little triumphs: a wound that closed over on a child's arm; a safer place to sleep at night; a better mask to keep out the dust— these things began to consume her. It was not like the old days when she had hungered for status and recognition. But then she had been one of the people in the high tower, one of those elevated above the filth she did not even know was there. This could be the hidden nightmare of her own world, easily, save for the fact that the days were longer here. She had stepped on plenty of fingers on her climb up the great social ladder, but now she walked with more care, mindful of those around her, taking no more than she needed, sharing what she could. Once it had been just a matter of survival, now there was something more to life.

～

THAT NIGHT, AS Cora went to work for the Waste Mining Company, she met a familiar figure in the street—a man who had helped her when she first arrived. She recognized the decorated mask he wore—unusual among the vagrants, but Rill was good at making things and he had connections. The warmth of his greeting was a pleasant balm.

"How you doing, kid?" he asked. He always called her "kid," even though she was probably of an age with him.

"Got a job, sorting and cleaning," she gestured toward her new workplace.

He nodded, "They aren't too bad, but get something to bind your hands with if you can."

She did not ask why; Rill had taught her how to survive and never asked where she came from, or why she was so naive and unworldly, her speech rough and broken like that of a young child. At first she had thought him soft, but his kindness had kept her alive and gratitude had eventually taught her to respect him for that.

"Where're you squatting?"

"Same place as before, not too good."

"Hmm. Look, I'm working days, if you're on nights we could share if you want, it's certainly a better class of hole I've got these days."

"I'll owe you one."

"I hear you've become one of the good guys."

She laughed, "Maybe, but if I did, it's all your fault."

Rill told her where to find the pad and she was impressed, it certainly was supposed to be one of the better places, a bit further out of the ruins of the old town. She had actually heard of it, and she wondered what he had done to get a spot in there.

"If you get any trouble, you just tell them you're with me."

She nodded.

Then he thought to add, "I ought to warn you, it's a pretty weird place. Some of the people living there—I don't know—a couple of them must be taking some heavy stuff. There's not much anyone can do for them. And don't ask questions, there's a lot going down there it's better to stay out of; you know what I mean?"

"I can hack that," she said, "it's got to be better than the old station."

He nodded, knowing that she was right.

IT TURNED OUT to be the biggest complete building Cora had seen since her arrival. She had seen the massive block of the main city, but that had been so vast as to be a touch unreal, like a grounded space station. This place had probably been a factory once. The roof was gone in several spots, but that was true of nearly every building in the old town, most others were missing areas of wall as well. People had set up little camps wherever they could find the room. Rill had made his home in the stairwell. It was sheltered and there was a fair bit of space, but people walked through constantly so there was no privacy at all and there was always something going on. The main advantage to the property was that there were places where a person could wash. The water seemed clean, and Rill said it was as good as it ever got in this quarter and safer to drink than most. No matter how bad things got, Cora refused to be dirty. It had become apparent that if you let the ash from the air cake on your skin, you transformed gradually into something less and less like a person, your mind slipping into apathy while your body slowly rotted. Most people apparently gave up in the end and let it poison them. There were all kinds of life-stealing things in the ash, from the factories that still ran, and the sinister leftovers from an almost forgotten war.

Cora had gradually come to realize that was probably why they had sent her to spend her days of exile in this particular backwater—so that she could see the legacy of chemical warfare for herself and to learn exactly how long and dire the effects of one simple device could be. You might win wars with it, but everyone else kept on paying. It was not as though she had not known this, but she was finding there was a whole world of difference between knowing something to be true, and being forced to live in its aftermath. If the same career opportunities came her way now, she was not so very sure that she would take them. Knowing what this year or so had taught her cast a long shadow over her previous calling. Cora might not have been able to dull her senses to all that she saw, but her ambition had certainly become blunt from lack of use.

For several days, she slept fitfully in the noisy stairwell, spending her nights sifting through buckets of recently mined rubbish, looking for the precious metals that could be reused; the plastics that could be sold for high prices. It was a filthy job that left her sore and aching. She could see why Rill had told her to bind her hands; the debris was full of sharp things, and a cut with all that muck about would have been dangerous indeed.

The sound of fighting from the floor above disturbed her equilibrium, and she tensed, wondering if she should move. It was the first time she had heard anything so aggressive. Most of the sounds from above were unsettling enigmas, and she tried her best not to listen to them. As she sat up in her blankets, there came a figure rushing down the stairs, someone Cora already knew. His name was Andreas and he could not have been more than fifteen. At night he dressed up as a woman and went out selling his body. She did not know where his money went, but he always had a lost, hungry look about him. Cora called out to him, but he did not stop. It sounded as though something serious was going on up there and, although she was aching for sleep, there was no hope the noise was going to end any time soon, so she went up to find out what was happening.

The elderly stairs groaned beneath her as she climbed. She could hear voices, but the words made no sense. There were figures in the semi-darkness of the roof-space. Cora felt a brief flash of pre-sentiment and realized that she could smell death in the air. There were three or perhaps four figures in the tableau. A man raving. A man restraining him. A man holding what she soon realized was the corpse of a woman.

"She isn't dead," the raver bellowed repeatedly.

Cora saw the flicker of a blade catching the light from the well. She knew no one there, this was not her problem, but even so she was loath to turn her back on it. A few paces placed her in the center of the room. Her heart was pounding wildly and around her she could smell the decaying woman and the sharp odor of unwashed human bodies.

"What's happening?" she asked, trying to wrap the sound of authority into her voice.

The man with the corpse said, "This idiot had a body up here. Could kill us all."

"She isn't dead," he screamed.

Although Cora had never knowingly heard the voice before, it filled her with a sense of eerie familiarity. She stepped between the corpse-bearer and the other two and, as she moved, the corpse-bearer made good his escape, hauling the dead woman with him. Cora attracted the attention of the distraught man. Standing closer now, she could see his face, and recognition flared up in her. This was the man who had kissed her in the street only a few days previously. There was nothing to suggest that he remembered her, and she could see little of the animation that had been in his face then.

"She isn't dead," he said softly, as though pleading with her.

"Who is she?" she asked.

"I don't know."

But he did know: it was written all over him.

The man with the knife had melted back into the shadows and the gloomy roof-space had become disturbingly quiet. Cora was alone with her familiar stranger. He began to laugh; a low cold sound that chilled her. Then he reached for her, covering her face with his ashen hands. She thought she could almost sense the poison that was in him and knew that without help he would die soon. She had seen it happen too often before. The toxins were driving him mad. If she could get him clean and let his skin breathe properly, he might stand a chance, but at best it would be a small one.

He kissed her and there was life in him yet, despite his closeness to death. His mouth surrounded hers, opening her and rendering her utterly vulnerable to the insistent penetration of his tongue. There was fire in him still, and it roused her from her stupor. She let him fill her mouth with the taste of his deadly ashes, knowing that so small an amount would do her little harm. She was more resilient, it seemed, than those who had lived among it all their lives, although she had not yet determined why this might be. She did not want him to stop, but eventually he drew away from her, leaving her empty and dazed.

"Let me help you," she said softly, uncertain as to how much help she could give him, but desperate to prolong this contact.

He backed away.

"Leave me alone."

"Come with me."

Her command startled him into attention, and she saw his whole body stiffen. Still he refused to follow. He was distracted though, and moving forward, Cora was able to knock him off balance before he knew what was coming. This life had taught her many little tricks. It was not an ideal solution, but sometimes you could not afford to wait around until people asked for help. Once the insanity started to creep in, all sense of self-preservation seemed to evaporate. Groggy, he stumbled. In his condition, it would not have taken a forceful blow to push him to the ground. She hoisted him up over one shoulder. It seemed as though his bones must be made of air, for although he was tall, he weighed no more than a child.

In the basement there was a tap and some large drums to wash in. Cora laid the disorientated man down, resting his back against the wall. She stood for a few moments, absorbing him with her eyes. Filthy and poisoned as he was, Cora knew she wanted him. There was something compelling about his fragility, and she was almost certain he was the hypnotic stranger who had pressed his mouth to hers in the street. It was as insane as chemical poisoning, more wild and uncontrolled than any want that had ever before born down upon her. She needed to connect with this man, to touch his experience, to let herself tumble a little way into the profundity of his demise. More than that, she ached to know how his skin would smell once she had worked the magic of cleaning upon it. She longed to see his eyes again, to taste his lips and feel his hands upon her body. No one had loved her in such a long time and unexpectedly she now hankered after such satisfaction. Why it was this man that had suddenly sparked her lust, she could not have said, but something in him reached through her defenses and set her soul trembling.

She would have kissed his ash-encrusted skin, had she not been aware that his life might hang in the balance. She tried not to damage his ragged clothes too much as she undressed him. There was still a little wear in them and otherwise she could only offer a blanket to cover him with. Then she filled one of the vats with cold water and sought out the rag and knob of soap she had secreted near the taps. Rather than hauling him into the vat, she began to dab at him, sponging the grime away. It was slow work, for the ash had mingled with his sweat to form a dense, almost impenetrable layer, like a second skin. The soap ran out while she was washing his body. Beneath the hard ash skin was a firm torso, almost as pale and graying as the filth that had covered it. Hunger had made him lean and she could see the grim marks of poison on him. He was almost certainly beyond saving, but she was not one to admit defeat so rapidly. She ran a finger across his shoulders, feeling where the bones were close to the surface of his skin, discovering the patterns of roughness, smoothness, vitality, and decay. His body was clean, the urgency was passed and she stooped to press her lips against his neck, feeling the pulse of his heart against her mouth.

There was a chill in his skin so she sprinted back up the stairs to retrieve a blanket. Her limbs ached from exhaustion and sleep-lessness, but she forced herself to make haste. His hair was still matted and filthy, and she set to work on it, wanting to know what color those locks would be once freed from the grayness of the ash.

It took her nearly an hour to clean his hair and untangle it with her fingers. Eventually she revealed black beneath the gray—dark curls that fell to his shoulders. The day was drawing to its end as she finally decided that he was as clean as she could get him. She had sweated through the afternoon while he moved between sleep and vague wakefulness. The sharp tang that rose from his body as she'd washed him had filled her with an intense yearning, but she'd forced herself to concentrate on what needed to be done.

At sunset, she should have set off for work, but decided to remain, to give this dying man what she could and bear the con-sequences later. As she wrapped the thin blanket about his shoul-ders, he returned once more from sleep. There was a hint of light in his eyes as he looked at her.

"You," he said softly, as though he knew who she was.

"How do you feel?" Cora asked.

"Like death."

"It's the ash. It's poisonous. It's been on your skin too long."

He nodded, this was not news to him.

"I can't do any more to help you," she added.

Cora knelt on the stone floor in front of him and placed her hands on either side of his head, torn between her own wants and her desire to help him. With time, she might have done more, but they had no time. She ran her fingers through his hair; it was soft now, clean and relatively good to touch. He smiled, leaning into her hand and she felt a rush of fire in the pit of her stomach. With her legs splayed, the scent of her body rose rapidly, and she knew he could probably smell her desire. She tried to concentrate her thoughts on healing him, on finding something to prolong life and give him a chance at surviving, but the tension between them was mounting and would not be denied.

It was the lightest touch, but it sent a shudder through her body. Cora felt his fingers through the rough fabric of her dress as he stroked her knees and thighs. Breathing seemed impossible; she was trembling with such force. Looking down into his dark eyes, she saw need burning there. She was the one who fell bewitched, abandoning all reason for the sake of a kiss. The taste of an ash-covered mouth in hers had haunted her, but now his flesh was uncovered and she did not have to struggle to find the warmth of life beneath his shell. The moist softness of his tongue transfixed her, her awareness filled by the closeness of his body as the desire to caress him overwhelmed her. The urge to snatch some moment of life back from the gaping maw of death was a potent aphrodisiac. Cora moved his hand up over her thigh, following the curve of her hip and waist, reveling in the roughness of his fingers against her skin. It was easy to push the blanket from his shoulders and warm his cold skin with kisses, to press her mouth to his neck and shoulders as though she meant to consume him entirely. It was easy to surrender to the joy of being touched by him, the glide of his hand under her clothing, over thigh and stomach, circling the curve of her rump and teasing her with easy familiarity.

"I'm dying, aren't I?" he asked her, his breath soft against her ear.

"Yes."

"Can I have a last request?"

"Of course."

"Stay with me."

It was all that she had wanted; some permission to remain and to give freely of herself. She looked into his eyes again. He knew death was coming and had resigned himself to it.

"I'm tired of this dirty world," he said. "You are the first pure, clean thing I've seen in such a long time."

"Let me warm you."

"Please."

She brought her body closer to his, feeling the coolness of him even through her garment. Cora smiled and kissed him, her heart aching.

"I'll stay for as long as you need me."

He discarded the blanket, baring himself to her, and she ran her fingers up and down his chest. He had been strong once and, in a cleaner world, with health and life, he would have been incomparable for beauty. Poisoned though he was, she could still love the light in his eyes, and the defiance in him that had sparked this last stand. She pulled the shapeless dress off over her head. There was nothing beneath it and he gasped audibly on seeing her. Not only was she clean, but her skin was still a flawless silk in perfect vitality. After more than a year in this ash-riddled world, she remained much as she had been before exile. There were tears in his eyes as he reached out to touch her again and she wondered when he had last looked upon skin free of sores and those dead, gray patches she had no proper term for. Perhaps he had never seen anyone like her before.

Though she could not drive the sickness from him, Cora hoped she could perhaps help him to forget about it for a time. As she bathed him in kisses, plunging her tongue into his mouth, she could hear the soft moans that escaped his lips, muffled by her own. These sounds were music to her. She ran her fingers down the bumps of his spine, over the hardness of his taut and toned muscles. She twined her fingers in his hair, letting the softness slide over her skin, leaning back so that her own hair brushed delightfully across her shoulder blades. From time to time she would pause in her touching and kissing, to look into his face, needing to check again that this was indeed what he wanted from her. He was weak and weary, but that did not matter at all in some ways. Each time his looks answered her with encouragement, and his hands would stray over her again, circling her breasts, or her hips.

His body grew feverishly hot as she caressed him, and she indulged a futile hope that he might somehow sweat out the poison. When he raised his hands to grasp her hips and pull her down upon him, she did not need to ask what he wanted of her. There was so much hunger in the alignment of his lips, such need burning in those exquisitely dark eyes. She wanted nothing more than to take him out of the world of death and insanity for a while, to let her health ward off his sickness for a time. She sank onto him, surprised at the sudden hardness between them, the rising masculine power she thought would surely have been ravaged away. This was a gift she could not refuse. He was unmistakably hard for her, and she slipped her hand down to test the potency of his desire. He gasped deliciously as she squeezed him, and grew harder yet against her hand.

The flame of his life burned brighter as death approached. He was utterly present now, no traces of confusion or failing awareness in his face. Looking into his eyes, she straddled him, and slid her body over his, drawing him deep inside her. Her insistent lust demanded speed and quick release, but she rocked slowly against him, not wanting to exhaust him and needing to prolong the intimacy, to draw out every last drop of wonder and feeling for them both. Each slow stroke brought new sensations. The sheen of sickness on his skin only made him seem more beautiful to her. Life was all around them then, strong and free-flowing as though the toxic world beyond were merely an illusion. His mouth on her skin sent shivers of pleasure through her and, delighted by these sensations, she threw back her head and laughed, letting the sound of her unleashed happiness echo through the empty basement. This was a different kind of insanity altogether, something rich and vibrant and joyful, a madness that could shake off the horrors she had witnessed and make the world afresh.

She clung to him, fingers digging into his shoulders, panting shallow breaths as every part of her strained toward new levels of feeling. She was beyond lust, now, beyond need or simple sexual hunger, moving in a slow, certain rhythm toward something else, something too mysterious for names or human constructs. She felt his hands on her hips, holding her steady, helping her onward, and buried her face against his shoulder, feeling his hair against her neck and arm. Time had lost all form or meaning for her, she knew only the slow unfurling of her being as her spirit unraveled, opened, blossomed, trembling in a slow eruption that took her, wordless and overwhelmed into a moment of pure bliss. She shook against him, and he held her firmly, not letting those violent tremors separate them. She could feel the throbbing gush of his release, the warmth of fluids shot into the core of her being. For a few seconds, or perhaps longer, she knew that they inhabited the same transcendent place, bodies and souls mingled in absolute harmony. She could hear the beating of his heart, the rattle of his breath.

"I love you," he said, and she knew it was true.

Surfacing was like emerging from the brilliance of a sun, or stepping from the vast darkness of space into something more solid and familiar again. They lay together, limbs entwined, bodies flushed with warmth and a buzzing energy that seemed to dance and sing through Cora's veins. For a long while they remained silent, inhabiting the aftermath of passion, the sense of unity found and lost again.

"You are an angel, a goddess," he whispered to her, his fingers in her hair and trailing over her face.

"No," she answered gently, "just another lost soul."

She kissed him softly, wanting to cling to this enchantment for as long as she could.

She had seen it all before, sitting as a silent witness to lives as they ended. The ash could leave you sick and depleted for years, and then one day it would become more than the body could bear, then you melted into a final fever and the true madness that came just before death. It could come at any time, without reason. She had seen men they had to hold down to stop them from harming others as the final moments came, but it was not that way for everyone. Perhaps Rill had been right she thought, perhaps she had finally become one of the good guys.

When eventually Cora's lover was too weary to do more, she held him, stroking his long dark curls with her hands and yearning once again to heal his dying body. It seemed so unjust, having made so deep a connection and seen the possibility of such profound love, to have it all torn away.

"Stay with me," she pleaded. "Stay with me."

"I would . . ." his voice was weak suddenly and the sound of it frightened her.

Too much time had passed and there was little to do but wait and watch. He was growing still, and silent, slipping away with each slow breath. There was no fighting it.

She knew he was there long before he emerged from the shadows. The dying man in her arms looked up, a faint smile playing on his lips. For a while these three regarded one another.

"Don't take him," she asked, knowing even then that it was pointless to do so. There is no bargaining with Death.

"It is his time."

Cora's lover turned to look at her. His dark eyes were bright with tears.

"Thank you," he murmured.

Then he was gone and the body in her arms was already growing cold. It was a sudden ripping away of life and hope, a loss that pierced her to the core and she bent over him, letting her hair fall into his face and her tears wash his cheeks. It was only then she realized that she had never asked him his name.

⁓

AT THE WAR crimes trial nearly two years previously, they had said a lot of things about redemption, and she had thought at the time how smug and self-assured they had sounded, even through the translators. She had listened with dull hatred to the presiding powers of the conquering race. It was evident that they meant to foist their dubious values on everyone else no matter what. She had not regretted her work then, nor the weapons that her research had created, only that there had not been time to make more of them, and that in the end they had lost. When they sent her to end her days on a poisoned, dying world, she thought their remarks about redemption were just another vile hypocrisy. Looking through a veil of tears at the dead man in her arms, Cora wondered. She was not who she had once been. The last year, the last few hours even, had changed her beyond all recognition. It did not matter if they came and swept her away, sentence completed, or if they left her here to rot, she was moving on. Slowly, she lowered the dead man to the floor, pressing a final kiss to his forehead before standing awkwardly and walking away.

Hubris

Jean Roberta

I: Kore

I've never seen a whole unit of the women warriors, although I sometimes used to see a scout on the horizon, usually at twilight. How I want to see them, and how I dread such a terrible sight! The women who ride horses are said to bring death and sorrow to everyone who sees them. Why should such a fate excite me?

Those who challenge the will of the gods are possessed by hubris, the arrogance which can never be forgiven. My father claims that the Amazons will be broken because they cannot accept the way things are. It is said that they cut off their own breasts and train for war until they no longer look like women.

News comes to us from bigger towns about the great losses men have inflicted on them. They don't seem to make as many raids now as when I was a child. If their tribe is growing smaller, what will happen to us civilized women once the wild ones are gone? Men will lose a word they use to terrify us, and we will lose a secret source of hope.

I fear for them. I fear for myself.

As the date of my wedding approaches, I am haunted by dreams of the women warriors. I feel as if their great leaders of the past—Penthesilea, Hippolyta—have ridden into my unguarded mind at the head of an army which has set up an enemy camp within the walls of my skin. I know they have come to burn our houses and our crops, and to kill our men. They are as relentless as the Furies. In my dreams I am always spared, but everything I depend on is destroyed, leaving me alone and free.

I am no longer a true virgin: self-contained, unpossessed. Jason, named after the great captain of legend, came to me soon after our betrothal. He followed me to the river, where he playfully lifted me in his arms and threw me into the water. I splashed him with it as he waded toward me, laughingly threatening to teach me obedience. When he held me and kissed my wet mouth, I could accept his threats as those of a lover.

He entered me with one finger under the water, as though I were a captured naiad. I cried out, more from surprise than from pain, and he soothed me with kisses. He promised me that his love-spear would bring me great pleasure on our wedding night. Does he want to give me pleasure for my sake, or for his?

Jason is the finest man my father could find for me, and I would not exchange him for another. I know that he expects me to grow into a grateful and loyal wife, one with no trace of Amazon willfulness. I cannot become what he expects.

My aunts would say that my thoughts come from my womb, which needs a man's seed. They think I must be married soon because my honor is in danger. I know the truth of that. Marriage would destroy any honor I have left.

I will not marry the man chosen to be my master. There is a monster, a snake-haired medusa, inside me who could free herself by strangling her bridegroom while he is weak and trusting. I will not expose Jason to an enemy who is still hidden from him. I will not grow a poison crop of hatred for him, or provoke his contempt for me.

I know of no way to prevent my marriage, but it must not happen. What if hubris is inborn, and not chosen? I know so little and feel so much.

II: *Amazon*

I will never forget the sound of earthbound thunder as they rode into our village, the winking tips of their spears forming a shield before them. The sky was black and almost moonless as though to cloak their intentions. I had not slept that night, as though I were a guard on watch for the raiders.

I screamed, whether in fear or welcome I am not sure. In an instant, the sound of my voice was drowned out by the crackle of flames as their archers set fire to our houses. There was no safe hiding place, so I ran into the streets. Some of our snipers fired at them, but our unprepared men were no match for the ranks of warriors and their stamping horses.

If they were going to kill me, I wanted them to do it fast. "Take me!" I shrieked, wondering if the barbarian women could understand Greek. Like gods, however, they seemed intent on a mission in which my life played no part. It seemed as if my people were invisible to them until one of us tried to defend what little of our property was left.

They were trotting past me, leaving as quickly as they came. Our village, our familiar houses and fields, our terrified goats and useless amulets, were their strategic target, marked for destruction as I had been marked for marriage. Civilized people, Greeks of both sexes, seemed irrelevant to the wild women.

"Take me with you!" I screamed. I would have preferred the shock of a spear in my heart to the desolation in which they seemed willing to leave me. On a whim, a hawk-nosed rider slowed enough to reach for me. I climbed onto the horse's back behind her.

We rode across the plain for miles under a black velvet sky dotted with stars. As the horse beneath me ran with her own gait, the lips between my legs met her backbone over and over until I was sore and breathless. My breasts pressed into the back of the warrior who had claimed me as I clung to her with the strength of my desperation. *Use me as you see fit*, I told her silently, *but don't leave me alone.*

At length, we stopped beside a river. The sound of flowing water under the tender pink sky of early dawn was like the music of Orpheus. Like the water, I trembled and swayed after jumping off the horse. I lay on the warm breast of the earth, entranced by the rhythm of my own breath.

One woman made a fire, and by its light I could study my strange new companions. Some set up portable houses made of hide to form a village as temporary as a dream. Someone kicked my bottom, urging me upright. I seized a length of hide and held it so that one of the warriors could secure it to the ground with a peg. I hoped I was useful enough.

As soon as I could be spared, I crept back to the warmth of the fire and gazed into its leaping flames as though they held visions of my future.

I awoke to feel strong arms holding me and someone's hot breath on my face. I drank from an old wineskin which was held to my mouth, and then chunks of cooked meat were fed to me. The woman who held me had brass rings in her ears and her beak of a nose. She looked barbaric, but her smile was as warm as the heavy breasts that pressed moistly against me.

The food and wine restored my energy, and I felt as though I could fly. The Amazon who held me spoke to me in her harsh language. I could feel the question in her arms. I moved so that one of my breasts brushed against her as I forced myself to look into her eyes. She uncovered me with one firm gesture that pulled the hem of my chiton up to my collarbone.

I wondered whether the women warriors ever violated unwilling women prisoners, and whether the victims ever went mad from the humiliation. I wondered what it would feel like to be a proud, trapped captive or a rebel caught trying to escape, and to struggle frantically while being held and entered ruthlessly, invaded in the private parts of my body that even I had never searched so deeply for fear of hurting myself. I believed that such a thought should inspire fear or hatred in me, but the thing I feared most from the warriors was their indifference. Only that, I thought, would drive me out of my reason.

Someone spoke to the woman who held me; her name sounded like that of Hera, queen of the gods, and that is what I have called her ever since. She answered her fellow tribeswoman, and all the surrounding women laughed. I was afraid of the laughter of killers.

Hera stroked one of my nipples. A bolt of desire shot like an arrow from my aroused breast to the center of pleasure between my legs, and I almost cried out.

Someone played a song of longing on a reed flute while someone else beat time on a drum. The melody suggested secret pleasures, while the rhythm of the drum was like pounding hooves and a pounding heart.

Hera shifted me so that she could kiss my lips. The hot blood taste of the meat she had eaten entered my mouth with her tongue. It tasted like the blood of virginity, offered and accepted. I gasped for breath, panting against her heat, her desire, her strength, and her sureness.

Hera spread my legs apart with one hand, and dipped a finger into my wet entrance. She spread my fluids over my clitoris, the little button that some Eastern people call the most shameful part of a woman, the one that must be removed. Mine was shameless, and it responded to her at once.

My seducer spread my own nectar on my face, a smear on each cheek. Thus was I adorned.

I wanted to be her bride or her companion, according to her culture. My new lover had a charisma that invited my trust, and I needed to have faith in the kindness of at least one of the wild women.

Hera pressed her warm, hairy lower mouth into mine and began a kind of horizontal dance on me. I moaned, wanting her. She slid down my body. Before I could see what she held in her hand, she had pushed a smooth metal rod up into me. The pain was like a lightning flash that soon gave way to the pleasure of cool water in a hot mouth. Hera worked her merciless, satisfying tool in me as though she wanted to claim the unexplored wilderness in my body and my soul. I felt I was being ravished by Aphrodite herself.

My pleasure became almost unbearable. When Hera gently stroked my swollen button to the rhythm of her strokes and our breathing, I shuddered in uncontrollable ecstasy.

She slowly removed the instrument of my violation and plunged it into her own mouth to taste my essence. I felt myself flushing with a confusion of shame and pride.

I knew that if I ever saw my father again, he would say I was ruined. I felt more truly married than he could know.

When at length I fell asleep again in Hera's arms, I dreamed about the dead men of my village crossing the river Styx. They seemed to be grieving for me as I grieved for those who had cared for me in their way. I hoped that Jason was still alive, and I wished him a loving wife who would bear him many children. In the land of dreams, I kissed him farewell.

In the days to come, I was betrothed to the spear, the arrow, and the sword. I soon lost my maidenhood in a deeper sense than ever before when I first shed blood not my own. The path of a warrior is not easy, but I have lived more fully in the turmoil of war than I ever did in my protected girlhood.

I grieve for the men I have killed, although they were my enemies. It is a paradox of manhood that many are made hard with life by mortal wounds. I have ushered many of my victims into death with the comfort of my hands and my mouth. Perhaps we will be at peace when we meet again.

My tribe has been dying, woman by woman, for two generations. My beautiful Hera died with her spear in her hand, leaving this world with her honor intact. The rest of us will follow her, sooner or later, and our culture will be buried by our conquerors.

I hope I will breathe my last while lying on the earth's breast, kissed by the sun and serenaded by the songs of birds. I can imagine my bones crumbling, preparing to roam the world on the restless wind. I will not be remembered by name, but a generation of kores I have never met, the maidens of the future, will feel my touch on their skin. It will be enough.

Filoxenia

Sage Vivant

*C*LAIRE DID NOT know how she got home from Kapos's market. Her breathing was a bit faster than usual and dust from the road coated her black shoes. The merest suggestion of moisture between her legs led her to conclude she had walked the dirt road through the village. But she remembered nothing of that walk.

Resignedly, she lifted the two heavy bags to the fine wooden table Yannis had built when they were first married. Since his death, she floated through her days. It wasn't that she forgot things; she simply did not observe them as they happened.

Sometimes this disturbed her. Often, it did not.

In the eight months since his death, she continued to wear the traditional black. She did not socialize. Her neighbor, Eleni, often came to sit with her in the afternoons until the woman had to return to the maintenance of her own home.

Eleni meant well with her encouraging words and cataloguing of all the eligible men of Moulos, but Claire had little interest in the future. No man would replace Yannis.

Yannis, with his booming voice and soft touch. The way he could purr a command at her and make her wish she could obey him twice to ensure his pleasure.

As she unpacked the fresh lamb shank Kapos had cut for her,

her eyes filled with nostalgic tears for her strong husband. She trembled, recalling his lesson about the beauty of the flesh.

Walking by Kapos's market one day, a slab of finely veined lamb hung in the window. Its flesh, a succulent rouge, drew her eye and evoked both hunger and embarrassment. Yannis turned to her as they stood transfixed by the meat.

"Do you feel the stir of blood at your sex?"

She flushed and dared not look at him, else he would read her thoughts. But she knew she must answer.

"Yes, Yanni."

"Do you know *why* you feel it?"

"No."

"Because you are the lamb. The shy beauty who builds its deliciousness under a thick coat. It lives, feeding its flesh, yet it does not fulfill its destiny until it displays its juicy, tender meat. It is most desired when it is viewed by those whose hunger it promises to satisfy."

"You would have me displayed in Kapos's window?" She teased, hoping to deflect him from his line of thinking.

"I would have you displayed for all! In a window far larger than Kapos can provide," he said definitively, leading her away from the window.

They walked home with no further reference to the lamb. But once they were home, he removed her clothes with wordless, gentle efficiency. Her naked, eager gooseflesh blushed in anticipation. He did not touch her but sat at one of the kitchen table's chairs (perhaps the one she now sat in herself, she mused) and let his eyes slowly roam her compact body. He asked her to show him her backside.

When he'd stared at her nakedness for a period that seemed to satisfy him, he commanded her to follow him to the small attic. The driest place in the old house, it was where they sometimes placed meat or basil from the garden to extract excess moisture. Small windows let in surprisingly abundant sunlight. Old meat hooks and randomly placed bars protruded from the walls and ceiling.

"You must be displayed like the tasty lamb," he explained softly as he collected ropes and rags from around the room. "Make me desire you, *minorio*," he instructed his "lamb" quietly, looping knots in torn sheets he wound around her small ankles and wrists.

She swooned now at the memory of her buttocks in the air, facing the largest window. Bent at the waist, ankles tied together, her wrists connected to a drying rod attached to the wall at waist level, she displayed herself to him for nearly an hour.

Sometimes, she felt he'd left the room. But then, suddenly, he'd speak to her and she'd feel his breath on her firm, round, exposed cheeks.

"The neighbors can see your juicy fullness, Claire. They watch you spread your legs and see your pink, ripe center. Their hunger makes them think only of feasting at this glorious bounty that they know belongs only to me."

His slaps to her bottom warmed her and she imagined that tendrils of smoke must be curling upward from her sex. She could smell her own arousal and grew increasingly less concerned about the neighbors. When he finally penetrated her, her inner walls pulled him up into her with wild gratitude.

Her reverie was abruptly interrupted by a knock at her door. It was a stranger's knock and she hesitated to answer. The insistent knuckles rapped again.

"*Neh?*" She called out, approaching the door.

"I come on behalf of your husband!"

Her hands fluttered to her face and tiny sounds choked in her throat. Surely, no one would mock the dead with such cruelty as to disturb a grieving widow? Had her unpredictable imagination conjured this visit?

Fueled by the longing for any connection to dear Yannis, her feet propelled her forward and she opened the door.

A handsome man of her own height stood framed in her doorway. In his Greek soldier's uniform and his dark hair combed neatly, he exuded authority and credibility. Yet, a visit by any of the Greek military was rarely cause for celebration. She stared at him with fearful hope.

"You are Claire Tsafutis?"

"*Neh*," she affirmed hesitantly.

"I am Kevin Kandaris. I have searched many months for you!"

She blinked at him, wondering why finding her should be of such importance. Some schoolchildren walked by and stared at the soldier on her doorstep. She invited him in, although she knew this visit was already being discussed among the villagers.

She served him water and ouzo and began to boil some coffee. He explained his close friendship with Yannis during the war, how often her husband had spoken of her and his love for her. He pulled a worn, creased envelope from his breast pocket and asked that she read it. It was written in her husband's hand; of that, she was certain. Trembling, she read the contents.

> Dearest Claire,
>
> I write this letter to be given you by Kevin in the event of my death. He is a man of the finest character and I trust him as I would trust you, dearest lamb. He is unmarried but healthy and strong. He needs a good woman to provide him with those comforts of home otherwise unavailable to him. It is my wish that you serve Kevin as you have served me; with sweet obedience. Out of respect for your heart, I ask that you marry him only if you come to love him.

SHE NOTICED THE letter had been sealed but opened by someone who was not she. Mr. Kandaris knew of Yannis's plan before she did!

And what of Yannis's request? Surely, he would have realized that she would show proper *filoxenia* to Kevin Kandaris, especially when she knew his relationship to Yannis. To open one's home, and purse, to a friend or stranger in need was the duty of all Greeks. She would not fail in such a duty.

But her blood ran cold at her husband's request to "provide him with those comforts of home otherwise unavailable to him." If it meant what she thought, how could she not marry him? Why would Yannis place her in such a vulnerable position? If the villagers found out, she would be a social and moral outcast.

His steady watchfulness made her conscious of her silence. She knew this man required some response from her.

"You are welcome in my home, Mr. Kandaris," she said quietly, then added, "Every Greek is bound by *filoxenia*." The tiniest wet trickle worked its way along her most private folds as she thought of her duty to this man.

"I know you are a good and kind woman, Mrs. Tsafutis. Your husband explained to me in fine detail your wifely gifts. While I am here at the request of your husband, indeed in place of your husband, I expect your hospitality would extend beyond that of traditional *filoxenia*."

"You have been sent by my husband and yet you are not my husband. How may I act as wife without bringing disgrace upon myself?"

"I am willing to marry you."

She turned away as her eyes threatened tears. "I cannot marry a man I do not know!"

"Then you must come to know me. I will teach you who I am and what I like, what I need and what I desire. Let me prove that I am trustworthy."

"It will take a long time and I still grieve—"

"No. I can show you in a short time that to obey me will suit you better than to deny me. You will see that trusting me is easier than avoiding me."

She shook her head unconsciously as she moved to the rumbling coffeepot on the stove. Her back was to the man at her table.

"You would not refuse your husband if he were alive. Why do you refuse him in death?"

She instantly swung her small frame around to face her guest. The blood in her body flowed like a wild river, close to the surface of her skin, vainly seeking escape through her pores.

"How dare you accuse me of such disobedience! I never refused him! But this is so . . . it's just . . . different." She began to weep, furious with herself for doing so. He immediately rose and went to her, embracing her protectively. The weave of his uniform felt rough against her cheek.

"Forgive me for upsetting you," he cooed. "I should have more respect for your modesty. Yannis told me you were a faithful, compliant wife. I know you do not desire to refuse him, but that you do not know me. Trust me to win you. Can you try? For Yannis?"

She sniffled and remained in his embrace. "For Yannis," she whimpered. *Oh, Yanni!* Her heart wailed. *Why have you asked this of me?*

"You will do as I ask, then?"

"Yes," she sighed.

He took her shoulders in his hands and held her eyes with a kindliness she had not seen earlier.

"Remove your blouse and your undergarments."

Her gaze locked to his with an eerie, magical strength that jellied her knees. Her fingers worked the small buttons efficiently and her blouse and undershirt were soon strewn on the kitchen tile.

He returned to his seat and finished his ouzo with one decisive swallow. Eyes closed, he let the resultant burning in his throat subside. When he was ready, he viewed her exposed breasts like a patron at an art show.

"Yes, Yannis was correct. You are very small," he mused.

Her color deepened with her shame. She hated her breasts and believed the bosomy neighbor women who pronounced her unfeminine. They warned her against having children, who would most certainly starve at her boyish teats.

"How beautiful and youthful they are," Kevin continued. "Move about the kitchen as you normally would and see how they never impede your activities!" He paused as she struggled to consider whether his observation was actually a command to her. "Go ahead! Move about!"

She busied herself with unpacking the bags from Kapos. His eyes on her breasts made the nipples poke forward with curiosity. She wanted to keep her arms over them but knew he would scold her if she did not move naturally. He continued to stare.

Her industry pleased him and allowed her to avoid eye contact with him. She began with washing the potatoes for the stew she planned to prepare.

His hands, now encased in his leather gloves, suddenly covered her naked breasts and began to rub. The soft, worn leather over her nipples produced a sharp, exciting friction. Smooth as skin but without the moisture, the cowhide boldly tantalized what it caressed.

He increased the rhythm of his strokes and she instinctively pushed out her chest to revel in the soothing currents of near-pain circulating around her nipples. Faster and faster he rubbed, faster and faster came her breath. The sensation sent messages to her awakening sex, now engorged with need.

"You have never felt such pleasure from your breasts, have you, Claire?" he whispered.

She dropped the potatoes and clutched the edge of the sink. His stroking was rapid now and she bit her lip to keep from asking him to touch the slippery, hidden spot under her skirt.

He removed his hands suddenly and she grimaced with unsatisfied desire. But then his hands were pushing up her skirt, past the back of her thighs and then over her bottom. He gripped the edges of her cotton unmentionables and ripped the delicately woven garment open, tearing until she felt cool air licking at her buttocks. The waistband still encircled her waist and she realized he'd slit the undergarment wide open to reveal her. With one hand, he held her skirt up while he inserted his other hand between her warm thighs. She prayed she'd kept her juices contained and that he would not think her wanton if he discovered the release of her enjoyment along the inside of her leg.

He spent little time at her thighs. His small, agile fingers probed and tickled her curled tufts of hair through the torn cloth until they found her opening.

"You have shown me much respect and welcome by letting me excite you," he proclaimed in a most understated way. "I think I should like you for dinner." He picked up one of the carrots she'd bought that day and returned yet again to his seat at the table. She turned to face him and her skirt covered her once again.

"Let us make a special stew," he said, motioning her to approach.

When she was close enough, he held her hips firmly and positioned her between himself and the table, with her back to him.

"Bend over and lay on the table," he instructed.

She obeyed, placing her torso prostrate on the wooden expanse. He slid her skirt up over her raised bottom and ripped her private clothing completely open. The very sound of such aggression brought color to her body and she feared her bottom reddened most visibly.

He gripped her legs near her knees and gently separated them. The carrot hit her blushing derriere unexpectedly and with a force that made her gasp. The vegetable slapped her repeatedly. But between contact with her sensitive skin, Kevin rubbed her private lips with wide, circular strokes. His caress seemed to take some of the pain away.

When the carrot had touched her often enough to leave welts, he inserted the carrot into her succulence. The mottled exterior sliding along her dark tunnel stimulated unfamiliar sensations inside her. She could not allow herself to think that it was a carrot from Kapos's market pleasuring her, else she could never purchase produce from the kind old man again.

Kevin drove the long vegetable into her with long, slow, rhythmic strokes. The trailing green stems brushed her legs suggestively. Unlike Yannis, he spoke as he had his way with her.

"Oh, yes! See how it parts your thick lips, collecting your precious juice as it enters. How deeply it impales you, my sweet!"

As he pushed the vegetable into her and titillated her wet, swollen sex, another knock sounded at the door. Eleni's knock. The woman must have known Claire had a guest and came now to satisfy her curiosity.

Kevin continued to slide the raw carrot in and out of her as if no danger or interruption threatened them. She raised her torso by pressing her palms to the tabletop.

"There is no need to stir yourself," he replied authoritatively. "I want you to ask who it is."

"It is Eleni," she replied. She moved her hips in small gyrations in spite of herself. She wondered how close his face was to her musky crevice and flushed again at her own unexplained ardor.

"If she is a friend, please invite her in."

"What?? No! I cannot!"

His teeth bit into one of the welts on her rosy bottom. She swooned silently and blinked back tears. She could not speak.

"Would you prefer that I ask her to come in?"

"Come in, Eleni!" She called out weakly. Such dread had never so consumed her as now. Eleni entered the house.

The scene, her widowed neighbor exposing her buttocks to a strange man who sat calmly as he inserted a carrot into her private parts, confused her initially. She processed what she saw quickly enough, though, and shut the door behind her.

"What goes on here?" She did not venture forward nor did she flee. The carrot continued its diligent performance.

Claire held Eleni's gaze as best she could. "This is Mr. Kandaris. He was a good friend of Yannis' in the war." The carrot pushed itself in rapidly and more deeply. "Uhhh!" She gasped in punctuation.

Eleni stood silently and then nodded. "Ah! *Filoxenia!*" She whispered knowingly.

"I see you are both good Greek women to so readily uphold such an old custom," he commented, pulling out the carrot completely. Claire heard the snap of his teeth on the vegetable and knew he was making a show of eating what had been so thoroughly inside her. Eleni watched with rapturous horror. He chewed for some time; Kapos sold only very fresh produce.

"Have you ever seen your friend displayed this way, ready to receive a man who desires her?"

The woman swallowed and wet her lips. "Yes. Yes, I have seen it."

"Eleni!"

"I saw her with Yannis," she continued boldly, looking directly at Kevin. "He would tie her to hooks or furniture or anything that would anchor her. She would be splayed like a fish at market, exposing whatever he wanted to see!" She hurled the words into the air, leaving Claire to wonder where the blame was being placed for what she saw.

"You watched such behavior often?"

"Yes. They did not bother about modesty near their windows."

"Well, then, what better punishment for our beautiful but immodest friend than to have her penetrated while you are close enough to hear her cries of pleasure?"

Eleni's bosom heaved with excitement. "You will have her now, in front of me?"

"*Filoxenia*," he reminded her. "Stand up, please, Claire."

Her skin, drenched with sweat, separated from the table reluctantly. She stood upright but kept her eyes lowered, consumed by her own humiliation.

"Eleni, may I ask you to help in teaching our friend a lesson in modesty?"

Kevin asked Eleni to sit on the middle of the table with her legs open wide. But first she must remove all undergarments below her waist. This she did with great eagerness. Claire was placed on the table once again, this time dorsally. She was told to press the top of her head against Eleni's fragrant, bushy womanhood.

"You will carry the scent of your friend in your hair," he explained.

Eleni placed her fingers on Claire's tiny breasts and fluttered them over her nipples, again at Kevin's direction. Of her own free will, however, she pinched the nipples between her fingers and rolled and kneaded their pink hardness mercilessly as Claire squirmed with hot delight.

Kevin's solid flesh burrowed into her as he held her legs up high in the air. Every thrust pushed her head more firmly into Eleni's moistness. Her nipples grew in her neighbor's hands while her grateful sex hugged and squeezed its pumping invader.

Embarrassment gave way to desire as her body surrendered to the relentless attentions of her friend and visitor. Her insides contracted with violent spasms until she could not recall why restraint was necessary. Her release shook her body with joyful abandon, leaving her to weep with thanks.

IN THE YEARS that followed, the eccentric widow became a model of *filoxenia* for the villagers of Moulos, who marveled at how selflessly she served the man who had somehow been friend to her long-dead husband.

The Spunk Gun

Michèle Larue

Translated from the French by Noel Burch

*L*ÈA ROVED THE streets of Paris on her silver motorbike, water pistol loaded with egg white. It was near dusk on a summer evening, no city noises disturbed the classy 7th arrondissement. In courtyards and private gardens concealed behind imposing stone facades, birds were chirping. Gripping her see-through plastic toy, Lèa studied the rare pedestrians from behind the anonymity of her full-face helmet. An uptight looking man wearing moccasins had them dowsed with a long jet. She spotted an overdressed teenager—side-part, Bermudas, and yachting shoes. "Bourgeois!" she shouted, squirting him as he stepped off the curb. The boy sniffed suspiciously at his sleeve.

On rue Barbet de Jouy, Lèa tossed her weapon into a sewer mouth, and parked her machine on the sidewalk. She liberated her hair, locked the helmet into the trunk, and was soon taking two steps at a time up a stairwell too narrow for an elevator. Welcome Aboard! said the blue doormat with a jolly sailboat on it.

Fresh as a soap ad under blonde bangs, Clèmence met her at the door, wearing indeed a ship captain's smile of triumph, navy blue slacks, and a gold chain bracelet and signet ring. Lèa's blank stare, her tousled black mane when she looked down at the absurd doormat as if unsure about coming in, roused a surge of love in Clèmence which softened her eyes: the faded blue irises shined feverishly, only to go brittle and worried again when she looked away. Clèmence had a haughty, controlling voice that clashed with her short stature and doll-like wrists. She drew her visitor firmly to her. Playing hostess made Clèmence feel confident and she expected instant recognition for the meal she had cooked with pride:

"Come on, give us a kiss. I did everything myself again, you'll love it . . ."

Lightly, Lèa brushed her lips over the expectant mouth. Clèmence clung to her.

"You're not going to force me, are you?" Lèa protested grumpily, going to the sofa and plopping down on it. "I hate the way you're always demanding tokens of affection. The presents and all the things you do for me, they're just bargaining chips . . . Think I'm impressed with your money?"

Clèmence gave a little laugh that soured toward the end and murmured: "Now darling, you're not starting that again . . ."

Wedged uncomfortably against a heart-shaped cushion, Lèa bit her lips to keep from answering back and Clèmence dropped into her arms with a sigh.

"Fuck me."

Lèa pushed her away roughly and stood up brushing her jeans with the back of her hand, her tone aloof as she asked about dinner.

Back on familiar ground now, Clèmence pointed with pride at the table set for two. The folksy embroidered cloth was strewn with more of the nautical themes—aquamarine glass baubles. A possessive look crept into her eyes as she came on to Lèa again. Pulling her lover forcibly to her, and as if about to receive the Holy Spirit she opened her mouth, waiting for a kiss. But Lèa stuck to social amenities instead, prying herself loose and going over to a shelf where she eyed some sea-blue packages.

Playing fairy godmother always made Clèmence happy and she plunked herself down in the middle of the sofa once more, giving

Lèa permission to open "her" presents. Clèmence got a high from watching her protégée tear at the wrappers like a child, trying to guess what was inside each from the shape of the package. There were little balls of perfume for the bath called "Bleu Mèditerrane," seashell soap bars, an antique-style cut-glass bottle of Montana perfume—blue as well.

"You're hung up on hygiene!" Lèa chided her, sniffing the scent of soap in her partner's ear before she stuck her tongue into it. But the voracious kiss she finally begrudged her ended in an ugly sucking sound. Clèmence clasped her hands to her temples:

"Is that how you thank me, you nasty little brat!"

"You forget we're the same age, even if I do look younger," Lèa shot back. "And all these presents, it's just too much. There's no reason for any of this. You know I hate taking things from you, it makes me feel uncomfortable."

"You'll use them, though. And you'll think about me everyday."

"How selfish can a person get?" Lèa retorted, running one finger up Clèmence's cheek and along her eyebrow, gazing at her with petulant eyes. Despite the exasperatingly clean scent her benefactress exuded and the creases the iron left in her linen blouse, Lèa was jealous of her velvet skin. Here she was at forty, too, practically done for. She was annoyed at herself for all those cigarettes . . . that depressing thought made her sink her teeth into Clèmence's lips. After a few seconds of this—all too few, her victim thought—she released her grip and proposed they eat.

"Some Cuban music?" Clèmence offered, skipping around behind Lèa to serve.

"If you like . . ."

"Bring any black lovers back from the West Indies last time?"

"That's one of your favorite fantasies, isn't it? Deep down, you want to see me fuck a Black. That would really turn you on, wouldn't it?"

"I'm sure you have black lovers!"

Lèa was getting fed up with this masochistic talk.

Clèmence liked to picture Lèa, her dream woman, swarming with lovers she herself would never think of balling in a million years. The only time Clèmence had even seen a black man up close was at the *Palais de Bercy*, watching Prince through binoculars. She was a true-blue lesbian; the pleasure of choosing between cock and cunt was definitely not for her. She wouldn't admit it to herself, but in fact she was terrified by the idea of all that freedom, moving from one sex to the other, changing tack whenever an interesting new sail peaked over the horizon. At the same time, she was frightfully jealous . . . and it turned her on.

"I can still get married at forty, I've had several proposals. Good-looking men, divorced, all top executives."

"Their names?" Lèa demanded.

"You don't know any of them."

"And may I ask what kind of sexual relations you plan to have in this future coupling of yours? Fellatio? Missionary style?"

"Yeah, well, you know . . . that's just in case you ditch me."

"Oh come on, there's never going to be a bust-up between us because we're not 'together' that way! How many times do I have to tell you? The couple you imagine we form is just your narcissistic projection. You're seeing me as your other self, a person you think you know because you imagine we're alike. You even think we have the same desires and the same feelings. That's just not true! There's a sexual thing between us, but beyond that, I feel only sympathy for you . . . perhaps affection . . ."

"Ah, there you see! We do have something in common!"

During dinner, Clèmence carried on about films and books she knew only through reviews she'd read, a confused monologue which mixed them all up. The opinions she picked up from *Tèlèrama*, *L'Express*, and *Le Point*, gave her the illusion of existing separately from Lèa. The latter said nothing: she knew her lover was incapable of listening. But whenever Clèmence turned her back, she'd yawn behind her hand.

Clèmence served up a strawberry charlotte from the best pastry shop in the *arrondissement*, and after that suggested they watch a video in the bedroom.

Her relations to machines were plagued by the same communication problems she had with humans. The TV picture was poor and it got worse the more she fiddled with it.

Lèa undressed, pulled back the covers and stretched out on the sea-blue sheets, gazing vacantly at the scrambled screen. When Clèmence caught sight of those rounded breasts, flat tummy, and plucked muff, her fingers went wild on the remote control.

She stammered: "Should I undress, too?"

"You little prig! Always simpering! Suit yourself, what do you want me to say?"

Clèmence removed her clothes methodically, taking time to turn her tights right-side out.

From her spot in the middle of the bed, legs spread brazenly apart, Lèa reached down to the carpet, contorting her hips and torso now as she searched for the remote. She was still feeling for it when Clèmence's tongue began to explore her exposed crotch. Lèa moved but Clèmence pursued her, crawling over the comforter. Lèa found the remote, lay back and started surfing the channels, leaving Clèmence's tongue free to roam. She adjusted the TV picture, got rid of a rapper in a black sweat suit singing "Horny Devil" and muted the sound. "Clitoris," she ordered and clicked the remote.

Clèmence's tongue drew tiny circles around the clit and it began to swell. She took it in her mouth and sucked, gently at first, then voraciously. On the screen, an aging blonde presented a close-up of a man's underpants with a horizontal fly. Lèa arched her back. The blonde slipped her hand into the fly, took it out and put it back in again, spreading her fingers.

Lèa punched the remote: a gangster was crawling past a huge yellow fire extinguisher. "G-spot!" she announced.

Trained to bring Lèa to a climax, Clèmence's tongue moved down a fraction of an inch to the designated spot on the rim of the gaping orifice. She started to slip her tongue inside, then teasingly stopped, withdrew, hovered, came in strong again, backed off and froze like a retriever pointing. On the screen, the villain fired a harpoon at a white-coated professor who collapsed against a blackboard.

"Anus!"

Instantly, Clèmence stuck one, then two fingers into the pulsating cavern that opened like a tiny mouth. The variety of caresses the tongue was still lavishing between clitoris and wet vagina had a contagious effect on the anus: deftly manipulated, it began slowly to dilate.

Lèa's head began to float. The face of Dietrich the enchantress flashed by in black-and-white, and then the gangster came on again, clinging to the extinguisher and pulling himself to his feet. Overcome with lust, Lèa's mind was quite empty as she murmured "not yet, no, no, wait . . . ," trying to delay the explosive orgasm her lover was preparing with tongue and fingers. A lock of hair tickled her belly button. Immediately, an itch ran down her legs and up her sides. She waited until Clèmence wasn't looking and scratched herself, but there was no holding back the waves that thrilled through her ass and rose to the small of her back. She clenched her teeth and swooned, arching her spine and nibbling the corner of a pillow, then sucking at it feverishly. Bit by bit, the whole lower part of her body, skillfully kneaded by Clèmence's wiry fingers, had become one vast sea of spasms, with all tactile discriminations banished: a dildo, a stick of wood, or the edge of a bathtub would have done just as well, anything to rub against.

Clèmence took advantage of a fleeting opportunity to catch her breath and ease the stiffness in her neck. Her eyes flitted to the TV. On the screen, the gangster was untying a woman who lay spread-eagle on an iron cot. Lèa locked her legs around Clèmence's head, forcing it away from the screen. The tongue resumed its task and Lèa closed her eyes once more. She concentrated on relaxing her back muscles, letting her body levitate like some celestial canopy, open to every sensual delight. Forcing her eyes slightly

open, she caught a glimpse of Clèmence's delicate nose lined up
with her slit. The sight repelled her and she shut her eyes again,
walling up inside her own sensations. Thanks to Clèmence's
expertise, the climax finally came. Howling hoarsely, Lèa squirted
her juices into her lover's face.

Now comes the downside, Lèa thought to herself; returning the
favor. Clèmence's head was still between her thighs.

"You're too greedy," Lèa murmured as she tugged on her
friend's hair. "It's all over for me, beautiful." Sliding across the
quilt, Lèa pulled on the lips of the moist cunt in front of her now
and drew it firmly to her mouth. Clèmence's clitoris was amaz-
ingly long, nearly two inches. With her free hand, Lèa fumbled in
the pocket of her jeans in a heap on the carpet, took out a hair clip
and snapped it onto the stiff clit. Clèmence's vagina was gaping
like an ogre's mouth. Lèa began torturing the exposed pink flesh
and she could feel the contractions deep inside.

"Some day, teeth will grow out of these little horns of flesh I
feel in the mouth of this burning sheath of yours," she murmured, her inaudible monologue interrupted by a beseeching
gasp: "Hurt me." Clèmence's narrow ribcage and tiny breasts
arched upward in her desire for pain.

Sliding one finger, then two, then the whole hand into her
vagina, Lèa masturbated her. She repositioned herself. All her
energy was concentrated in her forearm. Her fist slid past the slippery, resilient walls, rammed against the back of the cavern again
and again. Sweat ran down Lèa's forehead and onto Clèmence's
breasts. When Lèa sensed Clèmence was ready to come, her
punches on the back of the vagina quickened. She lifted a blond
lock and planted a big love bite on the woman's neck. Out of control now, Lèa slid her fist out, lifted her partner and deposited her
at the head of the bed facing the wall, then buried her fist inside
her again.

Mouth pressed to a picture glass, Clèmence spluttered like a
worn-out lightbulb, moaned, and finally collapsed gently onto the
pillows.

But when she saw Lèa putting on her shoes, she bounced off the bed.

"Where are you going? Aren't you going to spend the night with me? Look at the pretty sheets I bought just for you!" she begged.

The pillowcases were embroidered with trumpeting elephants, and the look Lèa gave them was as scathing as the one she gave Clèmence.

"You bought those sheets to please yourself. You'll excuse me, but I'm late for my date with a Black in a café at *Les Halles!*"

She made a beeline for the door and trampled her presents underfoot as she left.

Market Intimacies

Kiini Ibura Salaam

"*I*'M GOING TO market," Sunshine announced.

Talley grunted in response. Sunshine stood behind him, looking at the dirty exposed skin on the back of his neck. Talley didn't move an inch. He stayed hunched over the mound of tobacco spread on the table in front of him. Sunshine backed away from her husband, barely trembling. She wanted to say something fast and hard, leave some wounding and hurtful words lodged in his back, but she could dredge up no poison from her heart. She settled instead for disgust. An irritated hissing sound issuing from sucked teeth. A cold, turned shoulder, as she swept from the dark shack as quickly as her big woman legs would carry her.

Once outside, she squinted at the piercing early-morning sun. The hand that shaded her eyes was shaking. She gulped down her rage in deep wild breaths. When her fingers stopped trembling, Sunshine placed her hands on her belly and looked out into the dead fields. They were barren as was her home, as was her womb. The soil beneath her feet was riddled with seeds yet empty of sprouts. Even the orange trees down the road hadn't grown an inch since she took vows with Talley. She glanced back over her shoulder through the open doorway and speared Talley's spine with angry eyes. She could almost hear the maddening popping sound of his lips sucking on his dry, unlit pipe.

Cursing herself and her tomb of a marriage, Sunshine picked up her basket, rested it on her hip and swayed out of the yard. She went to a neighbor's field to pick wildflowers and went down to the river to rest them on a small mound of earth. With fluttering eyelids, she imagined the twisted blue creature sleeping within. The seed, their seed, that never got the chance to become a boy. Who knew this mini mountain, this bump on God's land would suck the love from Talley's heart? A dead clump of flesh surrounded by red dirt buried every caress, every lustful look, every semblance of desire Talley ever felt for his wife. After evenings of singing skin, nights of fire and wet kisses, and early mornings groaning oh-my-god, there was finally silence. Nothing, no amount of whispered remembrances or pleas from Sunshine's lips could court Talley back into bed with her. His hands, no longer open and caressing, were closed bitter fists. He held them still, did not beat her with them, but blamed her with every withheld touch.

Sunshine tightened her arms around her basket as an arrow of isolation shot through her body. Everybody knows every seed planted wasn't meant to grow, the midwife had consoled her. She stood and turned away from the grave, her heart raging, her teeth biting irritation into the soft inside of her cheek. When her heavy steps had carried her to the market, she halted. She could see people milling around, produce in hand, but she wasn't ready to enter. She wished she wasn't so stubbornly proud, then she could sit down, rest her basket on the ground, and unpeel her sorrows. Sunshine wiped the dampness from her forehead and temples and turned away from the market. She took one step forward and almost ran into Miss Millie.

"Miss Millie!"

"How is you, girl child?" Miss Millie asked coaxing dimples to the surface of her face with a smile.

"I'm fine, Miss Millie, just fine."

"Well whatcha waitin' on, for the produce to jump in your

basket? You gon miss all the good stuff standing here like a frightened lil' girl."

"Seem like no matter how early I get here, everybody still here before me," Sunshine said with a pout.

Miss Millie laughed and tugged at Sunshine's arm. Sunshine followed, head down, barely taking in the chaos around her, keeping her eyes trained on her feet. Miss Millie deposited Sunshine at the tomato cart.

"These tomatoes is fresh, an' red as the devil. You start here," Miss Millie said wagging an authoritative finger. Sunshine nodded her head obediently.

"I going to Miss Jay's booth. Chile, I got to get my gossip before I market," Miss Millie whispered and pinched Sunshine's fat fleshy arm.

"OK Miss Millie," Sunshine giggled, "make sure you come by and tell me who's actin' up."

"Don't worry, honey. You come by an' help me make my stew and I'll tell anything you wanna know," Miss Millie said with a wickedly raised eyebrow.

Turning her attention to the tomatoes, Sunshine rested her basket at her feet. As she stood to collect tomatoes, she caught a child, maybe the daughter of the tomato lady, biting into a tomato as if it were an apple. The red fruit, the dripping juice, the child's unveiled hunger called Sunshine's attention. She stared, as the child bit and swallowed and wiped her mouth with the back of a sticky hand. After a couple of bites, the child looked up, locking into Sunshine's eyes with a glance. Sunshine immediately dragged her eyes down to her empty basket. Heat flared to her cheeks. She could still see the ravenous child and the half-devoured fruit, but she blinked away the vision.

She reached out and palmed a tomato. She lifted it and squeezed, testing its plumpness. Dissatisfied, she dropped it back into the pile. She went on lifting and squeezing until she found four to her liking. As her fingers grazed the curve of the fifth, something soft brushed against the sheltered flesh of her inner arm. Her head jerked up and she looked over her shoulder. A woman was standing next to her, taking no notice of her. Turning back to the tomatoes, she resumed her hunt, the touched flesh of her arm aroused. Accident or not, Sunshine missed the brush of skin against skin. The woman roused the memories of skin cells. They rose from slumber with a low dissatisfied hum.

Sunshine collected six, seven, eight more tomatoes. As Sunshine was stretching toward the ninth, the woman's breast collided with her arm. Sunshine froze. Her arm stayed extended, her eyelids slid closed. The pleasurable weight of the stranger's flesh caused her to breathe in deeply. Within seconds the contact was over. Sunshine opened her eyes to find the tomato lady staring at her. She forced a smile and glanced behind her, just in time to see the stranger plodding away from the tomato cart, unaware of her impact on Sunshine's day. Embarrassment spread over Sunshine's face as she realized the tomato lady was still staring at her. She quickly gathered up two more tomatoes, paid the woman in coins and left the cart.

The strange market intimacies continued at the doubly-crowded banana cart. Arms brushed against her waist, elbows rubbed against her back, wrists collided with her butt. She reached around an old man to grab a healthy bunch of bananas then paused to pay. She pressed her folded bills into the banana man's calloused hand. While he counted out her change, she noticed his smooth throat exposed by his casually open collar. She leaned forward, under the guise of waiting for her change, and inhaled his clean, fresh scent. Eyes glued to the hollow of his brown, brown throat, Sunshine resisted the urge to embrace him, to press tongue against chest and gather up his taste. Instead she turned away, dumping her bananas into her basket, twisting her change into her handkerchief and moving on to the onions.

There was no one gathered at the onion man's cart. He smiled at her with beautiful white teeth.

"No one is buying from you today?" she asked.

"They are," he said and stood, arching his body into a long stretch, "but they are all in a frenzy over the yams."

Sunshine followed the direction his finger was pointing in. Directly across from the onion cart, a crowd was gathered.

"He had a special crop this month," the onion man explained. "Word got out last week that he has double the sweet potatoes and they are doubly sweet. The people are going crazy."

Sunshine eyed the crowd.

"What are you waiting for girl? Leave your basket here, go get some. Don't you want to bring home a treat for your husband?"

Sunshine looked at him out of the corner of her eye and said nothing. He reached for her basket. She let him pull it from her hands.

"Go," he said. "Come back for my onions."

Without asking another question Sunshine hurried over to the sweet potato stand. She circled the outer rim of the crowd, but couldn't find an opening. She looked back at the onion vendor. He was motioning for her to go closer. She sighed and placed her hand flat against a man's broad back. As the man turned toward her, she squeezed into the crowd. Slowly she began moving forward, pushing herself between bodies with her elbow and her hip. When no amount of pushing would get her any further, she knew she was near the front. She clasped her hands behind her neck and waited.

The urgency of the market goers clustered around her was a thick tangible thing. A prickly heat slowly invaded her body. She lowered her hands and pressed her palms against her thighs. Something soft brushed against the back of her neck. Her hand rose up to rub it away, but it hit against something moist. She turned but could barely see behind her. Was that a mouth, she wondered? A sweaty cheek? The pace of her breath escalated as she imagined lips kissing the nape of her neck. A force she identified as body heat curled around her body. It dipped down her back, slid into the crease of her buttocks, and settled between her thighs. Without thinking, she began to rub her thighs together, coaxing the heat to her skin's surface.

Little by little, the crowd fell away from Sunshine's consciousness. The woman in front of her ceased to exist. The bony hip pushing into her side no longer disturbed her. Her muscles took interest in only one form—a hard chest resting against her back. Swaying in the airless crowd, Sunshine brushed against his pelvis. The minute she touched him, a current jumped between her legs. She immediately severed contact, leaning forward ever so slightly. She turned again to look behind her, but she saw only jaw. No identifying arch of eyebrow or curve of nose. She shifted under a sudden dizziness. She needed air, but her body needed the sensation that was making her dizzy. As she fought to hold her body still, her back was arching back, disobediently seeking him out. She took a deep breath and settled her softness against him. She felt his hand on her neck. She closed her eyes and began to tremble.

The man leaned toward her and poured his breath, strong and heavy, into her ear. "I want you," she heard his breath whisper without him saying a word. She opened her eyes abruptly, suddenly aware that she was surrounded by eyes. Eyes like Miss Millie's who wouldn't hesitate to spread the story around town. She could hear the sucking teeth now, whispering her name, shaming her for acting so in public with some stranger with her poor heartbroken husband at home and her dead baby cold in the ground.

All the faces around her were facing forward. No one seemed to notice her tiny pelvic movements, the stranger's hardness. Even in anonymity, she felt disgraceful. The heavy hunger of her body driving her into hussylike boldness. Without a warning, she lunged away without looking back. She pushed through the crowd, ignoring the grumbling irritated mouths as she shoved people out of her way. When she cleared the crowd and returned to the onion man, she was shaking.

"Are you alright?" he asked.

She pointed to her basket without a word. The onion man didn't move.

"Are you sick?" he asked.

She pointed to the basket again. He leaned down and picked it up. He placed it into her hands. She forced a crooked smile from her trembling lips and turned to leave the market. She hadn't gone two steps when she stumbled. Before she knew it, the onion man had his arms around her and was leading her back to his cart. He pushed her into a seat in the shade and motioned for her to stay put. He left and returned with a cool glass of lemonade. Sunshine drank greedily. The onion man kneeled next to her.

"Feel better?"

Sunshine nodded, still not trusting her voice.

"What happened?"

Sunshine avoided his eyes, and again hoped her blush wasn't obvious.

"Let me take you home."

"No, it's okay I'll be fine."

"If my wife was sick in the market, I'd want someone to bring her home."

"Do you know my husband?"

"No."

The onion man's eyes rested gently on the curves of Sunshine's lips. She ran her eyes over his face in a soft curious way. A wave of comfort washed over him. She offered up a weak smile.

"I know who you are," he whispered.

"How come?"

"I asked the first time I seen you in the market. Come on, I got a strong donkey, let me take you home."

"No, I'll walk."

He didn't hide the wrinkles of disappointment that creased his face. Sunshine felt sorry, but she couldn't bear a bumpy donkey ride, not with her hands wrapped around the tight torso of a man, not with her cheek resting against his back, not with her hunger, her need.

"If you want to walk with me . . ." she said with a shy smile.

He nodded his head eagerly and offered her his hand. She took it and let him help her to her feet. She brushed off her dress and straightened her clothes. Suddenly she felt formal. The onion man picked up her basket and leaned toward her with a bent elbow. Sunshine smiled and placed her arm in the crook of his. As they strolled away, she glanced back at his cart.

"Don't you need somebody to watch your cart?"

"Oh, Johnson'll do it. He'll see I'm not there and take over. Don't you worry. We're going to get you home."

"What's your name?"

"Simon."

"Simon, where did you come from."

"From the country."

"This is the country."

"Yeah but there are places more country than this."

Sunshine giggled. She couldn't help but notice the length of his fingers, the thickness of his wrists. She could feel the muscles in his arm through the thin fabric of his shirt.

"Simon," she said out loud.

He nodded his head and smiled. Sunshine caught the gleam of his teeth out of the corner of her eye. Although they walked along in silence there was nothing empty about the moment. Sunshine felt full and complete and light. A light happy tune burst forth from her lips. She covered her mouth with her hand when she realized she was singing out loud. Simon laughed and sang her a song back. As his voice rolled over her body, she absentmindedly rubbed her fingers against his arm. Simon stopped singing and turned his face towards Sunshine's.

"Sunshine, I hope you won't think me too forward if . . ."

"How do you know my name?"

"I told you, I asked about you."

"You know my name?"

"Yes."

"And where I live?"

"Yes."

Sunshine was quiet.

"I hope you won't think me too forward if I invited you to the river."

Sunshine's heart jumped. She had heard the stories of the river.

Upstream, far from where families picnicked and folks without wells washed their clothes was a spot where lovers met. She couldn't read in Simon's face which part of the river he was referring to. Recklessness tumbled through her body as she thought about the absence of intimacy in her life.

"Well, you know," Sunshine said, leaning toward him until her breast rested against his biceps, "I have a river on my property."

"Yes, and you have a husband on your property, too," Simon retorted.

"Are you afraid of him?" Sunshine asked.

Simon walked a little taller.

"Nope," he said.

"Would you come to my river?" she asked.

Simon nodded his head.

"Today?" she asked.

"Of course," Simon said with a crooked smile.

Sunshine didn't know how starved she was until this moment. She stood—need thundering through her veins—facing Simon, only their clothing and a basket of fruit between them. She took Simon's hand and led him through the wooded area behind the house. They brushed past leaves and bush, stepped over stones and fallen tree trunks, until they reached the clear rushing waters running through Sunshine's property. Sunshine paused to listen while Simon rested the basket on the dry earth. Nothing but the customary silence vibrated for miles around.

"This isn't a river," Simon teased. "This is a creek."

"Oh yeah?" she asked, turning to face him, "What's the difference?"

"The difference is," Simon said as he placed a finger on her forehead. "A creek is what you're feeling right now." He lightly traced down her nose, over her lips and chin. Sunshine drew in her breath. When his finger rested in the hollow of her throat, she exhaled slowly. Her skin tingled as his finger continued its downward path.

"A river," he said as he unbuttoned the front of her floral dress, "is what you will feel when I'm inside you."

Sunshine groaned when his finger skimmed the skin between her breasts. As his finger ran down her torso, over her abdomen, her heart pounded a staccato rhythm in her chest. By the time Simon's finger dove into her belly button, her skin was moist. Sunshine's knees were losing their strength to trembling. She grabbed Simon by his vest and pulled him toward her. She licked a patch of salty sweat from his neck. Kissing him from ear to shoulder, she lowered him down to the ground.

"Wait," he said, "your hair will get dirty." He took off his vest and spread it on the earth.

"You should take this off, too," Simon said as he pulled the dress from Sunshine's body. "You don't want to go back home looking like you rolled around in the dirt."

"I don't care," Sunshine said in a low voice.

Simon hung her dress on a tree and looked at her lying on the earth below him. Her fingers lingered over her nipples, the silhouette of her legs were clearly visible through her sheer slip.

"Take that off for me," he said in a low voice as he unbuttoned his shirt.

Sunshine bit her lip when she saw the muscles in his abdomen, but she didn't obey. She kept watching as he took off his pants. A low exclamation of approval escaped her lips when she saw the size and shape of his hardness.

"You want to keep this on?" Simon whispered as he straddled her hips with his knees.

"Uh-huh," she mumbled then held her breath, waiting for his next move. He knew her nipples, her pelvis, every inch of her was straining toward him. He rubbed his lips over her shoulder blades and down her chest. She traced patterns across his back and side with her fingernails pressing down hard every time his teeth pinched her flesh. When his teeth nipped at her nipples, she drew in her breath. He bit around them and licked them, nuzzling them with his lips until they stood full and tall. He moved to the right of her and laid on his side. As his hands wandered over her hips, down her thighs, her hand played in his mess of pubic hair.

Her fingers brushed over his shaft lightly, then took a hold of it with an assuredness that surprised him.

"Word around town is, you ain't getting any," he whispered, "but you touching me like you know what you're doing."

Sunshine pouted and gripped Simon hard. She felt his skin shift over his muscle as she moved her hand up and down over his penis. Then she paused.

"I didn't know my business was public record."

"Please . . . don't . . . stop . . ." Simon whispered. "I don't know what I'm talking about. Please." And he put his hand over hers and guided her into a vigorous hand dance. She obliged, adding pressure and speed to the rhythm of her hand.

"Just because," she said after a pause. "I'm not getting any, doesn't mean I don't know what to do when I do get some."

Simon was too involved in what she was doing to him to answer. Sunshine allowed a self-satisfied grin to break across her face. Then she slowed down, she didn't want to push him too far. She lifted the hem of her slip and slowly revealed the big tight curves of her leg. Simon placed a heavy hand on her bent knee, then slipped it up her inner thigh. He lingered there, brushing up and down the insides of her thighs, reveling in the trembling he was causing there. Sunshine pulled her slip higher until it rested, rumpled, around her waist.

"My God," Simon whispered when he saw the curve of her behind.

"Turn over," he said, "Let me look at you."

She giggled and turned over. She felt his finger skim over the mounds of her buttocks. She opened her legs without him asking. She sighed when she felt his fingers skimming the crease of her buttocks and probing the creases and folds between her legs. She closed her eyes and rested her forehead against the ground. Simon's fingers first focused on her outer walls, probing and circling. Then he slid his finger over her clitoris. She pushed against his finger and he moved his finger away.

"Don't move," he whispered.

She clenched her stomach muscles and fought to keep still. His fingers returned to stroke her clitoris again and again and again. She felt the wetness seeping from inside her. Her whole vulva started to hum. When she felt his fingers inside her, she began to push against them. This time, Simon didn't complain. She reached behind for him and pulled him against her back. She felt the welcome weight of his body crush her against the earth. She spread her legs even wider in anticipation of his entrance. When he finally pushed himself into her, a low moan escaped her throat. Tears sprung from her eyes as a sudden sensation of sweetness rushed through their bodies. She cried for the places of her that had been left neglected, untouched for so long. She cried out of gratitude for his tenderness. Her emotions rushed out of her chest through her throat in a jumbled mass of sound. The wind plucked the rough sounds from her lips and carried them miles away from her body. Talley heard them, but did not stir from his silence. He did not recognize the sounds as his wife's, he did not wonder where the moans were coming from. In synchronization with thrusts and heaves and sighs, seeds in the earth beneath them began to stretch and rip and explode.

A low whine slipped from Sunshine's lips as heat exploded in her pelvis and her orgasm momentarily stole her consciousness. She was too caught up to care that Simon had not withdrawn before the rush of his orgasm filled her body. Her womb greedily drank up the sperm as the air sucked in their pleasure. They lay together—chest to back, skin to skin—wet, sticky, and satiated. As Sunshine tumbled into sleep, Simon slipped into the river to wash. He dressed without taking his eyes from her face. He placed a lingering kiss on her cheek and paused, lips hovering over her ear. As she slept, she heard the whisper of his words winding down her ear canal into her dream: "Baby, I'll be there, behind the onion cart, waiting for you to call on me again."

Hedonics

Iris N. Schwartz

Hedonics: *n.* 1. *Psychol.* The branch of psychology that studies pleasant and unpleasant sensations and states of mind. 2. *Philos.* The branch of ethics that deals with the relation of pleasure to duty.

—*The American Heritage Dictionary of the English Language*, Fourth Edition

*M*ATTHEW **CONNOR SIFTED** through the crests of black hair atop his head, wishing to impart sense memory to his scalp. Of course self-stimulation wouldn't feel the same. His scalp, his whole being, had experienced wave after wave of thrills in Dahlia's masterly hands. Matthew thought of her white, almost translucent, skin and fleshy, cupid's-bow lips. He remembered the fine blonde hair that fell just below her delicate shoulders, and the startlingly dexterous digits that had found their way to his dark strands after he'd driven his tongue into her mouth.

Matthew squeezed his eyes shut and laid his hands upon his lap. He keenly felt the wooden bench slats under his buttocks, punishing him with hardness and late October cold. He accepted this harshness. No, he welcomed it.

Dr. Matthew Kevin Connor, New York State Board–certified

psychologist, son of Kinsale, County Cork, Ireland, six years now in his adopted country, lifted a notebook from the briefcase beside him. He cherished the seclusion of Northern Manhattan, the redemptive possibilities of hushed, hilly, Fort Tryon Park, seasonally splendid with arboreal towers of crimson and gold. Matthew worked and made his home in this community.

The psychologist started reviewing notes from a morning session, his nine forty-five with a gloomy tenth grader. After two paragraphs Matthew rested his cheek against his right hand. He gazed in the direction of the Unicorn Café, a branch-strewn, circuitous path away from the Cloisters Museum and the famed Unicorn in Captivity tapestry. Matthew returned to his notes, but realized he was reading the third paragraph for the fourth time.

The distracted doctor thought of Dahlia's hand holding his as they'd studied the revered cloth hanging. He pondered her second and third fingers tracing circles inside his palm as he spoke of the acceptance and grace he saw in the equine creature's gait. Dahlia had said that the unicorn, apparently loosely tethered, did not want to be free. Matthew sensed that he'd known this, but somehow "forgot." He'd always chosen to concentrate on the fence.

The psychologist preferred to think of his sullen student or, better yet, Dahlia. This beauty, like Rilke's unicorn, had "body wrought of finest ivory." Had Matthew told her this? He'd lost his train of thought as she'd touched him, his words circling in his brain like her adroit fingers in his palm, like the barrier enclosing the magical horned horse.

Matthew looked at his notes; he willed himself to concentrate, to try to distinguish this lad's tics and complaints from the other adolescents' everyday angst.

The Fort Washington High School psychologist shook his head, shut the book, and resumed fingering his thick locks. He must quit thinking of that woman. He massaged his scalp, then scratched it, and before Matthew could stop he felt pain at his temple and espied brick-red blood under the fingernails of his right hand. This was the same hand he'd been employing on himself late at night, obsessing on the schoolteacher Svetlana Dahlia Orlovsky: her silken hair, her pale flesh, her . . .

Matthew cleared his throat and sighed. He dove into his breast pocket for a handkerchief, but not before thinking, this harshness, this piercing at his right temple, this he comprehended. This he deserved.

The doctor stared at streaks of blood on his handkerchief. Again he pressed the cloth to the side of his head. He recalled Dahlia's supple fingers mussing his hair. Their date had been last Thursday; a scant five days had passed. With more audacity than he presently possessed, Matthew might feel the exquisiteness of this Bronx woman's touch once more.

Riverdale, he corrected himself, and briefly smiled. Denizens of Riverdale, teachers included, preferred the name *Riverdale* to *The Bronx*, though all knew the accuracy of either appellation. It reminded Matthew of his father Liam insisting they stop for pints at a "proper" local public house, not "theme taverns with their piped-in music," frequented by "know-nothings" and "tourists on the prowl for local color."

Liam's favored pubs sported families with children and little black dogs, and Kinsale musicians practicing their pennywhistles and strings. Respectable, according to his *da*. Sure: as respectable as Liam himself in his later years, whoring it up on a cold Cork night with whomever he'd chat up in one of his proper pubs, whomever he'd find to take the place of Matthew's dead ma. Matthew made the sign of the cross, then collected several tissues from his briefcase. He pressed them firmly to his burning scalp.

Here's your respectable: Matthew shivering under the finger-nails of Svetlana Dahlia Orlovsky; his breathing quickening as her hands traversed his upper torso, and Dahlia's exclamations over his manly muscles and chest. Even more respectable: Matthew's penis perking up within his trousers now, reminder of his tumes-cence then, when he'd had the unmitigated Gallic gall to usher the lassie round the back of the Unicorn Café and close in behind her to clutch her hips, his cock pulsing against the warm half-moons of her arse.

Without delay he'd whipped aside her still-open jacket, lifted barriers of sweater, blouse, and bra, and, finally, mercifully, read the fullness of her globes in the dark. Oh, how his mighty little man had respectably lengthened and firmed while he'd fondled her breasts, their exposed tips growing in autumn-chilled air. Eminently respectable psychologist Matthew Kevin Connor had spun Dahlia around, lowered his zipper, and urgently called on the girl to touch him, needed nothing but her deft fingers making motions on his swelling head and shaft.

At this point in their nocturnal romp the good doctor thought he'd heard rustling, and so had left off his wanton behavior. Now, five days later, aggrieved at his eruption of lust, stymied by his embarrassment, and maddened at his timidity at not having called this Russian-American lovely, Matthew prayed that Dahlia might forgive him his prurience and agree to see him once again, for a decorous, *grope-free* date. He was fearful that he might not be able to convince her—or that he might.

The psychologist reached for his briefcase. He should be reviewing his morning sessions, or grading Monday's word association tests, but kept circling back to the same deep-seated desires. He couldn't run from them while studying to be a man of the cloth, and yet could not embrace his cravings even after allowing himself to leave. *It is not good that the man should be alone*, he knew. Were the words of Genesis not enough for Matthew? What a wretched excuse for a man thirty-one-year-old Matthew was.

Perhaps Svetlana Dahlia Orlovsky could find it in her heart to accept him nevertheless. "Please excuse this overgrown lad's lasciviousness," he might begin a note to this teacher. Matthew laughed sharply and rose from the bench. He was tempted anew to scratch his scalp. He could not get Dahlia out of his mind, his heart, or, he winced, his loins. Matthew genuflected, felt some comfort in tawny and magenta leaves coolly, crisply cradling his knees and lower legs. He began a prayer for his transgressions, including those to follow.

~

DAHLIA LIFTED THE lid from her lunch container and immediately bolted back from an invisible, acrid cloud. She'd been wrong to microwave eggplant caviar. Microwaving it accentuated the vinegar. Now the high school drama teacher was left with nothing palatable but the potato *pampushki*, and she knew, as her mother reliably repeated—like a Sabbath prayer or an Old World curse—that carbohydrates were the last things Dahlia should eat.

Dahlia replaced the lid and folded her hands on her lap. She could buy wheat crackers from the vending machine, or an apple from the cafeteria. No, those were carbohydrates, too. She didn't need lunch today. She would take satisfaction in the hollowness that filled her belly. Dahlia unfolded her hands and hugged her size-six frame.

Svetlana Dahlia Orlovsky reluctantly stood up, exhaled loudly, and picked up her plastic container. She returned it to the refrigerator. Then she smoothed down her flyaway hair and exited the teachers' lounge.

This was not Dahlia's day. Her second-period students hadn't responded as she'd hoped they would to her idea of *West Side Story* as their spring presentation. Nor did they appreciate her other suggestions: *A Midsummer Night's Dream* or *A Delicate Balance*. Both Tiffanys agreed these had been produced so often they wouldn't be fresh. Jason—or had it been Jeffrey? It might've been Jonathan—immediately pronounced all of them dated.

Sondheim stale? Shakespeare dated? Albee old? Her students were brats. For all their exposure to the world via the Internet, they were provincial, ignorant brats. Dahlia stormed off to her next class and sat behind the teacher's desk. She had fifteen minutes before the kids bounded in, sufficient time to collect herself. Instead her face grew florid at the thought of her ungrateful students. When

Dahlia opened her day planner, however, and noticed last Thursday's scribbled-in appointment, she recognized the true source of her ire.

Five days ago Dahlia had gone on a first date with an ebony-haired Irishman possessed of a brogue that had made her panties damp, and sad, earth-brown eyes that had caused her heart to ache. Five days ago Dahlia had clasped the hand of this man, who'd spoken passionately, if earnestly, about the medieval tapestries in the Cloisters Museum. For five days since she'd been eating too much or not at all, and had been unable to maintain interest in any of her beloved dramatists, all because she could not forget a high school psychologist who'd abandoned her after feeling her up with the glee of a sixteen-year-old sophomore and, maybe, the subsequent guilt of a monk in an abbey.

Every night since their dinner date and grope-fest, every night that passed without a telephone call or e-mail message from the debauched school psychologist, every night, despite mounting rage and sadness, Svetlana Dahlia Orlovsky had imagined Matthew's large, slightly rough fingertips once more encircling and stroking her roseate nipples, first almost tentatively, then with vigor. She heard him, with that lilt of Eire, whisper, "Ah, beautiful," and tasted on his breath the darkly sweet Merlot they'd shared during dinner at the Unicorn Café. Dahlia then pictured him seizing one of her B-cup breasts, pushing it out of its lacy haven, and squeezing the tip until it turned rigid and red. Soon Dahlia would be writhing in her bed. She'd be spreading her thighs wide, wishing she could capture that County Cork cock, all the while frantically fingering her dripping, dark blonde pussy. She would moan, she would come . . . and then she would cry.

Every night since her debacle with Matthew, Dahlia swore she would not repeat this pain and passion that was far too dramatic and draining even for a Russian-American drama teacher, on-again, off-again actress, and more than occasional binge and starvation dieter.

Alone in bed five nights after that date, drenched in perspiration, feminine juices, and tears, Dahlia lived up to her hated childhood nickname—"Sweaty Ana." She had acquired this sobriquet due to a chubby childhood propensity to perspire. The moniker had stuck all through grade school and into junior high, long after she'd lost those extra pounds—and then some. The nickname had hurt her to her core.

Dahlia was tired of being hurt. Tomorrow she would call Dr. Matthew Connor, give him a piece of her mind. In this way she'd remove him from her mind, for good. One day she might play Tatiana to a deserving Oberon, even, someday, back in the theatre. She truly could, as her mother often facetiously advised, "Save the drama for the stage." Dahlia's talents shouldn't be wasted on ingrates.

Svetlana Dahlia Orlovsky felt shaky, but eager to instruct her Tiffanys and Jasons. She closed her day planner and stood up to write on the chalkboard.

⁓

AT 3 A.M., feeling fenced in by guilt interwoven with desire, having slept only fitfully, Matthew sprang from bed and began assembling ingredients for a few of his *da*'s Irish specialties. Matthew had dreamed up a way to win her. He would court Dahlia: call her, then come to her doorstep laden with roses, *boxty*, Dublin Lawyer, and the old reliable soda bread.

No. He had to do something more difficult, more inventive, to atone. Matthew pushed baking soda, flour, whiskey, and potatoes to the far side of his kitchen table. There would be time later to put these away. A woman of Dahlia's caliber would not wait, might not be waiting now.

Certainly he hadn't left the seminary to be alone and unloved in the material world. He hadn't rearranged his life for naught. Matthew believed he could be of aid to the sullen, the troubled, the tormented teens of his school. He knew a bit about agony. Perhaps he could share his heart with Dahlia and manage to torment himself in other ways. The psychologist allowed himself to smile.

Matthew Kevin Connor hurried over to his desk. He would search online for Russian recipes, and woo Svetlana Dahlia Orlovsky with the food of her forebears. She'd appreciate this epicurean propitiation. Besides, this beauty could use more meat on her bones. He'll share food with her and win her heart.

He won't touch her when he sees her, though he'll be aching to do so. Matthew closed his eyes and began massaging his scalp. He yearned to graze every centimeter of her smooth, fair skin with his fingertips, to press his thin lips to her bountiful ones, to feel her tongue dallying with his. More than that, Matthew wanted to pound his now-stiff phallus into what he knew would be an enveloping, gushing, perfect little cunt. A woman with the capacity to caress so imaginatively, kiss so passionately, give herself so fully to the joys of the moment was a woman who would surrender her pink, juicy folds to him completely. Indeed, Dahlia was a lass who could help *him* surrender.

The ex-seminarian laid his palms upon his thighs. He took many deep breaths. No, he will not touch Dahlia when he sees her. He'll simply feed her forkfuls of his cooking, much as his *da* had for Matthew's own mother—when she'd been healthy, and after she'd grown ill. Matthew will demonstrate his love for Dahlia with every offered morsel.

⁓

UPON ENTERING THE New Minsk Market in Riverdale, three blocks from her home, Dahlia caught sight of Matthew, this on the day after she'd vowed to confront him. Dahlia spotted in his basket marinated mushrooms, dill cucumbers, bunches of green onions. The nerve of that man not calling her, then shopping for *zakuski* in her neighborhood—and in her favorite store! He was flaunting his disdain. Dahlia's face grew almost as pink as the beet salad behind the counter. As she stood next to the front door, Dahlia watched the owner weigh three small carp for this cruel man, this heartless man in a helping profession.

The teacher's right hand shook as she reached for the door

handle. Her mother might say this was lucky; it would keep Dahlia from eating too much—or from eating at all. *Aren't you proud of me, Mother?* Dahlia bit the unspoken words. *This morning a size four suit nearly buttoned all the way up.*

Hot tears pelted down Dahlia's face as she exited The New Minsk; a dot of blood bubbled from her lower lip. Dahlia placed one hand to her lip, jammed the other hand into a coat pocket. Her legs scissored the block. At a curb, interrupted in flight by a flashing DON'T WALK sign, Dahlia felt a hand grip her lower arm, and then she heard the telltale brogue.

⁓

IT MUST HAVE been Providence that returned her to him, Matthew thought, surely not his own clumsy moves and miscommunications. As she lay with her back to him, Matthew brushed blonde wisps away from her cheek. Her eyelids rapidly fluttered. Was she dreaming of their lovemaking? Matthew hadn't believed she'd let him near her again, not with that fire in her eyes as he'd tried to apologize and explain. There was a tangle of their arms as she'd tried to disengage, and disapproving glances from strangers on the street. She'd screamed at him at length to do his shopping elsewhere, and he'd screamed back that the groceries were for her. Never in his life had he raised his voice to a lass, let alone on the street.

After this squall she'd agreed to talk, a block away, under the shade of a tree, and then had allowed him to walk her home. To his great good fortune and relief she'd let him unpack the *zakuski* and put them in her refrigerator, though she wouldn't permit him to assemble or cook any food. Dahlia would not let Matthew feed her.

Yet here he was in her bed! As he watched her pink-tipped breasts rise and fall he recalled the sweetness of them in his mouth, the nipples puckering and swelling as he drew on each one, back and forth, over and over, until she'd gently moved his head and gestured for him to journey further down.

Now his eyes traveled over her flat, quivering stomach, to that lovely thatch, nearly hiding what Matthew wished to spread wide, lick and suck. Ah, he was thirsty for her a second time. His penis ascended; he wanted to stretch her pussy walls as he had earlier, when she'd cried out in his ear, when he'd worried that he was hurting her—but then he'd thought not, not the way Dahlia had wound her legs around his hips, not the way she'd rammed her lower body into his, not the way she'd whimpered "please, oh, Matthew, please, oh, please" as he felt her pussy spasm and flow.

Matthew was ready to thank all Gods any person prayed to for Dahlia's willingness to come round, for his chance to circle back. He clasped her tightly to him and began to fall asleep.

DAHLIA FELT A weight upon her, but in her present state she couldn't move. The weight surrounded her. As she struggled, the chains tightened around the torsos and limbs of the two of them, the black-maned horse and the blonde. Dahlia's eyelids fluttered faster; her body could not budge. Then she felt the warmth of the weight, and found she could move if she didn't panic. She was not sure she wanted to be free.

The Longest Escalator in the World

Max Sharam

*W*HEN **CELIA TURNED** twenty-three and moved in with the uncircumcised kraut, she decided to be fitted for a diaphragm. She placed it, in its delicately decorated box, in the top drawer with her underwear. Every now and again sliding open the square lid to appreciate its aesthetic; affectionately fingering its chalky, rubbery-ness. She didn't linger long, just periodically checked in, rarely removing it from the box. Rarely removing the box from the drawer. It was fascinating for her long after the stormy affair with the French painter and long into the live-in love with the lawyer, and even throughout all of the miscellaneous romances and one-night stands. Her diaphragm sat silent, still with its faint coat of silky powder, like a soft miniature Frisbee. Pristine and intact. Still perfect in its virgin state and she had never gotten pregnant.

Celia's tender affection for her unused diaphragm continued for over a decade and only began to fade after having an extended discussion with a friend about Celia's continued success with the timing method. Her friend had joked that the 'fram was now as good as an artifact and that Celia dare not use it as the rubber would probably perish if it came in contact with sperm; it would disintegrate in her vagina. She mused that likely Celia's vagina's shape had changed, after all these years of sex with well-endowed men, and maybe it was time she was fitted for another!

Celia had laughed it off, remembering the businesslike female doctor who'd first fitted her all those years back. After examining her uterus, she'd casually announced that Celia "had an unusually long vaginal canal." Celia recalled the lawyer once remarking that Celia's clitoris was huge, too. She wondered if she was the female equivalent of a well-hung man? She wondered if there was any correlation between this and her obsession with men who were six foot three?

THE HONG KONG escalator is said to be the longest outdoor moving sidewalk in the world, stretching eight hundred meters up Victoria Peak. This reversible people-mover was designed as an alternative to widening the roads. It was a success, easing traffic congestion while transporting thousands of commuters daily from the bottom of Hong Kong Central up the side of the steep mountain, depositing them at any one of the twenty exits along the way. The last ride up was at midnight; taking up to twenty minutes to reach the top, where usually the only people left riding were the wealthy and the business travelers staying in the five-star hotels built at the highest level of the peak.

It was 11:50 and Celia noticed as she stepped foot onto the first flight of escalators that it was an unusually quiet night for midweek. A late winter storm threatened to burst on the horizon and the air was balmy with humidity. The quiet amplified her restlessness. She felt her body talking to her.

She knew her body well—precisely why she didn't need to use contraception. She was ovulating. It was obvious. Her breasts and clitoris seemed in communication with one another. Her nipples would harden unprovoked, causing contractions at the entrance of her vagina. It would pulsate. Pulsations and contractions, migrating along the thick walls of her vagina, up through her body; making her push down on her pelvis and extend her waist and squeeze and curve, to curve her entire body. She became an S shape. S for sensual. Her shoulders dropped, pushing her breasts forward, her back slightly arched, the nape of her neck stretched to expose more skin to the slight breeze. One hand on the handrail, she moved the other up, unconsciously, over her breast. Pinching her hard nipple. She squirmed. She moved one leg over the other to increase the pressure on her clitoris. She was horny. She was definitely ovulating.

When Celia looked up she saw his eyes burning into her, stunned and full of desire. She didn't bother to adjust her pose. She just clutched the handrail more tightly and held her ground. Privately she exhaled, closing her eyes so as to not see him or that she had been so exposed. In her mind's eye she saw his eyes, dark and aroused yet innocent, probably as taken by surprise by her public instant—a moment snapped by his stare—as she was. How long had he been looking? It was as if he were reading her mind. Had it been his scent on the breeze that had aroused her? She could hear a Latin beat coming from a café below. She opened her eyes. He turned his face away. His body was as she had pictured it. Shapely. Statuesque. Dark. Well-dressed. Long arms. His energy emanated grace and calm. She watched him with a firm interest. She studied his hands. There was no ring. His fingers were long. His hands smooth. Maybe the hands of a man who draws? She leaned over the railing a little, feline, the bodice of her dress tightened around her heavy breasts. Peering down onto the street to see how busy the restaurants were, only a handful of people could be seen. All seemed to be moving indoors. He moved to watch her. She wanted his eyes on her.

They reached the next landing and walked forward the few steps to the next escalator. She was on his tail. She delighted in the shape of his arse, his long legs. He calmly looked over his shoulder. She dropped her head but kept her eyes on him. Then a moment of shyness came over her, she had been so bold, he had seen her watching him, and now she coyly grinned. He leaned back on the moving rail. This time he looked at her a little longer. She stirred. He was gorgeous.

They reached the next level and moved by the flow of the railing to the next landing, crossed the bridge that connected one side of the street to the other then ascended the next walkway. She reveled in his uninterrupted pace. Confident. Something casual yet striking about his stride. He mounted the next steps turning to look at her close on his heels—her body alive with the excitement of attraction. He had noticed her. She saw softness in his eyes. And they both smiled, faintly. Another rush of warmth. Her senses heightened, the subtle vibration of the conveyer belt resonated through her body.

The next adjoining landing was brief. They moved swiftly, inconspicuously falling back into the rhythm of the motorized stairs and a revised version of their previous pose. Alert to the patter of rain on the roof above them that was washing out the sounds of the streets below. In motion; she now only four steps below him, the only people visible on this 135-vertical-meter climb. Their eyes engaged, unsure what to do next. It seemed inappropriate to speak. The moist air and the monotony of motion had cast its spell. He angled his well-defined torso to face her, his back to the hill, his elbow slightly bent and his hand on the railing. The sleeve of his body-hugging pullover slightly pushed up, revealing his muscular lower arm. Her eyes drank in the shape, the contours—the color of his veins. Sliding her stare down the side of his body, across the front of his jeans where the bulk of his sex seemed to mold the denim into an inviting and sizable package. His body was at ease with her visceral explorations. Her eyes rested on his. And sank. His graceful gaze hypnotized her. They said nothing.

Together they traveled up the next portion of moving sidewalk—this section flat, faster. Its vertical incline steepening as it moved up the mountain. His chest still squared with her body. Their eyes still fixed. She felt the pulse of her vagina-blood pumping through veins. Her breasts heaving gently against the buttons of her low cut silk gingham dress. He could see down into the smooth crease between her cleavage. One leg was on the step above the other. The pale flesh of her thigh laid open. She stared with moist eyes up into his refined face. She felt a fierce magnetic pull, her clitoris swelled, her whole being sucked into his essence. Not a word spoken. A clumsy word would break the spell. His nationality would need to remain undefined. He lowered his chin, looked deeply into her hungry eyes and removed his hand from the rail, carefully laying it on the indent of her waist. He stepped down, she moved forward, their bodies melting into one another. Their lips met. Tender then vigorously, never breaking contact, pushing his body hard against her, and hers against the side of the escalator, still moving up, the rain beating down. His hand reached under her dress. Lips still locked and tongues tasting the insides of one another's mouths. Her body wet and hot, the hardness of his sex pushing heavy against her. Her hand extended down to his zipper, unzipping it. She eagerly took hold of his penis. Heavy and hard in her hand, her finger tracing its length and size. She pushed the palm of her hand against the head, wrapping her fingers around the shaft. She squeezed. He groaned. She needed this inside her. His fingers pulled aside the thin line of her G-string and slid along the mouth of her pussy. The juice was thick. Rich. Tight. Hot. Slightly slipping one finger in then pulling out. They kissed desperately, one another's lips, then faces, her neck, he fell to his knees pulling her toward him, his mouth still on hers, his finger back in her vagina he laid her carefully down onto the moving floor, the rain now beating down with full force on the concrete on the other side of the railings. And on the roof. Encasing them in a vacuum of sound and motion—in their own personal compartment. And the air fresh and his odor divine. The final incline was steeper. Darker. Their bodies flat on the metal floor, he looked deep in her eyes then penetrated her. Slowly his long penis deep and hard filled her void. He was a perfect fit. It took but a moment, thrusting, her head jolted forward, her throat tightened and there came the uncontrolled scream of delight. She convulsed. Her body heaved. He groaned a deep, guttural growl. Their juices entwined. They shivered. Her vagina clamped down hard on his cock. Then they lay there for a moment. Aftershocks.

Before the escalator reached the top, they pulled themselves to their feet. And with a deep and satisfied stare into his now searching eyes, she smiled warmly, placing her finger on his mouth. Still rich with desire she could take him again and again but instead, ran her hands down her damp dress and stepped out into the rain. He still in the shelter of the structure. They had reached the top. The quiet secluded end of the rail. The rain poured down. She threw her head back and looked up. Then turned toward the lights, she could see the entrance of her hotel ahead. Lights spilling out onto the street. Her saturated dress now clinging to her impassioned body, she watched him watching her. His raw sex appeal, the ambient magic of the night. She took one more hard look at his divine package and let out a light exhale. Pleasured. Flashing him her smiling eyes she then turned to traverse the path back to her hotel. Quickening her pace as she ran down the empty street.

This was going to be a close one—simultaneous orgasms on a moving sidewalk—while ovulating? Where was her diaphragm?

'Til Death

Marilyn Jaye Lewis

How could it come to this, that I could be such a creepy loser? I used to have so much to offer, to dream about. Now I'm pushing fifty, for chrissakes. And I'm nearly flat broke again. Earning just enough each day to secure a room in this dive motel from one shaky night into another. With maybe a little change left over for beer and smokes when I don't blow it all on food.

Waiting tables again at my age. It's such a glamorous life. The breakfast shift, no less. Up at 5 a.m. Walk across the parking lot to the diner while it's still dark. Sticky eggs and greasy bacon, over and over. Morning after morning. Not exactly a cash cow, like the cocktail shift always was—in the years when I had better legs. When I could drink like a fish and not feel so god-awful hung over the next day. Not that they were any longer or slimmer back then—my legs. And yet they were somehow sexier in those days. They were shapely legs, just made for those short black cocktail skirts and a cheap pair of sling-back Kmart high heels.

The booze was definitely where the money was at for me—back then. It was all mine before I decided to give it up and get married. Now those were the years to be waiting tables, when I was young and had energy to burn. Always getting the prime shifts. Not like it is now—breakfast. Because who cares what a girl looks like at breakfast? Nobody's gonna cough up some huge tip because they have a hard-on for your ass at breakfast. No one's even *got* a hard-on that early, or if they do, who has the energy to do something about it? Not me anymore.

And here I thought I'd turned my final table that first time I said, "I do." How many years ago was that first marriage, fifteen? No, it was closer to twenty years ago, maybe twenty-five. Jesus, life was exciting back then, before the marriages. Even the fights. The fights were exciting, too; they were mean but very sexy at the same time because those fights were just a prelude to giving up the goods, to getting nailed hard. Sometimes right here in this motel, in fact. "Fucking" is what we called it back then when we thought no one could hear us. Nowadays, people use the f-word as if it's just a regular part of the English language. They use fuck to describe every mundane thing.

However, my life in this motel room is no longer the hopeful smell of whiskey and sloppy sex it once was. It's now the smell of burnt coffee and grease. It underscores my thoughts all morning at the diner and has saturated my clothes by the time I come back to the room after lunch. And then here I sit clear into the night, until I'm almost in complete darkness except for the monotonous steel blue glow of the TV. Cable comes with the price of a room.

This is a big night for me, though. A six-pack of ice-cold beer in that tiny refrigerator under the sink. All of it mine and the night is young, the cigarettes, fresh. I know this motel too well, from when it was first built and didn't seem quite so tacky. Back when it was considered to be on the very farthest edge of town. It used to be that after the Lone Tree Motel, there was nothing but scrub grass and empty desert with no wells dug, yet, for drinking water or indoor plumbing.

We used to come around here on Friday nights. Right after high school—that summer when everything was on fire. My heart, my dreams, all that impatient virgin ignorance galloping between my legs. Or practically virgin, anyway. Technically, nothing about me was virgin by then, that summer after high school, but it turned out that there was so much more to know than just the technicalities. . . . We'd all pitch in whatever money we could scrape up in those days and we'd rent rooms here at the Lone Tree to party in, or we'd use the swimming pool. Management didn't care. Those were different times. Kids were kids and they drank, got loud, had fun. So what? They got laid, got married—if they couldn't get out of town and stay gone for good, that is. And the pool . . . in those days the swimming pool was new, a glistening, pristine blue, just like you'd picture some pool in Hollywood might be, especially at night. Brightly lit and nothing but black sky and stars up above. It was glamorous, that pool.

Look at it now, the faded blue paint peeling and the fence a rusted mess. Lights burnt out. No white patio chairs or tables with the striped umbrellas, those are long gone. Just like me, or the girl I used to be anyway, and Saint Christopher. Both of us long gone. Good lord, wasn't he the boy of my dreams then?

James Christopher Loggins, Jr., but we all called him Saint Christopher. He was quieter than the rest of us, less likely to get into trouble. The first to say, "No, we shouldn't do that, we might get caught." And so we all called him a saint. We thought he had more willpower or restraint than the rest of us had. Turned out that it couldn't have been further from the truth. While the rest of us were exploding, Saint Christopher was quietly imploding, living in dread fear of his alcoholic father. A man who, from the moment Christopher could talk, beat him with a belt; hollering obscenities at him and sometimes shoving him into furniture or across the room hard into a wall. Saint Christopher played it safe on the outside, but on the inside he had us fooled. He was no saint; he was just living in fear and biding his time.

But back then, boy, I was head over heels in love with him. I almost chewed off my own tongue in search of the right words that could convince him to love me in return.

It happened right here in this motel, in fact, the night I found out that he did love me. We were all down there by the pool when it started. All the craziness, those tentative gestures so full of juvenile hostility that are only meant to be overtures to getting some sex. What the hell did we know about it? Sex was a weird thing. You could see the pictures in the dirty magazines, watch a porno movie if you were lucky—all of this was even before videos, not to mention the computers that everyone has now. But it all still came down to feeling your way blind when it was finally you and another person, getting ready to have sex. Verging, verging, verging. The energy push-pulling you toward the other for hours, it seemed. The horny frustration could make you crazy-exhausted.

That night, it was down to me and two boys. Funny, I wound up marrying them both at different times. Saint Christopher and Randy—the man who's divorcing me now after twelve years of marriage because I can't come to terms with the idea that Christopher is dead. Randy says that I still love Christopher more than I ever loved him, loved Randy, I mean. This impending divorce that I never asked for is the reason I'm living alone now in such high style at the Lone Tree Motel.

But it was me and Christopher and Randy carrying on down there by the pool that night. Everyone else was up here in one of these rooms that overlook the pool, blasting music, eating pizzas, and getting screaming drunk, as usual. Lord knows, we were drinking, too. But what is the lure of a pizza when you're caught in that magnetic web of desire and near clueless about how to proceed? And what the hell do you do when it's three of you, and not the accepted—or the expected—two? You're only eighteen years old. You can't know better. You dance on in that sticky web, hoping it'll all get clearer as the night unfolds, the lust barreling down on you and you can't get out of its way.

I was so desperately in love with Christopher, in the way only a teenager can love, deep infatuation. But he was shy. I think he *wanted* Randy to take the lead. I think he wanted to live out some thrill through Randy first, to learn what route to follow when it came to sex with an actual girl. Randy was always bombastic, even then. Loud, bold, the fool always willing to rush in. We were in the deep end of the pool. Partly treading water, partly holding onto the side. Circling closer and closer, all three of us, until it couldn't be denied that we'd have to either start touching one another or start wearing one another's skin. We couldn't get closer.

To be honest, at first when I felt the fingers creeping up inside my bathing suit bottoms, I wasn't entirely sure whose fingers they were. That was a peculiar thrill. The kind that jump-starts your urge to misbehave. I think I wanted to believe it was Christopher, that it was his fingers down there between my legs, discovering the secret of my very wet hole. I moved closer to him, in fact, hoping to kiss him at last. But Randy yanked my hair suddenly, pulling my face up close to his, his open mouth latching on tight to mine.

When it happened, when that kiss erupted, devouring my mouth, my eyes were open in shock, taking in the equal look of awe and surprise on Christopher's face. For the entire time we were in that water, he watched. Sticking incredibly close to us in that glamorous well-lit pool on the black edge of nowhere, never once touching me in any overtly intimate way. Yet having him that close to me as Randy's bold exploration of my private parts continued, Christopher's dark eyes wide, his breathing as erratic as ours as my bikini bottoms were inched down my thighs and my top was pulled discreetly up, my hard nipples exposed in the water. Having Christopher that close to me watching and breathing heavy, felt as exciting as if he were the one touching me instead.

I didn't have sexual intercourse that night in the pool. Fucking was still too new to me and in my limited experience it was an act that required, if not privacy, then at the very least a bed. I did let Randy put his fingers in me. Then I let my bikini bottoms come all the way off so that I could spread my legs in the pool and in full view of my companions, yet again let Randy's fingers go in and feel around. I let him pull on my tits in the water. I let these things happen because they felt incredibly good, but also because I had only Christopher's gaze to work with, I wanted at the very least to show myself to him.

Saint Christopher. He was so hot. My young imagination wanted to try everything with him, everything naked bodies could do together. When at last we got out of that pool, Randy bolted up the motel steps like a shot, eager to get more beer, to get loaded, to eat pizza. But Christopher stuck close to me, his wet hair dripping and slicked back from his face, making him look more noticeably handsome than even I, the worshipper, had seen before. We were freezing outside that pool but our clothes were up in one of the rooms and we didn't want to encounter other people, not yet. Not even Randy. Although he would resurface in our sex life later, after Christopher and I were married and it became clear that Saint Christopher's lust was more suited to watching than to participating—unless, of course, he'd been out on the prowl in some bar; a secret I didn't find out about until the minute it was too late and the cops were banging down our door with a warrant for his arrest. Something about a missing girl, and another warrant to impound our car and comb it for evidence. It all came down to carpet fibers and two blonde hairs.

Who would have thought that happiness could hinge on that, could get smashed up against carpet fibers and two blonde hairs and be obliterated? Something that normally you can't even see and here it turns out to be so sinister, so very, very telling. But in the years before the nightmare came? Well okay, right off the bat I found out that Christopher was a little peculiar in the sex department. Still I thought of it as "unusual," the way he acted. And that alone I found erotic. In a way that words, or my feeble grasp of them, could not adequately explain. I simply responded to him, my whole body did, as I tried so hard to accommodate his tentative cues, to figure out what it was he really wanted.

Like that first night down there at the pool. Shivering cold in our wet bathing suits in the night air, wanting to be alone, far away from the noise and the prying eyes. We found our good fortune in the motel's housekeeping closet. A maid had left the door unlocked. Inside that windowless little room it was warmer and best of all, there were towels in there. Clean, folded, bleached-white towels. Stacks of them. It somehow felt safe. There were no maids in that motel at night. I wanted out of my wet bathing suit. I wanted to spread out a stack of towels and lie down on them, be underneath Christopher and let him do what it was boys did. That alone would have made me happy, because that was the thing that made boys happy: Fucking made boys happy. I knew that, and in this instance, it was going to make me happy, too.

But Christopher didn't follow the expected route. Instead, he wanted me to lie there alone on the towels and touch myself. "Try to act like I'm not even here," he said. Well, that was impossible. How could I lie there naked, right there in front of the boy I was so hopelessly smitten with, touch myself in a way I never did with the lights on and act like he wasn't there? As far as I was concerned, nothing else in the entire universe was there *but* him. His eyes. My world was right there in his eyes. *Respond to me*, was all my heart wanted. And the only way my heart could know for sure that it was getting what it wanted was by gauging the expression in Christopher's eyes. How could I pretend he wasn't there?

He didn't even want to take his own wet trunks off. I had to beg him to at least do that. For a long while, he hid himself under a towel. I wasn't even sure if he was hard. And since he didn't want me to look at his face, I had to proceed on a hope and a prayer that what I was doing was arousing him and wasn't just making a complete fool of me.

Eventually he got rid of that towel, though. He tossed it aside in earnest when I was finally putting two of my fingers up my own hole. He nearly straddled me then, leaning over me in all his gorgeous handsomeness but still not touching me. He had a hard-on then for sure, it was undeniable. It was out there in plain sight and he jerked himself off furiously, the sperm shooting out suddenly, startling me, landing on my tits, spattering my face, clinging in gooey drops to my hair.

Whose secret was worse? The way I'd exposed myself to him with the lights on, touched myself in ways I wouldn't even do when I was alone? Or the way he came all over a girl, right out there in the open like that, with no dignity, with abruptness? And yet with a gesture that had at once made something so distasteful feel more like a misplaced gift. I couldn't feel defiled by what he'd done. It had been too unexpected. And afterward, he kissed me. When we'd cleaned ourselves off, he kissed me and he said, "I'm sorry. I don't know why I did that to you. You're not going to tell?" He was back to being a saint.

Boy, the looks we got. Wearing nothing but towels when we finally came back to the noisy rooms off this second floor balcony here in search of our clothes.

That night, I didn't really mind that we hadn't fucked. Any intimacy at all was enough for me then and the peculiarity of Saint Christopher only felt like an added bonus; we now had a dirty secret between us. We were bound together in the erotic thrill of strangeness, something outsiders wouldn't understand.

It was only the other nights that came later, when I kept wondering when something normal, like fucking, would finally start. That's when there was all that whiskey to try to calm everything down. But mostly the whiskey just made us fight. On the rare times that we did eventually fuck, he was violent. Sometimes slapping my face. Sometimes shoving me onto the bed with all his strength, wrenching apart my thighs and then fucking me too hard. I used to chalk it up to the booze. I figured the whiskey made him violent. I didn't know better then.

When we got married, I tried to keep the whiskey out, but it always found its way back in. It was just as much my fault as his, back then. The lure of a brand new fifth on payday, gleaming and then splashing down over the ice into a waiting glass; that smoky, warm aroma. I learned to equate that smell with getting fucked. It was too erotic, whiskey was. Whiskey meant fucking like wild dogs, even though it brought Christopher's buried rage right along with the intercourse.

When I found out what he'd done to that girl, that blonde who was too young to know any better, who'd tried to seduce him because he was good-looking and she was drunk and horny; the one he choked the life out of after fucking her orally, vaginally, anally; tying her first, punching her—the works, right in our car. It got to the point where I couldn't figure out how to keep myself planted in that courtroom another minute. My whole world was shattering in public. In a court of law, in a town where I lived. At least they didn't show me the photos. I was only there as a wife. I wasn't required to be the actual judge. But when I heard what he'd supposedly done, I believed it on the spot. It just seemed like something he might be driven to do. His name was written all over that crime. When it came to sexual intimacy, once you exhorted him to move from watching to any actual touching, then he could only take and that he did with rage. When you tried to give to him freely what any normal woman wants to give a man, something short-circuited in him, something between his cock and his brain, like an electric shock shooting off deadly sparks, his heart fleeing away from the confusion like mad until you felt so sorry for him, for his paralyzed core.

Well that poor girl's parents didn't feel sorry for him. No one in town felt sorry for him—I didn't mean it quite like that. But in the years before the crime, I used to feel sorry for Christopher. I knew something was wrong inside him, I just didn't know what. Randy, our off-and-on sex compatriot throughout my marriage to Christopher, was an oak for me through the trial. Although I wouldn't say he felt sorry for Christopher, either. He did however tend to blame the girl. "She shouldn't have been drunk, flashing her goods at some married man. She was just asking for trouble," was how he justified it.

Randy, in his way, tried to encourage me, to give me hope. "The death penalty is for spics and niggers," he explained. "They don't kill white guys in this state." But it turned out that he was wrong. Sometimes they make exceptions and they kill a white guy, too. Especially white guys who choke young blondes, raping the bejeezus out of them in the process. On the day the judge was set to announce the sentence, I was almost too conflicted to attend. I wanted to be there somehow for Christopher's sake, to create an

invisible net for him to fall in when the inevitable decree came. But
I didn't think my own heart could withstand the impact of the
words it would have to hear, the words my heart knew were coming. Death by lethal injection. That's how they do it in this state.

We got the divorce because Christopher wanted it, insisted on
it. He thought it could somehow salvage my reputation, prove that
I was blameless and deserved to be allowed to go on with my life.
As if I could go on with my life, when all my dreams and everything I'd ever believed about love, sex, desire; the tender intimacies that are handed to you by God—all those things were subject
to the same lethal injection that killed James Christopher Loggins,
Jr.; snuffed out, all of it together.

Of course it took years of appeals for that to happen and in
those ensuing years, I married Randy and got old. But when the
years ran out, when Christopher's number was finally up and there
was no frantic last-minute call from the governor like you see in
old black-and-white movies, everything in my world died an ago-
nizing death, except for maybe bitterness and a touch of exhaust-
ing rage.

Then when Randy wanted a divorce, too, that was the final
icing on the proverbial cake. "You don't *love* me," he railed one
night, "you love a ghost. A son-of-a-bitch ghost who was never
any good. And he never loved you, honey, you should get that
straight in your fucked-up head right now. If he had loved you,
how could he have sat there all those times on the couch, watching me fuck you? Think about it. I put my goddamned cock in
your mouth, woman, and all he could do was sit there and jerk
off. You were his fucking *wife*, for crying out loud. How could a
pervert do that who feels any kind of love at all? It's not natural.
Tying up some girl in the car and forcing it up her ass—that's the
kind of man you prefer, you worship in fact, like he was all that
there was in life. You're nuts, you know that? You're one sick fuck
and I can't even feel sorry for you. Just get out."

It was Randy's house long before I married him so I figured,
why put up a fuss? I'll leave. And I didn't come back to the Lone

Tree Motel for the ghosts, either. I came back here because I needed a job and I got one here in the diner. But the ghosts have been okay companions, regardless. Sort of an added bonus to keep me company at night, to reacquaint me with what was once the glory of love as I find my way back to the dust.

Contributors

KIM ADDONIZIO is the author of several books, most recently the poetry collection *What Is This Thing Called Love* (W. W. Norton). Her first novel, *Little Beauties*, is upcoming from Simon & Schuster. She has received numerous awards for her writing, including two NEA fellowships. She is online at www.addonizio.home.mindspring.com.

DOROTHY ALLISON is the best-selling author of *Bastard Out of Carolina*, *Cavedwellers*, and a memoir, *Two or Three Things I Know for Sure* (all available from Plume). Born in Greenville, South Carolina, she currently lives with her partner and her son in Northern California.

MARGARET ATWOOD is the author of more than twenty-five books, including fiction, poetry, and essays. Her most recent works include the best-selling novels *Alias Grace*, *The Robber Bride*, *The Blind Assassin*, which won the Booker Prize, and *Oryx and Crake*, short-listed for numerous literary awards. She lives in Toronto.

SELMA JAMES BLAIR is probably best known for her versatile film roles. Her breakthrough performance in *Cruel Intentions* as the young Cecile Caldwell led to starring roles in other critically acclaimed projects such as Todd Solondz's *Storytelling* and Guillermo Del Toro's *Hellboy* as well as the hit *Legally Blonde* opposite Reese Witherspoon. Selma graduated from Cranbrook Kingswood preparatory school where she won the Strickland writing award while in her freshman year. She attended Kalamazoo college and NYU before graduating from the University of Michigan with a BA as well as a BFA. Selma lives in Los Angeles with her husband and one-eyed dog, Wink.

TULSA BROWN is an award-winning Canadian author who's been having a ball in erotica since 2003. In 2004 her work appeared in over a dozen anthologies, and her gay romance will be released in 2005 by Torquere Press.

RACHEL KRAMER BUSSEL (www.rachelkramerbussel.com) is senior editor at *Penthouse Variations* and a contributing editor at *Penthouse*, and writes the Lusty Lady column in the *Village Voice*. She is the editor of *Naughty Spanking Stories from A to Z*, co-editor of *Up All Night: Adventures in Lesbian Sex*, with several more books on the way. Her writing has been published in over sixty erotic anthologies, including *Best American Erotica 2004*, as well as publications such as *AVN, Bust, Curve, Diva, Girlfriends, Gothamist.com, On Our Backs, Oxygen.com, Penthouse, Punk Planet, Rockrgrl*, the *San Francisco Chronicle*, and *Velvetpark*.

BRYN COLVIN is a British author with a passion for all things strange and unusual. Other examples of her work can be found in the anthologies *Swing, Leather Lace and Lust, The Best of Both Worlds: Bisexual Erotica*, and in the upcoming Thunder's Mouth Press anthology, *Confessions: Admissions of Sexual Guilt*, as well as online at Extasy Books. In the rest of her life, she is an active member of the Pagan Federation, and runs a folk club.

ROSEMARY DANIELL is the author of the revolutionary memoirs, *Fatal Flowers: On Sin, Sex and Suicide in the Deep South* and *Sleeping with Soldiers*; the novel, *The Hurricane Season*; two books of poetry, *A Sexual Tour of the Deep South* and *Fort Bragg & Other Points South*; and a collection of essays, *Confessions of a (Female) Chauvinist*. Profiled in *People* and *Southern Living* magazine, she is originator of the Zona Rosa creative writing workshops and the author of *The Woman Who Spilled Words All Over Herself: Writing and Living the Zona Rosa Way*. Her work has appeared in *Harper's Bazaar, Mademoiselle, Mother Jones*, the *New York Times Book Review*, and other publications.

M. M. DE VOE is a prize-winning author, whose short fiction has been published in *PRISM: International*, the *Spectator, SLANT*, and *Bee Museum*. Her translations are forthcoming in anthologies in Canada and the EU. Her poetry has won first place nationally, and has appeared in *The Lyric, America, The Idiot's Guide to Form Poetry*, and the *New Yorker*. Her YA novel, *Burn in our Hearts*, was a finalist for the 2004 Bellwether Prize; she is at work on another. She holds an MFA from Columbia University, hates acronyms, loves gorillas, has a son, and lives a block from Ground Zero.

Novelist, short story writer, and essayist **JANICE EIDUS** has twice won the O. Henry Prize for her short stories, as well as a Redbook Prize and a

Pushcart Prize. She is the author of the story collections, *The Celibacy Club*, and *Vito Loves Geraldine*, and the novels, *Urban Bliss* and *Faithful Rebecca*, and is co-editor of *It's Only Rock and Roll: An Anthology of Rock and Roll Short Stories.*

HOLLY FARRIS is an Appalachian Pushcart Prize nominee who has worked as an autopsy assistant, restaurant baker, and beekeeper. Her work appeared previously in the Venus *Big Book of Hot Women's Erotica* and *Foreign Affairs: Erotic Travel Tales.* Her newest literary fiction is forthcoming from *Home Planet News* and *The Greensboro Review.*

BEVERLEY GLICK was born in London in 1957 and thought she would grow up to be a secretary. Fate had other ideas, and she has now been wielding a pen for twenty-five years. For the past ten she has worked as a writer and editor for a range of national newspapers but, for the fifteen years prior to that, she was a leading music journalist. She interviewed many of the biggest names of the eighties, including Duran Duran, Spandau Ballet, and Soft Cell, and somehow found time to become a fetish model. She has recently completed her first book, *Hit Girl*, about her adventures in the shiny worlds of pop and rubberwear.

SUSIE HARA'S stories have appeared in several anthologies under the name Lisa Wolfe, including *Best American Erotica*, *The Big Book of Hot Women's Erotica*, and the upcoming *Best of Best Women's Erotica*. Writing erotica is the most fun she's ever had with a laptop.

LAUREN HENDERSON was born in London, where she worked as a journalist before moving to Tuscany and then to Manhattan. She has written seven books in her Sam Jones mystery series, which has been optioned for American TV, and three romantic comedies—*My Lurid Past, Don't Even Think About It*, and *Exes Anonymous*. Her latest book is *Jane Austen's Guide to Dating*, which has also been optioned. Her books have been translated into over fifteen languages. Together with Stella Duffy she has edited an anthology of women-behaving-badly crime stories, *Tart Noir*, and their joint Web site is www.tartcity.com.

Celebrating the power of the erotic word, **DEBRA HYDE** is delighted to stir things up here and in many other major anthologies. Currently, you can find her short fiction in *Naughty Spanking Stories A to Z, Dykes on Bikes, Mammoth Book of Best New Erotica, Best of Best Women's Erotica*, and *Best S/M Erotica 2*. An opinionated sexinista, Debra tackles storms of controversy at her long-running weblog, Pursed Lips, and she invites you to visit her there.

BIANCA JAMES is a writer, translator, and lady vagabond living in Kyoto, Japan. She is currently plotting her escape to San Francisco in order to perform drag and burlesque under the stage name "Tittycat Von Scan-dalpants." Her writings have appeared in various anthologies, magazines, and Web sites, including *The Best of the Best Meat Erotica*, *Ultimate Lesbian Erotica 2005*, and Larry Flynt's *Barely Legal*. She is currently revising her second novel *Mono No Aware*, set in postmodern queer Japan. Her hobbies include drinking tea and coffee, astrology, high faggotry, and the pursuit of scandal.

J. S. JORDAN began writing her first book when she was nine and she has been writing steadily ever since. Her fiction and nonfiction have appeared in numerous online and print magazines including *Deadly Pleasures*, the *Mysterious Web*, *January Magazine*, *Plots with Guns*, *Shots Magazine*, and *Crime Spree Magazine* (www.crimespreemag.com) where Jennifer is the short fiction and special features editor. When not reading, working, and blogging, Jennifer is working on her first book, *A Day in the Sun*.

MICHÈLE LARUE, a Sorbonne educated journalist, has used her six languages freelancing around the world. As a film director, she made two documentaries in Cuba and another on the European SM scene. Les Editions Blanche (Paris) has been publishing her erotic short fiction since 1996. Editore Mondadori (Milano) picked up two of her stories for their collection of erotica, *Spicy*, in 2002. Her short stories have appeared in English translation in *Erotic Travel Tales* and the *Mammoth Book of New Erotica 2003*. Her collection of Cuban erotic tales, *Cuba Satissima*, was published by Descartes & Cie (Paris) in 2003. She lives in Paris.

MARILYN JAYE LEWIS'S erotic short stories and novellas have appeared in over forty anthologies in the United States and Europe. Her erotic romance novels include *When Hearts Collide*, *In the Secret Hours*, and *When the Night Stood Still*. She is the award-winning author of *Neptune & Surf*, a trio of erotic novellas, and *Lust*, her collected erotic short fiction. Upcoming novels include *Twilight of the Immortal*, *A Killing on Mercy Road*, and *Freak Parade*. She is the founder of the Erotic Authors Association. Visit her at www.marilynjayelewis.com.

CATHERINE LUNDOFF was scarred for life by working in the bar with "the largest collection of Elvis memorabilia outside Memphis." Her writings have appeared in such anthologies as *The Mammoth Book of Best New Erotica 4*, *The Big Book of Hot Women's Erotica 2004*, *Erotic Travel Tales II*, *Shameless*, *Naughty Spanking Stories from A to Z*, *Best Lesbian Erotica 1999, 2001,* and *2005*.

JOYCE CAROL OATES is the renowned author of many novels, including *Big Mouth & Ugly Girl*, *Freaky Green Eyes*, and her latest, *The Falls*. Her novel *Blonde* was a National Book Award nominee and *New York Times* bestseller. A recipient of the National Book Award and the

Pen/Malamud Award for Excellence in Short Fiction, Ms. Oates is the Roger S. Berlind Distinguished Professor of the Humanities at Princeton University. In 2003 she was a recipient of the Common Wealth Award for Distinguished Service in Literature.

JEAN ROBERTA teaches English at a Canadian prairie university and writes in several genres. Her erotic stories have appeared in over twenty anthologies as well as Web sites and print journals. Her reviews and opinion pieces appear in her column, In My Jeans, on the Web site *Blue Food.* She and Kayla Kuffs, editor of the Web site *The Dominant's View,* are currently co-editing an anthology about first-time BDSM experiences.

KIINI IBURA SALAAM is a realistic woman. She knows her nine-to-five threatens her fragile relationship with writing. So, she begs writing's absolution with essays published in *Colonize This!*, *When Race Becomes Real*, *Utne Reader*, *Essence*, and *Ms.* magazine. She prostrates herself with fiction published in *Mojo: Conjure Stories*, *Black Silk*, *Dark Matter*, and *Dark Eros*. She tithes her art form with the KIS.list, a monthly e-report on life as a writer. She produces www.kiiniibura.com as an altar, an online offering of words. She writes with holy gratitude, forever in love with her craft.

LYNDA SCHOR is the author of two collections of short fiction, *Appetites*, and *True Love & Real Romance*. She has had many stories and articles published in a variety of magazines including *Witness*, *Gargoyle*, *Ms.*, *Playboy*, *Fiction*, *Redbook*, and others, and her stories have been published in many anthologies. She's won a number of prizes, including two Maryland State Arts Council grants. She is the fiction editor of the online magazine *Salt River Review*. A new collection of short fiction, *The Body Parts Shop*, will be out from the Fiction Collective Two (FC2). She teaches at the New School University in New York City.

SOLVEJ SCHOU will graduate with a master's degree in journalism from the University of Southern California in May 2005. In 2000, she earned a BA in Creative Writing from Barnard College. Her work has appeared over the past five years in a number of print and online publications, including *L.A. Weekly*, *Fashion Wire Daily*, *Yahoo! Entertainment News*, *Mean* magazine, *New York Press*, *CMJ New Music Report*, *People* magazine, *London Evening Standard*, and the *Associated Press*. Her name is Danish, she loves music, film, performance, and art, and at times considers herself a bit of a muckraker.

IRIS N. SCHWARTZ is a fiction writer and poet whose erotic novella, *The Fruits of Her Labors*, is included in the anthology *That's Amore!* Her erotic fiction has also been anthologized in *The Big Book of Hot Women's Erotica 2004*, *Down and Dirty 2003*, and *Best Bondage Erotica 2003*.

She has had poetry anthologized in *An Eye For an Eye Makes the Whole World Blind: Poets on 9/11* and in the UK-based *Listening to the Birth of Crystals*. In addition, her writing has appeared in numerous online and print publications, including *Ducts Magazine, Ludlow Press*, and *Pikeville Review*.

LORI SELKE'S writing has appeared in outlets as diverse as the Best Bisexual Erotica series, *Asimov's Science Fiction Magazine*, and the *Children's Advocate* newsletter. Most recently, you can find her fiction in the pages of *Bottoms Up!, Ultimate Lesbian Erotica*, and *Glamour Girls*. She's the editor of *Tough Girls: Down and Dirty Dyke Erotica*, and of the zine *Problem Child*. She lives in Oakland, California.

MAX SHARAM was recently a clue in the *Sydney Morning Herald* crossword puzzle. Having made a name for herself as a recording artist with Warner Music, Max's unique blend of pop and classical opera ("P'Opera") has quickly become her trademark. Her award-winning, platinum selling debut album *A Million Year Girl* was nominated for eight Aria Awards in Australia. Her written pieces have appeared in numerous anthologies and magazines and her self-penned and produced orchestration *Crashlanding!* will be featured in *Frozen Angels* at Sundance Film Festival 2005 and on PBS Television. She is now an independent producer for Manhattan Neighborhood Network. She recently performed *Butterfly Suicide*, her latest one-woman Virtual Variety/Multi Media Musical at the Hong Kong Fringe Festival 2005.

SAVANNAH STEPHENS SMITH is a secretary by day and writer by night (and occasionally during her lunch hour). Her work has appeared both online at *Clean Sheets, Scarlet Letters*, and other Web destinations, as well as in print anthologies. She finds it hard to resist chocolate, good whiskey, and buying more books. She struggles to quit smoking, but can't resist smoldering a little. She lives in Canada.

Born in 1960, **CLAIRE THOMPSON** didn't find the courage to write about her deep-seated submissive yearnings until her mid-thirties. Now with fifteen published novels, including the international top-sellers *Sarah's Awakening, Slave Girl, The Stalker, Tracy In Chains*, and *Hard Corps*, she seeks not only to tell a story, but to exalt in the potential of a loving exchange of power. She writes about the timeless themes of sexuality and romance, with twists and curves that examine the "darker" side of the human psyche. Ultimately her work deals with the human condition; the constant search for love and the intensity of experience. Visit her at www.clairethompson.net.

ALISON TYLER is a shy girl with a dirty mind. Over the past decade, she has written more than fifteen naughty novels including *Strictly*

Confidential, *Sticky Fingers*, and *Something About Workmen* (all published by Black Lace), and *Rumors* (Cheek). She is the editor of *Batteries Not Included* (Diva); *Heat Wave*, *Best Bondage Erotica*, *Three-Way*, and the upcoming *Best Bondage Erotica 2* and *Heat Wave 2* (all from Cleis Press); and the Naughty Stories series, the Down & Dirty series, *Naked Erotica*, and *Juicy Erotica* (all from Pretty Things Press). Please visit her at www.prettythingspress.com

SAGE VIVANT operates Custom Erotica Source (www.customeroticas-ource.com), where tailor-made stories are created for individual clients. With partner M. Christian, she is the co-editor of *Confessions: Admissions of Sexual Guilt* and *The Best of Both Worlds: Bisexual Erotica*. She is the editor of *Swing!* Her stories have appeared in numerous anthologies, including *The Mammoth Book of Best New Erotica*, *Best Women's Erotica*, and many more. She is the author of *29 Ways To Write Great Erotica*, available at her Web site.

SHARON WACHSLER is a poet, essayist, short-story writer, and reformed cartoonist and playwright. She is the cofounder and editor of *Breath & Shadow* (www.abilitymaine.org/breath), the only literary journal written and edited entirely by people with disabilities. Sharon's erotica has appeared in *On Our Backs*, *Best Lesbian Erotica 2003*, *Best American Erotica 2004* and *2005*, *Harrington Lesbian Fiction Quarterly*, and *Down and Dirty 2*, among many other anthologies. She is a Peregrine Prize winner and a Pushcart nominee for poetry. As a humor columnist, she has a small, cultishly devoted following. Visit her at www.sharonwachsler.com.

SASKIA WALKER is a British author who has had fiction published on both sides of the pond. She lives in the north of England close to the wild, windswept and inspirational landscape of the Yorkshire moors, where she writes erotic romance, fantasy, and erotica. Visitors are welcome at www.saskiawalker.co.uk.